CONTENTS

Copyright   2

Dedicated to all my fellow beautiful disasters.   3

1. Dizzy.   4

2. Zeke   23

3. Lin   28

4. Zeke   38

5. Kieran   39

6. Monty   40

7. Connor   41

8. Dizzy   45

9. Connor   54

10. Monty   60

11. Dizzy   68

12. Kieran   72

13. Monty   76

14. Dizzy   85

15. Lin   94

16. Monty   98

17. Dizzy   107

18. Connor   122

19. Dizzy   130

20.	Zeke	146
21.	Dizzy	151
22.	Kieran	153
23.	Monty	159
24.	Dizzy	173
25.	Dizzy	182
26.	Monty	210
27.	Connor	216
28.	Kieran	229
29.	Lin	233
30.	Zeke	248
31.	Zeke	255
32.	Lin	262
33.	Dizzy	264
34.	Lin	277
35.	Dizzy	285
36.	Monty	292
37.	Lin	297
38.	Dizzy	308
39.	Dizzy	316
40.	Kieran	335
41.	Connor	344
42.	Connor	351
43.	Dizzy	361
44.	Zeke	367
45.	Dizzy	374
46.	Dizzy	388
Want to stay up to date?		393

Afterword   394

About the Author   397

More by Kat Quinn   398

I'm CURSED

Disaster Zone Jones • Book One

Kat Quinn

COPYRIGHT

DEDICATED TO ALL MY FELLOW BEAUTIFUL DISASTERS.

I LOVE YOU.

1. DIZZY.

When you've survived as many curses and near-death disasters as me, having your hotel go up in flames the second you leave, YET AGAIN, feels like just another Tuesday. Shit, is it Tuesday? How do people keep track of what day of the week it is, anyway? I've got so much other crap to deal with.

So far, it's really becoming a D-A-Y dayyyyy. And yes, I know that's just me spelling the word day out, but enunciating every letter really makes me feel like I'm somehow expressing just how jacked up it is. Sure, everything's going normal enough, all things considered (yes, the spontaneous hotel fire is included in my normal). Even getting doused by my own boiling hot coffee after a couple of sips (heck, I might even say it was an exceptionally lucky morning because I usually don't even get to sip it first before something goes wrong); but of course that means I burst out into a spontaneous "wow that is some boiling hot liquid" dance smack dab in the middle of the shop! My panicked flailing leads to knocking over some poor old woman in the cafe, likely just waiting for her tea or spark-ling water or whatever it is elderly women get in coffee shops these days. I'm pretty sure the look of shock on her face as I rip off my shirt to escape the painful but delicious beverage is only partly due to the horror of suddenly seeing a stranger's gold-skinned breasts. I mean, who's dick enough to knock over an old lady and then wave their non-saggy titties around like some sort of boob braggart? Me. That's who. Ugh. At least this time I whipped my shirt off before the skin was burned to blis-ters; believe you me... this ain't my first lava java rodeo.

Good thing I've always got my trusty black cotton jacket on. Before helping the woman up, I zip it over my goodies so the whole place can stop inserting me into their wet dreams for the rest of eternity, mostly because it's not fair for me to show them mine without them showing me theirs. What? I've got some good goodies goin' on. I would have shouted "You're welcome!" at the folks gawking at my money makers, but the poor old gal sprawled out before me really did need a bit of an assist. My flailing may have tossed her cane way across the building... and also may have smashed it against a table nearby... and may have caused it to shatter into roughly four zillion pieces. Oops. To be fair, it was apparently pretty hid-eous and had a bunch of deep gashes and gouges in the practic-ally toxic lime green paint anyway. Smelled like literal shit, too, so the insides were probably all rotted out and ready to give any day now. Nobody should suffer the fate of having a shit cane; I totally did her a favor, right?

Staring up at me, opening and closing her mouth like some kind of freaky old-lady fish, I help her over to a table and tell her to wait for just a bit. There were a couple of trees planted along the sidewalk to make the city feel more in touch with nature or whatever, so I figured odds were pretty high some kind of walking stick could be procured amongst their branches.

In true Dizzy Jones style, I actually manage to get a good one, but it cost me a tumble halfway down the tree I'd climbed up just to find something suitable; ensuring I become intimately familiar with the sting and vengeful immobility of every darn branch on the way down. Inanimate objects can be real turds sometimes, and I'm convinced this particular plant has an agenda of some sort against me. Man, if this were the ugly tree I'd be hideous by the time I got to the bottom. Though, given the number of burning scrapes and aching bruises I've earned all along my arms, legs, and torso, I'm not entirely convinced it isn't the ugly tree's first cousin at the very least.

Limping like a true champion of battle, I make my way back to the woman who still looks as though she's participating in some kind of really trippy dream. Yeah, that happens sometimes.

Okay, Dizzy, be polite and kind. You've already done enough damage here today so it's time to smooth it over with your best not-at-all-a-madwoman-and-totally-have-manners charm.

"Sorry I broke your cane, ma'am," I say as sweetly as possible while presenting her that bastard twig across both open palms, "I hope this walking stick will do for now. As evidenced by the fall both it and I took out of the tree it came from, I can pretty much guarantee it's unbreakable; should hold you over for a good long while. No need for me to find someone to repair the old one, right? Good as new is good to do?"

Blinking a couple more times as I hand her my hard-earned trophy, her sudden hyena cackle causes me to jump back; loud and manic barks startling the bajeeebers out of me.

"No, no, I don't think I ever want to see that rotten thing

again," she grins while wiping a gleeful tear from her eye. "You've done me a bigger favor than anyone could possibly understand. Those bastards will never keep me now." She leans in close and whispers in my ear, "I am completely in your debt. If you ever need any help, just whisper the name Jacinda and I will be there before you know it." Spinning her new stick like a ringmaster's baton, she saunters off way too peppily for how old I swear she looks.

Great, another crazy person for my collection of complete wackadoos. At least once a week somebody says something along the same lines, giving me a business card, or a phone number, or half a hot dog, or a carrier pigeon, or a hunk of stone that they claim is some kind of thanks. Yeah, sure, whatever you say. Thanks for creeping me out with your crazed laughter pretty much every time, you're welcome for me crashing into you, hurting you, destroying your property, and then trying my best to make things right even though it practically always turns out you're too nutso to really be aware. Man, being such a freak magnet has got to be some part of my own personal curse.

The rest of the day is really just more of the same-old same-old. Wander down the street for a bit and see a cool shop full of gorgeous antiques? Why not go in there, trip over absolutely freakin' NOTHING and smash an entire case of old-lookin' shit. Don't have enough money to pay for half the store? Good thing you're wearing sneakers today because this is one of those instances where you've got to haul ass out of there and hope the furious shopkeeper never ever ever finds you again. Too bad your giant ball of frizzy purple hair is distinct enough that if he ever sees you again, you'd for sure be picked out of a lineup. Unless there's coincidentally a troupe of purple-haired clown criminals in town at the same time, but that hasn't happened yet.

Maybe when you're done running for your life you decide it

might be nice to relax with some nature around you or whatever, so you just keep walking until the city starts to look and sound suspiciously like a park. Which is to say you happen to wander into a park because that is actually what happened; you didn't just wander into some fairy forest accidentally. Hey, it's a more common occurrence than you'd think, honestly.

And when you get to that park, you find a nice shady spot under a tree to just lie down and relax for a bit because why not, you're worth it, aren't you? Even an antique-smashing criminal on the run from Johnny Law deserves a bit of a lie-down in the shade from time to time. Like I said: totally same-old same-old.

But of course, I'm not allowed too long of a moment of peace before the utter disaster that is my life decides to kick it up a notch and I'm practically trampled by a herd of elephants.

Okay, they aren't actually elephants this time, but they are like 10 dogs that don't seem to have someone to keep them guided by leashes. To be honest, getting murdered by a mess of adorable little monsters isn't the worst way to go, but their dog breath is pretty rank and they are kind of freaking my furry BFF Aria out. Most of the time, she's totally content to just nap in my hood or across my shoulders, but she's desperately scrabbling her sharp nails against my neck in an attempt to break free and I'm so not a fan of adding more on to today's war wounds. I can't believe she managed to sleep through that whole coffee shop disaster, but she's been with me my whole life and we're both apparently unbreakable so it probably all feels like just another Tuesday to her. Shit, I really gotta find out if it's Tuesday, now. This is going to drive me batty until I get it settled.

Reaching out with both arms wide, I snatch up the three closest escapees and give them my best cuddle, rubbing my face all over them to mark my territory and show them who's boss. The display of dominance manages to calm both the dogs and Aria down a smidge, so I take a moment to just enjoy being surrounded by all the warm fuzzies. Gosh, if we could have a dog on the road I'd totally be all over it, but they seem like a lot of responsibility and my mom was apparently prophetic when she decided to name me Disaster Zone Jones. Any little pooch who decides to make its way into my life would likely be doomed to utter insanity, but gosh would it ever be loved like all heck. At least Aria's always good for cuddles.

With three of them distracted by me, including just the absolute cutest, chubbiest, little white Frenchie, the rest of the pack starts running around us while barking and howling and jumping around playfully. Did I win a game of dog tag or something?

Well fine, if we're playing tag and I'm "it," then I'm going to win this darn thing! I'm the nine-times tag world champion, they don't know what they're up against! Falling a lot and needing to bolt for freedom right afterwards means I'm a pro at getting up quickly, so I'm on my feet and bounding away with my hostages before the rest of them even know what's happening. Look at any one of us and, aside from obvious incurable madness, you'd see nothing but glee and joy in our free-spirited play. My cackles join their rambunctious howls and we dash like lunatics across the lawn. Of course, twice the feets is how you cheats so the group is on my heels pretty much within a few seconds, though it doesn't really matter. I boop the little white Frenchie on its nose and set it free, shouting "You're it now, Frenchman! Get 'em!"

For nearly half an hour we chase the rest of the pack around a giant fountain and over benches and through huge clusters of people before finally calling a truce and collapsing on the warm grass, every single one of us panting with our tongues hanging out. Despite a most glorious and valiant effort, my little white Frenchie didn't manage to catch any of the others with his stubby little legs, though we clearly had a blast anyway.

But of course, as soon as we get comfy in our honestly disgusting, sweaty, dog breath-scented puppy pile, this woman comes running up to us with tears streaming from her eyes and like a thousand leashes in her hand. Yeah, it's pretty obvious I'm about to lose all my new friends, but at least the dog-walker let me give them some good scritchens before hooking them all up and taking them back to home base. Given the desperate look on her mascara-streaked face, I have a feeling that she would have been murdered by somebody somewhere for losing their precious pooch, which is pretty much the only reason I restrained myself from "accidentally" shoving my new friend into my jacket and whistling innocently. Wouldn't want her severed head on my conscience.

Tears aside, she was pretty sweet about the whole thing, and at least she didn't give me a secret password after I broke her arm or something crazy like those wackadoos. For once, it feels kind of nice to have been part of a sort of normal disaster moment instead of a creepy-crazy one.

As I watch a flurry of paws eagerly thunder away, I'm suddenly reminded of something. "Hey, wait!" I yell, just before she's out of range, "what day is it?!"

She swivels to look at me with an expression on her face that could only be described as the visual embodiment of a heartfelt "huh?"

"Um... it's Tuesday?" She replies, cocking her head and questioning more than stating a fact.

"Oh hell yeah! I knew it! Thank youuuu!" I fist-pump my victory.

Chuckling, she stumbles and turns back around, very much

getting dragged by my bestest buddies. No wonder they got away from her in the first place. My heart clenches just slightly at the view of retreating tails waving like a parting farewell; I'm really gonna miss those rascals.

Aria pops her miniature fox-ish, furry head out and nuzzles my cheek, cooing in that way she knows makes me feel a little better. It's always just been her and me pretty much since forever, and sometimes it gets a little lonely being constantly on the road to nowhere with nobody but her. I don't know what she is, with her long, thin muzzle, pointy cheek tufts, velvety bat wings, and beautiful, complex vocal melodies, but she's my best and only friend. When we were little, she'd hum quiet, calming tunes until we fell asleep at night, and she'd trill happy melodies during the day while we played. The midnight fur of her long, ferret-like body is the perfect concealment for her inside the shadows of my jacket's black hood, even though she usually wraps her fluffy tail around my neck and ruins the camouflage. Though people still don't tend to notice her unless I'm suddenly stripping off a soaked shirt in the middle of a coffee shop or something crazy like that.

"I'll be fine, girl. It was just nice for us to have some more friends for a little bit."

She looks at me with bright gold eyes laced with shimmering bits of green; a perfect copy of my own. Even though she doesn't speak with words, I've never had trouble knowing what she means with a single glance.

A small, hand-like paw caresses the curve of my cheek before she slips fully from my jacket and flies away, slender body rippling in time with each rhythmic flap of her leathery wings. She'll be back when she's good and ready.

Of course, it's that moment that some asshole somewhere decides to curse somebody, a familiar pinprick tingling starting in my hands and a light tap beginning to work its way behind my eyes. Great. Just GREAT.

You see, I'm pretty much cursed to always be cursed. If anyone tries to curse someone else while I'm around, my lucky lottery ticket gets scratched and I win big instead of whoever the prize was meant for. Yippie!

Thank fuck it's just a mediocre one, because my prance through the park has me needing to catch my breath for more than just a hot second. If my whole body was locked up on top of being exhausted, I'd probably be stuck with it for a week before breaking it. Trying to explain why you're just totally immobile somewhere is super hard when you can't talk, and even if you can make noise it's usually just a scream. Finger tingles and brain taps? That's practically a walk in the park! Although apparently I don't walk in parks so much as run around with a mighty stampede so maybe that's not a good analogy.

My hands run themselves along the dozens of pockets hidden inside my jacket's lining, snatching up herbs and ingredients of their own accord. At this point, I trust my instincts more than I trust my brain to think through things consciously, although my love lumps are on full display in a public place again, so maybe I should have stopped to have a talk about discretion with my hands before letting them get to business. Too late!

Now for the fun part! And by fun, I mean gross. Like mega gross. Pretty much all my counter-curses require a bit of blood to activate, and they've pretty much all got to be eaten. Yuck.

Herbs in one hand, small blade in the other, I slice open a cut on the heel of my palm from yesterday that barely even had time to scab over. Because of course this shit happens pretty much daily.

A couple of drops of blood plus a good squish of random plant life later and I'm licking my hands clean of the gritty, herby, metallic mixture. Mmm, just like momma used to make. Gross.

Good thing whoever cast this piece of garbage isn't that skilled, because I manage to get my cure ready before it really starts to ramp up in intensity. Still, those tingles in my finger turn to a full on frostbite while the jackhammer going in my head stops my brain from making much think good. I mean brain think thoughts think. Fuck. Whatever. I caught a case of the dumbs.

Probably some asshole was trying to give someone a permanent brain freeze, maybe in the 'you ate ice cream too quickly' way but possibly in the 'you are now encased in ice, literally' way. I can't really judge them too well any more, since my body has kind of racked up an immunity to harmful magic. Super small curses, like making someone's shoes always be untied, or causing them to vomit up spiders for a day, or starting an unstoppable itch? Those usually just give me a little tingle here and there for half a moment before dissolving by themselves. Thank goodness, too, because people are ALWAYS casting petty curses like that and I used to have to cure myself dozens of times a day. Have you ever had an unstoppable itch? They'll drive you crazy if you can't cure them. And lucky me, that's an extremely popular form of revenge. Yaaaay. Thank goodness I don't feel those ones any more.

And big ones? Even if I don't manage to counter them in time, my body can pretty much naturally fight anything off at this point, it just takes a heck of a lot more time if I don't interfere quickly.

Still, while this curse isn't a doozy or anything, I'm stuck motionless for an hour of focused breathing and meditation, trying to shake the effects. I wouldn't really call "sitting cross-legged in a park while repeating 'get the fuck out of me' in my head over and over" a real form of meditation, but it looks fairly quiet from the outside, so let's go with that description.

Finally free, I slump back onto the grass with a huff of exasperation. Oh great, feels like there's some sunburn on my tits, now, too. Yep. Today's going great. Completely great. Perfectly great.

Aria chooses that moment to float her fluffy butt back over to me and give me this look. A look like she's scolding me as though she's somehow my mother or something. I get the point and fix my jacket, wincing slightly at the discomfort of its soft inner lining brushing against my poor, raw bazoombas.

"Look, I would have zipped back up but I was already halfway to the cure trance once I realized my boobs were hanging out. At least I've still got on a bra this time! Last time was way worse! Although it was probably less public. Okay. Yeah. You're right, okay? But I couldn't really do anything about it. I'm not going to apologize, so you're just gonna have to eat tough cookies." Defiantly, I stick out my tongue before changing the subjects like a super smooth subject-changing pro. "Where'd you go off to, anyway?"

Totally avoiding the question, Aria gently slides a bright pink leaf into my front pocket and pats it with her tiny grabby hands. Lord knows what the little treasure hunter needs that for, but after 28 years of them being forced upon me, I don't really question her random gifts any more.

We lay next to each other in the grass for a while as the barest tendrils of sunset start to creep in, enjoying the cool breeze and relative quiet out here in the park. You've got to take the good moments when you can get them, y'know? My thoughts slip away from me for a moment, leaving me with a small helping of peace.

Tender nibbles from needle-sharp teeth on my hand let me know that my little love muffin has had enough of this lollygagging and needs a proper meal soon or else those delicate nibbles will become full-on chompies.

"Alright, miss thang. Let's get going."

My shoulder pops loudly as I sit up and a groan comes barreling out of my mouth. Right. Fell from a tree and then chased a bunch of dogs. Of course everything hurts. Curses always make everything worse, too. Mostly just a small, residual headache this time, but it's really not a welcomed guest at this already bumpin' pain party if I'm honest.

"You hitchin' a ride or makin' your own way?"

Aria responds by trotting away delicately on graceful legs. I respond by stumbling just far enough to crash into the side of the fountain I ran around earlier, knocking off a hunk of one of the stone statues around it and cracking some decorative tile inside. The water practically starts glowing with how the ripples catch the dwindling sunlight. Or maybe the water was glowing for real, you can never really tell... especially when you're busy trying to casually saunter away from yet another scene of public property damage. Crazy shit always finds me and I'm at about my limit right now so I'm really not ready to face anybody's consequences.

Thankfully, we make it out of the park with what one might call minimal incident and manage to find a pub just over a block away that looks good enough. Well, it looks good enough to Aria anyway because she slinks her slender ferret of a body in through the door just as someone else walks out. Okay, guess we're in the mood for booze? Actually, you know what? Sure. We're in the mood. It's almost evening and I've survived more than enough trouble to deserve a brew or two.

The tall, thin barmaid looks tired but friendly as she makes her way over to me, long silver ponytail swaying with each step.

"What can I get you, sweetie?"

"Do you guys do food here? I'm about ready to find a horse to eat and I'm hoping there's a better alternative available."

She stops for a second and her face lights up before letting out a sort of amused chuckle. "Yeah, I think we can wrestle you up something a bit better than a horse. Where you'd find one at this time of day is beyond me; last I heard we stopped using mounted police a few years back and there aren't really any stables nearby. Seems like it'd end up being a lot more work than what's worth doing to try and hunt down something you're not going to find within a hundred miles of here. Let me get you a menu and then we can talk drinks." She places one dark finger on her plump bottom lip thoughtfully, "And maybe about the logistics of being so hungry you could eat a horse if no horses are readily available."

I'm beaming as this chick sort of skips away because she's weird, and I like me some good weird. Aria made the right choice, clearly. Speaking of, the little furball winds her way up the stool next to me and sits herself regally like she's some sort of queen, slim muzzle held high in the air as though she has even an ounce of authority. Never trust a …whatever she is when she tries to look trustworthy. The little minx will swindle you out of everything you've got if you let her, and she can't even talk! Her ways are a mystery, even to me.

My new temporary best friend, weird barmaid, comes back with a thick menu in her hand that has to weigh at least. thousand pounds from how it practically covers the entirety of her lean torso.

"There you go! We've got like 20 pages that are just cocktails and wines and beers, but there's plenty of food, too. Between you and me? Don't get any of the burgers. Jerry's shit at cooking them less than full charcoal but he makes a mean steak, somehow. It's got to be some sort of grudge against grinding up meat rather than serving it whole, that's the only explanation I've got. Other than that, pretty much everything is great!" She finally notices the stool next to me as she passes the monster menu over my way. "Ooh! Who's your friend?"

"This is Aria," I jerk a thumb towards my companion, "you got some water I can give her? Bowls are better but she's surprisingly good with a glass if there aren't any."

The barmaid looks around for a second and asks "How about a tea cup? My name's Lilly, by the way. Forgot to say so."

"A teacup sounds great, Lilly! Call my Dizzy. How do you feel about grabbing me a water as well? I'm not nearly as fancy as Aria, though; a regular cup'll do me just fine."

"Sure thing, Dizzy, be back in a second."

I glance dubiously at Aria out of the corner of my eye as we watch Lilly scoop ice into a glass and reach under the counter, seeking a smaller cup for my incredibly suspicious companion.

"What are you up to, Aria?"

Her golden eyes look at me wide and innocent, trying to play up how gosh darned cute she is to convince me her intentions are always pure and she has never ever caused a bit of mischief in her life.

"Yeah, I'm not buying it you little miscreant. Whatever you're up to, at least wait until we get our food if it's going to get us kicked out." There's no point telling her not to do something, and frankly, I'm more likely to get us booted for suddenly making every chair splinter into pieces, or accidentally chucking my drink into the face of exactly the most angry person in the place. It's only half-full in here and nobody looks particularly angry yet, but give it a couple of drinks and let my particular brand of chaos loose and this currently fine atmosphere can go south real quick. Nothing crazy has happened for basically ten minutes so we're more than overdue, anyway.

"Here's your water, ladies, I've got to check on some other folks but I'll be back in a bit to talk turkey. Or horse. Whichever you decide on! Give me a holler if you need me!" She gives a twiddling finger wave before walking towards a group of guys sitting around a circular booth. They came in a little while after me, but they look at Lilly welcomingly so this is probably their usual hang. Seems like I'm the only weirdo stuck sifting through an enormous menu tonight.

Shit. She wasn't lying when she said there were 20 pages of drinks. How are there even that many different options? Some of these have to be fake, surely? What the hell is a Caribbean Cowtown Cocktail? Yankee Doodle Don't Mind Me? Late Night Train to Alcatraz?

I'm too caught up in my astonishment at the ridiculous abundance of choice to notice Aria's gone off somewhere until I feel her hand digging in my pocket again, slipping in some mint leaves to join the pink one from earlier. Her cheeks are swollen like a greedy chipmunk, bright red cherry juice dribbling out of the corners. She looks at me with pride and victory, clearly pleased with her stolen bounty. I just roll my own eyes and give her a scratch behind a pointed ear.

Figuring it's probably a safe bet to stick with a sandwich, my stomach gurgles at the turkey Lilly's now got me craving.

I lean back to see if I can spot where Lilly's gone off to and, of course, manage to bump into someone even though I seriously barely moved. A chill runs up my spine at the contact, but when I whip my head back to see who it was, there's nobody close enough. I'm not a fan of spooky feelings, and a sudden chill at grazing an invisible stranger definitely falls under that category. Damn it. I'm probably not even going to get my food before something stupid happens. My stomach rumbles its discontent in solidarity of our inevitable future. Damn it, damn it, damn it. Now I'm gonna be on fucking edge until whatever it is finally hits me.

Deep breath, Dizzy. Deep breath. Don't will the bullshit to happen, it'll happen when it's good and ready. Just try to get your food anyway.

Lilly, blessed angel that she is, chooses that moment to make her glorious return and ask me what I'll be having.

"If you give it the green light, I'm game for a turkey club with fries. And maybe literally any vegetables that you have, like cooked carrots or a salad or half an over-boiled zucchini. Surprise me." My hands shoot up like an explosion, sharing how razzle-dazzle I feel about surprise vegetables. "And then maybe also an iced tea and a shot or three of rum. I've got a feeling my long day's about to turn into a long night and I'm just in no way ready for it."

"Oh yikes, starting off with three shots as your appetizer? Well if it's like that, I'll make sure to whip you up something real special to go with that club. Good choice, by the way, they actually roast the turkeys in house, of all things!"

"Sounds good to me, then," I say as she yet again heads off into the distance, my dreams of dinner squarely placed in her capable hands.

Aria climbs up my arm to drape herself across my shoulders while my gaze travels around the room. It's pretty cozy in here, and the warm lighting above the tables and booths makes it feel inviting. Sure, it's a little dated-looking with the green pleather seats and an overabundance of wooden everything else, but there are framed pictures and little trinkets all around that declare this place home to all the locals. There's even a small area cleared out near the back where it looks like they probably have a band every now and again, though I always wonder if people like the extra noise when they're working on earning a hangover.

Just as I'm wondering about the music situation, two people head up to the very squat platform that could arguably be called a stage and start setting up. Seems like it'll just be the two of them with a guitar and a microphone, but the uncomplicated act feels right for this atmosphere. Which may explain why more people start filtering in as soon as it looks like they're getting close to go time. Guess music is a draw for the place, after all?

The rough, scraping sound of glass sliding along the wooden bar top brings me out of my musings. I look over to see my obviously now permanently temporary best friend passing me not just a cool glass of iced tea, and not only a tumbler half-filled with rum, but also a slice of chocolate cake that practically glistens with the promise of perfection.

Eyes opened wide, I say "Are you an actual angel? I think you're an actual angel. You have to be. It's the only explanation."

Lilly grins like the Cheshire Cat, "Figured I'd save the shot glasses and just go for gold with the one cup. Less dishes for me later, anyway. And if you're having a shitty day, then chocolate is always the answer, on the house. Made it myself, actually, so I can promise it's better than the burgers." She winks at me and starts to walk away, long silvery ponytail whipping around like a single enormous feather from her invisible wings of glory.

"Marry me!" I shout over the growing sound of the crowd.

She laughs and does an awkward double finger gun winking combo that only convinces me she's clearly my soulmate even further. This town is lucky to have her. Given my continuous state of perpetual homelessness, though, guess I'll have to call off our engagement before I hit the road tonight. Usually it's about the time that the hotel I'm staying in burns to the ground that I figure it's time to move on, so today's clearly the day. Yes, this is a regular occurrence. It's not always burning, but I'm pretty sure my curse has destroyed way too many buildings and rooms and park fountains to count.

"Check one two, one two," The girl up on stage taps the microphone while the guy next to her lifts the strap of their guitar over his head. She clears her throat. "Hey everyone, thanks for coming out to The Wood Liquor tonight, we're Jessie and James and we're here to play a few songs for you."

James starts plucking a few chords on the guitar and humming, then Jessie starts to sing a soft and calming melody. Shockingly, they aren't a Pokémon cover band; their names may very genuinely be Jessie and James because their sound is all folk and clearly original. Jessie's voice is gentle and a bit haunting, but James's deeper humming helps to ground the sound.

Two songs in and I get the surprise of a lifetime: my massive turkey club has arrived and I may very well actually get a chance to enjoy it! Aria wastes no time snatching a fry off my plate before it's even hit the bar. My empty cake plate is swapped out for a mountain of mixed vegetables sautéed with herbs and probably butter given how shiny and delicious they look.

"Wife," I declare, "I have decided that on this, the night of our wedding, you will receive the most generous of tips for having brought me this glorious bounty. Clearly, I'm a lucky woman."

Lilly swats me on the arm and giggles for a second. "You're ridiculous. It's great! You want another iced tea before I make my next round? It might take a bit for me to get back since the band always seems to bring people in."

"I would love another tea, thank you. And it looks like my little fry thief could do with some topping off of her water as well."

"Sure thing! Back in two shakes."

Half of the sandwich is practically shoved into my face within seconds, so I can only nod my appreciation when the refills arrive. It's not a pretty sight, given that I basically had to unhinge my jaw to even get a good bite, but damn if it ain't delicious. There's probably half a gallon of mayo and turkey streaking down my chin right now, making me realize that Aria and I both apparently have the same table manners. Given that I'm now a married woman and I've clearly got no one left to impress, though, it doesn't really matter. So I might've been a little ravenous and not noticed. Oops. This dinner might not be fancy but it is definitely bliss right now.

Total. Fucking. Bliss.

And then a familiar tingle forces its way into the base of my skull as I am smacked in the back of the head with a force so strong my face actually slams down violently into my plate of food. My beautiful, beautiful plate of food.

Goddamnit. What the fuck is it, this time? Ruin my perfectly good goddamned club. Motherfucker.

But the pain is gone before I even have to figure it out.

2. ZEKE

"Zeke, you ready yet?" Monty pops his head into the doorway of my room, "We were planning on leaving in five if you've got the charms together."

"Almost."

"Right on! You need my help with anything before we head out?"

"No." I wave my hand distractedly in his direction, my entire focus on the project in front of me. Tonight, we're trying out one of my latest concoctions. In theory, combining a luck charm and a spiritual connection sigil should result in something that encourages encounters with a potential partner. True connections-not artificial ones created between incompatible mates-but ones teased out of those who would have enjoyed one another if their paths had crossed organically. The goal here is to find real love, not hypnotize someone only somewhat willing. Nobody's ever tried to combine these two before, but the theory is sound and my success could lead us to be lucky in love.

I inspect the bracelets once more to ensure they're constructed firmly. Each thin band made by braiding finely-woven rabbit fur into twine is securely fastened to the small golden medallion in its center via two punctures on opposite sides. The medallions have been painstakingly engraved with the sigil for spiritual connection, two overlapping circles with a line fully crossing through them horizontally, symbolizing the sharing between both. There is no fraying in the braid. There are no gouges or scuffs on the newly minted coins. Everything is precise and identical and balanced. Perfect. These will work.

When I look up, I'm surprised to see Montgomery still casually leaning against my doorway, arms crossed. He's wearing a ridiculous navy blue polo shirt littered with pink-maned unicorn heads. His electric pink sneakers were clearly selected to match precisely with the coloring on the creatures, though the stark white cargo pants are possibly the boldest choice of his ensemble.

He raises a thick black eyebrow at me in question and jerks his head slightly in the direction of the stairs. I nod sharply in response and stand from my work bench, grabbing the five immaculate charms made especially for tonight, then head towards him.

My progress is halted when his dark hand is placed gently on my lightly tanned chest. My bare chest. Ah. Clothes. Yes.

Monty smiles politely while I head to my closet and don a soft, cotton tunic with a small criss-cross of lacing at the chest. Its off-white color is at home with the brown trousers I was already wearing and the worn brown shoes I'll slip on by the front door. The black sleeve of tattoos on my left arm is almost a stark contrast to the muted tones of the rest of my adornments, but I like to display it to have easy access to its stored spell work.

I look to Monty for his approval, making sure I haven't forgotten anything. He squints at the scruff of my week-old beard and the strands of deep brown hair that always seem to fall into my eyes while I'm working, then gives me a shrug. Apparently it'll have to do.

"Come on, man, you'll be fine. You've got that sort of 'rough around the edges' look going for you right now and I'm sure there's someone who's into exactly that."

We head to the front door and I grab the keys from the bowl right next to it. On nights we test a new spell, I'm always the designated driver. Makes it easier to keep my head clear and note accurate observations in case it requires future tweaking.

Kieran looks like he's ready to jump out of his own skin by the way he's pacing next to our SUV, the fists he keeps clenching and unclenching pairing perfectly with the deep scowl he's sporting. "Let's get out of here, I hate standing around and doing nothing," he declares while crossing thickly muscled arms across his broad chest, shooting me an irritated glare. I don't mind.

Ever the peacekeeper, Monty steps between us and gives Kieran an almost patronizing look.

Kieran rolls his eyes and lets out an exasperated growl while throwing his head back, but he does exhale a slow breath and manage to settle. I've slipped into the driver's seat by the time he's calmed down enough to climb into the middle row without complaint. Connor's already tucked himself into a corner in the back, quietly reading a book while waiting. Lin is to my right in the passenger's side, grinning from ear to ear while tapping his long fingers together in a triangle.

The back door slams shut and Monty clicks his seatbelt into place.

"When we get to The Wood Liquor, Zeke will hand out the charms. If anything feels hinky, or it doesn't work well, or it works TOO well, let him know so he can make a fix before we risk giving it to customers. And take it off IMMEDIATELY if it causes you or anyone else harm."

"Yes, dad," Lin rolls his eyes at Monty over one shoulder while giving a little salute.

"Don't make me put you in a time out, young man," Monty teases back.

He's not wrong to give them these guidelines; we've experienced plenty of failures before. Better to risk a mishap with the guys while I'm around than with a customer when I'm not.

We're leaving the driveway when Connor's soft voice carries from the back. "What if it doesn't work for all of us?"

He's afraid of being left out, but my charms are identical. There's no reason one should be any more effective than another, although I didn't consider the possibility that a person's personal magic could interfere. Or their own biochemistry. The theory of the charms themselves is sound, though still untested, but all of the variables might not have been considered.

Surprisingly, Kieran's the one to answer for me. "If it doesn't work, it doesn't work. Zeke will try again, you already know that. Don't worry about it, Connor, you know he won't stop trying until it works for everyone, every time. Our genius is a dog with a bone when there's a problem around to solve."

Lin flicks through the stations on the radio, clearly not sat-isfied with what's on offer. "Besides, hotcakes, you don't need a silly charm to get a girl if you want to. You're far too sexy to spend the night alone."

Connor ducks his face further into his book to cover his growing blush while Lin continues to grin to himself, clearly pleased that his teasing has flummoxed its target.

The rest of the guys chat in the background while I consider Connor's question from a practical standpoint. Is it possible for my design to only work for some, but not all? Luck charms on their own have a failure rate, but that's usually due to sub-standard materials, not due to the individuals who use them. Spiritual connection sigils only work for those who are open to them working, but that's the whole basis of my design; making sure that the only people who would happen to be at-tracted are those who would be open to it in the first place. True, charms and sigils aren't often combined by other spell crafters, but the rings and earrings I wear daily are a hybrid of these philosophies and have yet to fail me.

3. LIN

Oh, tonight is just going to be the best! Our mad scientist has weaved together something undeniably special and I can't wait to see what mayhem ensues! The other guys may think they're ready for true love, but Kieran and Connor are terrified of screwing up while Zeke and I are too …different… to be tied down. Monty's got a pretty good shot, though. It's almost exciting enough to take bets on who's going to run away screaming first! Part of me thinks it would be Zeke himself when he finally understands that his charm is actually meant for true and lasting love, not just a temporary girlfriend to prove his experiment works.

Kieran's already on edge tonight, so maybe he'll make a run for it before the evening even gets started? No idea what's gotten up his kilt to get him so bothered but the gigantic red head's constant twitching and fidgeting makes him a pretty good candidate for first flee of the night.

The devil inside me smiles and I decide to poke the bear a bit. Or the wolf, as it were.

"Want to take bets on who will find their soulmate first?" I drawl, "I think our handsome rogue of an alpha wolf will be first to lock down the love of his life."

Kieran's face almost goes green as his mind undoubtedly replays the words "Soulmate" and "Love of his life" over and over again. His panic is delicious.

"Woah woah woah, soulmate? Fuck. Shut up, that's not what's happening here is it? Are we about to get fucking married in one night? That's not what this is for, right Zeke? It's just to find.... shit." His twitchiness only intensifies.

Zeke's clearly lost himself inside his mind, so I answer. "Well it's sure not to find a one night stand, sugarplum. This one's for love, not lust. You ready to meet your destiny tonight?" I snigger under my breath while turning halfway in my seat to see his reaction. Yeah, Kieran's going to be first to fuck up.

"Lin, lay off," Monty chastises me, the spoilsport. You'd think a man in a unicorn shirt would be more fun. "We don't know for sure what will happen tonight and even if this does lead to something big, do you really want to lose that chance?"

Connor smoothes down the front of his endearing little sweater vest, a faraway look in his eye as he obviously replays the words "Soulmate" and "Love of his life" in his head as well. He might be shy, but the illusionist is clearly the true romantic of our group. How could he not be, with all those things he dreams up in that adorable blonde head of his? Some of the things he creates are so beautiful it could make anyone fall for him if he'd just share them with someone. If this works for only one of us, I do hope it's him. Kid could use a boost of confidence to get him out of his own imagination and into someone else's pants.

"Well I'm looking to find two or three soulmates tonight, no reason to limit my love!" I declare.

Connor looks at me with bright turquoise eyes and uses long, slender fingers to push gold-rimmed glasses back up his nose. He tilts his head to the side slightly and says "I don't think that's how soulmates work, Lin. It's two halves of a whole, no?"

I tap an index finger to my chin in what most would classically consider the pose of a great intellect. "Ah, my sweet little angel cake, who says a soul can only be split into two parts? It's about finding the other pieces to your puzzle, and who ever heard of a puzzle that only has two pieces? Why couldn't someone have four or five or a hundred soulmates? If they fit together then they're meant to be together."

He seems to contemplate what I've said for a moment before nodding just slightly, as though it makes sense to him. Who knows, maybe it does make sense and I've just unlocked the secret of true happiness by talking out my ass to a long-limbed book nerd in the back seat of an SUV. Maybe this is how all great philosophers get their best ideas?

Kieran looks about ready to shit his kilt at the thought.

Monty shoots me a look of utter exasperation and I cock my eyebrow while giving him my best shit-eating grin. This night is going to be glorious!

Zeke parks in the lot behind The Wood Liquor and we stroll through the doors to head for our usual booth. For better or for worse, we're here and ready to give this experiment our best try.

Lilly's at the bar, leaning over and talking to a woman with the biggest curly mess of bright purple hair I've ever seen. Do the curtains match the drapes? What a delicious prospect! Oh, I do so hope she's on the menu for tonight. Lilly backs away from the woman while smiling and giving a flirty finger twiddle. Do they know each other? She makes her way over to us while I'm still inspecting the gorgeous bit of intrigue at the bar.

Monty waves and blasts her with one of his warm smiles. "Hey Lilly! How are you tonight?"

"Monty! I'm great!" She laughs with real delight, "Just had a kind of ridiculous conversation and it feels like tonight's going to be plenty interesting, in a good way. What can I get for you while you're here?"

"Three pints of lager, a coke, and a water sound good to start us off," He replies. "And a couple bowls of snack mix, if you could."

She gives a thumbs-up in acknowledgement.

I catch her eye before she can bustle away, "Gorgeous, what do you think about the crowd this evening? I know we'll never catch a gem like you, but we're on the hunt for our soulmates tonight and the bigger the sea, the more fish for our nets!" The dastardly grin I flash her is all show and she knows it, but I turn the charm up nonetheless.

"Lin, you incorrigible flirt!" She swats in my direction, "There's a band on tonight, so give it less than an hour and I'm sure you'll have plenty of company. Don't go harassing people and scaring them out of my pub with your wickedness, you devil!"

"Why Lilly," I say, gasping and placing a hand on my chest as though I've truly taken offense, "I'm nothing but the perfect gentleman. The complete Prince Charming package, truly!"

"Sure you are, and I'm a 10 foot tall parakeet named Duke," she says, rolling her eyes, a stifled grin just barely holding back laughter.

"Well then, Duke, you are looking lovelier than ever." I give a polite bow of my head in reverence to her parakeet charms, now holding my hand over my heart in what may look like a playful mockery of respect.

"Okay Lin, you win!" She laughs and backs away with a little bounce in her step. "Drinks! Back soon!"

Looking around, this place really hasn't changed much over the years. Thankfully, it's not one of those loud sports bars because it lacks even a single television on any of their wood-paneled walls. The "stage" that will be performed on tonight is probably the newest addition, and it's really just a couple of wooden palettes that have been lined up next to each other, the normal gaps filled and reinforced to discourage broken ankles. We've been coming here for years because it's always felt like part of the neighborhood, but more importantly it's only a couple of blocks away from our shop, making it damned easy to get to if we need a bite to eat or a bit of extra info after we close up.

Most people loosen their tongues a smidge after a drink or two, and why wouldn't you spill all your secrets to a familiar face in the pub you feel at home in? We've gotten a lot of good intel here ever since we started our side gig a few years back.

"Let's just get this over with," Keiran grumbles and holds out his open hand to Zeke, the brute bouncing his leg so violently the entire table shakes.

"No." Zeke responds, incredible wordsmith that he is.

"What the fuck do you mean 'no?' You dragged us all out here for this bullshit so let's just fucking do it and get it over with and go home. I need to go on a run or I'm going to lose my fucking shit." Oooh, he said that with a bonus snarl. So intimidating. Rawr.

"We need to wait until there's a large enough sample size to pull from here. Lilly said more people are coming to see the band. We wait until then." Dry as unbuttered toast, that Zeke is.

"Reel it in a bit, Kier. Why don't you go take a lap around the block and then come back to us?"

"Fine, Monty, sounds good," Kieran grunts out as he practically shoots from the booth like his ass is on fire and the closest bucket of water is three miles away. Oh, hey! Guess I won that bet with myself; Kieren WAS the first to flee. Does it count even though it happened before we activated the charms? I'm going to say it counts! Winning feels too good not to.

Lilly comes back with our drinks and I run my index finger fully around the rim of my beer as she passes Connor his Coke. "Thanks, Duke. You're a doll."

She rolls her eyes again but is still clearly tickled at having called herself a 10 foot parakeet, given the slight upturn in the corners of her mouth.

Connor grabs a small pile of snack mix and starts fiddling with it on the table, making designs out of the various pieces. We settle in for a bit and wait for things to pick up. I don't mind; so far there's been plenty of entertainment to keep me happy, and the band hasn't even gotten here yet.

"Who's going out tomorrow? We still need more steel and copper for the project on Walker street." Monty takes our downtime as an opportunity to get us all on the same page. To be fair, nobody else is going to do it so he might as well. "Lin? We haven't been to this site yet, it would be good if you were there in case we have trouble getting in. And Connor, I could use your help if we need to split in a hurry. If Kieran's up to it, we could use him for the harvest but we can just take tools if he's not. What do you say?"

"Secret midnight missions with the potential for a wild getaway? Of course I'd be delighted to join!" A thrill brushes its way up my spine at the possibilities. So few of these things are as dangerous as they could be, but it's ultimately for the best. Monty's good at keeping us prepared for the worst case scenario, so I shouldn't complain that I've never almost died while we take on our tasks... I shouldn't, but I'm tempted to.

"I'll help, too." Connor looks up from his snack mix designs through the curtain of blonde curls that have fallen in front of his glasses. He's the tallest one of all of us, but for some reason he insists on hunching over as much as possible and tucking himself into the smallest corners, almost always managing to look up at us rather than down. Who told him he's not allowed to take up space?

"Great! Zeke, are you okay to open the shop alone in the morning? Let us dastardly villains sleep in a couple hours extra?"

"Yes, Monty, that's fine. What do I need to do to prep your clinic?"

"Don't worry about it, buddy! I'll make sure everything's ready for me when I'm ready for it. Worst case scenario, Lin brews up a couple of small cure all potions for anyone with a minor problem so we don't end up getting behind. Right, Lin?"

"You've still got a full drawer full of them in the office; I could probably snatch 20 off your hands and it wouldn't matter for weeks."

"See! The clinic's covered. Just man the counter for a few hours. Take Stubbs with you if you need extra muscle to keep the riff-raff out." Monty takes a swig of his beer through a small grin, no doubt imagining Colonel Stubbs trying to intimidate anyone.

"Okay. Do you need me to make anything for tomorrow night?"

Monty pauses for a second, glass still raised to his lips, and I can see him going over scenarios in his head. "Actually, Zeke, do you still have any of those strength bracers? And protection gloves? If Kieren isn't coming they'll help us move the load."

"Yeah, I always keep extras in my work bench for us."

More people start filtering in, so we leave the details of our nefarious schemes to peter out in favor of drinking and people-watching. Seems like we're pretty well settled on it all anyway; not like this isn't basically par for the course at this point.

That delectable violet-haired woman is still at the bar, sitting alone. No, wait, not alone? There's a creature draped across her shoulders that she seems to be talking to. Is that hot? Is it crazy? A part of me wants to slink up to her and ask about it but Kieren chooses that moment to barrel back through the door and storm towards us. It might not sound graceful, but he's clearly blown off enough steam by the time he reaches the table and guzzles his beer down in one go. Slamming the glass down, Kieran slides back into his seat next to me, as smooth as his bulk can muster. Honestly, this really is about as calm as that maniac gets.

The band starts to introduce themselves as Kieran gets down to business.

"We ready yet?"

"Give it just a little bit more, Kier," Monty calmly states before cocking his head slightly to the side. "You okay to come out tomorrow night?"

"Walker street?"

"That's the one."

"Yeah, of course I'm in." Kieran shoves a fistful of snack mix into his mouth and nods a couple of times, not minding the peanuts he sends scattering everywhere in the process.

We listen to a song or two from the duo up on stage, and even Kieran seems to be soothed by their calming vibe. We're all sort of unconsciously nodding or swaying or tapping lightly along with them. Good music really is its own kind of magic, in a way. I get lost in their sound, just a little bit, letting it seep into my soul and pull out a memory or two that feels called to it. The singer has heartache dripping thickly from each word, sharing the ghost of love that now haunts her through every room in every house, no matter how many exorcisms she holds. Like me.

"It's time," Zeke states, shaking me from my memories. He hands each of us a small, woven bracelet with a golden medallion in the center. The ends are set up so that all you need to do is pull each one and it can be tightened to the most comfortable size without getting frustrated by a stupid clasp or cumbersome knot.

"Put these on, medallion against the inside of your right wrist with the sigil facing outwards. Pull the ends tight and I'll activate them all when we're ready. Last chance for questions."

"I'm good." Monty says as he twists the charm to the right spot.

"Same," Kieran mumbles through the end of the knot he's pulling tightly with his teeth.

"How do we turn it off if we need to?" Connor asks, biting

his bottom lip nervously.

"Just take it off. Nothing else required." Zeke looks to me since I'm the last to respond.

"Oh, I'm soooooo ready for this. Let's toast for good luck, gents!"

We all raise our glasses and clink the rims together, Zeke says whatever the magic words are and we all take a swig as the gold medallion on each of our wrists starts to glow.

I feel a tingle at the base of my skull and then something slams my head forward so hard I smash my face on the table and practically hurl my empty glass straight at Monty's face.

4. ZEKE

Something tingles at the base of my skull after I activate the charms.

Goddamnit. What the fuck is it, this time? Ruin my perfectly good goddamned club. Motherfucker.

"What? Who said that?" I shout.

Kieran growls loudly. Lin slams his head down onto the table and throws his glass at Monty. Connor's eyes grow impossibly wider as he watches the rest of us.

Well, that did not go as expected.

5. KIERAN

Something feels like it pricks the back of my neck and I go from irritated to fucking PISSED. And sad? Longing? What the fuck do I have to be sad about? I growl because this is bullshit. Fucking Zeke's goddamned charm is broken or some shit and I'm going to break every single face in this building right after I rip off this dumbass bracelet and maybe get some goddamned dinner. Fuck this love bullshit, I want a turkey club, not a fucking soulmate.

6. MONTY

The back of my neck starts to tickle, but I don't have time to question it because Lin chucks his glass straight at my face. Thank goodness trained reflexes kick in and my left hand shoots up to catch it before it can hit home and smash my nose in. A problem that Lin seems to need help with himself, given the loud crack coming from his side of the table and the splatter of blood above his lip. What just happened? Good thing I've always got a couple of his potions in my pockets because we have definitely got a broken nose on our hands right now.

7. CONNOR

The charms all glow brightly for a moment like miniature suns being born on each of our wrists.

A touch caresses the back of my neck, sending gentle tendrils of warmth flowing through my veins, extending their reach with each heartbeat until I can feel their heat in every part of me. Is this what love feels like?

To my left, Zeke shouts loudly while to my right, Lin's face hits the table. I reach out to him to check that he's okay but pause when I notice the charm is no longer on my wrist. It's gone! No, not gone, I realize. Absorbed. On the inside of my wrist there is now a light brown impression of the sigil that was on the medallion, and a thin brown line wraps around my wrist where the woven band was before.

Monty leaps up to heal Lin and I grab his wrist when it comes into my path, letting go once I confirm. Zeke seems a bit stunned when I do the same to him. I can't reach Kieran with both Monty and Lin to go through, but I'm pretty sure I'm right. Looking around, it seems like every single charm has been absorbed into their skin.

"They're gone," I say, thrusting my now bare wrist in front of Zeke's face.

"Shit," he says. This clearly wasn't supposed to happen. Zeke studies his own wrist as though he expects it to get up and walk away from him if he misses investigating even a single centimeter of its secrets.

The right sleeve of Lin's crisp white button-up shirt is painted crimson with rough smears of his own blood, looking starkly out of place against his otherwise immaculate appearance. Even his black vest and slick black dress pants are flawless and free of wrinkles, making the blood trailing up to his elbow even more surreal.

Monty is holding Lin's chin still with one hand while he gently dabs at Lin's face with a beer-scented napkin. It's already soaked with blood. There's blood on the sleeve. Blood on the table. So much blood everywhere, we're drowning in a turbulent sea of red, coming up to claim us as its next victims. I can't breathe. How can they still breathe? We're sinking too deep and I won't be able to get back to the surface in time to survive. Everyone is gone as I'm dragged down, down, down to the bottom; alone.

Cold fingers on my cheek bring me out of my nightmare and Lin's orange eyes are inches away. He leans his forehead on mine and whispers "Come back. This is where you are. See the truth, not the illusion."

I take in a shaky breath and close my eyes slowly, remembering where I am. Remembering where we are. Remembering who we are.

"I'm okay."

He nods slightly, our foreheads still connected, before straightening back up and returning to Monty's care.

The band is still playing. People are still drinking and talking and dancing. Lilly is behind the bar, talking to a woman with purple hair who looks ready to leave. Nobody seems to have noticed the explosion of chaos erupting from our table. Sometimes I wonder if I'm the only one who sees the world around us, or if I'm making the whole thing up after all.

Kieran slams his fist down on the table and jumps straight up. "What the fuck just happened, Zeke?"

This must be another hallucination, because it looks a lot like Kieran is suddenly crying. Kieran's never cried, not even when he had every bone in his foot and half his leg broken by a falling steel beam last year. Not even when he got stabbed in the shoulder by a thug who caught us on his boss's property. I was under the impression that it was somehow physically impossible for him to produce tears.

"This should not have been possible. My spell work was perfect." Zeke pauses, "Out of curiosity, does anyone else hear someone ranting about pity parties right now?"

Except we don't get a chance to answer because Monty is suddenly ripped from where he's leaning against the table and dragged across the floor on his back towards the exit. Nobody's touching him; he seems to have acquired his very own angry poltergeist, being dragged out of the door with neither hide nor hair of a corporeal aggressor.

"What the fuck?!?" Kieran screams, turning to chase our mysteriously departing healer.

I throw some bills down on the table as the rest of us scramble out of the booth to follow on the heels of whatever this latest development is.

8. DIZZY

Funny how smashing your face down into your dinner will take care of any lingering appetite you might have. I mean, it's one thing to have food all over your face because you're a slob trying your best to french kiss a massive sandwich, but it's another thing entirely to have it all over your face because some asshole somewhere decided to mess with some magic and hit you with the whammy instead of whoever they meant to. It's fucking embarrassing! I'm so tired of not really having any control over what happens in my life and just being forced to barrel on through whatever just shoves itself into my path. Or shove me in its path.

Thankfully, Lilly doesn't give me the third degree when I say I've got to go and slam a wad of cash down on the bar next to my obliterated meal. I snatch a couple of napkins and scrub angrily at my face, storming out the door to head off in whatever direction my feet decide they want to go.

It's not fucking fair, you know? Who did I piss off in a previous life to deserve constantly having bullshit rain down on me at every turn? I don't even know if I've managed to have a single meal go uninterrupted in weeks; I certainly haven't gotten any proper rest in months. I'm frayed at every edge there is, not even remotely prepared to hold my shit together any more.

The sneakers I'm wearing are too soft to really make my tantrum feel like it's expressing all my aggression. Heavy boots. Heavy boots with steel toes. Yeah, I bet they'd clomp down nice and hard and loud so this show I'm performing for no one could really have the proper impact.

But of course, the only one who gets to see me like this is Aria, and she's just hanging out on my shoulders like it's any other Tuesday. Fucking Tuesday. I think I hate Tuesdays, now.

Goddamnit. Stop throwing yourself a pity party and buck the fuck up. If the only people you can invite to your pity party are yourself and Aria, who isn't even a person to begin with, then it's not worth putting in the effort. Maybe if you got some pitiful decorations, partially deflated balloons, a half-melted ice cream cake, and wrinkled paper hats... has anyone ever thrown an actual pity party? I wonder if they help.

There's a wild scrabbling sound behind me and I turn to see some beefy guy wearing a unicorn shirt, looking like he's struggling to maintain his balance. Dude looks totally freaked and I'm pretty sure he's just saying "Fuck fuck fuck fuck fuck" over and over again. Shit, it looks like there's four other guys chasing him and I do NOT have the patience to deal with whatever this new fuckery is, so I just bolt out of there. I can't. I really, really can't.

It's a good thing I've got cutoff shorts on today, because running and getting all sweaty while wearing a dress is just asking for chub rub. Fucking hate chub rub. You ever had it? It's like diaper burn for your inner thighs and it will RUIN your life.

I keep shooting glances over my shoulder every once in a while and the whole group of guys look like they're charging in my direction while arguing with each other. Are they after the unicorn king or are they after me? Look, I hate to throw someone else to the wolves but it would really be great to get a moment to collect myself and have this not be some kind of perpetually cursed garbage, though I already know that's way too much to ask.

Still, I make a couple of random turns to see if it shakes them, accepting that I'm clearly the target once it doesn't. Shit. Good guys or bad guys? Am I being chased by your average, every day psycho mob of men, or the stabby stabby murder murder kind of man mob?

Shit, is one of them the guy from the antiques shop, earlier? Ugh. I knew that one was likely to bite me in the ass later.

No, none of the guys in this herd of hunks is middle-aged and balding. Yup. All of them seem to have hair.

Aria lets out a trill that sounds a lot like her version of a whoop, clearly enjoying herself while she clasps my jacket tighter with all four of her little grabby paws. So happy to keep you entertained while trying not to get us both murdered, oh mighty fluffy one.

Probably the only real athletic skill I have is running away from trouble since it happens a lot, but I'm still beat from all the arguments with gravity and canine-based galavanting earlier. The tops of my thighs are starting to scream at me and my lungs are begging to tap out and have some other organ take over. Tough luck, lungs, there's no understudy waiting in the wings for either of us.

My feet slip on what is now familiar grass; looks like I took us on a circuitous route back to the park from earlier. At least it's a recognizable landmark of sorts, so why not have it be the site of my last stand? Maybe I'll accidentally develop a sudden mastery of Judo and knock them all out with my mad skills. Hey, stranger things have happened!

Stopping suddenly and jumping to turn towards my pursuers, my mistake becomes obvious right about the time I'm tackled by our wide-eyed unicorn enthusiast. Oof. Momentum is one hell of a thing to try and halt when you aren't expecting it, so he hits me like a train made out of other, more powerful trains and the wind gets knocked out of me as my back hits the ground. Pretty sure I blacked out for a second there, too, but it could have just been an exceptionally long blink. The world may never know!

I open my eyes and take in the horrified expression now hovering on the face above me. Thick black eyebrows are practically shooting high enough up his forehead to join the long dreadlocks framing his face. His violet eyes are wide, practically glowing in contrast to his deep brown skin. It's not every day that I get tackled to the ground by a handsome man, but at least that can get checked off my bucket list now.

Breathing apparently isn't a possibility right now, either because he's leaning on my desperate lungs or because of how his sudden presence quite literally took my breath away. My mouth opens but all I can manage is a pained wheeze around the tightness in my chest.

His posse reaches us in an explosion of sounds and movements while I try to tap one of the arms he's got up against my side, my weak attempt at escape apparently doing nothing to dislodge my captor. Welp. Guess it's time to get murdered.

"Monty, what the fuck?"
"Why did you chase her?"
"Did she do this bullshit to you?"

"Why are we in the park?"

"Why hello there, gorgeous."

"Who said anything about murder?"

They all start shouting over one another and I have no freaking clue what's going on but I'm starting to panic a little bit because I can't move with the one big dude pinning me to the ground, and all the yelling from the other four is definitely not giving me good vibes.

Aria shoots her way up to me from wherever she must have been tossed to when I got knocked down, sharply nipping the arm I tried to push away from me moments ago. My assailant yelps and seems to snap back to reality. He lifts himself up and reaches a hand down to help me as well.

"I am so sorry, miss. Really. I don't know why I couldn't stop following you, well, maybe I know a little bit, but I'm so sorry. This definitely wasn't supposed to happen, but I guess we're here now, so it has. Sorry." He rambles as I take his hand, after which he runs it through his dreadlocks sheepishly. It's kind of adorable in a 'thought I was going to get murdered but it turns out to hopefully be way less scary than that even though murder still hasn't been fully taken off the table as their intention' sort of way.

"We're not going to kill you." The tattooed one with dark, shaggy hair and tanned skin says.

Okay, then. Murder is DEFINITELY back on the table because only someone who's going to kill you would make that the first thing they say. Nice try, stabberman, I'm not falling for that one today.

He snorts and covers his mouth with a ring-littered hand, "Stabberman? I don't even have a knife."

Fuck. Did I say that out loud? Or can he read my mind. Shit, if he can read my mind then how am I going to get out of this?

He'll know every move... Uhh...uhh.... I mean, nothing to think here.... doot doot doot....uhhh... uhhhhh.... POTATO.

He throws his head back and just laughs. Fuck. Potato.

The brick wall of a redhead wearing a kilt and pacing back and forth shouts "I'm freaking out, guys! I feel like I want to piss myself and run far, far away right now and this is not good. Not good. Lin, I think I'm losing it, do I need a reality check? Is this a panic attack? Lin!"

The skinny Asian guy wearing a black vest over a white shirt practically covered in blood saunters up to the kilted guy and grabs his face with both hands. Fuck, all that blood, I knew they were going to kill me!

Their foreheads tap together for a second while I wonder about the logistics of trying to escape again. That traitor Aria seems to have ditched me for the unicorn guy, though, and there's no way in hell I'd leave without her. I love the bitch, but she's got to work with me here.

"Hey," a soft voice says near my left ear. I turn slightly, startled at the sudden appearance of a very tall, very thin man to my left. The turquoise of his argyle sweater vest perfectly matches the bright color of his wary eyes. "Are you okay?"

I want to say no, but he's looking at me in a way that makes me think he really needs me to be okay, so I say....

"No. No I'm not okay." Darn. Went with the truth this time.

And then everything suddenly goes quiet. All the yelling from the other guys is gone, and I look around to see that the park is now empty except for me and the tall man before me. A light breeze blows and brings with it the scent of honeysuckle and lavender. An owl hoots twice. The night sky is clear and full of stars. In the background, the fountain splashes gently, somehow making me feel a little more grounded with its constant presence.

He gently sits down on the ground and crosses his legs, making me notice the high top converses peeking out from the rolled cuff of his skinny jeans. Idly, his hand plucks up blades of grass while he looks up at me with those damned beautiful eyes and asks "You wanna talk about it?"

Not really knowing what else to do, I flop back down onto the ground and join him, crossing my own legs and letting out a long sigh. My fingers get stuck a bit in my hair as I try to run both hands through it. What even is happening, right now?

I look at my new...friend? Not really sure what I'm doing or where everyone else went but I'm grateful that the panicked feeling crushing my chest is mostly gone. We just sit together quietly for what feels like hours, watching each other. His long fingers keep plucking up blades of grass until a bare patch is revealed in front of him. Time goes by and he doesn't push me for anything, just waits and lets me do the same. Crickets chirp their nighttime chorus. My heart stops trying to jackhammer out of its prison.

Those eyes. His eyes... they're so clear and pure and he's looking at me like I'm the only thing in the whole world to look at and something shifts inside me, feeling a little like gratitude and a little like longing and I just.... cry. I cry because it's been a long day and a long week and a long lifetime and I've been alone for so long and nobody even cares at all. But this stranger? He looks at me like I matter at all; like I matter to *him* and I don't even know what to do about it. Why is he looking at me like that? It's so much pressure. I cry and cry and he just lets me, not looking away and not moving to leave this crazy woman whose name he doesn't even know.

I sniffle and wipe my eyes with the sleeve of my jacket. "My name's Dizzy."

"I'm Connor."

We look at each other a little longer.

"I've had a pretty bad day and I just don't think I can take any more right now."

"I figured you might have. I'm here, if you want to tell me. Or we can just sit here until you're ready."

So I tell him. I tell him so much. How I'm cursed to always be cursed, and how crazy shit always follows me everywhere I go. I tell him I've been on my own since forever, except for Aria, but that I've been on the road since I was 16. We talk about how the hotel I was in burnt down to the ground this morning and I don't have anywhere to stay the night. I tell him about the coffee and the broken cane and falling out of the tree and running from the antique shop and breaking the curse in the park and the sunburn and the loneliness and my smashed up dinner.

He listens patiently, not asking questions even when I start rambling about how I was sure they were going to murder me and I'm not convinced I'm not already dead and did he know he has the most gorgeous eyes and why is he being so calm towards me?

When I'm done, he stretches his right arm out to me, palm up, and I tentatively place my hand in his. He runs slow circles over the back of my hand with his thumb and still maintains eye contact.

"Dizzy, it sounds like you've got a lot that you're carrying around with you. I think we were supposed to meet tonight, and if you'll let me I'd really love to help lighten that load you're burdened with. I'm sorry we scared you, but if you're looking for a place to stay for however long you need, the guys and I have a house just outside the city and I promise you'll be welcomed. We can talk more in the morning if you want, or more now, or you can go and I promise I won't try to stop you but I think you could use some company. Will you let me do that for you?"

Where did this guy come from? Despite all rational reasoning saying stranger danger, Connor seems utterly sincere and every instinct in me whispers to go on. I don't have it in me to run away any more; I'm so tired of always running. I'm a little choked up with feelings at the moment, so I just nod and squeeze his hand.

"Will you be okay if I leave you here for just a minute and tell the others you're coming with us?"

I don't know where "here" is compared to "there," but I trust him when he says he'll come back so I nod.

He squeezes my hand back and stands up, dusting off loose strands of grass from his skinny jeans and pulling at the white tails of the short-sleeved button up under his sweater vest. The quick way he tidies up for his friends is sort of curious, especially given that he got untidied in front of a total stranger.

"Give me just a minute," he says, and then he takes a step backwards, disappearing.

9. CONNOR

By the time I step out of the illusion, things seem to have calmed down significantly. Zeke is perched on the edge of the nearby fountain, twisting one of the rings on his fingers and staring up at the sky. Monty is sitting on the ground, tossing an acorn back and forth with Aria. Kieran seems bizarrely at peace and is laying down on the grass with his arms behind his head, eyes closed. Lin's lounging with his hip against the trunk of a tree, one hand resting on his chin contemplatively, the other draped across his chest.

He looks at me and says "Well?"

"Her name is Dizzy. She's staying with us until she doesn't want to any more. She's had bad days on repeat for a while now and I'm going to do something about it if she'll let me. Oh, and our spell led us to her so, Zeke, I think it worked."

Lin hooks both his thumbs into his pockets and straightens

up to walk slowly towards me. "It more than worked, muffin. When Kieran thought he was having a panic attack, I opened the truth for him but it wasn't what we expected; I saw a thread going between him and her and the emotions he was feeling were hers. Zeke already figured out he's been hearing her thoughts since we activated it, and it seems like Monty has to physically stay near her. All of us have a golden thread leading from our wrists towards her, it seems. Whatever the charms did, we're all tied to each other through her, so of course our violet beauty is welcome to come along. In fact, I wouldn't dream of having it any other way."

"It's the least we can do after I nearly crushed her flat," Monty says while reaching out his arm so Aria can climb up it. She rests on his right shoulder and wraps her tail around the back of his neck, flicking the fluffy mass against Monty's cheek in a sort of petting motion. They appear to have bonded while I was gone, then.

"She is an anomaly. I would like to learn more." Zeke gives his agreement.

"Yeah. What they said." Kieran slowly rolls to his side and angles to get up.

"Then we'll be out in a little bit."

I turn and take a step forward to re-enter the pocket illusion I built for her. Dizzy's still sitting on the grass, but seems to have braided her hair over her right shoulder while I was gone. Golden eyes find mine as she gives me a nervous smile while fiddling with the splayed ends of her plaited locks. I reach down my right hand and she delicately slides in one of her own, letting me help her to her feet.

"Are you ready to go?"

"I guess so." She looks down briefly and lightly kicks the grass with one of her feet, shrugging.

I link our empty hands together and lean down until I re-capture her gaze. "We can wait if you want to, there's no rush. The guys are all happy to have you come with us but we can stay out here forever if you're worried they don't want you around."

"It's not that," She releases a heavy sigh, the forceful breath fluttering a few loose strands of hair like wispy butterfly tails. "I don't really... everywhere I go, something bad always happens to the people around me. Or the buildings around me. What if an earthquake rips your house apart because I'm staying there?" Her voice lowers to a whisper and she closes her eyes with her head tilted down again. "It's not safe to be near me."

I squat down, still holding her hands, and wait. Her brows are furrowed and I can see the weight of all the hurt she usually hides as her shoulders tense up. She prepares for my rejection, but I would sooner go swimming naked in a tank filled with piranhas than let her down right now. She cracks one golden eye open slightly and sees me waiting.

"You're going to have to do better than that if you want to scare me away. I've had daydreams worse than a broken house before. If you'll let me, I'd love to take you home. Don't worry about anything else except for what kind of ice cream you want once we get there."

So much relief slowly creeps into her features. She's warned me of the dangers and I've accepted the terms, our contract sealed with promises of dessert and dreams.

I straighten up, and so does she; determination working its way into the ample chest she's starting to puff out as her walls against the everyday rebuild themselves. She gives me a nod and I go to drop her hands, but she keeps my right one clasped in her left. No complaints here.

The illusion drops and everyone is still roughly where I last left them. Monty takes a step forward with his right hand stretched out and she leans ever so slightly closer to me, but doesn't let her nerves betray her.

"Dizzy, I'm so sorry if I hurt you before. Please, forgive me. My name's Monty and I promise I don't make it a habit to tackle people to the ground." She eyes his hand suspiciously but takes it, shaking it firmly. "I run a healing clinic and I'd gladly look over any wounds on your body you might have, if you want me to." His eyes run over her bare legs as he takes in the accumulated scrapes and bruises, likely feeling guilty from the assumption that he caused them.

"I'll gladly just look over your body, sweet thing."

"Lin!" Monty hisses quietly, shooting him a warning glare while Lin very slowly skims over Dizzy with his gaze. She rolls her eyes, but a soft pink blush tints her freckled cheeks all the same.

Weirdly docile, Kieran languidly walks over to us and extends his right hand, palm up, bowing slightly. She places her caramel hand into his and he gently presses his pale forehead to it. "I'm Kieran. It is very lovely to meet you, Dizzy. Apologies if I frightened you earlier, I was a little more worked up than usual." He rises calmly and releases her hand, convincing me in the process that he's been body snatched and our next mission is going to be evicting a skinwalker. Kieran's not even fiddling with anything as his arms rest lightly by his sides.

Zeke rises from his seat on the fountain and approaches, a slight quirk on his lips before he looks her dead in the face and just says "Potato."

Dizzy's expression falls just slightly until she whips around and buries herself into my shoulder, shaking. I almost reach out to push him away until I realize she's starting to laugh.

The sound is muffled by my body but it's unmistakable once it reaches my ears. Her sudden, restrained joy has the rest of us quirking an eyebrow at Zeke, but he just crosses his arms and looks inexplicably smug.

Laughter peters down to small giggles until she snorts just slightly and lifts herself from me, wiping under her right eye. "God, I'm such a freak. Potato. What was I even thinking with that? Oh right, I was thinking potato!" She starts laughing all over again, clutching at her belly as it gets hard to breathe, this time baring her glee loudly for us all to be immersed in.

Nobody but Zeke seems to really know what's going on, but it's hard not to laugh when someone else is enjoying themselves so much, so we all end up making mad fools of ourselves in an empty park over a mysterious tuber.

Dizzy gently shoves Zeke's shoulder in a somewhat affectionate way.

"I won't. You're welcome. Zeke," He says. She beams in his direction and gives my hand a quick squeeze.

"Well then, guys, I was promised ice cream! Why don't we blow this popsicle stand for the clearly superior frozen treat? Lead the way, oh mighty herd of hunks!" Dizzy looks up at me playfully as she unclasps our hands and links our arms instead. Again, no complaints here.

Zeke takes the lead as we all head out of the park, back towards The Wood Liquor. When Monty falls into step with Dizzy and I, she reaches out towards Aria but her friend seems content to remain on Monty's shoulders. She looks disappointed briefly, but shrugs and keeps heading onwards.

A companionable silence begins to blanket our journey, warmly embracing but never smothering us. It's broken up by quiet but happy humming from Lin while he lopes along behind us with his hands deep in his pockets. From Monty's shoulder, Aria begins to sway and adds a harmony to his song with small trills and hums of her own. Dizzy's whole face lights up as she bounces and sways with every step, adding a third layer of sound with wordless vocalizations. The music builds and swells as Lin lets his humming grow stronger, and Dizzy bumps my hip with her side as she starts to lose herself in the song. She swings us both around and uses my hand to twirl herself before flitting off like a fairy towards Aria, circling around Monty whilst running a light touch along her friend. The trio's sound crescendos and all hints of former quiet are lost, filled with joy and brightness and playfulness. Kieran's deep baritone adds a note or two and Dizzy weaves her way among us, twirling and bouncing and clapping as she pleases. Her long braid whips around in whichever direction she's come from, leaving a streaking after-image of purple in its wake.

She grabs Lin's shoulders and he wastes no time lifting her up into a spin, moving both their feet to the beat whilst still somehow managing to stay on course. The song starts to taper back, Aria letting her notes become fewer and fewer. Dizzy's golden eyes gleam as she lets her part end, her dance partner providing the last few hums as we approach our destination.

"You're a wonder, Love. Can we keep you?" Lin gives her one more twirl as she giggles and gives him a brief but happy hug.

"Thanks for the song!" She kisses him on the cheek and bounces right back up to me, smoothly sliding her arm into mine again, this time leaning her head against me.

Can we keep you, indeed.

10. MONTY

Wowie zowie, that woman sure is something else.

Zeke unlocks the doors to our SUV and I happily open the back for our newest passenger. Her and Connor are apparently attached at the hip, so they both slide all the way back into his usual spot. Lin slips into the empty space in the back row, sandwiching Dizzy between Connor and himself. They look happy back there, Dizzy leaning against Connor who, for once, isn't curling himself into a tight ball. Kieran and I buckle ourselves into the middle row, leaving Zeke alone in the front as he turns the key in the ignition.

My new buddy leaps off my shoulder and lands in Dizzy's lap, stretching up to rub their noses together as Dizzy whispers "Oh, Aria, I've missed that. Thank you." She strokes her right hand down the length of her companion, stopping to give a few scritches at the base of Aria's tail.

Lin cautiously reaches out to Aria, pausing to let her assess him in the way you would any new animal you're not sure of your standing with. She hums out a few bars of his song in approval and rubs her face against his fingertips.

To my left, Kieran starts to pluck at the hem of his plain white t-shirt. Whatever high he was riding from experiencing Dizzy's emotions must be wearing off because he's starting to fidget again. He keeps glancing backwards but doesn't try to make conversation. I worry he'll lose control.

Hushed conversation and occasional giggles float forward from the backseat as we hit the road to home. It occurs to me that Dizzy is a wrench that's been thrown into our plans for tomorrow night and I wonder if we need to abandon ship, adjust the rigging, or bring her onboard. Things are especially complicated if I can't be far from her; maybe it'll still work with just Kieran, Connor, and Lin? As long as things don't go sideways, they won't need any major healing and Lin's potions should be enough.

An uncomfortable knot of anxiety forms in my chest at the idea that I might be letting the guys down, or that something big might happen and I won't be there to take control. Stepping back and letting other people take risks without a safety net has never really been one of my strong suits.

It kills me to admit this, but the safest bet for now is probably for me to stay behind. We need to get those materials as soon as possible and there aren't that many options when you have to raid condemned and partially demolished buildings to get them. It's a risk every time we take on one of these projects, but the rewards have *always* been worth it.

I scratch the back of my neck and run through scenarios in my mind, trying to anticipate every possible outcome so I can prep the guys as best as possible. They'll need strength bracers and impenetrable gloves for the work, but I'll have to mix up some salves and binds tonight in case they get hurt without me. Connor will have to bottle an illusion if they need an extra distraction; a dupe of the truck should be enough. Maybe a cover of darkness or two for if they get spotted. Kieran should have some manipulations for the others to help bolster collection. Can Zeke whip up something for speed and sound? If I can't be there to protect them, then there need to be as few risks as possible.

Snores start to build in intensity and I peek backwards to see Dizzy with her mouth hanging open, head still against Connor's side, Lin gently massaging his fingers in her scalp. He looks amused with her and pleased with himself as his hand lowers to give the same treatment to Aria, currently curled up in his lap.

Zeke pulls up to the gravel driveway of our large tan cottage house, parking in front of the detached 3 car garage.

"WHAT?! I'm up!!" Two pained "oofs" come from the backseat as Dizzy jerks upright and whacks her arms out wide, knocking both of her seat mates in the chest with a loud thwack. How is that even an instinct? Who flings their arms out to the side when they wake up?

"Oh shit. Sorry, guys." Her hands awkwardly retreat to her lap and she looks pretty much anywhere except at the men she just mildly assaulted.

Lin chuckles and gives a sly look out of the corner of his eye, "What, you're not going to kiss it better, beautiful?"

She rolls her eyes but clearly thinks he's funny from the smile blooming on her face. "Nope!"

"But how am I to survive such a mortal wound? Surely, tonight I shall perish. Woe! Woe is me!" Lin really plays it up, but she rewards him with a giggle snort so he's only going to lay it on thicker from here. "Please, Dizzy!" He turns and grasps the sleeve of her jacket with both hands, "I'm on my deathbed here! Will you not tend to a poor fool such as myself? Take pity, oh mighty mistress. My life... is in... your hands..." he says the last few words while slowly sinking backwards, raising one hand to his forehead and closing his eyes for added effect. Lin's tongue flops out once he's fully resting against the window, the perfect touch to add to this already ridiculous show of drama.

"Welp. Guess that means more ice cream for me!" She un-buckles and grabs a groggy Aria from her cruelly discarded victim, gently placing the creature inside her hood. "Let's go!"

Kieran already bolted out the second we stopped and dis-appeared into the surrounding woods, so she climbs out of his still-open door and promptly falls flat on her face. Dizzy hops back up almost immediately and raises both arms in a vic-tory pose, "And she sticks the landing! Whoo! The crowd goes wild!!!"

Lin rubs his nose as I grin and wonder what the heck kind of crazy ride we're in for with this girl.

Connor crawls out from the same door she did, looking her over while the rest of us step out and let Zeke hit the lock on the key fob. She flicks her hand a couple of times at Con-nor's concerned expression, clearly dismissing his worry as nothing. She's not bleeding or freaking out so I respond to the glance he gives me with a shrug and head up the walkway to our front door. Dizzy elbows Connor in the side playfully and follows the rest of us while looking slack-jawed at her sur-roundings.

"Woah, you guys have a lemon tree? That's so cool! And all these plants? Lamb's ear? Calendula? Sage? Is this a witching garden?! Oh my gosh, the flowering ivy is so beautiful! Are you guys fairytale princes? A huge gorgeous cottage surrounded by nature; next thing I know you're going to trot out your royal unicorn and let me wish on a magic mirror!"

"No unicorns, I'm afraid, but we do have a magic mirror." Her eyes light up at my response.

"No shit. Does it grant wishes? Or show you who's the fairest of them all?"

"It lets you see places," Zeke opens the door and flicks on the lights while giving his response.

"Cooooool. Like, anywhere? If I wanted to see the moon, could I?" She crosses the threshold and her thoughts are cut off as frantic scrabbling and a few gruff chuffs make their way around the corner towards us. "LITTLE WHITE FRENCHIE!!! Buddy, you live here, too?!" The lucky dog gets scooped up and squeezed tight to her chest briefly before she bolts deeper into the house, laughing hysterically the entire way.

"Did she just steal our dog?" I look at the other three guys for confirmation as I hear the back door slide open, triggering the motion-sensor lights. "I'm pretty sure she just stole our dog."

A huge smile breaks out across Lin's face as he starts to jog backwards in their direction, "Well then, gents, looks like we're on a rescue mission! The Colonel needs our help!" He hops a couple of times and turns around, not waiting to see if we're going to follow. I don't get the chance to decide for myself because within a few seconds I can already feel my chest pulling slightly towards the direction of our devious dog-napper. As if I would choose to miss a minute of whatever new crazy this girl has decided to whip up a feast of.

By the time we reach the back door, she's already halfway down the backyard, whooping and laughing while making some of the most ridiculous evasive maneuvers I've ever seen. She's zig-zagging around the yard, occasionally back-tracking and jumping over the dog who's clearly chasing her. How is he the one chasing her when she's the one who spirited him away in the first place?

Lin keeps laughing and running down towards them, so she makes a beeline at him. "Pick me up! Pick me up!" Her words only just barely give him warning as she takes a flying leap right into his arms. "Mua ha ha ha ha! Try catching me now!" She sticks a pink tongue out, clearly mocking the beast jumping as high as his tiny little legs will let him. Her laughter only grows more crazed as she curls her feet further out of reach.

Connor and I just watch from the edge of our wooden deck, but Zeke casually walks his way towards the mayhem. I notice Kieran at the perimeter of the yard, crouched in front of one of the surrounding trees, obviously baffled by the same scene we're scoping out.

"Nooo! I have been betrayed!!!" Dizzy is on her back in the grass where Lin's pinned her, "Curse you, Lin! Curse you!!!" She declares while receiving an extra sloppy helping of puppy slobber all over her scrunched-up face.

Zeke finally reaches the cluster of limbs and looks Dizzy in the eye while bending his knees just slightly. She shoves Lin off her using both hands, screaming "Tag! You're it!" At the same moment that Zeke scoops her off the ground and runs like mad towards a wide-eyed Kieran.

"Catch!" Zeke tosses Dizzy at Kieran, provoking a squeal from her as she soars the short distance.

Kieran rises from his crouch and snatches her right out of the air as Zeke spins a moment too late to avoid Lin's outstretched arm. "Colonel Stubbs, I'm coming for you, boy!" Zeke declares his intent and shoots off in the direction of our pudgy little pupper.

I look to my left and see Connor gripping the railing and

leaning as far forward as possible, riveted by the scene in front of us. "Why don't you get down there, too?"

"Why don't you?" He responds.

"Good point!" I take the couple of steps down the deck into our yard as Connor shrugs and follows. He heads straight to the tree line where Kieran and Dizzy lurk while I get to experience firsthand what it's like to be head butted in the leg at full steam by a 10 pound French bulldog: adorable, but not at all devastating. Clearly, I'm now "it." I glance to my left and find that the tree trio are missing. Seems as though I'll have to settle for Lin or Zeke as my target.

I casually walk towards them, arms clasped behind my back and looking up at the stars like I haven't a care in the world. They frantically wrestle to push each other forward in an attempt to sacrifice one another, Zeke being somewhat more successful at keeping himself behind Lin.

Trying a new tactic, Lin digs his heels into the ground and pushes backwards against Zeke, jostling him off balance just enough to spin to the side and break away from the now fallen spell crafter. I stalk towards him slowly, hands curled into claws as he scrabbles to back away. Just as I'm about to pass on my cursed position to a new victim, a weight suddenly attaches itself to my back, a pair of soft hands covering my eyes while muscular thighs wrap around my waist.

"Run, Zeke! To freedom!" Dizzy's orders are shouted with glee from above my head. She lowers herself just slightly and whispers in my ear "Tag, I'm it," causing goosebumps to rise all over my skin. She slowly slides every inch of herself down my back to firmly plant her feet on the ground. The liquid way her body flows across mine is a very welcome surprise, a movement sadly completed far too soon. What I wouldn't do to feel her up against me like that again... She lands a playful swat on my ass and my cock twitches in response. "You'd better go, too. It won't be safe for long." I don't even get a chance to think before she's turned and run away from me, sprinting towards the deck that Kieran and Connor appear to be hiding under.

In a few swift moments, she launches herself straight at them both, arms outstretched wide enough to simultaneously capture each in her grasp. "Tag! You're both it!" She starts to turn to make her escape, but Kieran and Connor both wrap an arm around her waist and hold her hostage, pressing her as close to them as they can. Connor whispers something in her ear and Kieran growls playfully while chomping his teeth together. She throws her head back and laughs some more, raising her hands in surrender. "Okay, so maybe it's a bit like cheating. You win! You both win! I'm it forever!" she crows.

I notice Connor's hand has switched from holding her in place to stroking up and down her back lightly, leaving Kieran to detain the wild woman. Connor's looking at her like a loyal puppy dog craving a cuddle or biscuit, which actually, is a pretty accurate description because Colonel Stubbs is sitting at her heel giving a roughly similar stare. Looks like somebody's got a crush.

"Come on, guys, seems prime time to head back inside." I gesture for everyone to follow me as we climb back up the steps and walk through the sliding glass back door, collapsing into a pile on the L-shaped couch in our TV room.

A collective sigh leaves our lips as we settle in after a tough battle. Colonel Stubbs lets out a huff in solidarity from the floor, having clearly exerted himself the most out of all of us.

"Soooo.....about that ice cream?"

11. DIZZY

With a groan, Monty dislodges himself from our pile and heads into the kitchen. Connor gently smoothes a hand across my legs and slides out from underneath them, disappearing up the stairs behind us. I'm still sprawled across Kieran, and Lin slickly takes up the space Connor just vacated. Guess that's what happens when you don't call fives! The calf massage I suddenly find myself getting is a very welcome surprise. Oh gods is it ever welcome. Mmmm.

Sounds of cupboards opening and closing and the clanking of dishes waft from the kitchen I could easily see if only I had the will to lift my head and watch. My eyes are closed, anyway, and that would be a whole extra step so it seems like Monty will just have to go unsupervised. Oh no, what a shame.

I let my left hand grope around on the floor until it finds the little white Frenchie, rewarding my partner in playtime with many a good pat-pat.

"Not that I'm complaining about that sudden outburst of excitement, Love, but why did you snatch up Colonel Stubbs and haul that cute little ass of yours out of here?" Lin's strong fingers move up and start applying pressure to a particularly sore spot on my upper thigh. With so much running today, I don't even try to hide the moan that he works out of me. His fingers still for just a moment and I sigh contentedly before he continues on.

"Stubbs and I are best friends, in case you didn't know. We chased around a whole bunch of other dogs at the park today and it was probably the most fun I've had in a long time. Who says you can be too old for tag? Not me. I'm never going to say that."

A gentle stroke on my dangling arm has me turning my head and, fine, opening my eyes. Connor's kneeling on the ground in front of me, offering up one of his short-sleeved button-ups. This one's emerald green, and I realize it matches the small flecks scattered throughout the golden irises that Aria and I share in common. I don't think this is by accident. Be still my heart, this boy is going to have me swooning hard if he keeps making me feel all kinds of special.

"Aw, you remembered about my shirt? Thank you, that's so sweet." I try to sit up but I'm kind of having a turtle-stranded-on-its-back moment, except I don't have a cool shell to hide in when birds try to snatch me up as a snack for their bellies. So, I wiggle back and forth, almost getting enough momentum to roll off of Kieran and Lin's laps even though my butt is dipped into an empty space between them and is the real reason I'm having a bit of difficulty. This is taking a lot more time and effort than it really should if you ask me, but at least I get to spend this time feeling more and more of the men I'm sprawled across. A large hand pushes my shoulders up from underneath and I'm able to swing my legs forward at the same time. I reach my hands out to the side to stabilize myself and hear Kieran groan when I grab his thigh to get my balance.

Aria hops out of my hood and flies off towards the kitchen as I unzip my light jacket and reach for the offered garment. As I stand up and slip off my outerwear, a naughty little part of me gets a thrill from how Connor's eyes go wide and his pale cheeks burn up from the inside when he sees my silky black bra. On one hand, they're just boobs; it's no big deal. On the other hand, I very much want them to be a big deal to him and it's looking a lot like dreams really do come true.

Connor's probably six and a half feet tall and I'm only just barely topping the charts at 5'4", so his shirt reaches pretty far past the little jean shorts I've been wearing today. I plop my butt back down on the couch and swivel sideways to resume my place draped across the two men who are very clearly staring me down like I'm the only snack in town and they're about to raid my vending machine. Ooh, that went better than expected! There's no way I'd ever be able to hide the look of satisfaction I've got from shamelessly flaunting my body so I don't even pretend to try. Who wouldn't want to be the center of attention in this crowd? I eye Zeke, who's propped up in the corner on the other side of Lin, facing towards us from his exceptional viewpoint. He's got one eyebrow quirked up and a knowing smirk on his smug mug. Yeah, I know you can hear me. I know you know I did that on purpose and I'm pleased as hell it's worked out. What are you gonna do about it? Hmm? What are you gonna do? I dare you.

Quick as lighting, he reaches across Lin and snatches my arm, yanking me back up until I'm sitting with the side of my hip firmly against Lin's bulging erection. Zeke fists my hair and crashes his lips to mine, hard. I gasp because holy shit this is the hottest thing that has ever happened to me in my whole life and he wastes no time thrusting his tongue forward. I'm squirming in Lin's lap as Zeke's other hand reaches up and tweaks my nipple hard. Lin groans and wraps his arm around my back, pulling me closer to him and grinding his cock against me slightly. Fuck, I would jump either one of them right now, I'm so turned on. The desperate need inside me has only grown stronger and stronger throughout the night as we've talked and touched and flirted and now trapped with searing kisses. I start grinding my ass in Lin's lap in time with him, trying to get some friction where I definitely need it. Zeke's kiss is hungry and relentless as he devours every single fire he lights inside of me. Still, I'm burning up and need him more the longer we stay connected like this. And then he pulls back, taking my lower lip in his teeth and applying just enough pressure to hurt so good.

He nips at my ear and murmurs "Dare accepted. Your move." Zeke releases my hair and walks away.

"Holy shit," Connor whispers from the floor in front of me, making me wonder if he can hear my thoughts, too.

Lin buries his face in the crook of my shoulder and leaves a slow, needing kiss on my neck. I let out a tiny mewl as the sensation sends hot and cold pleasure coursing through my body. We both shiver at the same time. Oh sweet baby buttermilk biscuits, what a kiss. What a more than a kiss. Hands start stroking up and down the length of my legs and Lin hums his appreciation against my skin.

Right on time, Monty shows up to cool us the fuck off with a tray full of ice cream and sprinkles and cherries on top. Aria's clearly already gotten into her treat because she's dripping bright red juice all over Monty's shoulder. The intensity in his gaze lets me know he saw every single damned second and wants more.

Good.

12. KIERAN

Fuck. What just happened? This chick is like a goddamned roller coaster and damn, it's a ride I sure as shit want to get on. She's a burning ball of life and excitement and I want to get close enough to singe my fur in her heat.

We're all just processing and wondering what to do next, frozen like a bunch of fucking teenagers who've never used the dicks in their pants before. Can't say I ever saw it coming that Zeke would be the one to make a move like that, but what are the rules here? She's been stuck on Connor since minute one, but I saw how she's been letting Lin touch her after they had that crazy ass song and dance moment. Not to mention she damned well was stroking my biceps in appreciation while I carried her around out back.

I'm about ready to snatch her off of Lin's lap and see what happens when she just starts laughing, breaking up the shock we were all stuck in.

"Well alrighty then, that just happened!" She swivels herself to face forward, still sitting on Lin's lap with his left arm wrapped around her waist and his chin tucked over her right shoulder. Dizzy beckons to Monty with one arm, "You just gonna stand there and let that all melt, or what?"

He shakes his head and snaps out of it, coming forward to pass us each a bowl. Idiot. I would have let it all melt instead; let it melt all over her body and licked it right the fuck up off her. My lip rises in a snarl as I feel my wolf trying to come out for about the hundredth time tonight to speak his mind. Jesus hover-boarding Christ, I'm all worked up over here. I'm gonna have to fight or fuck or blow something up every 10 seconds at this rate.

Monty hands me my bowl and I snatch it away from him, almost not even bothering with a spoon. I'm hungry for a taste of the woman to my right, playfully swinging her feet back and forth like she didn't just get the shit kissed out of her, so I practically inhale the dessert to sate the craving. It doesn't work. I just fucking stare at her.

"Movie!" Connor pops up from his spot on the ground like a jack-in-the-box that got wound all the way up and snatches the remote from our TV table. The skinny little fuck wedges himself in the space between me and Lin, almost blocking my view.

Monty lowers himself into Zeke's abandoned seat, setting the tray down to his right on the short section of the L-shaped couch. "Yeah, Con, that sounds like a good idea. Diz, what are you into?"

"Hm?" She pops her head up, spoon hanging upside down on those wet fucking lips of hers. "Oh, anything, really. Musicals, action, sci-fi; whatever you guys want." She swings that spoon of hers around while talking, a conductor with her orchestra watching for their commands.

A long, loud exhale comes from Lin, but he sits up and plasters on his signature flirty, confident look. "Ah, Love, how about two out of three? Connor, be a dear and look for Galavant. It's a TV series instead of a movie, but I'm sure we'll manage to find a way to forgive it for the longer format."

Hell yeah I'm good with more time with this fireball of a woman, even if I'm not the lucky asshole she's using as a chair right now. It only takes Connor a minute to flip through Netflix and find the thing Lin told him to, so I stop attempting to burn a hole into the side of Dizzy's head and try to settle in to watch the damned show. Things stop being so fucking charged and we all relax enough to properly enjoy the show; it's actually pretty funny, which helps calm me from wanting to throw Dizzy over my shoulder and claim her down to just really really really wanting to bury my face in her skin and breathe her scent deeply. I know it's still fucked up, but at least it's slightly less crazy for having only met this chick a few hours ago when she blasted her way into our lives and burned up all my expectations.

I try to keep facing forward so I don't do something stupid, but can't stop being envious of the glances I catch of Connor's hand twined together with hers, resting on her thigh. His thumb caresses her in slow motions and I want to be that close to her, too. Fuck, I'm staring at their hands. Don't stare at their hands. Don't stare at both of Lin's arms dragging her deeper into his chest. Don't listen to her little sighs and hums, don't keep holding your breath until the next time she sneaks a peek at you out of the corner of her eye, don't think about what her caramel skin would look like against your milky complexion, don't wonder if the freckles across her face line up with your own, don't imagine waking up to her golden eyes gazing into your green ones like she's been waiting all night to see them again. Watch the show, dummy.

I'm still a bit wound up, but whatever this thing is that makes me feel her has me slowly mellowing enough to get to a place where the constant need I have to move is dampened. There's still a feeling of turmoil and want in the back of my head, but I'm also aware of that same wave of peacefulness that I felt in the park, soothing away my edges. It's weird, knowing now that she's basically manipulating my emotions with her own, but it's not like I've got a good hold on them myself so this isn't really that different from normal. At least this is a nice change from the rage, anxiety, and irritability I usually end up needing to burn off-she's burning it off for me, instead. Yeah, a real nice change.

Someone turns off the lights at some point. My eyes start to feel heavy, and I drift off to the distant sound of laughter; dreams of a warm breeze and gentle waves easing me away from consciousness.

13. MONTY

It's getting late, and as much as I'd love to spend the rest of the night finding ways to learn more about the woman we've suddenly been blessed to have join us, there's work to be done before tomorrow. I've still got to make some salves and binds. Crap, I didn't offer to heal the cuts on Dizzy's legs. Better make extra salve and use some on her in the morning.

I get up and grab the discarded dessert bowls-Kieran and Dizzy are the only ones who really ended up eating them anyway-and head back to the kitchen, flicking off the lights as I pass. Aria's zonked out with her head on my shoulder, long body draped behind my neck with her fluffy tail wrapped around the front, using the plush length as her own pillow. Dang, that's cute. We silently rinse off the dishes and head upstairs; hopefully Zeke's still awake right now.

His door is cracked open. There's a warm light spilling from it but I knock quietly anyway. "You up, man?"

"Yes."

I push my hand against the door and open it further, "Can I come in?"

"Yes."

Zeke's leaning back in the chair at his small work desk, staring upwards at the ceiling while idly flipping a thin rod of some kind of metal between his fingers. Based off of the towel wrapped around his waist and the fact that his scruffy beard has been trimmed neatly, it's a pretty safe bet that he went and took a cold shower after leaving us all downstairs, shocked. Part of me wants to ask him what the hell brought that all on, while the other part of me wants to slap him on the back and congratulate him on a job well done. It's not really any of my business, though, so I start in on what I came up here for in the first place.

"Hey Z, you up for making a couple extra tricks for the gig tomorrow? With me being stuck with Dizzy, I can't exactly go out unless we're bringing her along, and who knows how she'd take it if we offered." He turns his head to look at me as I continue, "So, if I'm grounded... I want to cover as many bases as possible to make sure it all goes smoothly. On the plus side, at least you don't have to open the shop on your own any more!"

"What do you need?"

I lean my back against his door frame, "What do you have in the ways of silence? Could you rig something up so the guys can't be heard while they're scavenging? Not just them individually, but for the whole area?" I start to tick off a list with counted fingertips, "And a speed boost for the truck if they get caught and need to make a break for it. Those plus the strength bracers and protection gloves should be everything."

Zeke scans the materials scattered around his room. He's

got a full workshop space downstairs, but it always seems like his projects make their way into the bedroom instead. If there's an organization system somewhere in this chaos it's one I definitely don't understand. Is half this stuff even finished?

He taps the metal rod against his chin and reaches out for a tall cluster of pink crystals practically buried under scraps of fabric and random animal bones. The wheels in his head are clearly turning as he rotates the crystal while squinting his eyes in concentration at it.

"Yeah, I can make this work. And I'll set up the truck tonight. There's a swift travels blessing anyone can activate."

I step forward and clasp my right hand over his tattooed left shoulder. "Thanks man, that's a real relief. You know I always go on these things and the idea that I won't be there this time is really messing with me. It's not like our lives weren't already wacky enough, but..." my thoughts trail off. I'm not really sure how to end that. Our lives weren't already wacky enough, but now they're even more wacky? More complicated? More exciting? More confusing? How do you describe the effect one single night of being literally pulled to a stranger can have on the rest of everything? And if Zeke's charm actually worked... what does it all mean?

I start to step back to leave him to his work, but pause. Looks like I'm asking this after all. "Why'd you do it, Z? Kiss her, I mean."

A slow smile creeps across his face, breaking up the distant look in his eyes from planning whatever that crystal in his hands is going to be used for. "She dared me." He turns his stormy blue-gray gaze in my direction, "If you could have heard her voice in your head all night long, egging us all on? It's improbable anyone could have resisted."

Dropping my arm from his shoulder, I take the step my curiosity had interrupted. I give him a nod as his attention moves back to the crystal, a grin still plastered on his face even after he starts to slip into that hyper-focused thing he does.

My footsteps are silent as I retreat back downstairs, but my mind is swimming with that one statement he made. Egging us all on? All? I scratch the top of Aria's soft head distractedly, causing her to readjust slightly to get a better angle on my affections. We pass by the kitchen and TV room to the hallway on the other side, going through the first door on the right to my office. Bright lights from the alcove in the back greet me even before I flip the switch on for the overheads. Closing the door behind me, I pass by a padded bed against the wall on my left to head for the stacked garden in the alcove on the right. There are already shears hanging on the wall to the right of the plants, so I grab them and take a few cuttings to work with.

Stroking some of their leaves tenderly, I appreciate just how well they've been flourishing ever since switching over to a self-sustaining hydroponics system. Even the little fish in each of the tanks have grown and multiplied over the last couple of months; we may have to start selling them in the shop as pets soon. Might as well sprinkle in a couple extra pinches of fish food for them while I'm here.

There's a small basket attached to the wall with all the other gardening tools, inside which is their food. Absent-mindedly, I sprinkle some in each of the three levels, still running over everything that happened tonight. This could be a good thing, right? Maybe even a really good thing.

A few errant flakes fall from my hands as I dust them off together, turning towards the long work table lined up against this room's only window. The screensaver on my computer in the corner lets me know it's just past 11PM; I hadn't even noticed how late it had gotten. Better get to work, then.

Pushing off against the wooden floor with a small kick, my chair wheels and spins towards the apothecary's cabinet behind me, on the wall across from the padded bed. Mortar and pestle, long straps of cotton cloth, squat glass jars; everything I need is within reach.

Worries seep in as I crush a combination of fresh herbs and leaves with willow ash, creating a thick paste. What if they get caught? Strictly speaking, breaking into a demolition site and stripping it of raw materials isn't exactly legal. Sure, Lin could always conceal the truth or Connor could cover up their identities with an illusion, but what about the supplies? We've got less than a week to get this job done and that's already cutting it way too close for comfort. The scraping and grinding sound of mortar against pestle offers no solution to my fears, so I find myself only anticipating the worst and then some. Dread chokes me as visions of the whole building falling on top of Kieran, or the cops swarming the site and shooting Lin to death, or Connor breaking his neck while falling in a sudden sinkhole completely overwhelm me. They can't go without me, they can't. We'll have to tell Dizzy and bring her and hopefully she'll understand why we're doing this and everything will be okay as long as I'm there to make sure nothing happens. Nothing can happen.

The rough, wet texture of a small tongue against my cheek halts the frantic grinding my hands had built up to without notice. I reach up for Aria, who rubs her muzzle against my palm and gives a playful nip to my index finger before slinking down to the table and sniffing at the bowl of paste. She chirps at me and spreads her bat-like wings, hopping up in the air and flying over to my herb garden with a body that undulates up and down like rolling waves. Her little hands grab around some sprigs of thyme, which she clips with a few quick snaps of sharp teeth. She drops them off with me at the table, but apparently isn't done yet as she heads to my cabinet, sniffing each drawer until finding the one she's apparently looking for. With surprising ease, Aria grabs the small handle and pulls back, opening the compartment to snag her prize without even landing. I'm still watching her with amused interest as she heads back my way.

Sitting on her haunches in front of me, Aria offers up the dried plant with both hands. Witch hazel. Thyme and witch hazel. Thyme's good for cuts and can help stave off infection and witch hazel promotes coagulation while reducing inflammation. She's not wrong, but.... what?

"... Thank you?" I tenderly pluck the plant from her little hands and give her a sort of quizzical quirk of my eyebrow. She nods quickly, huffing in a way that both says "you're welcome" and "now use it, idiot" at the same time. The mixture I'd been working on would have been plenty effective to heal minor cuts pretty much instantly while taking away any residual pain, but adding the thyme and witch hazel would definitely pack a bigger punch.

Sure, okay, let's listen to the mysterious, singing, flying, bat-ferret-fox-cat thing. Why not? It literally can't hurt to add them into the mix. Guess I've got a new supervisor, now?

Much more gently than before, I add in the new ingredients and grind them until they're evenly mixed into the paste. Looking to my boss for approval, she sniffs the bowl with her long, thin snout and sneezes, but steps back and appears to think it's done. There's a good amount in there, so I grab four of the cotton strips to turn into healing binds and get to work spreading out a dollop in the center of each. Aria hums and purrs and trills out a cheerful song while I work, keeping me company and lightening up the mood far away from where it was before. Without even realizing it, my own whistling starts to join her and we're tucked away into our own little pocket of productivity.

With the binds finished and rolled up, we grab some aloe, lavender, and lemon balm to add to the leftover paste, making a thinner and less heavy-duty salve. It only takes a couple of minutes to mix up and place into a few squat jars, our job done once the lids are screwed on tightly.

"You're a clever little thing aren't you, Ari?"

Clearly pleased with my compliment, she lets out a brief, happy chirrup and hops up my arm to reclaim her shoulder-based throne. I'm starting to think that Dizzy's not the only one we're lucky to have met tonight.

Quickly, I wipe up my work top and scrub clean all the tools in a small sink between my table and the garden alcove on our right. The clock on the computer lets me know it's nearly midnight; much later than I'd normally be up with such an early start in the morning. Eh, worst case scenario we open the shop a bit late tomorrow. Not like I'm going to fire myself or anything.

Chuckling at the thought, I head back into the hall and flick off the lights to my office, turning left towards the TV room the others are still assumedly in.

Dizzy's still mostly sitting on Lin's lap, but she's leaning over with her head resting against Connor's shoulder, both men with at least one arm wrapped around her in some way. Kieran is decidedly completely knocked out and the other three don't look too far behind him in that respect. Still, it's nice seeing them all at peace, tangled up in one another. From the way Aria nuzzles my cheek and sighs, it seems like she's pretty happy about the sight as well.

We stand there a couple moments more to take in the view before walking the few remaining steps towards the large couch.

Sitting on the portion adjacent to them, I lightly tap Lin on his shoulder. "Hey," I say softly, "you guys should probably head upstairs."

"Hm?" Lin turns his head to me in a daze, only just barely processing what I said.

"Why don't you lead Dizzy up to Kieran's room, since he's already down for the count. Oh, and show her the bathroom, too?"

Lin strokes a hand gently across Dizzy's waist, stirring her slightly. "Love, why don't I take you to bed?" He smiles sleepily at the thoughts I'm sure he's had. "Come on now, up with you."

She stretches backwards before slowly getting to her feet, Lin's hand in hers. Connor mumbles a protest as they retreat towards the stairs, but he's clearly not entirely aware at this point.

"Con." I gently shake his now Dizzy-less shoulder. "Hey, Con, get up buddy. I need to talk to you before you go to bed."

He blinks a couple of times until he's finally able to focus on my face. "Oh, Monty?" His gaze flicks to the empty space on his right side.

"They're headed up to bed, bud. Diz'll stay in Kier's room for the night. You awake enough to talk for a minute?"

He rubs his eyes, but nods quietly.

"I can't go with you guys tomorrow night. I have to stay here with Dizzy."

His brows furrow in confusion for a moment before it hits him, and he looks at me with a bit of shock and fear. "You can't leave her, and she can't come."

"Yeah, that's the gist of it. So, listen, I just want to keep all our bases covered. Would you be able to bottle up some spare illusions in case they need to be thrown in a pinch?"

"Sure, what were you thinking?"

"Maybe a duplicate of the truck? One that goes off on its own direction when it separates from the real one? Even better if you can build a cloak for the real truck into it but at least a dupe or two will spread some confusion if you're followed. Maybe even a cover of darkness for while you're at the site? Zeke's already working on a silencer so nobody will hear what's going on out there, but you can't be too careful. Especially in these corporate industrial areas; never know who's got what security where."

"Yeah, Monty, I'll whip those up in the morning when we're at the shop. I'm out of vials anyway so I'll snag them from our stock."

Grabbing the abandoned remote, I pause their show before turning off the TV. "That's fine Con, why don't you head upstairs and get some rest. You've got a long day ahead of you tomorrow."

He groans slightly while standing up, "Yeah. Night, Monty."

"Night, Con."

14. DIZZY

Lin guides me upstairs and takes me to the end of the hall, saying something blah blah Kieran blah blah bathroom next door, shower blah blah. Not sure if he buys me pretending to pay attention but I'm too exhausted to care. He opens a door and I just look at him like some kind of idiot until he kisses my cheek and gives me a nudge through it. Oh, bye Lin. Pretty, pretty Lin.

He walks way more steadily than I did back towards the stairs, opening a door on the opposite side of the hall, catty-corner with the exposed railing. Look at that butt. Mmm, butts. Who came up with that word, butt? Butt. Butter. Butler. Better Butt Buttler.

"Get some sleep, gorgeous." I snap my head up and realize Lin's making little shooing motions at me from his doorway, that butt of his hidden from me by that front of him. Oh, that's fine. I like the front, too. Wait, sleep. Okay.

Slowly turning around, I head into the room he brought me to, zeroing in on the enormous king-sized bed. Oh, that looks like a good idea. I stumble towards it in near darkness, moonlight trickling in from a window behind the headboard the only reason I don't immediately bash my shins open on the bed frame. Thanks, moonlight!

Kicking off my socks, shoes, and shorts, I crawl under the blankets and bury my face in a warm tan pillowcase. It smells rich, deep, and musky, with a hint of something animalistic around the edges, like warm leather. Mmm, that's good. I breathe it in deeply, letting that manly man musk envelop me until I'm fully submerged in its comfort. Sleep takes me easily.

***

I've finally found her again, and this time she's not getting away. Mother's binding spell is ready, darling. I'm not going to let her out of my sight until her and that little bellirae are tied to me for good. I can't help it, the anticipation has my skin tingling with all the possibilities success will bring me. I'll know everything. I could change everything. No one can stop me, could stop us. We could have everything.

I slip behind her and inhale, shuddering at her sweet burnt caramel scent, laced through with hints of something floral like jasmine. Soon.

Suddenly, she leans back slightly and raises her arm, bumping her shoulder against my chest. Not yet, my darling, we only have to wait until sundown. I slip into the shadows of the bar before she turns around and ruins my surprise. Soon. Be patient. Soon.

The bellirae looks straight at me, despite the concealment. It knows I'm here, but can't stop me from achieving my goal. I use the shadows to travel across the room, never letting my eyes leave my prize.

Two idiots start to play something almost like music right next to the darkness I've cloaked myself in. Hideous. Music should be a crime. Maybe it will be. It's okay darling, I forgive you for bringing us here. You didn't know I was coming tonight or I know you wouldn't have made me suffer like this. Made us suffer like this.

I can feel the sun lowering, finally almost plunging the outside into full darkness. I've been waiting 12 years for this moment, but these last 12 minutes have felt like the longest stretch yet. Almost... almost... I shift to the wall behind her in preparation.

The second it's time, I make the necessary motions, say the words, and break the cylinder filled with her blood and hair. My power bursts forth with such force that she feels me and her head slings forward. Yes, my darling, you are mine. Finally.

For the first time in a long time, I feel myself smiling fully. "Come to me, darling," *I command through the shadows.*

The bellirae glares at me, obviously furious at the hold I have over it, now. Neither of them make a move toward me, as I instructed.

"Come to me. NOW." The bellirae's face transforms from a glare, to something almost mocking. My darling finally starts to get up from her seat, powerless to deny me what I demand.

No, this can't be right. She doesn't even look at me before storming out of the bar. I did not give you permission to do this! I've waited too long to let her leave, but my exit is interrupted by five assholes cutting across my path, one of them seeming to be dragged by his back along the floor.

***

There's a sickly feeling in the pit of my stomach when I wake up, but I shake it off as awareness pulls me out of the depths of a dream that's just on the tip of my memory, right outside of the thoughts I could catch if I had a big enough net. A last whiff of unease causes me to shudder before I completely lose whatever it was that had me feeling that way in the first place.

My eyes crack open, gentle beams of a newly born dawn only just bearable. It must be early. Like... really early. And I need to pee. Like... really need to pee.

One problem, though: seems a lot like I'm trapped here. A pale, heavy arm coated in red hair is draped across my midsection, really not helping with the pressure demanding attention in my bladder. Well, I never expected to start my day off with a round of pee-or-death arm wrestling but weirder things have happened, so why not?

Not wanting to wake who I'm going to both hope and assume is Kieran behind me rather than some super beefy stranger, I try to gently dislodge myself from the muscular arm's grasp. The slow, even breathing behind me is replaced with a low growl now coming from the face tucked into the crook of my shoulder. Given what I can see in my peripheral vision, the mystery arm definitely belongs to Kieran, but I'm not entirely sure he's actually awake right now.

"I've got to get up and pee."

I squeak when he just squeezes me tighter and growls even more. "No." His voice is gravelly and hoarse with sleep.

"If I promise to come back, will you let me up? Otherwise, you're going to need to air out your mattress and change your sheets, and I'm not doing either of those things because you had fair warning."

Time passes and it almost seems like he's really going to make me go through with peeing myself before he finally loosens his grip and grumbles "fine."

"My bladder thanks you!" I slip out from under my restraint

and dart for the door. Well, that's a pretty generous description of how uncoordinated my body is feeling right now but whatever, the porcelain throne beckons and there's no time for semantics here.

Thankfully, the first door to the right of Kieran's turns out to be the bathroom, which I almost remember Lin pointing out but was way too zonked to actually retain. Ah, sweet relief. Remind me to start worshipping whoever invented indoor plumbing as a god because this is definitely heaven. Wait, was that the Romans or something? Whatever, they deserve it.

This bathroom's pretty nice, now that I'm doing more than turning into a toilet-seeking missile and can actually appreciate it. Most of the room is sleek with glossy black, white, and teal tile, giving an understated look to the whole room. I'm in the corner, doing my business like a super secret squirrel hidden spy agent. The basin of the sink to my left, hiding me from view of the door, is modern and round, sat atop a large square wooden structure that's been stained so dark it's almost black. It has little shelves instead of being closed in, so you can see all the things being stored under it. Hm. Wonder whose nail polish that is.

Directly across from me is a large white shower/tub combo, surrounded by an opaque black curtain. It's actually pretty classy in here, especially considering I've been led to believe that guys have absolutely no taste. Shows how much I know!

Finishing up, something about the idea of wearing two day-old panties after multiple dog-based tag exertions makes me decide to go without until I can get more. Luckily, there's a hamper to the left of the tub, so I ditch them before washing my hands at that gorgeous sink. The mirror above it screams an unruly ball of purple frizz back at me. Yikes. That braid did NOT fare well at all. Oh well, that's a problem for future

Dizzy to deal with; there's a warm bed and strong arm calling my name from the other room and who am I to ignore them?

Kieran looks and sounds like he's fallen back asleep already, if he ever really even woke up in the first place. As soon as I start to put a knee on the edge of the bed, wondering about the best way to get back in there, his bright green eyes pop open and that beefy arm of his shoots to grab me around the waist and drag me in like a human tractor beam. This time, I'm facing him and he is most definitely awake. And shirtless. I can tell he's shirtless because he's jammed my cheek up against his broad chest, letting me get a hit of that intoxicating man musk straight from the source. Mmm.

"Uh... Good morning to you, too, Kieran." He lets out a huff against the top of my head. "Sorry I took over your room last night, I kind of don't really even remember invading it if I'm honest." Guilt twists and pinches the edge of my stomach. Should have asked permission.

The iron hold he's got on me loosens just enough for me to arch slightly and look him in the face. Well, mostly in the beard but close enough. He turns his head and clears his throat gruffly, "It's fine. Better than waking up on the couch alone, I hope."

"Oh shit, did we leave you down there by yourself?" My fingers lead a lazy trail up and down his bicep on their own, tracing the dips and swells of his muscles.

"Like I said, it's fine." His own broad fingers make a path up and down my spine, increasing in pressure with each pass they finish. "Is it okay that I came in here while you were sleeping?"

"It's your room, I'm the one who should have asked first." The fingers on my spine curl slightly, dragging blunt nails along my borrowed shirt, sending shivers throughout my nervous system and building an ache in my core.

"And is it okay that I'm touching you like this, right now?" My own fingers have jumped ship and are exploring his chest, raking my nails through the light covering of soft orange hair.

His hands keep dipping lower and lower with each stroke, so my voice is much more breathy than usual as I say "Yes. Very yes."

"And this?" he ducks his head down and, more gently than I would have expected, places his lips on mine. We share a long, torturously slow kiss before he pulls back and looks at me for a response.

"Definitely."

This time, his lips are demanding as we crash together in a frenzy. Our tongues explore each other in a desperate way, like lovers who've been separated by a lifetime and are finally reunited. He hitches my right leg over his hip and drags his nails up the back of my thigh, growling when he finally makes contact with my bare ass. A quick swat shoots unexpected vibrations straight through my pussy, shock and pleasure stealing a gasp from my throat and breaking my mouth away from his. Kieran takes the opportunity to trail kisses along my jaw and neck, pushing me down onto the bed until I'm pinned under him, his mouth continuing its rough exploration along my collarbone. One arm next to my head supports his weight, while the other glides under the shirt I'm wearing, up towards my heaving chest. He slips his hand inside my bra, freeing one breast from the cup, massaging it as his mouth heads downwards. In this moment, the flashing pain from my still-raw sunburn only serves to enhance the dangerously addictive sensation of each touch. His teeth find my nipple through the shirt, clamping down hard as my nails instinctively claw deeply into his back and drag him tighter to me.

Kieran's knee is shoved right up against my throbbing

pussy, the pressure of his weight enveloping every inch of me an enticement my life has apparently been craving. I don't know exactly when I started to grind my hips, but god if it isn't sending electricity through me every time I rub my needy slickness against his upper thigh. I'm dangerously close to coming already, in bed with a practical stranger I'm impossibly desperate to tie myself to, despite normally avoiding lasting connections. And he's not the only one I'm deeply drawn to. This realization scares me a little bit, halting the ecstatic whimpers I didn't even know were escaping from me with each breath. I grab Kieran by the beard and drag his lips back to mine, needing to maybe calm things down a little with this man I've known for less than a day.

He gives my nipple one last, hard squeeze before trailing his hand out from the bottom of my shirt and bringing it up to cup my cheek. Our kisses transform from violent to softer, sweeter, more exploratory. I run my hands through his long, wavy hair tenderly, just enjoying the texture of each strand against my fingers as they glide through. We share one last long, slow kiss before he pulls back and gently strokes my cheek, bright green eyes locked on my own golden ones.

We stare at each other for a little while, gentle caresses the only movement either of us make while time passes. Waking up like this every morning wouldn't be so bad.

He plants a soft kiss on my nose. "Come on, Fireball, might as well get up now. No way I'm getting back to sleep after that. You can have the shower first... Unless you want me to join you?"

Damn, I'm tempted despite my recent hesitation. Really tempted. "Maybe next time, Beefcake. I'm a solo artist for now. Let a gal up, would ya?" I say, tapping the arm still pinned above my head.

He chuckles, but rolls onto his back and lets me free, watching with both arms tucked behind his head as I "dart" towards the door even more unsteadily than I did last time.

15. LIN

An intense feeling of pleasure rips me from sleep, letting me experience that aching, pent-up sensation that precedes a release, but it suddenly retreats from my grasp. My heart races as I bolt upright in bed, wide awake from the near-orgasmic sensations still pulsing along the base of my spine. Such wonderful torture to wake to, no doubt courtesy of dreams about our new enchantress. My dick is rock hard when I push down my black boxer briefs to fist it, no way can I make it through the rest of the day if I'm pent up and chasing the orgasm that almost was.

Pressure builds as I pump my fist, bringing with it the feeling of climbing higher and higher on an impossibly tall roller coaster of pleasure. I close my eyes and remember the curve of Dizzy's bare back, the swell of her barely-contained breasts in that enticing black bra, the little motions of her hips against my cock on the couch last night while Zeke tongue-fucked her mouth. Now it's my mouth on her, my hands fondling her through her shirt as I thrust harder into my hand. Already so close, I can feel the muscles throughout my whole body tensing up in anticipation of release. Dizzy's full breasts bounce as she replaces my hand, crushing my cock tightly between them while she grips her own nipples and moans my name, letting me fuck those gorgeous tits of hers. The tip of her tongue flicks out as she laps at the head of my dick every time I thrust upwards and I lose it, finally free falling-down the edge of that roller coaster as I come hard, all over the fantasy of this woman I never saw coming.

Never saw coming. Ah, that will certainly need to change.

Sated, I flop back onto my pillow, careful to keep the evidence of my very good morning from spilling onto the black bed sheets. My heart rate gradually returns to its natural rhythm, slowly returning worldly awareness to my still-tingling body.

Doors down the hall open and close, someone starts a shower, I try to remember what it feels like to have bones. My arm flings out towards the small bedside table on the left, groping around until my fingers finally make contact with the cool surface of a phone that annoyingly declares it to be just after 6am. Should I try to catch an extra hour, or just get on with it?

Fuck it, I'm up. I scrub the sleep from my eyes and they're drawn to the left. Against the wall, a table mockingly displays my tightly-closed violin case. Last night was the closest I've come to making music again in... years. After Miriam... well, it got harder and harder to find the notes and get them to stick together. I hadn't even realized that playing had taken a backseat to the rest of everyday life; caught up in whatever it takes to survive to the end of each day to get to the next mind-numbingly identical day. Yes, there were fun distractions like mischief, empty lovers, and missions, but last night reminded me what living is really like. Not just going through the motions, but actually grabbing a moment by the balls and enjoying whatever comes of it. That used to be something that came so naturally to me, I really hadn't noticed my joy getting cast aside in favor of a feeble facade. Why did I start to make excuses to banish it to the back burner and take the easiest, safest, least attached available options instead?

Dizzy stumbled, no, stormed into our lives like a whirlwind and already it feels like she's forced me to wake up from a haze I really thought I was enjoying. And why shouldn't I have thought I was enjoying my life? There certainly hasn't been anything to complain about. No, enjoying life looks like running from a little white Frenchie because you're excited to see him. It looks like dancing among strangers with wild abandon just because you feel the music in your soul and have to express it in every way possible. It looks like freedom from fear and judgement and loss and what-ifs and ghosts, or maybe even freedom despite those things. It looks like Dizzy.

Have I really spent the last seven years letting myself be so haunted by the ghost of a dead woman that I forgot to really come back to the land of the living? Was I too scared of an encore that I refused to take the stage ever again? That's not who I'm supposed to be; it's not even who I thought I already was.

One night, and already my life is shaken up enough that I want... More. I want to feel the music, again. I want to be the composer of my own life, not the poor sap at the back of the stage waiting for their chance to hit one note on a triangle every now and then.

Suddenly, I'm hearing music in a world whose silence I'd gotten used to. Silence I hadn't noticed creeping in and taking over.

The song from last night comes back to me, swimming through my thoughts and breaking the spell of sorrow I'd cast on myself long ago. I feel more awake, more alive, and more optimistic about what's to come than I can remember having been in the longest time. It's almost as though a weight I've been carrying around without even noticing has finally lifted itself, lightening my spirit and giving me permission to fly again. Maybe it's time to really spread my wings and take chances again.

That sounds great.

The absence of noise from the bathroom down the hall is also a glorious tune to my ears on this early morning. One chance I'm not going to take is someone else getting into that shower first!

16. MONTY

Setting the tray aside to cool, I take in a deep breath of the savory, acidic scent of roasted tomatoes fresh from our oven. They've been in just long enough that the outer skin has shrunk and separated from the inner flesh, giving them access to the salt, pepper, and olive oil they were coated in before being cooked. Perfect timing! The goat cheese grits are done and my white wine vinegar-sautéed mushrooms just need a sprinkling of parsley before they're ready to serve. All that's left is to poach enough eggs for the house and toast up some sourdough. Oh, and the juice. Have to make the juice.

"Mornin', Monty." Lobster pot holder still in hand, I look up to see Dizzy traipsing down the stairs in the same long green button up Connor lent her last night, chest-length hair damp from the shower. "Whatcha makin'?"

"Ah, let's just call it breakfast to keep things simple. You hungry? There's plenty for everyone."

"Definitely!" Dizzy slides into one of the barstools on the other side of our island, across from where I'm just setting some water to simmer on the built-in gas range. Aria leaps from her perch on my shoulder and makes a high-pitched warble of excitement as she lands right in front of Dizzy, chittering and chattering up a storm. They have their own little conversation, catching each other up on their version of last night's events even though neither one of them is actually speaking in the same language. I kind of get it, though, because after spending the night working with Aria it seems almost obvious what she means whenever she communicates.

Digging through the refrigerator, my arms become loaded with eggs, oranges, carrots, ginger, and lemons. A quick trip to the cutting board and my bounty is roughly sliced and diced, though I only cut the lemons in half to squeeze them in the poaching water for the eggs. Everything else is destined for a glass eventually, so knife cuts don't really matter.

"Hey Dizzy, how do you feel about carrot, ginger, and orange juice? Or do you prefer tea? Coffee? I don't really know what you like, aside from ice cream." And making out with Zeke.

She already looks happy, but her whole face lights up with a beaming smile, "Ah! The juice sounds fun! I've never had carrot juice, but I'll try pretty much anything once. Really, I'm more adventurous than picky." Her fingers tap against the dark marble countertop in front of her, head bobbing lightly to whatever melody's bounding around in her head. It's infectious, and I find myself adding a little bounce to my step as I grab one of the sourdough loaves from a cooling rack behind me, deeming it ready to be sliced and toasted.

Light footsteps descend the stairs and I turn my head to see Lin making his way down as well, trademarked black vest and crisp black slacks looking impeccable as ever over yet another white button-up, this one devoid of blood on its long sleeves. He takes the seat to the left of Dizzy, tenderly trailing his fingers down one of her arms as he takes his place. "Hey Lin, you're up and about early this morning."

"I could say the same about you, Monty. Did you even sleep last night?"

"Not really," the obnoxious whirring of produce being processed in the juicer likely drowning out my pathetic reply. Back turned, they don't see me blink to clear my eyes and let out a deep yawn. Between the anxiety of not going out tonight and just generally being too worked up from all the excitement, getting to sleep and staying asleep really wasn't in the cards. Two hours was all I could eke out until I gave up and decided that if I insisted on being awake, I may as well bake some bread and tend to my sourdough starter while everyone else was asleep. The guys aren't really a fan of the mother's pungent, sour smell in her raw form, but they sure do love all the bread babies she helps birth.

Grabbing a few glasses from the cabinets overhead, I pour us each some juice and turn back to face my audience. Lin accepts his lazily, but Dizzy snatches the cup from my extended hand with excitement.

"Thank you!" She takes a huge gulp immediately, clearly a fan of diving straight into the deep end of things rather than just getting her toes wet. A thin line of juice tries to dribble its way down her chin, but she quickly swipes it away with the back of her hand, "Oh wow, this is great!" Already, the glass is nearly halfway drained but she still tilts it towards Aria, who manages to lap up a little of the orange liquid.

"Yes, thank you, Monty." Lin takes much more reserved sips, though I already know he enjoys this particular combination.

It's impossible to miss Kieran's thunderous descent down the stairs, so I take that as my cue to put the kettle on and start some calming tea, trying to get an early start on reeling in his beast. Shirts during breakfast are apparently optional now, but at least he's wearing his trademark kilt, this one a tartan of multiple blue shades. At this point, it shouldn't surprise me when he takes the empty seat to Dizzy's right, leaning in to kiss her neck while her head is tilted back to take another gulp of juice. I can see her lips curling up at the corners through the glass, so it seems his affections are neither unexpected, nor unwelcome. Good for them; Kieran could do with a little extra happiness in his life.

"Ah, welcome to the party, Kieran," Lin says between sips from his glass.

"It's not even 7am yet, is everyone already up," I ask, "Or is this it for now?"

Dizzy and Lin shrug in unison, but Kieran lets me know Zeke and Connor are still out for the count. Looks like I don't need to poach the full dozen just yet.

As I crack an egg into a ramekin, swirling the lemony poaching water with a spoon, Dizzy snaps her glass onto the countertop suddenly. "Oh, shoot! Monty, I didn't even offer to help! Like, I don't know what to do or where anything is and I'd probably just throw your stuff everywhere and ruin it but… It's polite to offer to help, right? Am I the worst guest? I'm so sorry. Do you need help?"

I chuckle at her misplaced concern, but it's kind of adorable in its own way. "That's okay Diz, I'm almost done anyway. I'd love your help next time if you'd like, but I do most of the cooking here by choice so it's really no trouble."

The electric kettle pops, signaling that the water inside is finished boiling. I grab a mug for Kieran and add my custom calming tea blend, plus some honey. "Actually, though, Dizzy, if you're up for helping out down at the shop today it would be great to have you along. Otherwise, you and I can do something else for the day since it seems like I kind of can't wander too far away from you." Kieran takes the steaming mug I offer him, blowing its surface gently.

"Shit, that's right. I'm sorry you guys got caught up in one of my curses, I guess..." She trails of for a moment, "Wait, shop? What shop?"

Curse? Is she sure about that? I'm starting to think this might be a truly unexpected blessing. "Yeah, the guys and I run a magic shop in the city, pretty close to The Wood Liquor, actually. The Tea Kettle and Cauldron; have you heard of it before?"

She shakes her head. "Nah, I'm not really from here."

Realizing I don't really know anything about this woman I'm physically tethered to, I ask the obvious next question. "Oh? Where are you from, then?"

Her face falls, and an agonizingly long series of seconds pass before she quietly says "Nowhere." Well, that's clearly a sore subject. Not sure what else to do, I stall for time by grabbing some bowls and starting to scoop goat cheese grits into the bottom. She lets out a rushed breath as I add tomatoes and mushrooms to the bowls. "When I was a kid, I didn't have a dad so my mom was always out working, or with one of her boyfriends, or just gone somewhere to get away from me. I think she was afraid of me a little, but she was never mean or anything, and I guess she did the best she could in her own way. Pretty sure she named me Disaster Zone Jones for a reason; my whole life it seems like I've actually been cursed. Well, not even seems like, she told me that's exactly what it was. Things or places or people literally go up in flames around me. Or they break or get lost or flood or any other number of things, so mom wasn't really around much. It's hard to blame her though; just being near me puts everyone in danger, so I stopped bothering with keeping anyone around for too long. Aria's been with me for as long as I can remember though, and she's the only one who's gotten through it all okay.

"Anyway, I was basically on my own until 16, when shit got real crazy and the neighbor tried to kill me or lock me in her basement or something after I... kind of... sent her son into a coma. So I just bolted out of there, scared as shit and figuring living on my own somewhere else wouldn't be that much different than how things already were. Joke's on me, though, because at least I never burned down my mom's house. It's been 12 years and I've never been able to stay somewhere longer than a month before the building collapses, or is hit by lightning and loses power indefinitely, or is flooded, or suddenly falls into a sinkhole, or an earthquake destroys it, or a demolition crew accidentally knocks it down instead of the building next door."

Her hand stills around the lock of hair she's been nervously twirling, golden eyes locking on mine "So I'm not really from anywhere, I guess. Technically, I guess I'm homeless, but Aria and I always manage to make do with whatever we come by." Her caramel-colored fingers resume their nervous twirling, eyes once again hiding themselves from view.

That is not the answer I was expecting. Not even close.

In a way, though, it's a familiar story and I should have seen the signs. The way her face falls sullenly when she thinks no one's looking, how manic she is about trying to steer a moment towards happiness even if it's a bit risky, the way in which she pulls people in instantly, even if their interactions are meant to be temporary. How she makes snap decisions and barrels into things with abandon. Some of my brothers and sisters were the same, and all of them did it to hide themselves from their own pain.

Lin gently takes the hand from her hair with one of his while using the other to delicately turn her face to him, index finger curled under her chin. "Not any more, Love. You're from here, now. Our home is yours."

We've known her for less than a day, but it feels like he speaks for all of us.

The eggs are done poaching, so I place two in each bowl and distribute them, grabbing spoons for all of us. She turns her head away from Lin and stares into the breakfast before her, a forlorn expression swallowing her face. "You don't understand, Lin. Twelve years. Twelve whole years and I've never been able to stay anywhere for too long without it ending in complete disaster. I can usually get away with a week or two at most, but in the end... I'll just wreck your house. And I'll hurt you. I can't stay here and risk it." The pain is thick as she adds, "I'm always alone. That's just how it has to be."

Left hand still in Lin's, her right hand idly spins the spoon through her grits. Kieran's shoulders are slumped and it looks a whole lot like he's nearly crying, but his expression hardens quickly. He yanks Dizzy's head in his direction much less gently than Lin, firmly kissing her before staring at her with a dominating fierceness and certainty. "Not. Any. More." Kieran repeats Lin's sentiment and, impending typhoon be damned, I have to agree.

"It doesn't matter. They mean it. We all mean it. We'll find a way." Zeke comes up behind her and strokes a hand from the back of her head down to her shoulder, pausing to briefly give it a squeeze. He comes around to my side of the island and grabs a mug to make tea for himself. I didn't even hear him join us.

Brows furrowed and bottom lip sucked into her mouth, moisture starts to well in Dizzy's eyes. "I have to... I'm...." She grabs the bowl in front of her and shakily slides down from the barstool, heading towards our back door. Colonel Stubbs uncurls himself from where he was sleeping on the couch and joins as she passes, trotting after her out to the deck table.

I move to follow, but Zeke's firm hand on my shoulder stops me. "She's fine. She doesn't know how to feel. Give her space."

Nodding, I change course and grab the rest of the eggs. Might as well make Connor's too, if I'm already setting up Zeke's.

We all stew in silence for a bit, undoubtedly running through what Dizzy told us. To basically always feel like you're not welcomed? Not wanted? No wonder she connected with Connor so quickly.

"Hey, Z?" I start to plate up the last two bowls, "If she really is cursed... Do you think you could dig into it? Maybe we can check her out tonight?" Shit, tonight. I almost forgot. "Right. Lin, Kier... With me leashed to Dizzy... I can't go with you guys tonight. Connor already knows, and Zeke set up some extras, just as a precaution.

"Kier, do you have any Manipulations around? We only need one tuned to steel and one to copper on this so you could give Lin and Con a Manip each, just so it isn't all on you to collect?"

"Nah, the last ones I had broke down a couple weeks ago and I forgot to make more. It's fine; I'm good to do the gather if Lin and Connor are doing the carry. Besides, the Manipulations can't compact an element as tightly or as quickly as I can. Makes more sense just to let me cube them up fast and have both guys lug them away if we're trying to be efficient here."

I still think it would be best to have a backup strategy, but it is what it is, I guess. Looks like that just leaves one last thing... I let out a long exhale because this is honestly the hardest part for me; letting go of my control.

"Lin," I turn to look him in the face, "if I can't be there, I want you to take point on this."

He looks at me like I've got a screw loose and, fair enough, but... "I know you can think on your feet if something comes up, and I trust you to make the right decisions. We all know you like to mess around, but I also know you can reel it in when you need to. You'd be the first one to know if Con starts to lose himself, and if Kier gets too worked up and has to go wolf, you're the best bet to take charge of wrap up and get everyone home safe and undetected. We don't have the luxury of enough time to do this later or else I'd just say we call the whole thing off, so it has to be you."

A few moments pass before he nods, "I'll do my best."

"I know you will."

Zeke takes his now-empty bowl and rinses it out before loading it into the dishwasher. "Lin, I'll show you the setup. Come on."

They finish cleaning up and leave just as Connor finally makes his way into the kitchen. Wordlessly, he pours himself a glass of juice and carefully takes the bowl I offer him. Looking around quietly, he spots Dizzy out on the deck with her back to us, knees pulled up to her chest. I don't try to stop him as he softly pads out the back door to her; they're good for each other.

17. DIZZY

Breakfast was stupid delicious, but the conversation was kind of a bummer. My fault, really, but I don't get to talk to people much so I blame it on being raised by wolves. Well, actually, being raised by Aria I guess, but she doesn't talk to people much either so it's not like I ever had a shot at learning real manners or how not to make a total sap of myself in front of a room full of people.

Nope, we're not doing this pity party thing again. Remember? There aren't any decorations. You can't have a proper pity party without pitiful decorations.

Connor comes out and just sits with me for a while, not even saying anything or making it awkward or trying to pry about why I'm by myself. Well, by myself aside from my growing portable menagerie, I guess. Maybe we'll get a talking squirrel next, or a miniature dragon.

The point is, it's nice; just us sitting out here together without any expectations or shame or whatever. If I wanted to, I know Connor would let me talk but sometimes you just need to be left alone, together.

It's silly, really, getting all worked up over nothing. The way things are just are the way they are, and I'm fine with pretending I'm fine with that. Really. But it's hard to hope that... maybe... I could have this; have a place I belong, and people I belong with. But I can't. If I let myself think that I can get a whole meal instead of just a taste of what stability and family and love are like then it'll crush me when the fit hits the shan and I have to make a break for it again.

But I really, really, really want to believe it. So badly. I'm so tired. Just for a second, can I have this? I don't want to just enjoy it for now, I want to enjoy it for longer, maybe forever. But I'll take a second if it's all I can get. Please, just let me have this. Or don't. It's fine. It's silly to want things. Hope for things.

It's fine.

I'll be fine.

I'm fine.

Brave face, Dizzy. You're alive, you've got a belly full of breakfast, and you've got your best friend Aria. It's even been a solid 12 hours or so since anything ridiculous has happened. That's got to be a record of some sort, right? Maybe today'll end up being a winner and I'll find that miniature dragon I now definitely want. Or a full-sized dragon if that's all that just happens to be lying around in this imaginary dragon pit, but it'll sure be hard to keep fed if that's the case. Do you have to feed dragons horses or something?

Didn't I just have a conversation about how hard it is to

find horses around here? My poor dragon! It's going to starve! Maybe I can train it to survive on tinned beans and fresh grass? Or milkshakes? Nah, it would be too hard to break it of a 30 milkshake per meal habit when the milkshake money runs dry. Though that's never actually been a problem for me, despite not having a steady job or secret inheritance or anything. Those crazy people who screech their thanks and run away after I break their stupid crap? Sometimes they'll throw money at me before leaving, or find me later and do it, or cash will appear where they disappear from. I have gotten odd jobs here and there, but they only manage to last about one paycheck before the nonsense takes over and an enormous swarm of territorial bees comes flying out from the drain pipe and takes over, permanently. One time I found a scratch-off that someone lost and it won $200, so that was neat.

Still probably couldn't keep a dragon in milkshakes longer than a couple of days, though.

Then I start imagining a giant milkshake with a dragon swimming around in it, lazily doing the backstroke and kicking through ice cream with its taloned feet. Vanilla? Chocolate? What's the best flavor to swim in? What's the swim speed velocity of an unladen dragon through milkshake?

My laugh comes out more like a super duper sexy-hot snort/huff combo, which is absolutely why Connor finds me so irresistible at that moment and just has to take my hand. Obviously, the key to catching a man is to just be a total nut job and go from sad to dragon milkshake in 60 seconds or less. Take note, ladies!

It's at exactly that moment that I remember Zeke can hear what I'm thinking and I just fucking lose it. Head back, teeth all the way out, laughter so hard it makes you cry when you realize how manic it is; the works.

Truly wooed by my amazing and definitely absolutely normal moment of mirth, Connor gently tugs on the hand he's still holding and stands up. Yeah, sure, let's go back inside. Monty said they have to go to that magic shop so it's probably time to leave soon, anyway.

We grab our dishes and head back in, Colonel Stubbs and Aria in tow. Connor only lets go of my hand long enough to slide the glass door behind us closed, taking it back again as we head through the TV room to the kitchen. I'm still feeling a little off-kilter as we rinse our bowls and load them into the dishwasher, but Connor's hand moving to rest on my lower back while we're at the sink lets me know he doesn't mind. Even when little giggles just pop themselves out of me for no reason.

"Do you want to come with us today?" Connor ducks his head to look at me and ask in that quiet way of his.

Pretty sure something stupid like fire or spaghetti or words will come out of my mouth if I open it, so I just nod a couple of times, deranged grin still ruling entity over The Great Dizzy's Face Empire™.

"Okay. Shoes?" He glances down at my bare feet. I jerk my head in an upwards motion, mostly certain I left them in Kieran's room. He gently pushes the hand on my back to encourage me toward the stairs, walking side-by-side up them. We both turn right at the top, Kieran's room being the last on the left side and Connor's apparently being directly across from it. "I'll be right in here when you're ready. Do you want to borrow another shirt?"

I look down at the emerald green button up he lent me last night, long enough that it covers the frayed jean shorts I'm still wearing. It looks like I may as well be naked under here at this point, but it's not like there just happens to be a pair of pants I can snag out of the pants dimension, so my options are pretty limited. This shirt isn't exactly dirty or anything though.

"I should be okay, thank you." Well would you look at that, not spaghetti.

He nods and slips into his room, letting me step into Kieran's on my own. Looking around, there are a lot of things I missed in the dark about this space, like how pretty much all of the furniture is made out of a dark, slightly reddish wood. Even the large wooden chest at the foot of the bed. What is he, a pirate or something?

The short headboard of his giant bed is pushed up against the only window in the room, on the wall across from the doorway I'm standing in. One of my shoes is just barely peeking out from underneath the still very rumpled bed itself, reminding me with a small thrill why the green plaid comforter is in such disarray. I flop down backwards onto the mattress and take a minute to reel it back in. I really am fine, now, just need a moment to compose myself.

Eyes closed, hands on my stomach, I take in the silence of what seems like a nearly empty house and let it settle my thoughts. Trying to regroup, I hum the slow, low notes of a tune Aria used to sing to me at night when I couldn't sleep because I was too worked up, or scared, or worried, or excited to properly relax. It works. The hysteric and volatile explosions of an emotionally unstable weirdo start to melt away and I feel more like myself again; actually ready to tackle the day this time.

With a long exhale, I sit up, root around under the bed with my bare foot for those sneakers, and put them on. Sans socks. I know, gross. But probably better than putting on the sweaty ones from yesterday again.

When I head to Connor's room, he's sitting cross-legged on the queen-sized bed, reading one of the apparently zillions of books he has, judging by how many are neatly stacked in bookshelves to either side of the bed. There are more piled up on multiple wall shelves as well, accented with random pieces of artwork and origami and toys. Some of them even look like sketchbooks, and I take note of multiple glass jars filled with various art supplies as well.

He pushes up his gold-rimmed glasses with long, slender fingers and it doesn't escape my notice that he's changed into a pale golden yellow shirt, topped with a knitted green sweater vest almost the same color as the shirt I'm still wearing. "Ready?" He asks.

"Yeah, where's everyone else?"

"Monty sent a text to let me know they're out by the car, but there's no rush," he politely lets me set the pace I'm comfortable with. But I'm pretty comfortable with barreling on through right now, especially now that my head's feeling more sorted out.

"Nah, I'm ready. Let's go!"

He unfolds his long legs, exposing argyle socks under cuffed skinny jeans and standing with way more quiet grace than I could even if I tried my hardest. His hand finds its home in mine once again and we make our way downstairs to the front door.

Aria nips at my ear as I watch Connor snag a pair of high-topped converses from a nicely organized shoe rack and then I remember something, "Oh, wait a sec!" I jog back to the TV room and find Colonel Stubbs curled up on my cotton jacket, still right on the couch where I left it last night. I pick both Stubbs and the jacket up and walk back towards the front door, happy to see that Connor has, in fact, waited more than a sec. It's kind of difficult to put on a jacket while cuddling a sweet little 10 pound pupperoni pizza, but I surprisingly manage it without any incident or injury. Hooray!

"Nearly forgot my swag!" I shift Stubbs so he's in the crook of one arm and snatch Connor's hand back up. Connor wordlessly grabs a blue leash from a hook beside the door frame before we make our grand exit. Knowing firsthand how adept at escaping captors this pooch is, this appears to be a wise move.

Monty's leaning up against the side of the same giant black SUV we came here in last night, watching Kieran pace around the front yard while Lin and Zeke sit sideways inside the vehicle, legs hanging out of the opened doors. They each look up and give various greetings, but we manage to all get seated and buckled quickly despite having so many bodies to coordinate. Nobody tries to take my best bud Colonel Stubbs away, either, so I basically become a human seat belt for him. That's probably safe enough, right?

The drive back into the city is only about 20 minutes, 30 tops, that time spent chatting about nothing particularly important.

We pull up in front of a surprisingly tall one-story building with huge glass bay windows. There's an awesome wooden sign spread across the door's overhang, smack dab between those two massive windows. From the slightly rustic texture in every scooped-out area of the work, I'm pretty sure that wooden sign is hand-carved. It's got an image of a squat cauldron with both the spout and handle of a tea kettle attached to the sides, smoke coming from the cauldron's open middle to form an ampersand in "The Tea Kettle & Cauldron." Smaller text beneath the cauldron-kettle says "Spells, Cures, and Custom Teas."

"Everybody out!" Kieran gives us enough time to clamber onto the sidewalk before pulling the SUV down an alley to the left of the building, assumedly parking it somewhere down there. I forgot to charge my X-Ray vision eyeballs before leaving home, so that's my best guess without actually being able to see through the walls and whatnot around us.

Lin heads to the shaded door and unlocks it, shuffling us all in before spinning back around and locking the deadbolt behind us. Inside, the shop is both surprisingly cozy and spacious at the same time. In the two giant nooks on either side of the door, there are tables and cushioned chairs set up in front of crystal-clear windows. The windows themselves are curved around plush, attached benches. With the sun beaming in and a hot cup of tea to keep you company? Spending hours here settling in and enjoying yourself has to be easy.

A few slightly worn arm chairs are set up along the right wall, preceding what looks like a modest barista station. At the end of the line, there's a swinging door that likely leads to a secret kitchen, only accessible from behind the bar. A few small end tables are scattered close to nearby chairs, and there are even a couple of large ottomans nestled within certain seating clusters. The wall behind the barista counter is lined with dozens and dozens of glass cylinders filled with a rainbow of dried herbs and leaves and flowers of all sorts. The canisters are stationed above two metal sinks and a long steel counter covered in a whole bunch of tools and machines.

On the wall to my left, there's a wooden counter with intricate Celtic knot work carved along the edges, clearly being used as their checkout station because of the iPad cash register set up on its surface. Plus, there are containers full of little minor charms and dolls and smudging sticks that I'm sure people impulse buy right as they're checking out.

The cash register area stops right before a hallway that goes off to the left, but the rest of the store is filled with shelves and shelves of books, stones, raw ingredients, bottles of all shapes and sizes, pendants, bones, candles, little potted plants, incense, and pretty much anything any magic practitioner could ever want or need. Despite being filled with so many different items, the entire shop manages to smell primarily earthy and spicy, like cedar wood and cinnamon; a warm hug by the fireplace on a cold winter night. It's making me want a steaming cup of spiced apple cider, even though it's only just barely Autumn. There's like....one almost sort of partly orange leaf on the tree outside, so It's probably not too early in the season to demand spiced beverages.

A hand finds its way to my lower back, fingers climbing up my spine like some kind of giant spider, except way less terrifying than if it were truly a giant 8-legged arachnid. It actually feels pretty nice, almost sensual in its crawly kind of way. "Like what you see, Love?" Lin's hand leaves my back as he smoothly swings out in front of me, "I'd be happy to bare it all to you; Let you see everything on offer?" Nudge nudge wink wink.

The...hold on, what's the male version of a temptress? Tempter? Temptation? Hm. Something to think about. Has there really never been a man as tempting as Lin before this moment to cause need for such a word? Impossible! I demand equality! Let's go with scoundrel for now.

The scoundrel certainly knows how to tempt a gal, I tell you what. After my morning with Kieran, despite everything else that got brought up, I'm still just the tiniest bit hot and bothered. I swear, my vagina has completely replaced my brain ever since I got over the idea that they might be a herd of hunky murderers. Though calling them hunky murderers sort of proves that my Chamber of Secrets may have been doing at least part of the thinking from minute one. Every look, every touch, just goes straight to the top of my growing trash heap of filthy fantasies. What would those roaming spider fingers have felt like if they'd roamed just a little further....shit. Come on, girl, you've been standing just barely inside the door like a frozen idiot for about six lifetimes, say something before they notice your vagina brain and send you off to science to be studied!

Zeke barks a laughs somewhere off in the distance and I glare in the general direction, knowing full well he can't see it to cower before my might.

What was the question again? "Um, yes. A tour would be nice. Thanks!"

"Wonderful!" He slides his arm through one of mine, linking our elbows as he begins to saunter through the store, detailing many of the things I'd already noticed. He points out the dried stuff behind the bar and talks about how they're well-known for their custom tea blends, which Monty sometimes also prescribes from his clinic for minor troubles.

"Some people come here to have their fortunes read, and I'll use the tea leaves for that, too."

Gasping, I ask, "Lin, you have future sight?!"

He grins devilishly, "Not even a little bit."

I cock my head and look at him quizzically, "Then how do you read fortunes?"

"Oh, this is going to be so fun!" He lets go of my arm and claps both hands in front of his face, bobbing lightly on toes primed full of excitement. Excitement I feel like I'm supposed to be wary of, given the scandalous gleam in Lin's impossibly orange eyes. The thing is, even though he's doing his best impression of a mischievous devil, it kind of just looks to me like he's eager and adorable, only serving to further fuel my curiosity. Especially when he places a hand on my chest and gently guides me backwards until I stumble into one of the plush armchairs, plopping down solidly and scientifically confirming their comfiness.

Lin sticks up his pointer finger in a "wait just one moment" gesture and heads behind the bar, humming a cheery tune to himself and bouncing around to grab things left and right off of shelves. Monty and Zeke are busy dusting off and wiping down and straightening things up, but Connor seems to have vanished. Kieran must have driven the SUV into a black hole rather than a parking lot, given his booming absence as well. At least Colonel Stubbs and Aria are keeping me company while the giddy madman plots whatever has him clearly so entertained.

Within a few minutes, Lin returns with a small cup and saucer, placing it on the extremely small table in front of us and claiming a chair angled towards mine slightly.

In one smooth motion, he gracefully deposits himself into the seat with impeccable posture, sweeping arm movements encouraging me to partake of the tea he's provided; a far cry from the stumble-flop I performed earlier. He even crosses his legs with more class than I do, especially given that mine are basically just kicked directly out in front of me, ankles crossed while I'm practically sunken down into a hunched slump. From this position, my dangling arm is just barely able to pet Stubb's head without needing to stretch too much.

Lin waves his hands theatrically around, "Now, my dear, drink deeply and we shall uncover what your fortune holds." Clearly, the showman in Lin enjoys a bit of drama.

The drink is actually surprisingly delicious, a blend of Early Grey with rose and almond; a combination I'd never have picked out in a million years but am now the number one fan of. There's just the barest hint of sweetness, but no cream or lemon or anything else. Funny story, the first time I ever made tea for myself, I added both lemon and cream because I knew they were both things that sometimes went in tea. That's a great way to make gross and instant cheese, so there's a top life tip everyone should follow. Or avoid? Don't put citrus and dairy together in your tea, kids, it'll taste like spoiled nightmares.

I'd heard of tea reading before, so the last sip was a somewhat dangerous one where I tried desperately not to disturb the dredges while getting every last drop of the floral nectar. I probably look like a giraffe trying to lick around ants in a swimming pool, but I felt my tonguing the tea cup was an important strategy. After all, Lin would need all the tea leaves to stay where they were to get an accurate feeling from them.

"Now, my dear, give me your hand and your cup and allow me to investigate," Lin leans forward eagerly with both hands extended, pulling me back slightly once our fingers gently clasp. His expression morphs into one of forced concentration as he turns the cup every which way possible while muttering "hmmm" and "I see" and "oh my." In a way, seeing the playful and dramatic man try to be so serious is funny, especially while his flirty thumb has been rubbing slow, tingling circles on the hand he's holding. The corner of one side of his lips has been pulling up slightly, despite his obvious best effort to retain a professional look of some sort.

Lin nods to himself a few times before setting down the cup on its saucer and grabbing my other hand in his, pulling me closer and staring intently at me with vibrant orange eyes.

"Tell me, Love, what do you want to know?"

The secrets of the universe seem like a tall order for a first reading, so I start with something smaller but still big to me. "How long will I get to stay here?"

Both of his thumbs trace circles on the backs of my hands and I feel a pleasant warmth slowly sparkle its way up my arms. "You are exactly where you're supposed to be, and you'll stay here for exactly as long as you want."

I scoff, because that's just patently untrue; I've never gotten to stay anywhere I really wanted to ever since this all began.

"Your doubts announce themselves loudly, having been on the run for so long, but I can tell you that you've been blessed with an unusual plethora of luck. Plus, word on the street is there are five guys who find you charmingly refreshing and want to keep you around if you'll let them."

Cue eye roll. Lucky? Me? Sure, as long as you count bad luck as well.

He continues, "You're a natural protector, and you've spent your life saving others as well as yourself, sometimes at what seems like great cost. You are truly meant to be here; I can see it as certain as an anchor around your hips, and this time you won't need to do the saving alone. You are destined to find more happiness than you could ever dream of, sooner than you'd think. Also, you're smokin' hot."

He says that last bit with another wink and I can't help the second eye roll I masterfully demonstrate. Cheese ball. There's a sharp clap as he slaps his hands together and rubs them against one other, standing to take an exaggerated bow accompanied by more flourishing arm sweeps.

"Thank you, yes, thank you, I know, I'm truly incredible. Please do come again." And with that, he gracefully returns himself to his seat, leaning forward with elbows on knees, fingertips splayed together in a triangle. "So, what do you think? Nearly as impressive as the real thing, no?"

"Pft. Not even a little! Do people actually fall for this?" My arms fling out wide, incredulous at the idea that Lin could ever convince someone he's psychic. "How could they possibly?"

"Now Love, I'm hurt that you'd think I'm a terrible fraud," he says wide-eyed while touching his heart in mock shock. "I am a fraud, of course, but not a terrible one! I assure you, everything I said was completely the truth."

"That's literally impossible. I'm probably the most un-lucky person on the planet, and you already know I never get a choice in staying anywhere for long, let alone for as long as I want. You're crazy if you think I'd fall for any of that nonsense, Lin. But it sure is a nice fantasy, I guess."

"Love, I promise you, everything I said was pure truth," his playful expression drops as he places one hand on my knee. "I'm not a fortune teller, but I am gifted with truth. And comprehension, revelation, manipulation, and opening; but mainly truth. I am able to see the truth of anyone or anything, and I promise you that everything I said to you was clear as day to me, and completely honest."

I want to accuse him of playing a mean trick, or tell him again that he's wrong... but the look on his face is so uncharac-teristically earnest. At the very least, he really believes what he's saying. Who am I to pick a fight over him trying to say something nice, just because I can't agree. Lin's been nothing if not... enthusiastic... about my presence since last night. It's been nice feeling like I have, at absolute least, friends for right now; I'd really rather not go rocking the boat over something silly. Time for a topic change?

"Well, since you guys have got me here today, where do you want me?"

He pauses only to bring back that glorious and mischievous smile and lean in, face barely inches away, "Oh, I could think of a couple places in particular that I'd love to have you, but a gentleman would insist the lady choose." His hand on my knee casually moves up just enough to allow the thumb to stroke my inner thigh slightly, a shiver shooting through me at his nonchalant seduction. As if the easiest thing in the world would be to just point my finger in any direction and let Lin fuck me stupid, right then and there. I'm tempted to raise my arm and do just that, but if that kiss from Zeke last night taught me anything it's to be careful with a dare if you aren't prepared for the follow through. Right now? I don't think I'm prepared. But that doesn't mean I won't be.

So instead of using my pointer finger to dare us both, I lift it to stroke under his chin and close the gap between our lips, teasing us equally with the briefest of stolen kisses. "Maybe next time, you scoundrel." His smile remains even after I remove my touch from his jaw and lean back fully into my chair. "In the meantime, where can I be useful today?"

"Well, like I said: lady's choice. We open in about an hour, so Connor's undoubtedly busy baking cookies if you wish to help him in the kitchen. Monty's likely moved on to the clinic now, playing with his plants and mixing up some common cures for the day. And of course, you're welcome to help me at the tea counter if you'd like-it's always useful to have an extra set of hands around if I need to do a reading."

I resist the urge to say something smart about his readings and instead, flick my head towards the swinging door behind the bar. "Kitchen?"

Lin hums his affirmative while nodding, "Have fun, Love. It would be my pleasure if you chose to join me later, though I know our boy will be delighted to see you by his side as well."

As I stand to head towards the kitchen, it doesn't escape my notice that Lin makes sure the hand stroking my thigh only loses contact at the last possible moment, long seconds before finally escaping the growing desire in his blazing orange gaze.

18. CONNOR

   Sugar. Butter. Flour. Eyes staring at me from deep within the shadows. Ovens at 340ºF. I might not be the best cook in the household, but ever since Monty taught me how to bake I've found a certain comfort in the calm of our shop's kitchen. It's hidden away from all the customers, but still somewhere that I can be useful to the rest of the team and feel like I'm earning my keep. Same goes for the roof garden I tend, and the stock in the back room I keep control over; it's all essential, but doesn't force me to face the swarm of strangers that buzz through.

   Sometimes my imagination leaks out when the anxiety gets to be too much, so it's better if I can work quietly while in my own little world, should I actually find myself in one by accident. Like the eyes in the shadows, glaring at me from the moment we crossed the shop's threshold, bouncing around every time I just barely catch a glimpse of them from the edge of my peripheral. It's not real, don't think it's real, it's not real-don't forget to add the vanilla. A few pinches of salt, 3 pounds of chocolate chips.

The door to my left swings open slightly and Dizzy pops her head in, glorious purple mane framing her intrigued face like a violet lion peeking out from deep within. She tucks a few unwieldy strands behind a pierced ear, revealing three studs up top and a small golden hoop hanging from the soft lobe.

"Hey Connor, can I help you out in here? Lin said you were making cookies? I don't think I've ever made cookies before and the last time I tried to make anything in the kitchen it kind of burnt down just a little, but third time's the charm, right? Or I can just stand still in a corner and not touch anything if that's better; I just wanted to spend more time with you is all. If I won't be in your way, I mean," Her bottom lip tucks itself away and briefly hides from view. "Maybe this isn't a good idea-I could really mess things up with an oven and knives around, and nothing freaky's happened for a little while so it's probably about time."

It looks like she's mentally scolding herself as her eyes roll skyward, Aria taking the opportunity to stand her front paws on top of Dizzy's head. The slender creature nearly looks to be pulled under by the swelling tide of purple curls swirling around its delicate legs. Is Dizzy feeling self-conscious? About me? I couldn't imagine why, and I can imagine a lot of things.

"Please, stay." I wave her in with a gloved hand, "But Aria will need to wait out there; food safety regulations. And we'll have to tie up your hair, too."

"Oh, okay!" She perks up and has a huge grin plastered on her face but promptly leaves anyway, door swinging back and forth at her abrupt departure. Small puffs of air from the motion lightly disturb flour dusted on the giant steel sinks next to it, swirling particles almost mimicking smoke dancing lithely towards the sky.

I'm just starting to portion out the dough onto lined trays with a scoop when Dizzy opens the door again, two white birch twigs securing her hair into a still somewhat messy bun, but as controlled as I suspect either of us could hope for. She heads straight to the sink and washes her hands as I grab a spare apron off a wall hook for her.

"You may want to take off your jacket for this, it gets pretty hot and messy in here between the oven and the dough." Plus, I love seeing her in my shirt. I'd give her my whole wardrobe if she wanted it, though I don't know if she's the type of person to ask something like that. It occurs to me that she likely doesn't have any clothes with her at all, given she didn't have a shirt of any type when we met up with her, let alone a bag full of them. Something to think on.

"That's okay, I like to keep my jacket close most of the time if I can help it. Besides, I'm not afraid of a little fire. A lot of fire, maybe, but not a little bit." She ties the apron over her clothes and takes a pair from the box of latex gloves I offer her. "So, what should I do?"

It might be showing off a little bit, but I flick my finger in her direction and an identical scoop pulls itself off the wall, floating directly into her hand. She looks at it wide-eyed, luscious lips stretched in full delight around an open-mouthed smile.

As soon as her fingers close around the handle, I catch movement out of the corner of my eye and all our knives fall from the magnetic strip they were just suspended on, clattering loudly to the ground in a heap. Dizzy jumps back instinctively, a tiny yelp escaping while she covers her head with both hands-as though she expects the ceiling to come crashing down on her and that her arms would somehow be a big enough barrier to prevent injury.

The scoop wasn't anywhere near there but it's fully possible I pulled them along as well, by mistake.

"It's okay," I duck my head and try to hide a blush behind my hair as a wave of my hand sets the knives back on their magnet. "It's my fault. Shouldn't have been showing off for you." Shouldn't have said that last part out loud, either. I can already feel my ears heating up even more.

She slowly opens one eye, the other still clenched shut tightly as her gaze roams suspiciously around the room. Both arms fling down and she pops straight up as if on a spring, "Are you kidding me?! Totally worth it! We're not dead and you've got flippin' telekinesis! Connor, that's so freakin' awesome! If I could move shit around with my brain, I probably wouldn't fall out of trees, or get doused with coffee, or trip into mud ever again! I may as well be a burlap sack full of marmalade right now because I'm totes jelly!"

A little chuckle slips from me despite my embarrassment because Dizzy's absurdity and enthusiasm are infectious, incurably spreading throughout everything they touch instantaneously. I don't really want to ruin it by mentioning that my strength with the skill is weak at best, small objects the only thing I can move with any real reliability. Or that marmalade isn't really a jelly.

She walks up next to me and playfully bumps her hip against my leg, "So, boss, what's next?"

I point to the sheet trays stacked on the metal under-shelf of our wooden work surface, ripping off a length of parchment paper from the roll attached to the table's side as she retrieves a tray and places it next to mine. It occurs to me that she might not be tall enough to comfortably dig into the over-sized mixing bowl, so I tip it on its side and swirl the scoop in my hand with a small flourish before reaching in. Pulling at the lever on the side of the portioner, a slight metallic scraping can be heard as the bar it controls passes behind the glob of chocolate chip cookie dough, sending it cascading towards my sheet tray with a fully anticlimactic plop. With all the showmanship I can muster within me, I wave the scoop in my left hand while reaching my right arm out wide, bowing as though I've performed the most wondrous of magic tricks for my lovely assistant.

"Ah, so it's rocket surgery, I see!" Dizzy giggles playfully and I can't help but throw her a cheeky wink.

"I'll have you know I studied for years at the most prestigious cookie university before they trusted me with these dangerous and complicated portion scoopers. Thankfully, I've been granted the power to provide temporary certification to probationary cookie-making agents as long as they solemnly swear only to use their skills for good. Or at least for kind of alright. Certainly not for evil, at the very least." I try to keep my expression as neutral as possible, hoping to convey an air of deadpan seriousness.

The musical laugh and brilliant smile she bursts out in light the whole room up with every bright note of her happiness. I find myself grinning like a fool, ensnared by the trap her joy laid out. We spend a few wonderful moments just enjoying ourselves, letting our laughter season the air around us and lend flavor to everything waiting to be cooked with our recipe of merriment.

She wipes an arm across her cheek at a phantom tear, "Okay Connor, sure, with great power, etc, etc. I do solemnly swear to only be up to kind of alright. Now let's get on with it!" Her right arm plunges into the overturned basin, scooping up a hunk of dough and depositing it onto her sheet. My left arm does the same, occasionally colliding gently with hers as we work side-by-side.

Within minutes the bowl is empty, each of us having finished prepping several trays worth of our sweet bounty. They're stacked on top of one another in a criss-cross pattern, making sure not to crush any one tray with another above it. Normally, I would have put them in the ovens in waves, multi-tasking to keep myself moving efficiently, but with Dizzy's help I have a feeling it'll all be finished with plenty of time to spare.

"Alrighty then, what's next, bossman?"

I can't help but smile slightly at being called bossman. Me? Far from it. "Would you mind washing up the scoops and bowl while I get these cooking and start setting up for the next batch?"

"Aye, aye!" She salutes, then whips off her gloves and tosses them into a nearby trash can, snagging the dishes and spinning towards the sink to complete her task. Meanwhile, I open up all four of the long, squat deck oven doors and start sliding trays in, beginning at the uppermost level of the four-tiered monster. Dizzy is singing something cheerful to herself as she uses a soapy brush to scrub out the last of the dough from our bowl, bouncing on the balls of her feet and popping her hips to the beat.

My own steps feel weightless as I reach for buckets and bins loaded with cinnamon, cardamom, star anise, clove, vanilla paste, sugar, and flour. I find myself bouncing slightly as I grab the sticks of butter that have been sitting out since we got here, the perfect softness to be creamed with sugar. There's no real reason for it but I find myself going to her, wrapping an arm around her waist from behind and bending down to let my chin rest on her shoulder. She smells like burnt sugar and jasmine; sweet, smoky, and floral. So perfect.

"I'm really glad you're here, Dizzy."

Lightness lifts my chest as she leans her head to rest against mine, lifting her shoulder slightly to cup my face in a hands-free hug of sorts.

"I'm really glad I'm here, too."

We let the moment settle around us for a bit, contented by the comfort of our physical connection. My mind has been clearer and more peaceful almost since she first arrived, making me unwilling to be the first to break the spell and tempt reality with its often cruel illusions. I nuzzle her hair and reach around for the bowl she's set aside, grabbing a towel to dry it down with both my arms still on either side of her. Little droplets of water glisten like diamond tears as she flicks her hands dry, not particularly well, I find, as she runs damp fingers up my arms and places them under the hem of my short sleeves.

Gathering the bowl, the scoops, and my courage, I turn my head just slightly and quickly place a gentle kiss on her cheek, pivoting and making a hasty retreat as my ears start to heat once more. Like lightning, she reaches out and reclaims my upper arm, spinning me to face her as she tugs me down and tenderly places her lips upon my own, just for a moment. It's soft and sweet and over quickly. I hope I didn't make a fool of myself. Bashfully, my gaze meets hers as I duck my head down to hide the furious blush further blooming. Her hand slides down my arm, fingers lacing into my own as she gives me another tug, bringing our mouths together again, more slowly this time.

"I like you, too," she whispers into the kiss, making my heart skip several beats at the quiet admission.

Our lips pull apart, both of us smiling softly, like we have all the time in the world for more than these small moments we've been collecting in jars and keeping safe to visit again later. Hands still linked, we take the few short steps back to our work table and prepare for our next batch of cookies, this one The Tea Kettle and Cauldron's specialty spiced variety.

My movements go on autopilot as I throw ingredients into the bowl, stealing glimpses at the goddess to my left paying rapt attention to the motions I'm personally barely conscious of performing. Cookies are scooped, baked, and cooled on repeat during a timespan that I could swear never existed. Even as we place the last tray to cool on the speed rack, clean up, and arrange some cookies onto a serving platter to display at the counter, there's only one thing running through my head that matters. Right before we walk out of the kitchen to hand Lin our treats, she stands on tiptoe and places one more quick peck on my cheek, pushing the door open afterwards.

She likes me, too.

19. DIZZY

My heart is warm and full as I skip out of the kitchen. All of these men have brought something out of me I didn't really know was waiting inside, and Connor is no exception. From the start, he's been patient and gentle and made the biggest effort to pay attention and listen to me. Aria's great and all, and she's pretty much the only other being on the planet who's taken the time to listen to my rambling stream of nonsense, but there's something special about how it feels to have a human being on the receiving end; a human with big turquoise eyes that don't miss a trick and soft lips that beg to be brushed against again and again. He's sweet, and I've always been a fan of dessert.

An arm snaps out, snaking out around my waist and pulling me into a lithe body, halting my frolicking days in their tracks. And here I was considering graduating to galloping! Ah well, I'll just have to slum it and accept the giddying spin I find myself in as a suitable substitute.

"Ah, Love, I gather from the smiles and wonnnnnnderful bouncing you had a good time with our boy?" Lin looks pointedly at my chest. Ah yes, boobs tend to bounce when you do, I get it! Frankly, I should be embarrassed at him bringing it up but why bother? I technically haven't even owned a shirt for as long as I've known them, and they've all already seen me about a half step away from naked at this point. No use borrowing a sense of shame, suddenly!

"Yes! Nothing exploded, and we didn't die! This has been my most successful kitchen adventure yet! Well, I've never died so that's kind of a weird baseline for fun, but I stand by it. Plus, Connor's just good company."

Speaking of, the man himself chooses that moment to finally come through the swinging door, arms loaded with two different trays of baked goods. I don't know when he made mini muffins, but they're adorable and I wish I'd seen them earlier. Is that blueberry? Oh, I will fuck up a blueberry muffin somethin' fierce.

"Hey look! A distraction!" I don't even bother pointing in a direction, but both of the guys look randomly elsewhere despite the ridiculousness of my declaration. It's enough for me to snatch one of them tasty little blueberry bites and slam it whole into my mouth, crumbs breaking free around my giggles. I realize too late that Lin still has me trapped in his arms, making a quick getaway basically impossible. Even a slow getaway seems out of the question given how the embrace has suddenly tightened, combined with the maniacal grin he's now blasting my way.

"Now, Love, would this be a good time to have a serious, life-altering discussion? No, that's okay, no need to answer, I'll take your silence as a yes." He shoots Connor a conspiratorial look. I may be panicking ever so slightly because while Connor may be sweet and thoughtful, I have a feeling Lin is part lord of mischief and may be up to no good.

Heart screeching to a halt, I wriggle and claw towards Connor, a desperate plea in my eyes because one can't make it through my lips due to an overwhelming mouthful of carbs. You'd think a mini muffin wouldn't set a gal back so far but clearly this has been one of my greatest mistakes.

At least Connor has the decency to look bashful as he slowly shakes his head and leaves me to the wolves, the traitor. It's hard to be mad at him even as he sidesteps my outstretched arm to whisper something in Lin's ear.

"Interesting. I was going to ask you something different, but it seems our little stud muffin here would like to request that you spend an evening with him, this Friday actually, and since you're in no position to argue..."

I nod my head enthusiastically because it is absolutely no kind of hardship. Lin could have committed me to juggling knives, or adopting a herd of baby goats, or going on a naked jog across town, or delivering a puppet show to the elderly, also while naked. Not that I wouldn't, just that I probably shouldn't. Going on a date with Connor? Definitely don't have to twist my arm!

"Wonderful!" Lin removes one of his arms from around me only to quickly circle it around Connor, dragging him in close to us both in a tight squeeze. "Now you two kids seal the deal with a kiss! Or I will, I'm not picky." He waggles his eyebrows and looks expectantly between the two of us.

Connor has this whole deer in the headlights thing going on, probably caught between wanting to kiss me and not wanting to do it in front of Lin. Personally, I'm looking to avoid the risk of spitting a bunch of muffin on him since I've only just barely managed to finally swallow it all down, though I'm pretty sure there's still plenty on my lips to give him more than just a small taste.

"Too slow!" Lin declares, having only given us a few short seconds to wrestle with extreme internal debates.

His lips rush towards my cheek and he makes an exaggerated "muah!" sound upon contact. To my surprise, he does the same thing to Connor's cheek as well before releasing us both, snapping both wrists quickly to slap each of us on the ass before we even knew it was happening. Lin wiggles his fingers in front of his face in farewell, walking backwards away from us as we recover from... whatever that just was? As he turns around, he yells over his shoulder "Let me know if you need a chaperone! I'd be happy to come between you two."

Wait, was that a double entendre?

Connor awkwardly laughs while his hands start to make random and unfinished motions, opening and closing his mouth a few times like he means to say something. Seems like he can't figure out any of what to do so he gives up and walks away, leaving me alone behind the tea bar.

Oh hey! Across the room I can see Kieran behind the checkout counter; looks like he escaped that car-parking black hole after all. Good for him! I should congratulate him on a successful journey.

On my way across the shop, I notice Colonel Stubbs curled up on one of the window seats, Aria draped over him as they both soak in sunbeams. Definitely looks comfy.

I swipe a finger across the top of the wooden counter, enjoying the smooth slide of lacquered lumber beneath my touch. Resting an elbow on the counter, I lean forward and kick one foot up slightly.

"Hey there Beefcake, whatcha doin'?"

Given that he's been sitting on a stool, scrolling through

his phone, I'm pretty sure the answer is "not much," but who knows! Maybe he's busy writing the next great American novel.

"Not much, Fireball." Ah. Called it! Finally, my psychic powers are beginning to develop! "Would you like to keep me company while we wait to open? Only another 20 minutes or so."

"Sure!" I hop around the counter and plop sideways onto his lap, forgoing the available empty stool beside him. It's probably not nearly as comfortable, nor welcoming. I mean, when was the last time you sat on a stool and it squeezed you tight against it, burying its face in your hair? Probably never. It would be really creepy if a stool managed to do that, actually, and you should probably call an exorcist or something if that ever happens. Or maybe Beetlejuice? Though he'd probably be the problem if you're getting squeezed by seating, now that I think about it.

My legs are pretty high off the ground, between the tall chair and the muscular man keeping me from succumbing fully to gravity, so I kick them freely back and forth. The hand I have wrapped around Kieran's shoulder makes its way up to his flowing orange waves, idly swirling random pieces between curious fingers. My other hand reaches out and grabs a wayward pen from the countertop, ensuring maximum possible fiddling can be achieved at this juncture.

A quick nip at my neck surprises me and I yelp slightly.

"If you keep wiggling your ass on my dick like that, I'm going to greet the customers with much more than an outstretched hand this morning."

Oops! .....Oops? Hm. Yeah, oops. Bad Dizzy, definitely say it's an oops.

"I've got all this pent up energy right now. Normally, by

the time I've been up this long, I'd at least have had to make a mad dash away from something or other so it's weird having the leisure to actually stay still. Not sure if I really know how to do it that well, if I'm honest." My legs continue to kick even though I thought I told them to chill out, "Is there something I can do before the doors open? Anything you want to show me so I can help out during the day?"

Zeke appears from between two shelving units and walks up to us, sitting in the stool I snubbed.

"Go for a run. Take Monty."

Isn't that a little… unwise? Two people who are supposed to be here in the morning and one super secret bonus person just up and leaving? I don't really know what opening is like here, but with the tea being a big draw I bet it's not NOT busy first thing.

"We'll be fine."

Man, having someone be able to read your mind is kind of weird but kind of cool. I wonder if he can see my thoughts, too? Like the milkshake dragon…

"Sometimes."

Hm. Interesting. How often does he get the pictures instead? Try not to think about dicks. Big, throbbing, thick, hard dicks. Big, throbbing, thick, hard dicks like the one definitely pushing against your thigh. Then try not to snicker when you fail.

I slide off of Kieran's lap and pop up, hands clasped behind my back. I'm already hopping from foot to foot, ready to get moving now that the option's on the table. "Looks like we're going on a run, then! Where to?"

Kieran's big, warm hand lands on my shoulder as he guides me out from behind the counter and towards the mysterious hallway. "Come on, let's grab Monty and we can go out. Although it would be kind of funny to see him get dragged out of the building, again."

"Oh crapdoodles, I hadn't even thought about that. Guess Monty and I are gonna get to know each other pretty well until we get this whole thing figured out, won't we? Wonder why all this is happening, anyway? It doesn't feel the same as the normal curses I get hit with."

Kieran puts one hand behind his neck and rubs the back of his head. "Yeah, I think that's kind of our fault." He shows me the inside of his right wrist, "We tried out one of Zeke's new spells last night and... Well, I don't think it didn't work, it just probably worked different than we thought it would."

I grab his offered arm and look at the faint brown tattoo, basically two overlapping circles with a line through them inside of a larger circle, a thin line encircling the rest of his wrist as though the whole thing were a friendship bracelet. The same design has been on everyone else, but I just figured it was some kind of secret boy's club thing or whatever.

"....Okay? What am I supposed to be seeing here?"

"We didn't have these marks before last night." He leads us to the first door along the hallway, knocking twice before opening it and strolling in. "Zeke can probably tell you more about the spell, but he basically told us it would help us find our soulmates."

Kieran turns his head away from me for a second, but I can still see his eyes trying to seek me out discreetly.

"Oh shit. Soulmates? Is that why I'm... Well... It's like I can't keep my hands off any of you, and nobody's gotten hurt yet either. Which is so crazy because I don't normally touch people on purpose in case I break them. Heck, I don't even remember the last time I actually had a friend, but it already feels like I'm connected to all five of you like it's easy and normal and we've known each other forever. Is that crazy? I haven't stopped to wonder if it's all that crazy."

Monty stands up from the swivel chair he was sitting in across the room we've just entered, stepping towards us to take one of my hands.

"I don't really think it's crazy. If it is, then I'd better start taking someone else's medicine because it's been incredible having you here with us, even after getting dragged on my ass around town," he flashes a toothy smile. "Your being here feels right, and I'd say I can't explain it but it seems like you already understand."

I didn't notice before, but Monty's outfit is a testament to lime green, today. He's wearing lime green sneakers, black cargo pants, and a navy blue polo shirt covered in electric green limes, accented by an occasional lightning bolt erupting from the citrus fruit. I'm beaming at this limey fool because yeah, I totally understand. And I have a feeling that a lot of people would keep their distance and think these guys are a bit weird, between Monty's unique fashion sense, Zeke's abrupt way of speaking, Kieran's intimidating bulk and ever-present kilt... Each of them has a uniqueness that I personally already appreciate so much. Plus, they don't really seem to be put off by my particular brand of hot mess. If they've ever felt out of place the way I have, I know exactly how they must be enjoying not seeming different, or weird, or freakish, or scary, or dangerous, or untrustworthy to a new person. To me, they're magnetic and I'm fully enjoying being pulled together.

"Yeah, I do understand," Strong in my convictions, I nod decisively. I'm not even bothered by the soulmate thing; it kind of just makes sense. It's also sort of comforting in a weird way? Like, no need to question how I'm drawn to them because it's already destiny or whatever, and why would I want to fight this kind of destiny?

Kieran visibly relaxes next to me, Monty smiles with his whole face and squeezes my hand.

"So, what are you both doing in my clinic? Ah! That reminds me!" He snaps his fingers, "Dizzy, I made up something for you last night." Monty pulls a small, round container from his pocket and unscrews the lid. "If you want, this should heal those cuts and scratches on your legs. I feel like a total jerk-wad for tackling you last night and figured the least I could do was fix part of the problem I caused."

"Part of the...? Oh!" I chuckle and shake my head, "Nah Monty, don't feel bad. Most of this is from falling out of a tree before I even met you guys. At worst, you might've put another bruise on me somewhere from knocking the wind out of my lungs but I'm good. Barely even feel any of it now. Trust me, this is practically nothing!" I wave my hand like a showcase display down my exposed legs, "Now, I was promised a run?"

Kieran jumps in, "Yeah, Zeke said they've got the front for a bit and our Fireball here is burning with excess energy. I haven't gotten a chance to shift yet, so we might as well go for a lap or two around the block and get it all out now to make sure we're good later on."

"Ah, and you're here to bring me with you willingly," Monty deduces. "Well, good news! I'd be happy to go on a run. Don't have any scheduled appointments until noon anyway, and it'll be good to run with you again, Kier. Let's get to it!"

Monty locks up the clinic behind us and we continue down the hallway, turning right at the end and going through a huge set of double doors that apparently lead to their back of house. It's way more warehouse-y back here, rows and rows of metal shelving units stacked high with what's probably extra stock. Or empty boxes pretending to be extra stock. Or box trolls equipped with the perfect camouflage.

We exit through the back, answering my question about where the SUV went: it's parked behind the building! There's your standard dumpster and loading bay nonsense back here as well, even though it seems like it would be difficult for anything much larger than an oversized van or trash truck to maneuver through the alleyways. Clearly, they've found a way.

To my right, rustling sounds catch my attention and HOLY SHIT WHY IS KIERAN NAKED?! THE FUCK?!!?

I'm not scared of his dingaling dangling about, just deeply confused by the idea that this dude is seriously about to streak through the city. Seems like a real good way to get arrested, though maybe it's a training technique? If you've got to run from the cops, you'll probably run a bit faster than if you weren't being chased. I certainly run faster when there's an angry pitchfork mob behind me than when there isn't.

It all makes sense when the man beside me falls to all fours and turns into an enormous goddamned wolf. The sounds of his joints popping and bones grinding aren't exactly pleasant, but it happens almost instantly enough to leave me wondering if I'd actually even heard anything at all.

The same green eyes I woke up to this morning look out at me from the face of a rusty orange, deep auburn, and white-furred wolf. He's about chest height to me, which puts him at roughly 4 feet tall without even trying; pretty sure that's basically double the size of a normal wolf. Holy shit!

Ducking his head, he shoves a cold, wet nose into my hand, rubbing the entire length of his soft snout against my palm. My free hand slaps its way up to my chest as I gasp in a tight breath. "Holy shit, Kieran. You're a wolf!"

He chuffs like "No shit, Sherlock. Glad you noticed." At

least, that's how I interpret it.

"Wow," His fur is rough-textured but thick and somewhat plush as I run my hands up his forehead to round his ears. I breathe out in wonder at his literal transformation, "You're amazing."

He bumps my side in response, letting me explore the rest of his body while walking a slow circle around me.

"Yeah, uh... Surprise?" Monty shrugs. "Guess we didn't tell you? It's not something Kier usually advertises but it's just a fact of life for us. You might want to take off that apron, by the way. Just leave it with Kier's clothes and we'll grab them when we get back."

Rolling up the sleeves of my unzipped jacket, I take off the apron and put it on top of Kieran's discarded clothes, helpfully on a small table just inside the door.

We take off at a slow jog down the alley, Kieran literally nipping at my heels from behind. Once we make it to the sidewalk in front of the building though, we start to put a bit of pep in our step. The slow jog builds up to a fast jog, then to a straight up run. Normally, running is something I do out of necessity rather than for fun so I've never really gotten to analyze the experience. The wind whipping across my skin, my legs burning with a pleasant pain, the companionable silence making it a sort of meditative activity as my mind empties. I don't know where we're going, and there's no true rush to get there despite our speed. We're alive, we're free, and we're only a little bit sweaty.

We've been at it for maybe 15 minutes but I'm already feeling way less worked up than when we started. The sexual tension, the insecurities, the nervous energy; everything's gone; all that's left is me and the pounding beat of feet upon pavement. Each step like a steady heartbeat, helping me shed anything that might try to hold me back-my only focus on that next footfall.

Laughter bubbles up and flows out as I spread my arms and feel the wind slip through my spread fingers. A wet tongue laps my outstretched hand just once, only making me laugh more at how weird and wonderful this whole experience has been; not just the run, but the whole morning, really. Yesterday started with light coffee burns and assault via tree, today started with grits and giggles. Definitely worlds apart!

Gradually, we slow our pace until we cool down and walk, just for the last block or so. I'm in my own little euphoria by the time we make our way through the shop's alley to head back inside. Weirdly, it doesn't feel too soon, even though we couldn't possibly have been out for more than half an hour at most. Who'da thunk I'd actually *enjoy* running as a hobby? Something to explore in the future, it seems.

By the time we're at the back door, my breathing has almost returned to normal and my spirit still feels wonderfully light. Unconsciously, I've started humming to myself with happiness.

"Well, that sure is a good way to keep the blood pumping," Monty says, holding his hands on his hips, chest puffed out in a clear attempt to finish catching his breath. He might look muscular and toned, but it seems like our lime-loving unicorn king may be behind me in cardio. Not gonna lie, I'm feeling kind of like a champion right now. Seeing this large, capable man having just a tiny amount of struggle while little ol' me is on cloud nine? Let's just say that my ego is like the Grinch's heart at the end of the story-it's grown three sizes today!

A few loud crunch-n-pops later and I'm getting the bajeebers squeezed out of me by a naked, beefy redhead. Arms pinned to my sides, feet dangling, this really isn't the ideal high ground for a mighty warrior such as myself. The fact that I can't stop laughing also, perhaps, wounds my fierceness. "What the crap, Kieran! Put me down!"

"Never. You're my prisoner now. You've been sentenced to a lifetime of running at my side every morning, just so you know."

"Oh, have I, now? And what's the crime I'm being punished for, hmm?"

"You're far too intoxicating, so much so that it must be illegal. You're weaponizing your incredibleness somehow, and I'm sorry to say that I can't let your charm spread to any unsuspecting victims." Hoisting me up further so I'm now bent over his shoulder, he walks us through the back door and straight past the table with our now abandoned clothing.

"Monty! Help me! I'm being abducted and it's not even by aliens!" I reach out to the totally rude dude who's laughing at my predicament. At least he's smart enough to grab the clothes, but I'm starting to get real worried that Kieran's about to go strolling through the store with his wang out. And by the way, what's with these guys and holding me hostage while another just watches and is totally unhelpful? I smell a conspiracy afoot.

"Uh... Kieran? Seriously, maybe put me down? Or at least put some clothes on? Or don't, y'know, you're a free man and you can live your life and all, but maybe don't go flashin' your phallus to the customers? Or at least charge them extra for the show?" Clearly, my business savvy is unparalleled.

He picks up the pace and swats my behind, weaving inbetween the shelves while whooping and hollering until we make it to a door that I'm terrified he's going to open right onto the main floor of the shop. Those customers better get ready to pay at least double for the MORE than eyeful they're about to get!

Much to my surprise, the door he opens leads directly into a bathroom, complete with shower. It's then that I'm finally released and able to fully appreciate the wild expression on Kieran's face. That fucker is grinning like he won the damned lottery ten times in a row and is about to cash in.

Monty jogs up to us and bumps Kieran aside, handing me my apron politely and haphazardly tossing the rest at our mad wolf man.

"Diz, if you want to take a shower in here you're welcome to it first," Monty offers.

There's sweat trailing tracks down my neck. "Uh, yeah. Sure. That's probably a good idea, actually."

He points to a second door in the wall, "That leads directly into my clinic. Come and get me when you're done? KIERAN" he coughs and looks pointedly at the naked man still grinning like a damned fool, "will get dressed now and head to the front. The lucky dog doesn't have to deal with sweat when he shifts."

"Wolf. I'm a lucky wolf." Which his wolfish grin only further emphasizes.

Monty just crosses his arms and gives him the daddest dad look that has ever been dadded. One eyebrow cocked like 'Listen here, young man, I will put you in time out and take away your video games if you don't get your act together right now.' Man, a look sure can say a lot of things even if your mouth doesn't.

Kieran lets out a long-suffering groan, huffs, and dramatically whips his blue kilt taught before stepping into it and pulling tight the straps on its sides. I'm super jealous of the huge pockets. Also, wow, commando? Guess that shouldn't come as a surprise, but it seems like Kieran is literally only wearing a white t-shirt, kilt, and slip-on shoes. Considering it appears he needs to be able to get in and out of his clothes quickly it's a pretty ingenious setup, but now I'm probably going to spend a large portion of the day thinking about his dick. Like oops, don't mind me, I just happen to be lying on the ground like a perv every time you're walking by, no need to stop unless it's directly above me.

He was literally just naked. What the hell is wrong with me? Why is wearing just a kilt somehow even more tantalizing than being straight up skin city?

Aaaaaaaaand now I've been staring at Kieran's covered crotch for an unreasonable length of time. Oops. Maybe he didn't notice?

I glance up. He's gone from "wolfish grin" to "oh yeah, I definitely saw you checking out my junk." I grimace at my own transparency.

"Need some help wiping up that drool, Dizzy? I'll be glad to stick around and show you how to use a towel if you want."

Monty rolls his eyes and literally grabs Kieran by his ear, dragging the smug man through the clinic door and away from my super smooth complete and utter lack of response. Yeah, Dizzy, you tell 'em.

The entire time I'm in the shower, all I can think about is trying to come up with some sort of witty comeback. Sadly, the best I've got is "You can show me how to use a towel if you also show me that dick again." Admittedly, it's pretty garbage as far as responses go. Even just saying "Okay" or "No thanks" would be about a thousand times smoother. I bet Lin could come up with something in his sleep.

I don't bother washing my hair so it only takes five minutes before I'm stepping out, thinking heavily about dicks as I grab a towel to dry off. Man, the zen from our run really didn't last long, did it?

When I do walk into the clinic, Monty and Connor are saying something about eyes to each other and looking a bit concerned. Monty's leaning against his desk, smooth brown arms crossed in front while Connor's hunched down, pale hands thrust deep in the pockets of his skinny jeans. They both look up at me, Connor straightening slightly and smiling as soon as he sees me, reaching out as I round the exam bed.

"Hey, how was the run?" He wraps his arm around me as our sides fuse together to reveal our true four-armed, four-legged form.

"Awesome. So awesome. Were we gone too long? Did I miss anything important?"

"Nah, people mostly just come in for tea the first hour or so. It's busy, but it's pretty easy."

"Ah, okay. I felt a little guilty leaving you guys, even though Zeke said you'd be okay. Is it still tea time out there? I'd rather help if that's an option."

He squeezes me tighter for just a moment. "Go on, Lin would love your help."

"M'kay." I plant a quick kiss on his cheek and return the squeeze, sharply flicking my hand once in farewell at Monty. "Thanks for the run, Monty. It's just what I never knew I needed."

He smiles and waves back, "Feel free to come and help me in here any time, if you want. And I'd be happy to run with you again, just say the word."

Amused, I wonder what the word I'd need to say is. Maybe potato?

20. ZEKE

Mornings are predictable. Open the doors at 9:30 am, the same 37 people filter in at their usual times. We sell out of muffins. Nobody buys spells until 10am or later. Even with Dizzy being an added variable, everything runs as smoothly as it always does. Realistically, just two of us could man the shop for most of the day if we had to; one at the tea bar, one at spell sales. The clinic would be closed.

Dizzy comes bouncing out of the hallway, not nearly as quickly or energetically as when she left but clearly still happy. Her hand reaches out and tenderly skims along my arm while she passes me at the cash register.

Thank you, that was exactly what I needed.

"Good."

She smiles and keeps going, skipping lightly towards Lin at the tea bar. I wish she'd take those infernal twigs out of her hair and let it flow freely down her back again.

Lin points out different things around his station, quickly showing her where the cups, lids, and hot water are. He waves his hand in front of the wall of tea ingredients and gives a lengthy explanation, making sure to always have at least one point of close contact with her.

Uh, yeah, no duh. I can read a freakin' label, I'm not some illiterate slug from a remote garden village that hasn't invented the alphabet yet. And even if I were, I assume I'd still at least know what dried rose petals look like as a slug. They're all just plants, and I've definitely met plants before-no slug-form required!

I snort. She's so bizarre. It's unique and perplexing and fascinating. I could study her for years and still never tire of finding her unpredictable.

Within minutes, Dizzy goes from obviously taking commands from Lin, to waving him off and doing as she pleases. Confidently.

"Excuse me, how much for the smudge stick?"

I look down at the well-dressed woman standing in front of the counter, digging her hand into the basket filled with sage bundles. It's very clearly labelled with a large price sign.

"$3.50 each."

"Ah, is there a deal for buying multiples? I may need a few!"

"Yes. 2 for $7, 3 for $10.50"

"Oh, excellent! I'll take 2, please!"

Customers. Unlike Dizzy, they follow a pattern. Everyone makes the same jokes, everyone ignores the labels and signs, nobody does the math to realize there isn't a deal at all; they're just paying the listed price.

"Do you guys take cards here?"

I glance at the sign in front of the Point of Sale, directly within her line of sight that says "Yes, we take cards!"

"Yes. We take cards."

"Excellent, excellent!" She digs into her large purse, "Ring me up for just them? And a bag if you have one please?"

Yes your hot tea is going to be hot and tea, what?! What kind of question even is that?! Has he been tricked before into cold cabbage soup or something!?

Hopefully, my smile comes off as gratitude towards the customer handing me her credit card and doesn't give away my amusement at Dizzy's reaction to what was likely an average customer encounter.

The transaction ends and I hand the woman her card back, providing the requested bag as well. She leaves.

The next few hours continue as they usually do, a good number of customers coming in and lingering for a while. Kieran and I take turns trading between the cash register and roaming the store. People start to filter in for the clinic. Dizzy and Lin build a rhythm as they dance around each other at the counter. He leaves her alone occasionally to do some of his "readings." Maybe he'll come back to us with some leads.

Connor quietly creeps up and waits for me to address him. I tilt my head in his direction.

"Connor."

"I was going to get lunch for us in a while. What do you want? We're doing sandwiches today."

"Pastrami on rye. Chips, too. Please."

He writes it down and nods before retreating to ask the

others for their orders. I assume I'm not the first.

Oh shit yes! Finally I'll be reunited with my destiny, a fucking beautiful turkey club.

Lin leaves with Connor, entrusting Dizzy to make the tea on her own. It's not that busy, but she's clearly good at it. A couple of times she's needed to climb onto the back counter to reach one of the jars that's on the top shelf. I'll have to remember to find a solution for her.

If I install a shelf with a pull-down rack, we could still store everything neatly but have a simple way for Dizzy to reach what she needs. We could also reorganize so the most common ingredients are lined up on the counter itself, freeing up the top shelf and avoiding the problem altogether. Or find space to expand horizontally. If she wants to keep helping there.

Goddamn, none of these dudes remembers ever being 5'4". Wish I was taller by like two inches, would totally make everything easier. Maybe I'll luck out and fall down some rabbit hole and eat some magic fungi. Or was it the drink me bottle?

Hm. I could probably devise a way to make her taller if she really wanted me to. Seems more practical to just adjust the shelves.

Two hours pass. Lin and Connor aren't back yet. I need to make more cleaning spells, they're almost sold out again. Connor needs to bottle more glamours.

Dizzy climbs up onto the counter again.

Fuck fuck fuck fuck fuck, not now!

She screams, falling to the ground and smashing the glass container in her hand.

Kieran rips through the crowd in front of the tea bar, jumping over it to get to her.

Fuck fuck fuck fuck fuck.

I'm up and running, yelling over my shoulder for Monty as I join a snarling Kieran. Aria hisses and snaps at him every time he tries to reach for Dizzy, whose eyes are glazed as she reaches blindly into her jacket pockets. She's whimpering. A lot. She won't say anything to any of us, though it doesn't stop Kieran from asking her questions.

Get the fuck out of me. Get the fuck out of me. Get the fuck out of me. Get the fuck out of me.

21. DIZZY

I don't know what it is with the people here, but it seems like everyone wants this blue cornflower stuff in their tea, and of course it's on the stupid top shelf. I'm about two more orders of Seasonal Prep Brew away from just leaving it on the counter so I don't have to keep climbing up there every time someone puts in an order with it-damn the fact that I'm basically a visitor and I'm sure the guys like the way things are organized already.

A familiar burning tingle slams into my whole body, more like a violent explosion of pins across every inch than the tolerable warning signs most curses make me deal with. Fuck fuck fuck fuck fuck, not now! A second heaping helping of holy-shit-that-hurts-a-lot knocks me flat on my ass, sending me crashing down from the counter onto the floor.

Dimly, I know things are happening around me, but they don't matter right now. Fuck fuck fuck fuck fuck. My hands are shaking so hard as I force them to get to work, throwing off the apron and opening my jacket, grabbing whatever I need to break this one. Oh man, it's a real doozie. Every single one of my joints feels like it's trying to pop out of the socket at the exact same time as every single bone in my body tries to snap in half. This is the strongest curse to probably ever hit me, and it hurts so so so so so much. Fuck. There isn't even time to grind everything together at all, I just start shoving leaves and buds and whatever else directly into my mouth and chew.

Something tells me this one needs more than just a small bit of blood, so I don't question it when I get the urge to slice open a long gash across my chest and shove some of the chewed-up mixture into the cut. The rest I gulp down, making sure to swipe up and swallow some of the blood now thoroughly soaking Connor's shirt to activate it. Fuck, this hurts so much.

There are definitely people nearby but I don't know who. Hopefully I'm safe here. There just wasn't enough warning with this one.

Get the fuck out of me. Get the fuck out of me. Get the fuck out of me. Get the fuck out of me. My mantra. There's nothing else I can do at this point except concentrate and fucking hope it goddamned works. Fuck. Get the fuck out of me. Get the fuck out of me. Get the fuck out of me.

22. KIERAN

"Everybody get the fuck out of here. NOW!" I don't give a shit if they never come back, either. Fuck them all. Something's wrong with Dizzy, and goddamned Aria won't let me stop her from cutting herself up, and I'm feeling really fucking panicked. This time, I know Dizzy and I are experiencing the same emotion at the same time and that only makes it worse on my end, knowing that she's also all worked up. "Where the fuck is Monty?" I'm screaming for him at the top of my lungs.

"I'm right here, what happened?" Monty practically screeches to a halt. "Shit, why is she bleeding?" He assesses the situation quickly and turns to the people leaning over the counter to get some new gossip instead of being actually fucking useful. "We're closed. Everyone leave, now. Thank you for your understanding."

Finally, after Dizzy stops moving and sits completely stone

still, Aria lets me touch her. I know it's not helping, but I don't know what else to do and it feels like I have to make contact with every square inch of her to be sure she's okay, though I'm pretty sure she's not. "Talk to me, Fireball." It's a desperate plea, punctuated by the frantic seeking of my fingers over her skin as she whines every few seconds, not actually saying anything in response.

Monty places a hand on Dizzy for a moment, clearly reading her injuries. He then reaches into one of his pockets and tosses Zeke a small, round container of salve. "Z, stop the bleeding with this. I'll get them out." He quickly ushers everyone out the front door and locks it behind them.

Zeke scoops up a small blob of goop from Monty's container, moving to spread it on Dizzy's chest. From atop Dizzy's shoulder, Aria hisses and reaches out one of her hands to stop Zeke's finger from making contact. She sniffs the substance he's offering, then swipes it for herself and gently pats it on Dizzy's wound, careful not to disturb whatever it is that's already packed on there.

Dizzy's still whimpering, sometimes making a sharp keening noise and it's making me absolutely lose my fucking shit. Last night I didn't think I was ready for anyone new to actually be a part of my life, but I will rip anyone and anything apart that thinks they can take her from me, now.

I grasp both her hands in mine and squeeze, but she doesn't even seem to know I'm here. "Please, please talk to me, Fireball. Tell me what's happening. Tell me what to do. Fuck. Just say anything." My eyes are starting to water and I don't even give a shit, I'm feeling her stress and my stress at the same time and it's scary as fuck.

Monty's phone rings, and he starts cursing up his own storm. I can hear Connor panicking on the other end, so it looks like we're all dealing with some kind of bullshit.

"We're on our way, Con. Stay with him. Give us fifteen minutes, okay buddy? We'll figure this out." Monty hangs up. "Fuck. Lin started screaming and collapsed, too. Connor can't move him and they're a few blocks away. Kier, you need to drive out there and..."

"Fuck you, I'm not going goddamned anywhere! Just try and rip me away from her right now." My eyes never leave Dizzy's face, but I can smell Monty's frustration and fear from here.

"Well I can't fucking leave her!" He throws his hands over his head. "I literally can't, Kier, and you're the strongest of us!"

"Fuck. You." I growl out. "I'm not leaving."

"I'll go. I heard her before she went down. She knows what's happening to her, but can't tell any of us right now. She just keeps thinking 'get the fuck out of me' over and over again." Zeke does something on his phone, "Connor and I together can lift Lin easily. He's sending me the address. If something changes, I'll likely know it before you two but update me regardless. If she snaps out of it before I return, tell her to let me know she's okay."

With that, Zeke turns and jogs towards the back.

My skin is starting to feel itchy and too tight. It's getting harder and harder to stay human, and I don't even want to. Stubbs has the right idea, he's curled up against her side and I plan to do exactly the same for as long as it takes to get her back.

My wolf shifts, not even giving the slightest hint of a shit if my shirt rips. The kilt and shoes will survive, they always do. I lay my head in her lap and circle my body entirely around her. Nobody's getting to her without going through me. And Stubbs. And Aria.

Monty kneels down in front of us and puts his hands on her arms, her back, her head, her stomach. He repeats this a couple of times before Aria snips at his hands, more politely than she did at me, earlier. Backing up just a step, Monty starts to pace, muttering to himself.

"There's nothing wrong with her, Kier. I can't feel anything inside her out of place. But she was screaming, you don't just scream for nothing so it has to be something. Why can't I feel what's wrong?" He keeps pacing, muttering, theorizing. I don't give a shit. She's still breathing and that's the only reason I haven't torn this whole block apart. Fucking alchemy and shifter magic are useless to her right now, I know it, and I can't deal with feeling like a worthless sack of crap. Monty's our fixer, and he'd damned well better be able to fix this or there will be hell to pay.

I'm still in a panic spiral. Dizzy hasn't moved an inch, aside from very tight breaths. Her eyes are closed and her back is ramrod straight, legs crossed under my head. I'm whimpering and whining, occasionally nuzzling her stomach with my cheek. Her body keeps heating up and cooling down uncomfortably, but there's no way I'm leaving her or letting go. Never.

Aria slinks down and lands between my shoulder blades. Her hands start to pet my face while doing that humming trilling song thing she does. I don't want it to but it takes the edge off of my own panic, though I still feel Dizzy's separately. She hasn't made any noises at all for a while, but I can feel her anxiety as a tight, hard ball straight in the center of my chest. Feeling what she does but not being able to do a damned thing about it or take it away from her is torture.

I know Monty is going through his own shit because he keeps stopping to put a hand on her every now and then before going back to pacing and arguing with himself. Seems to be trying to come up with a plan but it's pretty fucking obvious we don't know what's wrong, so it's not like we know how to make it right again.

Finally, FINALLY, after the longest half hour of my life, I start to feel her shift slightly behind me. Just a small twitch of her arm, nothing major but at least it's something. I lift my head the barest breadth away from her lap to look at her face, but she hasn't moved anything else. Licking her hand doesn't do anything, and I whimper in distress.

Connor and Zeke come zooming down the hall, Lin being wheeled on one of Monty's office chairs. Zeke must have told Connor about Dizzy because he makes a bee-line straight for her, not even pausing before crouching right behind her and immediately wrapping his arms around her. His face looks as panicked and grief-stricken as I'm sure mine would if I were human.

The second he touches her, she draws in a huge gasp of air, like she's been drowning this whole time and can finally come up for a breath. Her eyes snap open and she limply raises an arm just enough to point a finger at the sky and say "Not today, motherfuckers," before slumping backwards against Connor and passing out.

A small amount of relief passes through me at her emotions switching to triumph for just a moment before shutting down to nothing. It's not much, but it's enough. Her breathing is deeper now than it was before, her body way less tense. This time, it just feels like she's asleep. It's hard not to still be worked up over everything, but at least it seems less impossibly desperate than before.

Monty and Zeke each come in on either side of her, leaning over me to touch whatever part of her they can reach.

"Fuck, that hurt." Lin croaks out from the chair he was

wheeled in on. Connor is clutching Dizzy like his life depends on it, eyes squeezed shut tightly, lashes clearly wet. "Anyone want to tell me why I'm in this chair? And why you all look like someone died?"

Nobody says anything. I'm sure we will later, but right now we all need a moment to not think our girl is in the middle of some shit that some useless panicking idiots can't do anything about and just be grateful it seems like it's over.

23. MONTY

"Is this part of the curse she was telling us about this morning?" When I realized that I couldn't sense any physical injuries, magical distress became one of the top suspects for her inexplicable shutdown. It's the only thing that makes sense, if she was in pain but not actually hurt. Unless it was all caused by her fall from the counter?

Tucking a stray curl behind her ear, I let my hand linger as it grazes her cheek. It doesn't feel good being a healer who can't heal someone when they're hurting.

"She's not cursed." Lin's voice is still a little rough as he rubs his throat and rises unsteadily, "I gave her a reading earlier and didn't catch a whiff of anything nefarious. If anything, she seemed... blessed. Though who knows; too much of a good thing and all that."

"So then what the heck happened, here? And what happened to you, Lin? Connor said you screamed and just collapsed," I ask.

He dusts off the sleeves of his white shirt, brows furrowed somewhat uncertainly as he starts. "I'm not sure, actually. One minute, we're on our way back from the shops and the next it feels like every single part of my body is trying to rip itself apart. It was as though my bones were trying to break themselves into dust and my limbs were trying to sever, but I don't remember seeing anyone or anything when it began." He bites his lip and looks me in the eyes, "I felt it the whole time. Part of me almost knew Connor was probably nearby, and part of me thought that I was possibly being moved, but it was like the only thing I really knew completely and for certain was pain; pain worse than anything I could even imagine." He pulls at the bottom of his vest to straighten it out, obviously doing all this primping as a way to self-soothe. "I think... I think I almost died."

A chorus of curse words are thrown around.

With his head still buried in Dizzy's shoulder, Connor's muffled voice reaches my ears and throws a chill up my spine. "I saw the eyes. They were there before Lin fell. I don't think I'm imagining them any more, or if I am, they're a warning."

He told me earlier about how he's been feeling and seeing eyes on him ever since we got into the city today. I treated them like they were one of his flashbacks, but what if he's right and they're something else? Connor's been known to manifest nightmares into reality regularly, but he doesn't have the power of premonition. Though it wouldn't be far-fetched to consider he developed a sixth sense warning him of danger, given everything he's been through. Maybe he really did sense something, and we didn't think to wonder what it meant because it just seemed like another nightmare of his.

Sighing, I tie my dreadlocks back in a low ponytail and

stand up. "Lin, I don't know what happened to you or what happened to Dizzy, but it seems like too much of a coincidence that you both went down at the same time to ignore. If it's cool with everyone, I vote we close up and go home early. Forget everything else. If she's still not up by the time we get there, Dizzy can rest in my office and I can monitor her safely," I sigh again and mumble, "if I can even monitor her at all."

"I can combine an astral tether with an observation alert, so we know as soon as she's conscious. Even if she doesn't look it," Zeke offers. "And it will prevent her soul from wandering, if it was going to." He pauses for a moment, "You should probably know that I can't hear her right now. I don't know what it means."

I don't really care if that means our binding to her is broken, or if it means she's just sleeping too deeply to think. What matters is that nobody said no, so I place one hand on Connor's shoulder and one on Kieran's scruff. "Let's get her up, guys; let's get her home."

Kieran whimpers, takes a breath, and squirms out from around her. He shifts quickly, sliding back into his abandoned kilt and shoes in less than a minute. More patiently than I expected, Kieran runs a hand through Connor's hair, letting him bury himself in Dizzy's shoulder for a few moments more before reaching down and picking her up like she's the most delicate treasure in the universe. She lays cradled across Kieran's arms, limbs dangling limply in his strong embrace. Connor slips his hand into one of hers and holds it, a pained expression haunting his face as they steadily make a path to the SUV out back.

I know he's imagining losing her, likely already seeing a familiar bloody carcass in her place. It doesn't help that the front of her shirt is drenched in thick rivers of red, one of his worst triggers.

Always seeming to know exactly who needs her most, Aria crawls across Connor's shoulders and licks his cheek, rubbing her face against his afterwards. She purrs softly, and I'd swear that Connor's eyes become slightly more focused the longer she dotes on him.

Our drive home is solemn, Aria and Stubbs the only ones making any real noise until Lin finally turns the radio on, filling the silence with quiet pianos and strings.

Without needing to be told, as soon as we enter the house Kieran heads straight for my office and carefully lowers Dizzy onto the bed. I step up next to Connor, who's still clinging stoically to her, and place a hand over her heart. It's beating perfectly; no abnormalities there. Slowly, I run my hands over every inch of her body, searching for any sign of internal injury. She might not have worried about them last night, but I push a little of my energy into her and wipe away her bruises and cuts. It's all superficial healing, but just being able to do something at all feels better than nothing, even though this isn't really the problem that needs to be fixed. Normally, I'd rely on mixtures to do this minor work-to keep my magic stores stocked for bigger issues-but frankly, resigning myself to a small amount of weariness feels like penance for failing her earlier.

Moving around to the head of the bed, I trace along her neck, up her temples, letting my palms rest on either side of her face. There's no physical trauma anywhere on her, the worst reading I'm getting just an overwhelming sense of exhaustion. Whatever magic source she has inside her seems to be empty, leaving both her body and soul in deep need of rest and restoration.

Kieran and Zeke walk back into the room, dragging along enough chairs behind them for everyone. I didn't even notice them leave, or Lin stay for that matter-I was too focused on checking her over.

"She's okay, guys. She's just completely drained and needs rest. Magically, physically, she's got nothing in the tank right now but everything about my exam tells me she's in a restorative sleep." I don't tell them that this is only my best guess, not wanting my own anxieties to heap onto theirs as well. "If she's not up in a few hours, I'll see if we can bring her out of it, but right now it seems best to just leave her be."

"Ah, that's my cue, then." Lin collapses into the chair behind him and falls asleep pretty much instantaneously.

Zeke approaches the bed and pulls a piece of yellow cloth from his pocket with a small black stone tied to the end. He loosens her hair and braids it through a chunk of the freed tendrils. "When her mind resurfaces, these will warm noticeably." He hands out matching black stones to each of us, slipping one into the front pocket of Lin's vest. Then he just leaves.

"You have to wake up," Connor whispers. It's at this moment I notice the tear tracks working silently down his face. He hasn't made a single sound since before we left the shop, nor has he let go of her hand. I'm watching him do his best not to get overwhelmed, but having known him since he ended up in my parents' house years ago, it's obvious to me he's fighting off a flashback.

"Hey Con, why don't you take a seat? Keep her company for a while? I'm sure she'd be happy to see you when she wakes up." He doesn't acknowledge me, just stays standing silently over her, holding her hand like a lifeline and staring intently at the closed wound on her chest. I could mend the gash in the shirt, but that wouldn't take care of the blood-the bigger problem, I suspect.

Kieran's already pulled his chair up against the foot of the bed, his head resting on her legs, one arm draped over her thighs. There's no point in trying to ask him again to leave her, so I take it upon myself to head upstairs to get a clean shirt. My room's the master suite, directly to the left of the stairs. As I push open my closet door, I suddenly become self-conscious of my clothing choices. Personally, I enjoy the bright colors and funky patterns, but will Dizzy appreciate waking up to a shirt covered in bananas? I guess we'll find out if it happens. When it happens.

Stopping to grab a couple of pillows and blankets, I head back to my office downstairs to see everyone pretty much how I left them. One pillow gets tucked under Lin's head, a blanket draped across his lap as well.

Knowing full well how delicate the balance of Kieran's and Connor's emotions are right now, I approach slowly, placing the spare pillow and blanket, as well as my shirt, on an unused chair before standing between them.

"Hey. Would you guys help me clean her up a bit? Do something nice for her so she doesn't wake up like this?"

Connor doesn't respond, and I'm worried he's lost in his head until he lets go of her hand and heads to my work sink, grabbing a cloth and filling a bowl with water. Kieran and I work together to take off her jacket, which I fold and put on the nearby desk. It seems a little intrusive to take her shirt off while she's sleeping, but it also feels like waking up to your own personal horror show may be worse. I hope she knows she can trust us.

Tenderly, Connor wipes the wet cloth along her chest and midsection. He's still crying, but his eyes are clearer; more determined; more grounded. Maybe he needs to feel like he's in control of something, too?

I leave them to finish redressing her, pointing out the pillow and blanket before I go. They don't need me in there right now, and much as I want to hover and constantly read her just to feel helpful, I know there's not actually anything else for me to try until she wakes up.

Right now, the best thing I can do is not pile my stress onto anyone else's and just focus on keeping us all calm. Soup. Soup is always good to soothe the soul. We never ended up having lunch, anyway.

Stubbs butts against my ankles as we head to the kitchen, the little scamp knowing full well I'm a sucker and will always give him a treat for acting as sous chef.

I make short work of dicing an onion and setting it to sauté with some garlic in a pot. There's an instant comfort in the sweet and savory scent of them together over heat; as long as there's garlic and onions cooking, it smells like you know what you're doing. And it smells like almost every warm meal you've ever had lovingly made for you.

Food is its own language, and it always comes down to saying to someone "I love you, I care for you, I want you to be well." A good meal can heal wounds that run deep, even if you don't know they're there, crossing all boundaries to do so. Everyone understands what it means when someone, from scratch, bakes a pan of brownies especially for you, or when they spend two days straight tending a pot of beans just because you like them, or when you're not feeling well and a piping hot bowl of chicken noodle is conjured up to heal you from the inside out.

Most people don't know that there is magic in a meal, even if it's made by someone without any magic of their own. It's one of those things that calls on the latent power in the world around us. Normally, a caster is only able to work with as much magic as they have inside of themselves, limited to their own well of strength or from the essence they're able to manipulate from items. Like Kieran, who can combine his own magic with that inside of materials to create objects of power, or just shape natural elements as needed, or exchange them for others. Or my own abilities, using my source to heal bodies and objects and make plants grow, or listening to the power within nature and combining ingredients to enact change. Rare is the magic user who can sense and utilize the energies of the universe itself; we mostly rely on our own internal source and that trapped in physical objects.

But every now and then, like with the healing powers of a meal that brings people together no matter what their conflicts may have been before, magic is simply made into being because it's meant to. Because some things are magical on their own, without trying, and power comes to them externally, rather than relying on the energies stored within the ingredients themselves.

As I stir in dried lentils, cumin, and turmeric to the pot, I send a prayer off to the universe that this meal is one that can help heal. Still, it irks me how out of my element I've felt in the face of today's problems. Normally, it's a great comfort to me the idea that if anything ever goes wrong with anyone I care for, I'll be able to heal them. Even when Kieran's leg was completely shattered last year it was only a matter of minutes before I was able to have him healed up and walking around, despite the fact it nearly drained me dry. I'd pull on every ounce of power in my body to bring any one of my family back from the brink of death if that's what was needed.

But how do you fix something when there isn't an apparent problem? It's unsettling to think that whatever happened today is something far out of my control, and it puts my family at risk of pain and vulnerability. I can't protect them from something that, as far as I can tell, doesn't exist-though it clearly does.

Stubbs paws at my leg as I thinly julienne carrots for the soup, so I toss a couple of chunks down to him.

"You like those, buddy?" I pet his side with my bare foot, "Of course you do, you roly-poly pork chop." Like most dogs with food, he happily snorts and chews, completely ignoring me as long as the treats last. I appreciate his company, even if he is just using me as a snack dispenser.

Into the pot goes vegetable broth along with the carrots; all that's left to do is simmer until the lentils are plump and the carrots are just barely soft.

My parents always taught me the value of family, and how important it is to help others-especially if they can't help themselves. Growing up, I had over a hundred brothers and sisters; children brought into our home through the foster system. Sometimes they stayed for a few weeks, tossed around due either to fortunate or unfortunate circumstances, and sometimes they stayed for years until they aged out, like Connor. Every single one of my siblings was touched by something they never should have had to experience and, as the oldest, I took it upon myself to always care for them. Always make sure I could protect them for as long as they had me, sometimes even long after either of us expected. My instincts have always, always been to keep those around me safe and take on their burdens so they don't have to shoulder them alone, if at all. There's always been a way. For the kids that were afraid of the dark, I taught them to grow bioluminescent mushrooms so they'd have light no matter where they were. If they came from families of abuse, I looked for their triggers and found ways to avoid them while showcasing what a loving and supportive family can look like. Even our living situation right now is because I couldn't help but step in when Connor and Kieran needed somewhere stable to stay.

As I cut tomatoes into chunks and toss them with onions,

vinegar, and herbs, I start to let go of some of the anxiety of feeling helpless. I couldn't do anything in the moment, but I'll do everything I can afterwards to keep us going. It's hard to remember sometimes that bad shit has to happen, the real test being how you continue on and deal with the life you're in after. No matter how hard you try, how hard you prepare, how hard you train, there will always be the possibility of something going wrong despite it. Time to shake off the shock and just keep going.

I lower the flame on the burner and ladle some of the spiced lentil soup into two bowls, placing them on a tray with two glasses of fresh ginger-lemon seltzer, as well as portions of the tomato salad and some slices of sourdough from this morning. Kieran and Connor might not be in the mood to eat, but feeding them is the best way for me to deal with my own feelings. Some people are emotional eaters, I'm an emotional feeder.

Kieran looks up slightly as I walk through the door, watching me place the tray down on my desk across the room. "Any change?"

He shakes his head, clearing his throat, "Nothing yet, not even any feelings." His hand idly strokes the outside of one of her thighs, "Lin hasn't moved yet, either." He jerks his head towards the man still asleep in a chair against the wall.

As if hearing the comment, Lin chooses that moment to shift slightly in the way most people do while resting, as opposed to the complete stillness Dizzy's displaying. Hopefully he wakes up before developing 'Fell asleep in a chair and now everything hurts' syndrome.

Even expecting not to feel anything, I place my hands on our sleeping beauty's chest and seek out even the barest hint of anything I can. "Guys, eat. Please. She's not going anywhere, and you don't have to either, just don't forget to take care of yourselves, too." Unsurprisingly, Connor doesn't acknowledge my request, but Kieran gets up and stretches briefly before retrieving the whole tray to put it on an empty portion of the bed.

"I got it, Monty." Kieran nudges Connor's shoulder slightly, "Come on man, eat up so you don't pass out and miss it when she wakes. And sit down, geez. Your knees'll lock up and you'll drop like a stone if you keep this up."

I'm grateful for the fact that Kieran apparently used all the magic words he knows right then, because Connor does exactly as asked. From his shoulder, Aria lets out a big sigh and slumps over in relief; she must have been worried about him, too.

I reach out and scratch behind her pointed ears, "You want me to get you something too, Aria?" She looks at me, then at the food on the bed and shakes her head. Wearily, she slinks over to the tray and grips a slice of bread in her mouth, fumbling for a chunk of tomato with both hands before crawling over to Dizzy, curling up in the crook of one of the unconscious woman's arms to chow down.

Sending my senses through her system one last time just in case, I acknowledge it's not helpful for me to stay here and give in to the temptation to obsess. "If Lin wakes up, let him know there's soup on the stove? I'll be upstairs if you need me."

Kieran shoos his hand at me in an affirmative, basically being the only person in the room capable of response right now anyway.

I put together another tray for myself and Zeke, tossing a couple more carrot scraps to The Colonel to keep him happy.

As expected, Zeke's up in his room, immersed in some project at his desk.

"Z, you up for some food?" I present the tray like a question, though I have no idea where in all this mess to set it down. The bed, I guess? It's the only place for me to sit anyway, so I make my way to his small bed, decked out in a ridiculous mishmash of random sheets and pillows. The dude may be a genius when it comes to combining spell theory, but his design choices leave something to be desired. Looking around the room, not a single piece of furniture matches; it's almost as though he just bought the first thing that suited his needs at the time and never bothered to think about how they'd all fit together. Maybe that's part of why he's so good at combining unexpected magics to create something new, though.

I wave Zeke over to the bed, "Come on man, take a break for a sec. What are you up here working on, anyway?"

"Cleaning spells."

I pause, "Oh? Okay." He makes those all the time. Guess he just wanted to stay busy?

"We needed more."

Accepting this, I shrug. "Sure, fair enough." It feels a little awkward to be eating soup on another man's bed, but I guess that's just how today's going.

Zeke rolls his chair beside the bed, "I was thinking about what you asked this morning. Looking into what's wrong with her. How to do it." He picks up a piece of bread and pauses before actually eating any of it, his thoughts taking priority over baser functions, "Lin said she's not cursed. She says she is. How do you identify something when it isn't what it is?" A few more moments pass before he finally takes that bite.

I consider his question. When we thought it was just a trivial matter of investigating, identifying, and removing a curse, it was a somewhat simpler task than what it now appears to be. We need something that reveals the truth to us, except Lin already did his truth thing with her and came up with conflicting results. He said she was blessed, she says she's cursed. Can it be both?

Zeke spins one of the rings on his fingers, something he often does when lost in his own head. But seeing him play with some of his enchanted jewelry gives me a thought.

"No matter what it is, it's magic. Right? So then let's start by testing her magic, see if that triggers something. Do we know what her primary is? Physical? Mental? Spiritual? Do we even know for sure if she's magical? She must be, right? Of course she is; I felt where her power source should have been, even though it was empty." I realize how many things we still don't know about this woman that already has us bending over backwards to help. Not like we don't already do this kind of thing for pretty much everyone anyway, but that's usually a conscious choice after careful planning and investigation. With Dizzy it just feels... obvious. Natural. Instinctual. "It doesn't matter. Even if she doesn't have magic of her own, whatever happened today was definitely magical so we should start by identifying whatever magic she has, or has around her. Right? That might give us some idea of how to help her?"

"That will give us a place to start, yes."

Is it weird that I don't remotely care about figuring out what happened with Zeke's spell last night? Maybe we will in the process, but I honestly don't even consider it a priority; especially in comparison to figuring out whatever has been plaguing Dizzy.

I finish off the last of my lunch and lean back against Zeke's headboard, arms folded behind my head, legs straight out and crossed at the ankles. Zeke grabs a random notebook from nearby and starts scribbling in it, the rest of his meal obviously forgotten at this point. My mind wanders, sometimes worrying about the future and sometimes being excited for it. And I remember about the mission tonight, wondering if that's even still on the table. There are a lot of people counting on us whether they know it or not, but would it really be so bad to put the needs of the few before the needs of the many?

Of course it would. What am I even thinking? It's selfish to want to call it off to hover over the newest member of our own family when there are so many members of so many families whose lives could actually be on the line if we don't take advantage of the window we have tonight. It feels selfish to even consider abandoning Walker Street, though it also feels shitty to abandon a woman who will likely be scared and confused when she comes to.

So then, I bargain, as long as she comes around before the evening there's no real good reason to throw in the towel.

Each blink starts to get longer and longer the more I consider the possibilities of both now and later. The excitement from earlier, plus the run this morning and lack of sleep last night must all finally be catching up with me.

The next thing I know, I'm jolted awake by the sound of Colonel Stubbs barking his head off downstairs while something tries to burn a hole in my leg.

Zeke looks up from the desk he must have moved back to while I was sleeping and grins, "She's up."

24. DIZZY

"She still hasn't opened her eyes yet."

"My spell is accurate. The stone is correct."

"Be patient, guys, she'll wake up in her own time. Give her some space."

"Not on your fucking life."

"Please come back, Dizzy."

"Bark bark bark bark bark woof woof bark bark!"

There's a lot of rustling and scraping and overlapping voices wherever I am, and the pounding in my head is definitely not a fan of it at all. Without opening my eyes, I raise a finger to my lips and let out a solid shhhhhhh.

Many, many hands seem to be suddenly moving on my legs, my arms, my chest, my neck... Pretty much everywhere except for my back and butt, likely due to the fact it seems I'm laying on them. Well, that's nice I guess?

"Ah, Love, welcome back."

"See, accurate."

"It just took a little extra time, that's all. Z did say it would detect when she's conscious, even if she's not fully awake yet."

"Oh, thank fuck!"

"I was so scared we were going to lose you."

"Yip yip woof bark bark woof!"

Man. These guys really can not follow simple instructions. Against all of my better judgements, I let my eyes crack open just enough to take in the sight of silhouetted expressions ranging from calm to clearly disturbed and so many things in between.

"Ughhhh. What about shhhh do you not understand?" My eyes slam shut again and I raise an arm to clutch my aching head. One of the hands on my neck moves to cover the one I've placed on my own forehead, warming and sending a path of heat through my entire system. A whole lot of the pressure in my skull eases up, though it's not exactly perfect, at least I'm down to tolerable rather than raging.

Monty's voice whispers softly, "Better?" His warm breath caresses my ear, sending a whole different kind of heat throughout my system.

"Mmm, much. How long have I been out?"

Strong pressure on my back carefully lifts and twists me up into a seated position, other hands still holding and stroking me all over. I try this whole opening my eyes thing again with significantly more success, both shocked and comforted to see all five of the guys paying rapt attention to me, each with at least one point of contact to me.

"Too long." Connor is directly in front of me and he places both hands on either side of my face, pulling me in for a kiss that's so much harder, so much more desperate than the ones we shared in the kitchen however long ago. With his mouth, he shows me he was worried and scared, and may still be a bit scared now, but is relieved and grateful. One of his hands travels down and wraps itself behind my back, pulling me tight against him in a way that seems to try and make sure that this moment is real, we're here together, and everything's fine. There are still other touches trailing along my arms and legs, but they all seem content to give us this time to connect.

Having found the reassurance he was looking for, Connor's kisses start to soften and become sweeter; slower, less a desperate plea and more a display of grateful content and affection.

Eventually, he moves back just enough to capture my gaze with his clear, vibrant turquoise eyes, penetrating into my soul with an intensity not unlike when we were bubbled in our own peaceful reality and he made me feel like the only person in the whole entire world. Those eyes have a way of making the rest of our surroundings melt away and make me feel seen, really seen, and known.

The sound of a throat clearing shakes me out of the pleasant haze I was floating in. Lin is grinning like the cat who caught the canary, everyone else's smiles only about half as wide but very much still present. Kieran's sitting next to me on what looks like an exam bed for some reason, Aria pressed up against my other side.

"Diz, can you tell us what happened?" The bags under Monty's eyes are heavy with concern as his gaze slowly roves over my body, "You kind of passed out for about six hours and none of us knew how to help you. I couldn't even detect anything physically wrong with you and frankly, it scared the shit out of us. All of us."

Realizing how awful it must have looked to them, a little piece of my heart breaks on their behalf; healing a piece for myself at the same time from knowing they cared.

"It's part of my curse, I guess. Someone must have tried to cast a hex nearby and, lucky me, I get to absorb those and deal with them instead." I try not to sound bitter about it, but I honestly kind of am. Having to deal with this crap every damned day definitely isn't one of my favorite things. "Sorry if it scared you, but this is really just everyday life for me. This one was a bit of a whammy, though, otherwise I would have been up and ready to explain way sooner than now. Dealing with so many of these curses, though, I've gotten super good at breaking them so there's no reason to worry about me. It just is what it is, you know?" I shrug to show them it's no big deal and I'm totally fine with it all, but I'm feeling so much more worse for wear than normal. It really was a big one this time; bigger than I've felt for a long, long while.

"Wait, you have to deal with this shit every day?" Kieran growls, "It hurt you. Fuck that."

Lin bites his lower lip and looks at me with hesitation for a moment. "Love... Did it feel like everything inside of you was being ripped apart and smashed all at once?"

Flitting between his eyes desperately, I'm shocked because there's no reason he should know exactly how it felt, especially since this was unlike any other I've had to deal with. "How could you possibly know that?"

"I think... I think I felt it, too. Apparently we both went down at the same time, and I only woke up a couple of hours before you did. Love, is this what happens every time? Because I think I felt your pain, and that was nearly unbearable." He looks down and to the side, whispering, "I was trapped. It was terrifying."

Oh no, no no no. Is this what he's inherited by being linked with me? I shake my head violently, ignoring the slight spinning it causes the room to perform. "It's not usually that bad, I promise. Oh Lin, I'm so sorry... This is all my fault." Reaching out, I cup his cheek and try to push every bit of regret into the tips of my fingers, "There's no reason you should have to go through it, too; I know exactly how bad it was and I wouldn't wish that on even my worst enemy. I'd have to make a worst enemy first, but that's besides the point." My smile is half-hearted at my dumb attempt at humor to cover how much dread is creeping into my heart. The thought that anyone else at all felt how absolutely awful that episode was today kills me, especially someone I care about.

"Are you kidding me right now?" The anger in Lin's voice shocks me and makes me cringe, my hand on his cheek falling away. Given that I'm the reason he was trapped in a sudden nightmare of agony for hours without any clue about what was happening? I probably deserve it. "You're telling me that you go through pain every single day, pain that isn't even for you, and you're apologizing to me? No. No damned way." He sneers, "Love, you have nothing to apologize for and don't you dare feel guilty for a single second about this. I can't believe this is just normal for you, it's completely awful. And you've been dealing with it alone? For how long?" He pushes Connor aside slightly and grips both of my shoulders, furious glare boring right into my soul. "I swear to you, I will find a way to fix this. I'm GLAD I felt what you felt, because I know how serious it is and I refuse to let you spend the rest of your life being assaulted like this." My mouth is hanging open slightly, and he swipes a tear from my cheek that fell without my notice. "I don't care if you want it or not, you've got my help. We're in this together, Love, and I'm not letting you forget it. I won't fail you, too."

My heart catches in my tightening throat. These men. They're all just so... For the first time in my life, I actually feel lucky. Uncaring of our audience or the tears that seem to be multiplying by the second, I lean forward and wrap my arms around the back of his neck to bring him in for a soft, grateful kiss. This isn't the first time I've hurt someone and they've thanked me, but it's the first time I've been reasonably sure they weren't crazy, and the first time they haven't run away. Or driven me away instead.

Looking around the room, I take in the faces of these guys who've given me so much happiness and hope in such a short amount of time. Zeke looks contemplative, but there's a slight smile at the corner of his mouth that's trying to make its way out. Monty is clearly relieved, posture significantly more relaxed, one hand barely resting on my knee. Connor looks like he's fought a huge battle and came out the other end alive and happy, but terribly exhausted. Lin has fire burning in his orange eyes, determination etched in his gorgeous scowl. And Kieran? I can't help but laugh a little when I take in the face of the man next to me because it's just an absolute mess. He's also scowling, fire and determination burning in his green eyes, totally clashing with the tears streaming down his face, into a mouth open wide in a smile. It's not even possible to describe what the heck is going on with his expression but it's amusing in a way that isn't even really rationally funny.

I can't help but keep giggling, imagining that someone played Mr. Potato Head with Kieran's face and used way too many random pieces to make him look the way he does right now. He growls playfully and tackles me lightly, causing me to lie down on the bed again with my legs dangling off the side. Aria just barely manages to scurry away as he pins me like that, hovering on all fours to snip at the air near my nose.

"There she is," he forcefully rubs his cheek against my shoulder, inhaling deeply when he buries his face in the crook of my neck. "I like it when you feel happy. Even if it's at my expense." His beard tickles me slightly and only further incites the giggles. Again, how have I managed to get this lucky? A whole gamut of emotions have run through me over the last couple of minutes, but this is definitely one of my favorites.

"Alright you brute, let her up. Diz, you up for some food? You never got lunch, and it's practically 8 p.m. right now so I'd really like to get a proper meal in you." Monty lightly pulls at Kieran's shoulder, my wolf man still smiling broadly as he obliges, taking me with him so we're both sitting up again. "I made soup earlier and there's still plenty of leftovers, or I could whip something else up if you'd prefer."

"Oh, soup sounds good!" Lin performs a graceful bow as he reaches out his hand, so I take it and slide down to the floor. My legs are a little unsteady, and the slight stumble as I definitely don't almost fall on my face is halted partially in its path by his strength. He may not be as muscular as Kieran, or even Monty, but dude's clearly got secret guns under those long sleeves of his. "Damn though, that's the second sandwich that never was." I sigh wistfully, daydreaming momentarily about the meals that might have been, if only the turkey club gods had decided to favor me as I want to flavor them.

"Why don't you guys head to the couch, I'll get Diz her soup. Anyone else need anything while I'm in there? It's basically dinnertime, though it doesn't really feel like it given how everything's played out across the day."

They all decline Monty's offer, but we do manage to make it to the couch together. I flop down, still feeling a little rough around the edges and indulging in a pretty epic lean-back into the soft fabric cushions. At this point, I am yet again overcome with giggles at an unexpected sight.

"Bananas?! Monty, this has to be your shirt, right?" He looks at me sheepishly from the kitchen.

"Sorry, if you don't want to wear it, one of the other guys can get you one of theirs. And I'm sorry we changed you while you were unconscious, I just didn't want you to wake up in the bloody one you were wearing earlier."

"Oh no, it's great! Totally on board!" I laugh for a few seconds more before realizing something, "Shit. Connor. I sliced up your shirt! Do you want me to fix it? I've never been especially skilled at sewing but it's literally the least I could do given that you let me borrow it in the first place and then I went and attacked it with a knife and bled all over it."

He cocks his head to the side like I've just said something curious, "No, it's okay. That's not even close to anything I was worried about today." Unsurprisingly, Connor's put himself on my left side and is already holding my hand, which he gives a quick squeeze while smiling wearily.

"Anyone up for more of that show from last night? I really liked it!" The guys all either shrug or agree, so I nudge Lin and he gets it set up again.

Monty comes in and hands me a tray with a bowl of some kind of warm, spiced deliciousness and a tomato vinegar thing. He settles into the couch with us, Stubbs hopping up into his lap after the soup-er duper chef fantastic claims his spot to the left of Connor. Zeke's back in the corner space, and Kieran's leaning against my legs from his place on the floor.

Someone moves the tray from my lap to the coffee table when I'm finished, freeing up my hands to run through Kieran's long orange waves. Connor and Lin settle in on either side of me, leaning against a shoulder each and letting their fingers idly trace patterns on my skin. The whole thing is so cozy and warm and welcoming and just feels right. Two nights, and already this house feels more like a home than any other place I've ever been. No doubt that's entirely down to these men who, without question, welcomed in a crazy woman and have refused to let her go.

Belly full of soup, surrounded by warmth, actually feeling safe; it's not long before I doze off again.

25. DIZZY

Something jostles my shoulder slightly and I wake to the sound of whispering. Whispering whispering whispering. Someone groans, someone else sighs heavily. The back of a hand graces down my arm, another gives my shoulder a barely perceptible squeeze. My eyes crack open when I feel the men around me getting up, taking me out of my cuddle cocoon. Hazily, I'm aware of Kieran, Connor, and Lin standing. Something comes out of me that was definitely meant to be "Hey, where ya going?" but mostly sounds like squeaks and grumbles.

Lin leans down and comes fully into my field of vision, "We'll be back soon Love, just have to get some supplies. You can go back to sleep." He places a tender kiss on my forehead and goes to say something in Monty's ear.

Connor strokes my cheek with a feather-light touch before gently brushing his lips against mine.

The second Connor steps away, Kieran, incapable of subtlety, grabs me by the back of my neck and slams our mouths together. He devours my lips hungrily, tongue thoroughly tasting every single flavor bursting within. Well okey-dokey then, I'm wide awake now.

I lace my fingers through the ones behind my head, "Not that I'm complaining about the A++ top shelf way you guys say goodbye, but what do you mean you have to get some supplies?" I glance at the display on the box under the TV, "It's almost 10PM, why not just wait until tomorrow? I like our super snuggle pile." Yawning, I'm not exactly happy at my people nest being disturbed. It's warm and safe and also really ridiculously comfy.

"Sorry Love, it's a bit time sensitive and this is the only opportunity we have to gather the things we need for an exceptional project." Lin reaches over Kieran's arm and boops me right on the nose. "I'm sure Zeke and Monty can take over and keep you plenty cuddled. If you're a good girl, maybe they'll even let you 'cuddle' them. All. Night. Long." He says 'cuddle' euphemistically, pausing to run his tongue over his teeth and wink after emphasizing the last few words. I swat his hand away, rolling my eyes as he skips back a few steps, laughing. Still, he manages to coax a smile out of me.

Kieran gives me one more strong, possessive kiss and backs up a few feet, never breaking eye contact. I can see some deep feelings brewing in him, and if we're all honest here I know exactly what that's like. Them leaving feels a little like my kidney getting ripped out and casually tossed across the room like a useless hunk of flesh and blood, rather than an essential piece of my anatomy. "I could come with you?" The abandoning group pauses.

Monty speaks up, "Maybe next time, Diz; your body's still recovering from earlier. Tonight, actually, Z and I wanted to test your magic and see if we could work out what this curse of yours is about-try to figure some way to fix it for you." Aria's flopped lazily over one of his shoulders, letting him squeeze the pads on her squishy people hands while we talk. Colonel Stubbs seems to have abandoned his platoon of humans while I was knocked out, though.

"You really think you could do that?" Nobody's ever taken the time to figure out exactly what's wrong with me. Even my mom used to brush it off and let me know it's just how things are if I asked her how I got this way, telling me it's all part of the curse.

"We'll try." Zeke says, still perched in his corner seat, watching me with the rapt attention of a hawk. "No promises it will work, but we want to help. It'll be a start."

"If you're up for it, anyway. Z and I planned to test your magic tonight and see if it has any clues. What's your primary discipline?"

"Oh, umm... I don't have one?" My voice rises at the end like I'm asking them a question, even though I'm supposed to have the answers. "I... Kind of got kicked out of school before the testing. Just a couple small explosions here and there and suddenly you go from being a charming nuisance to a terrible danger overnight. It's not like they weren't already used to my brand of special at that point! Anyway, I was 10 when they told me to leave, so I never got my testing at 13 with everybody else. The neighbor used to sort of tutor me a bit and send me home with work for the week, so I learned a few things here and there but nothing really actually fully official. Mostly just identifying the plants in her garden, if we're talking magic. Though she did give me actual schoolwork, so I would have graduated, probably. Curse-breaking is the only hocus pocus I'm actually good at, and to be honest, I don't even really think about it any more so it's not like I could tell you how or why I do it, it just gets done."

Zeke raises an eyebrow, intrigued, but Monty raises one in confusion before speaking. "That's... Unorthodox. How did you start breaking curses? Was it the neighbor who taught that to you? Specializing in curses is essentially spell casting and dark arts, and I didn't get exposed to half of that until about the last year of high school."

"Nope. It's kind of just something I've always known? At least, as far back as I can remember it's something I've needed to do. When I was a kid, I remember there was someone in kindergarten that kept bringing in spelled cookies to give one of the other kids diarrhea. I broke that one pretty quickly, since I mastered its counter probably the first or second day that they tried it. So glad I don't have to deal with that shit any more!" I chuckle at my own joke. Diarrhea, shit? Get it? Eh? EH? Ah, thank you, my adoring fans, my comedic genius knows no bounds.

"You've been doing this since you were a fucking kid?!?" Kieran looks shocked.

"Well, yeah, but like... even further back than that. I remember a couple of times from when I was younger, before school, but it's really just been a part of my life as far back as I can think."

"Well that fucking sucks a shitload." Now Kieran looks kind of disgusted. He's not wrong, though.

"Gents, fascinating as this all is-and I assure you Love, it's quite fascinating-we've got work to do. Monty, you take care of our girl and I'll take care of our boys. See you all in a few hours. Ta!" Lin yanks on the sleeve of Kieran's shirt, dragging him away towards the door. "Don't get in too much trouble while I'm gone-you know I'd want to be a part of it!" Bet I know exactly what kind of trouble he'd want to get into with me.

I raise a hand to wave them goodbye, but they're basically already gone by the time I think to do it. Bye bye, my kidneys. I'll miss you filtering my blood or whatever it is that kidneys do.

Monty rotates sideways on the couch so he's looking at me but not actually any closer, a distance I notice he's always managed to keep despite the fact he's apparently unable to go too far from my side. Zeke takes a vastly different approach and crawls on all fours across the couch until he's right up in my space, a devilish grin plastered across his face. It's actually pretty sexy seeing him look confident and cocky in my direction. A couple of times now I've noticed that Zeke tends to give his entire focus all at once to one thing. Being that singular object of his focus is a bit intoxicating, and empowering. A shiver swipes its way up my spine as the intensity of his stormy blue-gray gaze makes me wonder what else he could give his whole focus to. An image flashes in my mind of that same grin between my legs, glistening with my wetness and the taste of smug satisfaction. In the real world, Zeke's grin only grows wider as he crawls even closer, one hand now planted on the couch in the space directly between my legs.

"I could worship you as a goddess, if that's what you want."

Well shit, who wouldn't want that?

His left hand pushes my shoulder until I'm lying down, my head suddenly in Monty's lap. The hand between my legs firmly moves up my body in a line, not shying away from touching me with strong and commanding pressure until it wraps itself around my throat. He doesn't squeeze, but he does hold me with enough control to let there be no mistake that he's in charge of this moment.

There is no gentleness as he lowers himself to me, still a

prisoner to his stormy gaze. He takes my bottom lip between his teeth and pulls, not bothering to kiss me first. I start to raise my right hand to touch him, but he uses his left to pin it back down, the other never leaving my throat, nor his eyes leaving mine.

"This is the only reason I want to see you on your back for hours, ever again."

This time, when he bridges the distance between our mouths, he does claim my lips with a slow, strong kiss. Monty hasn't moved an inch this whole time, but he can't stop his cock's stirring from making itself known against the back of my head. For now, it seems like we're both trapped in one way or another, at the mercy of Zeke's command.

Suddenly, in one smooth movement, Zeke rolls his body and yanks on my arm until we're both standing upright again. The hand on my throat releases and slowly makes its way back down my body, this time gently passing over my breast and tracing the length of my waist before resting heavily on the curve of my hip.

"So... We have work to do, then we can play."

Well shit, what do you want? I'll type up a dozen spread-sheets right now if we can get back to that second part.

Monty's already deep voice is a bit darker as he speaks up from behind me, "Right. Work." I look over my shoulder to see him adjusting the hard-on very visibly in his pants. "We should probably move to the workshop, if we're all done here." He cocks an eyebrow, loading that question and pulling the trigger right to my primed and ready lady parts.

Zeke spanks me, hard. "Naughty girl. Work first." Oh gosh, if this is what getting to work feels like, I think I'm going to enjoy earning my play. "Come, you two." He crooks a fin-ger and walks backwards towards the kitchen, disappearing down the hallway, just expecting us to be good little boys and girls and follow. He's right, of course, I followed the hell out of him and Monty followed the hell out of me but like... woah. Power move right there.

The workshop turns out to be a huge room at the end of the hall that Monty's office is in. I'm pretty sure it's either an addition to the house, or was once some kind of porch that got extreme makeover'd. Looking around, it's got plenty of tables, covered in a crazy variety of things from a tower of so many different plants it would be impossible to identify them all, to giant hunks of rock, and even a small easel that's set up with a canvas and some paints near a window. One table appears to be entirely dedicated to housing a cauldron and many many different vials and tubes, as well as scoops and spoons and even a Bunsen burner. Maybe I'm crazy, but it also looks like there's swords covered with random animal hides and rocks? Actually, since there's definitely some kind of giant fire tube and anvil thing going on in one of the other corners I'm probably not crazy. Plus there's a spouted cauldron used for smelting, and possibly a kiln over there. I'm getting sort of a "lumberjack steelworker dad workshop" combined with "science mom craft room" vibe out of the whole experience. Now seems like a really dumb time to make a "so this is where the magic happens" joke so I won't, but I know Zeke knows I'm thinking it so that's kind of pointless.

"It is."

Darn. Knew it.

"Alright, Z, how do you want to run this? Start mental and then move on to physical stuff? How were you planning on monitoring this, aside from the usual results?"

Zeke pulls a small wooden cube out of his pocket and sets it on the floor in the center of the room. It's engraved with multiple different symbols, some inlaid with different materials and whatnot so it's probably pretty magicky, though I couldn't tell you what it does.

"What it does is read the magic in the room and record it. It will analyze ambient magic, spikes or dips in power through-out the space and its inhabitants, direction that the craft came from, who or what used it, who or what is affected by it, and the discipline it falls under. If possible, it will also record the exact spell used to later be replicated or investigated."

"Holy shit dude, you pulled out all the stops for this one. When did you even make this thing?!"

"While you and Dizzy were sleeping, obviously. We talked about how to monitor her magic, and you were both out for a while. Plenty of time to build it."

Not to be left out of a good conversation, I drop my highly knowledgeable two cents, "I don't know what's happening, but it sure seems exciting! Or impressive? Either way, cool! What do I need to do?"

If this were the movies, now is when a super peppy mon-tage would happen where we stood in front of test tubes and cauldrons, poked at plants, changed outfits a couple of times, and did a series of push-ups while upbeat power music played. Sadly, this is real life and that sort of abbreviated time travel isn't possible (Or is it? Is that somebody's power?), so we have to go through it in real-time, without the outfit changes or power music.

Zeke pulls up two extra stools to a table already covered in items, stacked pretty high with all sorts of things in random storage cubes and containers and whatnot. There's a decently-sized space front and center on the table that's been cleared out. Curious, I start to poke at some of the things scattered around.

"What is all this stuff?" A box full of small wax circles imprinted with identical designs catches my eye and I poke at them.

"Those are some grow charms I was working on for the shop." Zeke indicates the box I'm digging in, "They were designed to mimic Monty's ability to make plants grow quickly, but to continuously affect anything they come in contact with until the wax is melted. It was a success, but they react even to dust particles in the air so I had to contain them until the design is refined to be less powerful."

Not wanting to suddenly have a hand the size of a cantaloupe, I draw it back back slowly. It's then I notice that there are also designs etched into the box. There are multiple boxes like this one, actually, all over and under random stacks of things on the table. Knowing me and my luck, I'd make sure to keep dangerous malfunctioning magic somewhere with a lid, but most people haven't been conditioned to expect disaster at every turn.

"Ah, got it. Don't touch if I don't know what it is. Anything else here to avoid?"

Zeke looks at the piles around his area and points out a few, showing me some spells that were meant to be used in survival or camping situations but also need some moderation, like the fire starter that's meant to work even on wet wood-and it does-but it does so by releasing a massive fireball that can only be put out by another of his works in progress, an instant water spell that does summon water... but does so endlessly. And any water consumed or used continues to multiply within its new container until the device that controls it is obliterated. I'm starting to notice that Zeke may be the mad scientist of spell work, and that's totally cool, but most mad geniuses go down in a blaze of their own glory. Zeke's pile-based organization system definitely lets me think that's part of the fate he's tempting here.

He also points out a small cup-like container just full to the brim with knives and other dangerous pointy things. Yeah, definitely getting the no touch-y vibe.

Both of my hands find themselves shoved very firmly between my legs, to keep them clamped together and prevent the temptation to get into trouble. Lin said we're not allowed to, after all.

"As Monty recommended, let's start with purely mental-based testing and move towards ones that involve outside elements. For the purposes of these experiments, I'll act as observer and document your results." Like a total nerd, Zeke pulls out a clipboard and pen from inside a nearby drawer. A sexy, totally prepared science nerd, I mean. In case you're listening. I meant it in a good way!

He winks at me and pulls his chair away, forming the furthest point in a long triangle with Monty and myself, ensuring the best vantage point.

"Monty, I want you to think of a number. Any number at all. Dizzy, when you're ready, tell me what number he's thinking."

Monty's eyes are closed, so I take his lead and do the same. I concentrate hard, and it takes a couple of seconds but then I'm struck with an instinct. I peek one eye open, "Four?"

Shaking his head and wincing slightly, Monty breaks my heart, "Sorry Diz, you're half there! 42. You know, the answer to life, the universe, and everything." Darn.

Zeke writes a note on his paper. "Two more chances. When you're both ready."

Monty nods his head once, and I close my eyes again. Just like before, a few moments pass before I'm snagged by the idea of a number, hard. "Sixty-three?"

"Uhhhh……….. Well, this is awkward." He grins bashfully, "I went for Sixty-three thousand four hundred and twelve this time. But you got the first part right!"

As encouraging as that is, I doubt it's proof of my latent telepathic abilities. We move on to our third and final number, this one being for all the pudding cups. Rather than concentrating and trying to think about slipping into Monty's head, I try and empty mine. I wait, letting the emptiness fill me and spread outwards, eliminating everything around me. A minute goes by, maybe more, and the emptiness doesn't fill with any ideas or numbers. If anything, the emptiness starts to feel right; like the answer itself. Then it hits me.

I open both eyes and look at the relaxed man in front of me, "Zero."

His face blooms a creeping smile, purple eyes glinting with excitement as they slowly open. "Bingo."

I jump out of my chair and hop up and down excitedly, "I did it! I friggin' did it! Holy shit, am I psychic?!" If I was psychic, I probably would have remembered that everything around us is terribly dangerous and would have seen me knocking over a pile of stuff coming. Thank fuck it was just random bones and stones; that could have been way worse. Immediately, I plop my ass back into its seat and slam my hands between their leg prison again for safekeeping. You never know what mischief those things can get up to when they're let loose.

Zeke barks a laugh, and Monty bends down to clean up my mess, Aria balancing skillfully on his shoulder without falling despite his change in position. I decide to feel like a queen and allow my squire to handle cleaning duties because otherwise I'm just an asshole who makes messes and leaves them lying around for other people while being totally capable of doing it herself.

"Well, your majesty, if you're ready, we can move on." Oh goddamnit, this is going to be a thing, isn't it?

"Yes. It is, your royal highness." Fine. Better that than something else... like a buttswatch. Or gutter turkey. Or donkwonkler. I'm content to be royalty, now guide me through the next test my loyal subject!

"As you wish." Zeke bows slightly from his seat mockingly, a smirk gracing the edges of his lips.

"Yeah, I get that you guys have some kind of wonder twins powers and all, but maybe share with the rest of the class so a guy doesn't feel left out?" Monty implores us.

"Her majesty has decreed that we are to begin the next test post haste." I glare at Zeke, not wanting to look like I'm on board with his sudden teasing. This feels like the opposite of bullying, somehow, though it's still highly suspect. But I do kind of like it a little. Shit. And now he knows that. Time to just roll with it!

"Chop chop, my subjects! Don't keep your queen waiting!"

Monty rolls his eyes and shakes his head but he's smiling. I'm glad he's good at rolling with it, too; it's an essential life skill as far as I'm concerned!

"Z, telekinesis next? Or object summoning?"

"Telekinesis, if it pleases her highness."

I straighten in my chair, assuming an unaffected tone, "It does."

"Very well then," Zeke bows his head yet again, "Sir Montgomery Ursanis Henderson, please select an item in the room for her royal highness Disaster Zone Jones to move with nary a touch of her delectable flesh. Nay, only the power of her enthralling mind may be what transports your quarry."

Now it's my turn to roll my eyes. Putting it on a little thick there, eh? Zeke winks and nods his head in response.

Monty continues to take this tomfoolery in stride and simply does as instructed, picking up one of the stones he just placed back on the table and holding it out in his open hand. "My lady? The stone?"

"You have three minutes. Retrieve the stone from your subject's grasp. Begin!"

The three minutes went by pretty quickly and let me tell you, I was closer to poopin' my own pants from extreme concentration than I was getting that darn thing to move. So I guess that's a no on the telekinesis? Darn. At least I can still watch Connor move stuff with his mind.

The next few tests were also pretty anticlimactic failures. Try to summon an object to appear just by thinking of it? Nope. See this candle? Light the wick with your mind. No dice. Okay, we lit it with fire, now put it out. Nosiree Bob. Can you make it rain? Why no, no I can't; thanks for asking. What about make the wind blow? Does from my mouth count? Can you detect what types of metals are in a hunk of mystery rock? Because I can't. Turns out even if I have the magic words, I can't cast incantations so that's kind of a bummer. And let's just forget about trying to see spirits; living or otherwise. I also can't see invisible things, in case that's something you were wondering, though it's not entirely clear to me whether or not that test was some weird form of hazing.

It wasn't until Zeke tested me on locating that I only just barely started to taste success again. First, they asked me to use a map to locate Lin and Kieran and Connor. For sure, I failed that one. It didn't matter if I randomly pointed, threw an object, or dangled a crystal on a chain; every time my chosen spot was completely random and fairly far away. Though at least usually on the same continent, at least.

Then they asked me to use the same map to locate us, so I flipped a coin and let it land where it would. Interestingly, it landed pretty exactly on top of the town we're in now, though the map is fairly zoomed out so the coin covered a large enough area that it might not be the most accurate or reliable method. So we moved on to closed-eyes-random-finger-pointing style, also hitting success! My fingertip is smaller than a coin, so there really wasn't much denying its accuracy. Using the chained crystal landed its point directly on our exact coordinates, pretty much solidifying that I have some sort of locating magic.

"I'd like to narrow this down more. Majesty, concentrate specifically on finding yourself on this map," Zeke asks, indicating I use the crystal still in my hand.

I swing the crystal around, concentrating on finding myself while letting it pendulum over the map. When finally I feel like relaxing my grip on the chain to let the point touchdown, I'm disappointed to see that it's off target again. Not as far as before, but still not really anywhere close.

"Now try to find Monty."

Swing, swing, swing, annnnnd... Hit? This time, it lands exactly where we are again.

"Find me."

Miss. Slightly closer than the other misses, so maybe I'm getting better, but still definitely a fail on that front.

"Dizzy, what number am I thinking of?"

I look at Zeke like he's grown a second and third head, but then go with my gut and answer, "Negative twelve?"

"Correct. What about now?"

It seems obvious, somehow. "You aren't, you're thinking about horses. Three horses?"

He seems to be getting excited at my responses and jumps immediately into his next request. "Close your eyes. Monty, get up and move somewhere."

I hear a rustling and footsteps. A hand touches my shoulder and guides me to stand before spinning me in circles a few times.

"Don't open your eyes, but point to Monty."

I turn to the right and jut out a finger, opening my eyes afterwards to see if I won the big prize. Spoilers: I'm takin' home the jumbo unicorn plush tonight!

"Dizzy, I don't know if this is already what you can control naturally and need more training or if it's part of our link. You can read my mind, I can read yours. Monty can't go too far from your location, you can find his instinctively. This may require further investigation when the others return." Zeke spins one of the rings on his fingers while speaking aloud, "We know Kieran experiences her emotions, though that may make it difficult to trigger his own and see if she can read them. Lin appears to experience her physical pain, and dealing injury to either party is not ideal but perhaps could be done in a safe environment to support the theory. Thus far, Connor hasn't exhibited any linked abilities, but we may not have had opportunity to understand his yet if he is also affected. The most obvious and easy to observe would be Lin, though again, not ideal. Still..." Zeke's gaze has grown distant, no longer really addressing me so much as thinking things out.

"Z. Come on man, maybe let's just take this win for now and not plan to stab our friends? Seems a little off-topic."

"Hm? Oh, yes." Zeke's eyes refocus. He pauses, "Well, maybe not. Monty, will you cut yourself to see if she can heal you?"

Monty groans, but reaches for the cup full of knives and grabs one, pointing the danger end in Zeke's direction, "Just because that happened to work out doesn't mean you can keep planning to wound people out of curiosity, you hear me?"

"No, I didn't hear you. Too busy plotting murder." If I'd been drinking something, it for sure would have gotten pressurize-sprayed out of every available orifice. Okay, officially on board with the playful side of Zeke. He can call me her majesty all he likes.

A long-suffering sigh escapes Monty as he melts dejectedly. "At least don't do it without their permission." With that, he quickly slashes the blade across his palm, which I know from experience hurts like a bitch. Holy shit! He went way deeper than I usually do!

"What do I do?!" There's a lot of blood very suddenly and I'm not so sure that surprise blood is my favorite kind of bonus feature.

"Just put your hand on mine and heal it," Monty looks calmly into my eyes. It's got to be years of experience that lets him keep his cool in this moment because I'm definitely freaking out a bit as I grasp his hand and blood starts to seep through my fingers, streaking down our clasped palms in thick streams. Looking away from the red goo and into his purple peepers helps a smidge to calm me down, and really all I want is for the blood to stop. When it comes down to it, that's what's actually making me panic; If I could just make the blood stop, then I could think better.

"Monty, I don't know how to heal you," I whine a little, not really meaning to-it's just a fear response knowing he's in pain and not having a way to fix it. Though he's still completely calm and not even wincing, like some kind of totally impervious, pain-proof hunky-dunk. How? HOW?!

"Let your power trickle its way into me. Then, instruct it to fill in gaps, mend seams, move things that are out of place; whatever your feelers tell you when the energy comes back and lets you know what's wrong."

I give him a pleading look as I try to do what he says, but it's not like I've ever needed to trickle my power anywhere before; I'm barely aware of what it feels like when it's inside me much less how to make it move around. The only time I really know there's magic afoot is when I feel the tingling of a curse coming on, and that's probably not very useful now, is it? Unless that's what I need to do?

My fingers start to tingle and warm as I remember the familiar feeling and try to call it forth to share with Monty. He nods, "Good, now let it examine me. You only need to focus on my hand for now, no use wasting energy exploring my whole system when we already know what your target is."

The sensations in my hand grow, but if that's supposed to be them reporting back I don't know how to interpret it, much less control it to give it instructions on what to do. For a brief second, I almost think that my own hand is the one that's been split open, but the feeling leaves almost as quickly as it came. Maybe that's my power telling me what's wrong? Come on power, we already knew that, now fix the problem!

Can you bleed out from a hand wound? I don't want to find out. Please don't let this be the day I find out.

"One more minute," Zeke amps up the pressure.

So far, the times when I've wanted something to happen and it's worked out okay enough have been when I've managed to clear my mind and just let everything go. Right now, my stress level from the blood panic isn't nearly as high as when it first started, mostly because Monty is kind of just ignoring it like there isn't a gallon of his life splattering all over the floor. Better close my eyes to stop seeing it, and pretend like I don't feel the sticky warmth between our linked palms. Breathe, Dizzy, breathe. Think healing thoughts, clean thoughts, scar-free thoughts. Think about peacefulness, and completeness; where there are no broken things to worry about. Think about what Monty's strong hands looked like this morning while he made breakfast, or how smooth his palms were as he wiped sweat from his brow after our run, or how alluring they looked as he held the stone I couldn't move with telekinesis. Nothing changes in how anything feels, and either I don't know how to do it right or this just isn't a skill inside of me.

"Time's up. Monty, heal yourself." Yeah, that's probably for the best. "Then take her down the hall to wash."

Monty gives me an apologetic smile, and I feel the space between our hands suddenly warm in a sort of 'hot cup of cocoa on a cold Winter's day' way. It's pure comfort, and any last icy shards of panic left in my psyche melt away into his inviting heat.

"Let's go get ourselves cleaned up, how's that sound?" He doesn't let go as we travel back down the hall into a room directly across from his office. Turns out there's a bathroom in here! Cool. And this is apparently where they hide their washer and dryer.

Monty turns on the sink and tests the temperature, then dispenses a couple pumps of soap from a bottle on the edge, moving me closer so my hand is under the stream of water. He rinses off his palms briefly, then tends to mine with care, making sure to let the lather build enough to wash away all traces of my failure.

"You know, I could feel your magic in me, and that's a great start." Lines at the edges of his violet eyes smile at me encouragingly while he tenderly strokes my fingers under the warm water. A shiver runs up my spine as I lose myself somewhere between his fingers and eyes for a moment. "Maybe you didn't get it this time, but if you want to try again sometime, we can. It almost felt like you were halfway there before Zeke called time so this might be a skill we can develop together, if you want to."

I bite my lip nervously, "Well, I do want to... but seeing all the blood sort of freaked me out and I panicked a bit. It's not like I'm afraid of blood or anything, I see it every day, but seeing it come out of you and just so much of it made my brain break or something and I couldn't focus."

He chuckles lightly, handing me a small towel from a nearby rack, "That's easy enough to fix. Most healers can also heal objects, since it's mostly a matter of reminding things how they're supposed to be, rather than how they are. We can just smash a bowl or something to practice with."

Now my jaw is dropping, and I shove his shoulder hard enough to almost hurt myself. "What the shit! Why didn't you have me do it that way in the first place?!" The heel of my hand connects with his chest in a furious display of absolutely wimpiness.

He shrugs. "Just didn't."

Yeah, okay, great answer there, buddy. Real enlightening. "Okay, well, next time maybe start with the option that doesn't involve actual wounds?"

"Well... maybe."

I glare at him, crossing my arm. "What do you mean 'maybe,' Monty?"

"I mean maybe. Might have you make some salves or something to heal minor cuts and that's something that would need to be tested on an actual wound, not on a bowl."

"Well then fine, *I'll* be the one to get cut up, not you! I've never minded little scrapes and bruises on myself but seeing you hurt kinda fucked with me. Guess I've never really had anyone I cared about get messed up and I freaked? Well, actually, that's not true; I did manage to send my first crush into a coma but that's... well, it's not different, but it's different. That was a whole mess anyway." I'm torn up by the memory for a sec, since it was pretty much the catalyst for how everything's gone wrong over the last dozen years. I can feel my face falling, my crossed arms loosening their defiance.

Monty rubs his hand up and down one of my arms, tender touch soothing away the ghostly ache of regret and reminding my head to wander back to the handsome man who's much better than a bad memory. "Hey, whatever you want... Your highness." He playfully nudges my foot with his, jostling a scoff out of me. Doesn't he know that queens don't play footsie? I swear, you just can't get good royal subjects these days. Aria takes that moment to flit over from Monty's shoulder to mine, burrowing into the cavern of my hood and loosely dangling her tail down my chest. Okay, well, you can get at least one good royal subject these days if you count her, and I definitely do.

We head back into the workshop together, his arm draped across my shoulders comfortingly. Rather than stopping at Zeke's disaster of a work space, Monty guides us to a table-based forest, bathed in moonlight spilling in from the window it's pushed up against. The entire surface is precariously overloaded with all manner of plant-life. Some in large pots that have multiple shelves of different things growing in them, others practically luxuriating in their own spaces carved out of larger explosions of greenery. Not even the sky is off-limits as I notice yet more plants stacked on top of one another in something that looks like two hanging fish tanks underneath glowing lights. The foliage is so dense in this area, If I were to lower my face to the table it would almost feel like being immersed right in the middle of a jungle.

Monty pops the clear, domed lid off a short, black, plastic container with multiple patches of dirt in a grid. Most of them boast little seedlings just barely starting to sprout, but some of the cells remain completely empty. Giving me a brief view of his tight behind, Monty bends and scoops bagged soil into some of the blank spaces. He pats it down, wriggling a small divot into each center with his finger. Into this dip, he delicately places two seeds each from a drawer he's slid open, revealing an entirely different grid filled to the brim with all sorts of tiny dots and balls and ovals of seeds. If the planet ever goes totally barren, Monty seems to have already built the plant-life repopulation ark in a single drawer.

Gently, he places a few pinches of dirt on top of the seeds, tucking them in to bed for the night. Then he walks over to a big work sink in the corner that makes me wonder why the heck we went out to the bathroom to wash our hands, even if it was nice to get out of this room for a bit. I glance over to where we were before and notice that the floor blood has completely disappeared, cleaned by Zeke while we were out. He's standing behind me with his clipboard, dipping his head once in the affirmative as I peek over my shoulder. Very likely, that was a move to calm me since he would know without question that seeing Monty's blood was what sent me into a panic. Aw, how romantic.

Returning with a watering can, Monty feeds our new little babies-in-waiting until their houses are just the right wetness to encourage a good start. Satisfied with his work, Monty sweeps a hand over the new spaces in presentation, "Help them to grow."

I rub my hands together eagerly. Oh! This one I know I can do! The tip of my tongue bleps out slightly as I hold a palm above the newly-dampened cells. My arm moves up, pinching all five fingers together like a jellyfish, almost immediately teasing forth tiny green leaves from the wet dirt. They poke their tips up and stretch to say good morning in the midst of this fine evening! I smile at my little loves, happy to see them waking up into the world. Encouraging them to grow a bit more, I tilt my hand to cup around the newborn life and make an upwards-sweeping motion, curling my fingers inwards with each elevation. Not wanting to choke the roots in such a small space, I only pass by three times until they're just a couple inches tall and ready to be transplanted to something larger.

Triumphant, my hands fall to my hips and I puff my chest out in the best impression I've got of a real-life superhero. Monty's totally slack-jawed at how awesome I am, especially since pretty much everything else we've tried has been lukewarm at best, as far as success goes.

"Holy shit, Z, she didn't even touch them."

"I saw."

I'm still in superhero victory pose, don't worry, but I do cock my head to the side slightly at their lack of thunderous applause, "Well, yeah. That's how it's done?"

"Diz, that's n..." Monty's cut off by Zeke placing a hand on his shoulder.

"Dizzy, how long have you been able to do that?" They both look at me with open curiosity.

"Well... A long time? When I got kicked out of school, the neighbor, Mrs. Williams, would tutor me on weekends and teach me Math and English and all, but sometimes she'd have me help in her garden. She doesn't have much magic of her own, but she can mix up potions and used to get me to watch over her plants. After a while, she showed me how to start new growths the regular way like you did, Monty, but then one day I got kind of impatient with some seedlings that were taking forever to sprout so I just… asked them to grow." I'm remembering the cute, detached greenhouse in Mrs. Williams's yard, littered with tables of different plants in pots. Not nearly as many as on Monty's table, but it was still like being in a totally different world. There I am, nearly eleven years-old, Aria tucked into the front pocket of my overalls, playing with the leaves of all my friends. When I showed Mrs. Williams what I could do, she had me help even more-even had her son David work with me despite the fact he couldn't talk to the plants the way I could. We used to be a good team.

"You just ask them to grow?" Monty's head shakes back incredulously. Did I do something wrong?

"No, you didn't do something wrong. What does it feel like when you ask them to grow?"

What does it feel like? Well that's a weird question. "Nothing?" I cock my head, "I just ask them in my head to come up, or sometimes I'll imagine how they'll look once they're big and beautiful, but it's not like thinking and feeling are the same thing."

Zeke writes something down on his clipboard and I feel like I've either failed a test or he's pranking me and just drawing doodles of kitty cats to build tension. Standing on tiptoe to rubberneck, I try to get a glimpse of his paper but the sneak just flips the page over and starts to doodle kitty cats in defiance. Darn you.

"Monty, would you explain how you do the same thing?"

"Yeah, yeah of course." Monty's looking at me in wonder

like I've performed the magic trick to end all magic tricks and his bulging eyes are kind of freaking me out. "When I want something to grow, the first thing I need to do is touch it, or if it's a seed, touch the dirt it's in. Just like with the healing, I need to send my power out and seek the subject with my magic. Then, once I've connected, I pump more energy into it from my own source, jumpstarting its metabolism and encouraging it to feed off of me so it can grow. The entire time, I feel a link to the plant and the warmth of my power courses through it the same as it would during a healing session, reporting back to me the progress of the plant as well as what it is and how it can be used. Though that's partly due to my naturalism abilities, some people can grow without the know."

I fidget with the edge of my banana shirt, "Oh, well, I guess that's kind of like me, a bit. The last part, I mean. The knowing. The plant you had me grow is good for detoxifying, expelling, and removing... but I don't know what it's called. This one doesn't feel like any of the plants Mrs. Williams had in her garden."

"Wow!" Monty's no-longer-bulging eyes light up with excitement. He points to a random pot on the table, "What's this one good for?"

I look at the clump of dark leaves he's gesturing towards, the answer sort of obvious as far as I'm concerned, "Secrets, in a nutshell. Hiding and revealing things overall, so really that just means secrets."

Practically giddy, Monty grabs my elbow and dances me back to the other table to sit again. "Wait right here, I'll be back in a sec."

Zeke follows me to our original spot and we both watch Monty hustle out of the room in a flurry of movement. It's awkwardly silent as I tap my fingers on my knees and wonder what's about to happen, Aria occasionally flicking her tail against my cheek while we wait. Maybe a minute or two later he comes back, arms loaded with bowls and scoops and clear, flat boxes. Most of it he hurriedly shoves onto the table behind Zeke, but places the small clear boxes, a bowl, and a mortar and pestle in front of me with focused purpose.

Inside the plastic cases are divided sections, filled with dried leaves and whatnot of all different kinds. The lid has a bunch of labels directly over each cell, but Monty takes the lids off each box and buries them on the other table, out of sight.

"This is just like making tea-all we're going to do is combine the inherent capabilities of plants to meet a certain goal, no magic needed to activate it or anything. Now, say someone has an upset stomach and needs relief, what would you mix together?"

Given that this is exactly the order that someone placed at the shop earlier, it seems a bit like cheating but I go ahead and grab the four ingredients needed and throw them into the bowl, making sure to add extra of the little yellow squigglies. I look at Monty like "Okay, now what?" as Aria resumes the rhythmic flicking of her tail, probably bored out of her squishy mind since we've been at this for a couple of hours.

"Yes!" Monty exclaims, grabbing the bowl in front of me and gesturing quickly behind us for Zeke to swap with an empty one. "Same thing, but now you're treating pain and inflammation from arthritis."

This seems like a five ingredient job, so I take a couple of pinches that speak to me and plop them in the bowl. Something still feels like it's missing. Tapping a finger to my chin, I notice larger nuts or whatever in one of the spaces that look right, but need to be ground up. I snap one up and huck it into the mortar, bashing it with the pestle until it breaks apart so I can grind it into more manageable pieces. It joins its friends in the bowl before Monty snags it and swaps with Zeke again.

"Now, it's the mother of all migraines. Headache, light sensitivity, difficulty hearing sounds without pain, neck ache, dizziness; the works." Dang, you'd think Monty was a sugar-addled kid in a seven-story candy shop with how hyper he is right now. Either that, or I'm a new toy he's excited to play with. Oooh, mama likey; I was definitely promised some play tonight.

Aria's tail slaps my lips and I get a nice big mouthful of fluffy black fur, narrowly avoiding choking on a hairball by instinctively exhaling at that exact moment. I swat her poof down slightly with one hand, reaching out towards the box of dried plants with the other. So many different ones call to me, which makes sense in a way since there are a lot of different symptoms to account for. Each one I add to the bowl makes a sharp metallic plinking sound until the bottom is covered in enough of a cushion to dampen the impact. At the exact moment I go to reach for what I think is one of the last ingredients I need, Aria's tail flicks directly into my line of sight, totally throwing off my hand-eye coordination. Y'know, given that the eye portion was suddenly eliminated from the equation.

This, of course, leads to going completely off-course and bumping something I had no intention of aiming for but can't currently see. As soon as her fluffy mass is lowered, I see chaos break out almost in slow motion. Of course my aim would be amazing and drawn straight towards that damned cup full of knives. Obviously, it makes sense that It would not only eject all those sharp blades from itself, but it would also roll across the table in the process, bumping into a large stack of books and papers. The books and papers, of course, were too sturdy to do any damage... But the large round ball of glass precar-iously balanced on top wasn't, so it's jostled by the impact and makes its merry way down the edge of the book tower. It crashes down hard onto the tips of a collection of sticks just barely peeking out from underneath an assortment of unsuspecting objects, sending them shooting off in all different directions. The Rube Goldberg machine of mayhem concludes its journey by directing a few of those sudden projectiles to fling one of Zeke's magic boxes into the air, causing its contents to leap out and wreak havoc throughout the land.

First of all, I fucking knew this was going to come back and bite me in the ass because there's really no way that an open container full of bad times is safe around me. And second of all, of course there are now dozens of those dangerous waxen "grow" charms being scattered around us, because that's exactly the kind of lucky I am.

A charm lands right on top of one of the spilled knives and, on instinct alone, I thrust an arm across Monty's chest to push him back like every female driver ever at a stoplight with her purse in the passenger's seat. We start to topple to the ground together as I essentially pounce him, thrusting my other arm out towards the danger at the same time. I don't think about it, all I know is that there's a threat to someone I already freaked out over bleeding today, and I'd really like for that not to happen again please. If these grow charms could be stopped before we find ourselves suffocated by enormous dust particles or shredded to bits by full-body paper cuts, that sure would be swell.

A humongous orange fireball erupts from the hand I'm using to ward off the problem, right before I pull my arm in to cover the back of my own head and twist to land on top of Monty. Hopefully protecting him with my body, even though he's significantly taller. The whole event spans across barely a few seconds, including the daring rescue. My eyes are squeezed shut tightly as I brace for whatever impact I'm about to take on Monty's behalf.

Nothing happens. I peek an eye open, taking in Monty's

shocked face. Maybe from the tackle? Oh, how the tables have turned; is our thing that we tackle each other every now and then? It sure was one heck of a way to meet him, can't imagine it's left any less of an impression on him than it did when I was in his position.

Behind us, Zeke starts clapping. Oh hey, there's that thunderous applause I was looking for earlier! Little late on that one, though; clapping should be used for when good shit happens, not when I almost kill us all with my clumsy ass.

"No, it's really not late at all. That was very good."

26. MONTY

I'm looking up at Dizzy, wild purple hair framing her face like a swirling halo, the stone Zeke wove through it tapping me lightly on the chest. Behind her, there's an even more chaotic explosion of items than was originally on the desk, some of them actively smoking and smoldering, others simply displaced. Or enormous. Or a combination of those things. Most notably, a giant, smoldering sword whose point is thrust directly where my chest just was. The chest whose heart is now pounding in an adrenaline-fueled frenzy just a few seconds late to the show. Holy shit, did Dizzy just save my life?

And was that a fireball? Where the hell did that come from?

Zeke is clapping, but I'm frozen stock-still by my inability to process whatever just went down. And also by the feel of Dizzy's warm body laying across mine, because believe me, it's a stunning addition to this sudden and unexpected turn of events. She and I haven't really gotten a chance to... connect...

the way the others have, and I've been happy that they've all found something with the woman who's apparently soulmate to all of us, but I've wondered if maybe I'd missed my window of opportunity somehow. Or maybe this is it?

"Monty, you okay? Did I hurt you?" She pushes both hands against my chest to sit up, causing her to straddle my crotch with her legs tucked backwards, knees digging into each of my sides. Her plump bottom lip tucks into her mouth, an expression of worry that only brings attention to the juicy bit of flesh. Well if that ain't a gorgeous sight I don't know what is.

"What?" I replay her question in my head until I'm able to actually process it. "No, I'm fine." Pushing up with one hand on the ground behind me, I place the other on the small of her back to steady her as I sit up too, both legs sticking straight out between hers. "Did you just save my life?"

She winces and tucks her head down, peering upwards at me reluctantly. "More like I think I almost just killed you, really."

"That's not what I asked, though. Did. You. Save. My life?"

"Umm… technically? Maybe? It depends on how you…" I cut her off by jerking my hand on her back closer, crashing her front tight up against my chest. I cradle the back of her head with my other hand, lifting her lips to mine in a firm but quick kiss.

"My hero," I croon. She gasps as I smile broadly, likely not expecting that response. Her golden eyes are wide, but she doesn't look pissed, which is a relief since it's not like I asked permission or we have an established thing already. If anything, the way the corners of her open mouth start to tilt up tell me she's glad I took that leap. I can see words forming in her throat, so I pull a dirty trick and go in for more.

This time, she's not nearly as surprised, returning the kiss eagerly. Though she looks a bit disgruntled when I pull away again.

"I'm sorry, what was that? I didn't quite catch it," I tease her. She takes in a breath to respond, but I'm already moving in again to take it away. When our lips come together, it's not hurried or rough, but exploratory; us getting to know one another in this small, intimate way. Neither of us is demanding in our kiss, something loosening in us both as we find easy comfort together. Her tongue seeks its way into tangling with mine, her fingers doing the same in my dreadlocks as we melt together. My hand on her back no longer forces her up against me; it supports her firmly as we discover how the shapes of our bodies best fit together.

The tips of her nails start to graze sensually down my biceps, across my chest, up my neck, around my back. She tests the texture of every inch of me she can reach as I do the same with my free hand, eventually finding its home stroking up and down her hip along the silky length of her thigh.

A gear shifts and we both become bolder, more forceful in our attentions. I lean forward, dipping her backwards to press my arm further up and claim her lips more firmly. Her hips start to snap, teasing the hardening cock she's sitting right on top of. We find a rhythm with our tongues that mirrors the frenzy the rest of our bodies crave, each thrust into her mouth timed with her sharp movements along my throbbing manhood.

She gasps as her lips are suddenly ripped away from mine, her head pulled back by Zeke's fist wrapped around her hair.

"Do you like the feeling of Monty's dick against your pussy, Dizzy?"

I grind up against her, causing her to gasp once more, one of her hands suddenly clawing at my back and forcing out a groan of my own. Even though our lips are apart, we continue the rhythm, the friction between us building up into little jolts of sensation that only make me want more, faster, more.

She tries to pull my mouth back to hers, but Zeke yanks her hair again and pulls her further away.

"Uh-uh, my queen, Monty needs to hear you say it." He kneels down behind her, straddling my legs as well, still fisting her hair in one hand while the other starts to stroke her waist.

She moans softly before answering, "Yes, I like feeling Monty's dick against my pussy."

"Good girl." He rewards her by relaxing his hold enough to let her mouth reclaim mine, much more forcefully than before, demanding I give her every last piece of me. She rubs against me faster, cock painfully pressing against my zipper in its forceful seeking of her wet heat. Zeke's hand roams along her body, knuckles brushing my chest as he squeezes her breast roughly. She hums in my mouth, making this moment feel impossibly more primal as I swallow the sounds of her pleasure.

Zeke yanks her head to the side slightly, not to force us apart but to give himself better access. From behind her, I see him start to place long, slow kisses along her neck, traveling down towards her shoulder. When he gets to the crook of her neck, he opens his mouth and bites down, causing her to grind even harder against my cock and moan into me once more.

Locking eyes with me, Zeke kisses the space he just clamped down on. "Do you want me to show Monty how wet you are for him?" He kisses her once again before pulling her hair to give her room to respond.

"Out loud, Dizzy. He wants you to share, remember?" This wasn't what I had in mind at the time, but there are definitely no complaints over here.

"Yes, show him!" She's almost desperate in the request.

"Monty, she likes the biting. Give her more." He tilts her head to the other side, giving me access to a fresh space of her skin. Happily, I oblige and trail little nips from behind her ear, along her jaw, down her neck. At the same time, I feel Zeke's hand glide between us as he lifts her shirt slightly and unbuttons her shorts. Her breath hitches every time I bite her, a deep moan rattling her throat as I clamp down firmly at the exact moment Zeke's fingers make contact with her core. She's still grinding up against me and I can feel his hand through both our pants, my own thrusting only forcing his fingers deeper inside her pussy every time we move. She rides his fingers while riding me and I'm about to come from knowing just how turned on she is by both of us. Zeke removes his fingers, dripping with her desire for us before he slowly licks one of his digits in the most erotic way possible, holding burning eye contact with me the whole time. My roaming hand finds its way to the breast he abandoned, both my teeth and fingers increasing pressure against her skin at the same time. Her breaths are getting faster and faster, her movements more jerky as she rides me harder and harder, both of us getting closer to release with each of her desperate moans.

I feel Zeke tug her hair back sharply again, "Out loud, Dizzy. Tell us what you want."

"I want Monty to fuck me with that hard cock of his while you rub my clit and bite me until I'm screaming so loud they can hear it from space."

"Good girl." He loosens his grip again, "What do you say, Monty, has she earned your cock in her pussy or does she need to beg for it a little harder?"

Holy fuck, how am I supposed to choose?

"Please, Monty. Please fuck me. I need you to fuck me."

Best of both worlds, it seems. I move up and kiss her fiercely on the mouth, her returning it just as roughly. We're both more than ready to follow through on what sounds like one of the best plans I didn't have a part in coming up with.

Of course, that's when my leg is jerked by an excruciating shock of electricity, the source unmistakable; my phone will only do this if it's an absolute emergency, an impossible to ignore feature I told the guys to activate if they got into trouble tonight. My libido is instantly extinguished by a freezing bucket full of dread.

Being the one who designed the spell in the first place, Zeke knows exactly what happened. He doesn't let on to Dizzy that anything's wrong as he leans in to kiss her neck, his free hand helpfully digging into the side pocket of my cargo pants to retrieve the phone. I take it from him, my blood running cold despite the heat coming from the woman still trying to get herself off against me. Her eyes are closed as Zeke continues to play his mouth and hand along her body so she doesn't notice as I raise the device to my ear. That changes the second I answer and distinctly panicked yelling comes from the speaker. All three of us pause, immediately shocked into stillness at the distressed voice heralding its very bad news.

27. CONNOR

I know why it's important that we go out and scavenge materials tonight, but after seeing Dizzy immobilized for hours-part of it spent covered in blood-I'm having a hard time keeping this on the priorities list. Watching a woman so full of life frozen in an imitation of death has me spiraling. Too many bad memories are scratching, scratching, scratching against the inside of my skull, trying to get out and keep me trapped inside them, instead of them trapped inside me.

Almost as soon as we leave the property line of our home, I start to feel the eyes again. Sometimes they're looking in from outside, nestled in a far corner of the truck bed. Sometimes they're inside the cabin with us, tucked within the passenger footwell near Kieran's shoes. I want to ignore them but I can't because they definitely feel malevolent; like something bad is waiting just around the corner all over again. Last time I saw them and we were away from Dizzy, she was tortured. This time I imagine something even worse will happen. She'll be ripped to pieces, flesh shredded and bones picked clean by phantom teeth and claws. Limbs strewn across a room. Blood painting the walls.

It takes over an hour and a half to get to the site we're scoping out, an abandoned glassware factory shut down a few years back that's finally set to be demolished this week. In a breathtaking display of poetic sympathy, every window has been smashed, twinkling shards scattered like thousands of tears shed from a multitude of eyes. It knows its time has come to an end, and it's mourning.

We arrive early and park down the block, like always, to make sure there aren't other souls nearby who might interfere with our activities; a practice we learned quickly to uphold. One over-ambitious security guard on patrol at a glorified heap of scrap can destroy even the best-laid plans if you're unprepared to make a discreet getaway. Now, we never leave home without a few tricks. Luckily, I remembered to bottle some illusions of the truck when we first made it to the shop this morning. Even made sure to include the whine of a belt skipping and the slight smell of exhaust. The rattle of a partially damaged muffler. Our pickup was inherited from the farm Monty and Kieran used to work at. The poor beast isn't in disrepair, it's just lived a long and hard life of service to people who expected it to perform heavy-duty tasks regularly. Here and there, small patches of light blue paint have bubbled up to reveal a spattering of coppery rust; an infection attempting to take hold and consume the mighty creature. Despite the taint, it fights on, conquering day after day after day with ease in the face of time.

Realizing I've lost myself in fantasy again, my attention draws back to our physical surroundings. Still paranoid about a bad omen, I'm relieved slightly to find the hateful eyes nowhere near enough to spot. No pupils, no whites; the way the fully red surface glints each time I manage to catch them is unsettling, as though hell itself is watching and waiting to claim what belongs in its depths.

Lin and Kieran are in the front seats, discussing strategy for extraction. Kieran will go inside the building and seek out the materials we came for, using his alchemical abilities to collect what we need and compress it into concentrated cubes. Lin and I are equipped with strength bracers and impenetrable gloves to aid in carrying the blocks back to the truck. We have a silencer Zeke rigged up to keep anyone outside from hearing whatever noise we make, as well as a cloak of darkness I bottled to deepen shadows around the area to make it more difficult for onlookers to catch us in the act without purposeful investigation.

"It's been over half an hour, are you both confident the way is clear enough for us to start?" Lin taking his role unusually seriously in Monty's stead; normally the one to charge in without observing first.

"I don't see anyone, I don't smell anyone, now's as good a time as any to get in there. The sooner we start, the sooner we finish and can head home. Today's been too fucking long for this shit-don't make it any longer than it has to be." Kieran snarls, one sharp tooth glinting from within the orange forest of his beard.

They look to me for a response. I shrug; it's the best I can do. If this weren't so important, I'd listen to my gut and stay far away, holed up in my room with something to read to become immersed in another world, or a sketchbook to capture the ones I discover on my own. So I might not be confident, but I won't be the reason anyone is let down. They can count on me, and I'll do my best to keep an extra eye out just in case.

"Well then, I'm going to pull up behind that construction dumpster to hide us from street view. Kieran, I want you to head in first to ensure the building is truly cleared out. I know you and Monty scoped out where the best spots are earlier in the week, so make a chalk path for Connor and I to follow." Lin hands Kieran a thick piece of blue, luminescent chalk, the latter rolling his eyes; likely due to Lin's almost spot-on impression of Monty giving us the same instructions as always. "If you're not out in five minutes, we'll head in to either help haul the bounty or save your delicious wolfy ass from whatever trouble it may have fallen into." A slight deviation, but still mostly mimicking Monty.

We glide down the street, lights off, and pull into the property. For whatever reason they didn't put up a full gate around the site, so we begin weaving deftly between various construction vehicles and cones until arriving safely behind the designated dumpster. Behind us, tire tracks through plaster dust declare our presence like a neon sign, pointing brightly to a prize at the end of the line.

Not wanting to leave our entry so obvious, I reach into the box sitting next to me and retrieve a cloak of darkness, popping the cork and letting the illusion loose. As it settles into the space, I feel slightly more secure in our secrecy; shadows a familiar protector in my world.

Kieran opens his door and solidly thuds out, looking both Lin and myself firmly in the eyes.

"Five minutes," Lin reminds him. Kieran grabs a small electric lantern from the floor, loosely salutes, and jogs towards the remains of a shattered door into the abandoned building. Lin gestures back to me for the supply box, selecting a pink cluster of crystals wrapped in thin leather straps twinkling with various pendants. A small piece of paper is produced from one of his vest pockets, which he studies briefly before twisting the dangling charms in a specific order. The crystal pulses brightly once, then dims to maintain a soft pink glow. It's placed in a cupholder from the center console, already occupied by a few stray napkins likely abandoned after an illicit fast food rendezvous. Monty would be so disappointed.

"Hey there hot stuff, you doing okay?" Lin twists around in his seat and looks at me, eyes soft and gently probing. Monty knows theoretically how bad my head can get sometimes, but Lin has actually seen it and is no doubt worried about me due to the events from earlier. There have been times when the only thing that can pull me out of a flashback has been Lin stepping in to set me straight. While it didn't get that far today, I'm sure he knows it was pretty close.

I nod, throwing in a shrug for good measure. There's an edge chasing me around, even now, waiting for me to be on it. I'll manage. They're relying on me, and I want to do some good in this fucked up world to make it better than it's managed to be for me.

Lin reaches out and delicately strokes my forearm. "We're in this together, you know? If you need me, I'm here for you, just like I know you're here for me. Okay? Let me help if you need it, whenever you need it." His hand slinks away to unbuckle his seatbelt. "Now, let's go hunt ourselves a wolf, what do you say?" Lin winks and opens the driver's-side door, pulling forward his vacated seat to make it easier for me to follow, even though the small second door already offers plenty of access to the outside world.

I slide down quietly, both feet barely making a sound as they land on the solid ground. Here and there, cracks in the cement make way for shoots of new life attempting to make themselves known. The hum of our truck's engine the only consistent noise, likely imperceptible to anyone outside the silencer's range. Lin pulls his cell phone from a pants pocket, glancing at the time as we follow each other towards the looming entrance. I double-check the fasteners on both my bracers and gloves, not wanting either to slip off at an inopportune moment.

A chill creeps up my spine as we approach the doorway, causing me to dart a look over my shoulder. This time, I know for sure I see the eyes because I watch them move from near our truck to the cabin of a tall construction vehicle. They're either watching over us to witness or to warn; I can't shake the sick feeling in my gut that this is more than an omen. Lin doesn't notice my attention fixate on the empty space occupied by a bit of extra nothingness, but it keeps me on as high an alert as I'm able. Instead, his gaze is captured by the time displayed on the phone within his hand.

"Come on, let's go."

We follow a thick stripe of glowing blue chalk drawn along walls that were likely white in a previous life. Now, they're dingy and grey, occasionally bubbled up to reveal rot beneath or covered in thick graffiti. I peek inside every room as we pass by, suspicious of what may lurk within. No one jumps out at us, no traps are triggered, and no monsters abandon their closets to consume our flesh and bones. We come upon Kieran safely, finding him already next to three condensed metallic cubes, his space illuminated by the small lantern casting twisted patterns of light and dark across the room. Both of his hands are coaxing out an amorphous silvery blob from a hole he's broken into one of the walls, it moves like a metallic underwater air bubble.

"You can start loading these up. A lot of what we're looking for is in this room since it needed more support beams for some reason. There's plenty of wiring to pull from too, so it'll be easy to clear the space fast and move on, if we even need to." Without losing contact with the form between his hands, Kieran gestures an elbow towards the square foot cubes at his feet. His work is precise, each corner sharp enough to justify using the gloves and, despite their somewhat diminutive size, heavy enough to require the strength bracers to retrieve repeatedly.

Lin and I each grab a cube, moving quickly back towards the entrance. It only takes a minute to return to the truck, depositing our load carefully in the bed so they're lined up evenly. I glance up at the space where the eyes wait, but they don't seem to be watching from there any more. The night around us smells cold, like Winter came early and wiped away all traces of spice and warmth from the Autumn we've just barely entered. It seems appropriate for a building condemned to death, surrounded by large, yellow, metallic executioners.

The solid sole of Lin's sleek dress shoes hit the linoleum floor with a whispered scuff, a deafening roar in comparison to the imperceptible footfalls from my rubber-bottomed high tops. I am a ghost.

Kieran is just finishing up a third cube when we reach him again, allowing us to relieve him of the two already waiting before he places the newest in his reformed pile.

"I really wish we'd grabbed something to eat before we left. This whole day has been so screwed up time-wise and I've suddenly realized just how hungry I am." Lin talks over his shoulder to me, barely a step behind him. "What do you say we raid the fridge when we get home and make a hero's feast? Eh? This is hungry work right here!"

My stomach growls its response for me, making its displeasure known. The last time we had anything was Monty's soup, hours ago, and it's just past Midnight right now.

"Maybe you can even bake us some of those cookies of yours as a treat?" Lin lowers his cube next to the others in the truck, mine following shortly after. "Or even better: brownies! You make a damn fine brownie, my damn fine man." He bumps his hip against mine, causing me to stumble just slightly off-course as we begin the journey back yet again.

Lin swoops down at the waist and scoops up the only cube waiting for us when we return, Kieran handing one directly to me almost immediately afterwards. We turn around and continue our repetitive path.

"Do you think we could bribe Monty to make pizza this late? You know how he is about that dough of his, though, might be past The Mother's bedtime right now or something."

"Pizza sounds good, but it's going to be hard to find the energy to actually cook after all this," I say as we continue down the hall. "I'd be happy with a handful of dry cereal before passing out, no need to get crazy."

"Well, maybe there's still somewhere that does takeout even at this hour? Between here and home I bet we can find at least one random place to pick up a hot meal. No reason to make you slum it with a handful of cereal, Connor. At least hope for some chicken tikka, or penne arrabbiata, or even a trashy drive-through cheeseburger. Heck, maybe we'll even get kiddie meals just for the toys! No one said being an adult means you always have to act like one." We drop off our latest haul, "Well, it might work out better if we pretend to know a couple of kids who crave burgers in the middle of the night, though."

It's a dumb idea, but I have to admit it does appeal to me. Some of those toys are pretty clever, especially for how cheap you can get them. I'm smiling at the idea that a 38 year-old man suggest we pretend to be children. At 26, I'm the youngest and even I know there's no way I could pass as a kid, or lie about knowing some that happen to be up this late. "You're an idiot."

"Yeah, but now you want to do it, don't you?" He twitches

an eyebrow up twice, a sly grin only adding to his devilish demeanor. Looks like responsible Lin has officially left the building, though he did stick around longer than expected so that's still something.

"And what would Monty think if we came home reeking of saturated fats and fry oil?"

"Oh, he'd be fine with it as long as we brought home enough for him, too, and never spoke of it again. I may or may not know he has a particular weakness for chicken nuggets."

This time when we make our way back to Kieran, he's just finishing up one cube, no others already waiting on the floor. When he holds it out for one of us to take, Lin snags it and spins on his heel, leaving me to wait for the next to be ready without him.

"I could go for burgers after this, if that's what you two are planning," Kieran says as he punches a new hole further along the wall. "It was stupid of us to do this shit on an empty stomach. Can't believe we didn't at least grab snacks for the stakeout portion." He shakes his head and grumbles, but continues to work the metallic mass growing in his palms.

"We had other things on our minds." I watch it as the liquified metal collects, eventually eclipsing Kieran's head with its mass before he begins to push and shape it into a familiar cube, identical in every single way to the others. He might not think of that as impressive, but the precision in his craft is difficult to master. The fact that he takes the time to make sure all of the resources he collects are untainted, completely separated from all traces of any other element or nearby scrap in addition to shaping them evenly? Kieran is skilled in a way that most craftspeople would envy their whole lifetime, especially at how casual he makes the process appear.

"Well, I'll be glad to get this over with and fix that mistake.

I'll skip the kiddie meal version though, get myself a couple of jaw-busters instead if that's okay with you two and your hare-brained scheme."

"Don't worry," I take the copper block he hands me, "we all know you don't like to have fun." My feet move quickly away from the burly redhead, a look on his face that clearly says he gets the joke but is shocked I made it.

"You little shit, you get back here!" I'm already striding down the hallway, long legs an advantage when trying to make a speedy getaway. If anything, now I *really* want to do this stupid thing, and force Kieran to only order kiddie meals. Mostly just because it seems funny to annoy him, though maybe he'd secretly enjoy a small army of cheap plastic figurines? Who knows!

I'm nearly to the exit when I hear a gasp, causing the dormant panic inside me to rear its head once again until the gasp is followed by a long, deep, sensual moan. The sight greeting me once I race through the doorway is confusing to say the least, and I'm stunned for a moment; my feet temporarily losing all sense of momentum.

Lin is leaning with his back up against the truck, one hand behind his head, pulling at the short hairs there as he holds the other over a spot on his neck. His hips undulate in a mesmerizing wave, calling attention to the very obvious erection pressing hard against the front of his pants.

"Lin, what are you doing?" I hiss out. Stepping towards him, I'm entranced as the hand from his shoulder starts to press its way down to his cock. As his fingers make contact, he moans once more, completely lost in... whatever this is. By the time I get to him, I very indelicately huck my copper cube into the truck bed and shake him by the shoulders.

"Lin, what the fuck?" His eyes snap open, but they look

caught in a frenzy, pupils dilated enough to nearly wipe out all trace of his normally burning orange irises. Quicker than I could ever react to, the hand behind his head snaps out and clutches the front of my shirt, pulling me into him hard to be consumed by a fiery kiss. When he kisses me, it's passionate and needing; as though he craves more from me than he's currently getting. I find myself lost in his desire, pressing closer against him and seeking out even greater pressure between our bodies and lips at the same time.

Then I remember this isn't the time or the place and push away with both hands on his chest, all kinds of confused about how and why and what. I'm gaping at him as he continues to rub himself against me, the hand grasping my shirt still attempting to pull us back together.

"Lin! Seriously, what are you doing right now?" My eyes dart around in a panic because this feels like the start of whatever the omen was trying to warn me about. Would I be able to call Kieran from here? Is this a trance like Dizzy was in and there's no way to break it until it's over?

I'm looking back towards the darkened doorway, but out of the corner of my eye I glimpse a flash of something shiny. My head whips to face Lin, lost in whatever's controlling him right now. Speeding towards us is a phantom, coated in swirling, curling tendrils of the deepest, darkest shadows. In its outstretched hand, a large knife is aiming straight for Lin's neck, murder reflected in its only discernible feature: solid red eyes.

As quickly as I can, I yank Lin and myself backwards, out of the range of danger. Thankfully, the strength bracers make it a much easier job than expected despite Lin's lustful movements being incredibly unhelpful. The phantom lands exactly where we were just moments before, knife thrust into a space its target only just narrowly vacated.

Something clicks as I recognize the knife from our kitchen back in The Kettle and Cauldron. All day I've been feeling eyes on me, seeing them, worrying about them. This isn't an omen, or a manifestation, or anything else-this is an actual creature out for our blood. When all the knives fell, it must have taken one. And when Lin was attacked in the city, I saw this specter in the shadows, likely behind it all.

"Kieran!" I yell, pushing Lin to the ground. He lands hard on his back, but is obviously too lost to care. "Help!" I yell out right as the phantom launches itself forward, knife now aiming for my chest. Instinctively, I swat my arm out and try to deflect the attack. If I hadn't been wearing these gloves, I'd be missing at least part of a finger.

"Why are you doing this to us?" I try to call up a double of myself, but the darkness swings its knife again and I'm just barely able to fling my hands out in front to take the impact in time.

Stepping back, I try to use my telekinesis to yank the knife away, but all it does is make the next swing jut off course, aiding in its successful connection with a bare portion of my forearm. The cut isn't too deep, but it stings immediately.

"Stop!" I thrust both hands out in front of me, trying to push a burst of telekinesis at my attacker, only doing enough to bump them back a step before they lunge once again. This time, I'm too slow in deflecting and it ducks underneath my outstretched arms. A searing pain shreds through my midsection as the knife drags across my stomach, cutting a long slash through both my vest and shirt to the tender flesh beneath. I stumble backwards once, still desperately trying whatever I can to get away but the phantom charges forward once more, plunging the blade deeply into my gut, leaving it lodged in there as I stagger two more steps backwards before falling.

My hands press against the wound on instinct, but my brain can't compute what's happening. The panic that's been bubbling and building all day finally boils over and I'm taken away from myself. There's blood, there's so much blood. And there's a man with a knife. I'm hiding in the corner, behind one of my illusions, but he knows I'm there and he's coming for me next. She couldn't protect either one of us, and now we're both going to die. It's only a matter of time before he finds me and snuffs the life out of me, too. All I can do is give myself over to the nightmares and hope they can protect me better than her.

Off in the distance, in another world, another life, a howl rings out. I wonder if the nightmares will win.

28. KIERAN

The extraction is going surprisingly fast in this room. Thankfully, the materials they used to make this building were good quality and have very few impurities to extract. Probably because it was built a long enough time ago that there weren't too many corners getting cut. The liquid copper pooling in my hand is almost half of what I need for another cube, it shouldn't take much longer to get the rest.

"Kieran!" My ears perk up as I hear Connor scream my name, sharp with panic; something the normally quiet man has never done before, "Help!"

I've already turned around and started running before he can finish the word. In my hand, malleable metal is still waiting to be formed into whatever I instruct it to become. Halfway down the hall, I catch the sharp scent of blood-Connor's blood-and immediately know now is not the time to fuck around. The metal in my hand lengthens into a deadly sharp spear just as I make it to the doorway. In front of me, I'm too late to stop the knife I see get plunged deep into Connor's gut. The attacker is too late to stop me from throwing my spear right at them, going straight through a shadowy area somewhere below the middle and burying its length halfway. In the same smooth motion, as I release the spear, the arm that hurled it continues towards the ground and I shift into my wolf seamlessly, barreling on all-fours towards the shadow that fucking stabbed a member of my pack. Connor falls to the ground and I leap over him, aiming to land on his attacker and rip its throat out, if it even has a throat. Before I'm able to taste revenge, it glares at me with hot red eyes. The spear drops uselessly into our truck bed as the shadow dissipates upwards into a fog, completely disappearing. Anger and fear take life in a mournful howl I let chase after our demon in my stead. I will not lose another pack.

I try to scent for its blood, but all I'm getting is Connor's; not even a trace of someone else. Whatever it was, it either doesn't have blood or doesn't have a scent.

There's moaning from the ground nearby, but it isn't Connor, it's fucking Lin who looks like he's about to come in his pants from how hard he's rubbing his dick. What the fuck?! I swat him in the face with a paw but it's like he's in a totally different world. We don't have time for this bullshit. Anger and anxiety and fear are almost as thick as the fur around me, but looking at Lin fucking himself and Connor fucking dying, I'm the only one who can get us out of here right now. And I can't do that as a wolf.

Forcing the shift back, my nature fights hard against the command, actually slowing and hurting for the first time since I was an adolescent. Parts of me still feel wolf, but I'm on two feet and have mostly human hands so it will have to be enough.

The first thing I do is grab my kilt and sling it onto the driver's seat-I know I'll need to use the phone in my pocket but it's more important to get out of here first. Gently, I pick up Connor and slide him into the back seat, head on a swivel as much as possible in case there are more threats to his safety. From the box we packed beforehand, I try to uncork a healing potion but my claws get in the way. Frustration comes out in a growl. There isn't enough time for this! We need to leave now! I throw it into the empty cupholder and shut the small back door to keep Connor safe inside the truck.

Lin is still on the ground so I hook both my arms under his shoulders and drag him into the passenger seat, doing my best to not scratch him or get humped by him. What a fucking mess. His door slams shut, I race around to the other side and slide bare-assed into the driver's seat, picking up my kilt at the same time. The engine's already running with the key in the ignition, so I fucking floor it out of there, digging around in a pocket to get my phone out.

Once it's in my hand, I push just the tiniest bit of my magic into the metal symbols inlaid on its back, letting it zap me to activate the emergency spell. On speakerphone, it rings a few times before Monty finally picks up.

"Monty, fuck, everything's all fucked up over here." My voice sounds unnaturally gruff and wild, a side-effect of my only partially human mouth. "Connor was fucking stabbed by a goddamned shadow, and Lin's practically jerking off right next to me and won't fucking stop. Connor's going to fucking bleed to death if I don't get him back to you but I'm out here doing this shit alone." Every word comes out with a growl on its edge, the panic making me want to shift into a form better suited to fight off attackers. I need to stay human right now. I have to push the wolf down. "I don't know if we're being followed or if there's more coming but it's all gone to fucking shit and I don't know what to do. Monty, you need to tell me what to do because I can't solve this by ripping something apart and that's the only instinct I want to follow right now."

"Kieran, we planned for this," Monty's voice is calm as he addresses me. "On the dashboard, there should be something etched over the speedometer-just run your finger along it and it should activate. The truck will go three times as fast as it normally could." I do it as soon as he tells me how. "There's healing materials in the box, and an illusion of the truck breaking away. If you're being followed, it can hide you." My grip on the steering wheel is tight as I focus on not crashing and killing us all. I quickly find out that whatever this spell is also lets us avoid obstacles automatically so it takes a small amount of pressure off of me. "You're doing great, Kier, you're bringing our family home. You're keeping them safe."

To my right, Lin has stopped his bullshit and starts to speak up, "It seems there's a new development with me," he grabs the box from the floor and starts digging into it, "We'll talk about it later. Kieran, get us home. I'll focus on Connor, we're going to be fine, just get us all home."

The drive passes by in an actual blur, the second we pull up to our house and see Monty, Dizzy, and Zeke waiting outside I bound from my seat and finally stop trying to force my wolf back down. Another howl leaves my throat, long and loud and weighted with every painful emotion inside of me that I don't know how to express. An unfamiliar call returns, feeling my pain and letting me know it hears me; that it will help me carry this sorrow and fear so I'm not doing it alone. I cry my thanks back up into the sky, a prayer to the moon that my pack stays whole tonight and we make it through this together. There is no return call.

29. LIN

I feel like such an asshole for laying uselessly on the ground and literally fucking absolutely nothing while Connor took a knife for me. What happened at the factory site felt suspiciously similar to the event earlier today, except obviously significantly more pleasurable. Thank fuck it passed and I was able to at least partially tend to Connor on the drive home. Even though he immediately vomited up one of my potions, its healing effects wasted on the floor below, at least some of the bleeding stopped with one of Monty's binds. When I pulled up the edge of his shirt and vest to take a look at the damage, a horrifically deep, long gash split apart his abdomen and threatened to spill his guts. Not to mention the knife still stuck inside him. Terrified of causing any further damage, I left it in place, but my poor sweet angel looked about to earn his wings. From the furrow in his sweat-soaked brow and his lack of responsiveness to anything I said or did, he was obviously trapped in one of his nightmares. A knife twisted deep into my own gut at the realization that I needed to abandon him to the horrors, but I honestly thought it would be worse to bring him back to this reality.

As soon as we pull up to the house, Kieran and I both fly out of the truck, Monty and Zeke already yanking open the back door to slide Connor out, stony expressions prepared for battle. Dizzy gasps and covers her mouth, no doubt shocked by how absolutely shitty our normally quiet and composed companion looks. His white skin is ashen and paler than usual, his normally voluminous blonde waves matted down and tangled with sweat. Tears well in Dizzy's eyes almost immediately, but then her jaw locks and those same eyes flame with righteous fury. If she's mad at me for failing to keep him safe, I agree and shamefully deserve it. Tonight was on me and I was utterly useless.

We place Connor on the exam bed in Monty's office as gently as possible, but I'm still grateful he likely can't feel any additional damage done to him in this moment. Our house is already warded heavily, but I recognize the symbols Zeke is lining the walls in as protection sigils; to reflect any ill-will and bar trespassers from entry. Normally I'd think going the extra mile a tad paranoid, but we didn't expect to get attacked at any point so this has twice proven to be an "expect the unexpected" kind of day. Now I welcome his overactive tendency to go too far.

Dizzy is standing with her arms clutched across her stomach, the small woman tucking herself away in a gap between the foot of the bed and the wall, angry tears silently burning a course down her face. Knowing what I do about her, she's blaming herself and her curse for what's happened to all of us today. Kieran remains in his wolf, pacing around outside the door; likely feeling more able to detect danger and protect us from it in this form. I'm still standing by the side of the bed, not willing to miss a moment until I know I've done everything possible this time.

Monty grabs a pair of scissors from a hook on the wall and cuts straight up through Connor's shirts, granting full access to his vicious injuries. He peels up a corner of the long binding cloth I hastily placed across Connor's stomach, revealing that the blood seems to have at least clotted, though the wound is still plenty deep. Monty places one hand on Connor's abdomen and one on a slice in the poor man's arm I hadn't noticed before, pushing his energy into them to close the gaps. I only realize we've both been holding our breaths when he lets out a tight one of his own, sweat barely starting to bead just as the edges of his scalp.

Monty moves to delicately probe around the knife still protruding from Connor's stomach. "Shit. It actually cut through his intestines. His whole circulatory system is tainted. It's a miracle he's not already in septic shock." Monty's brow furrows as he further assess the damage. "Lin, I need you to help me. The knife is lodged into his kidneys and his intestines. When I say go, pull it straight up and out as quickly as you can. I'll give him everything I've got, but if it's not enough I need you to do whatever you can to get him stable. Duct tape his torso shut, call someone in, kidnap a non-magical doctor; I don't care what you have to do, we fix this. We are not losing my brother tonight because some psycho decided to slash him up for no reason." The shadows starting to rim his eyes look dark in contrast to the bright purpose flashing through his gaze.

"I'll do anything he needs. Anything."

Monty looks me over, hands still on Connor. "I know you will, Lin. I know." He rolls his shoulders and cracks his neck, getting ready. I grab the handle of the knife. "I can heal his kidney and intestines for sure, but the real trouble is cleansing the bile and bacteria from his blood. Right now, his whole system is tainted and he's already lost a lot of fluids. When you take out the knife, it's going to bleed a lot. First thing I'll do is tell his body to amp up blood production to help refill and cleanse, but Lin…" he pauses, a small flash of doubt creasing lines through his forehead, "I've never had to do something this big before. Just… Be ready, is all."

"Don't you dare kill yourself, Monty. Don't you dare. I'm not losing both of you in one move just because you were stupid enough to pull on your life force to finish the job."

"Just like you said; I'll do anything he needs. Anything." His scowl becomes determined, and I realize there's a real chance I'm saying goodbye to two more people tonight. Monty turns his head back towards Connor, but closes his eyes, "Pull it, Lin."

I do as he asks, yanking the knife out as quickly and as straight as possible, hoping to everything that I didn't do more damage in the process. It's a good thing Monty warned me about the blood, because there's an impossible amount spilling from his wound at the moment.

Monty's teeth are gritted as he groans out "Artery," a word you never want to hear when sharp blades and an excess of blood are involved. My stomach clenches, only relaxing slightly a few seconds later when he says "Sealed." I can see the muscles in Monty's arms starting to strain, causing him to tremor slightly. Sweat now fully drips from his brow. "Kidney healed." The sound of Kieran's claws clacking on the hardwood floor somehow reminds me of the knife, still in my hand. I put it on a shelf in the apothecary's cabinet behind us and keep myself a step back, giving Monty space if he needs it.

There's still more blood gushing from the open wound, making me especially nervous because our healer's legs are now shaking, looking like they're having trouble supporting him. Fear grips my heart as Monty slurs the word intestines, not indicating if they have been fixed or if he's working on them. His knees buckle and he falls, forehead colliding with the edge of the bed right before limply dropping in a heap on the ground. Zeke is there in an instant, finger on Monty's neck.

"He has a pulse."

At least that's something, though now we have to help Connor without him. "Zeke, duct tape and a towel, seriously. We're doing whatever we can." I dig into my pocket and pull out my phone, searching through my contacts for the doctor we met last month at the Walker Street clinic. It might take longer to heal Connor through traditional means than with magic, but at least they'll know what to do.

Before Zeke can leave or I can hit call, the air becomes heavy and charged, then it's sucked from the atmosphere; my next breath feeling weak and insubstantial. I feel a pull towards the corner of the room, the one Dizzy is in, like she's a black hole ready to consume everything around her. Arms rigid against her sides, her hands are balled into tight fists matching the pure fury glaring out of her golden eyes; golden eyes that are now actually glowing. In fact, all of her is glowing; as though she is a goddess and a light is shining from within her. Aria is sitting regally upon Dizzy's shoulders, emanating a low, constant hum from her throat.

"No. I already told you, not today motherfuckers." Dizzy's steps are sure and powerful as she claims a space beside Connor's bed, kneeling to place a soft kiss on Monty's damaged forehead. She rises and settles a hand on the wound gushing rivers of blood, Connor's body still reproducing the crimson liquid at an alarming rate. Before my eyes, the glow surrounding Dizzy starts to melt off of her and transfer to Connor's still form. The furrow in his brow softens, feverish expression relaxing to something more neutral. She looks lovingly at Connor's face and tenderly strokes his cheek, bending to whisper in an unexpectedly nurturing way, "Not today, mother-fuckers."

The last bit of gold seeps out of her, fully encasing Connor in its shine and she starts to collapse. Zeke rushes forward and stops her from hitting the floor, slowly lowering himself down with her in his arms until they're fully seated on the ground. Kieran rushes in and is immediately hovering over them, burying his snout in her skin to sniff out any wounds.

I leap forward and check on Connor first, shocked to find that beneath a thick swath of blood, all his injuries are sealed. When I touch him, the golden aura feels warm and comforting, like... well, like love and protection. It immediately makes me think the word "safe," and I know instinctively that he'll make it through this night.

Crouching down, I clasp one of Dizzy's hands in my own, her fingers icy cold. She's slumped in Zeke's lap, his arms circling her waist protectively, keeping her in place. The steady rise and fall of her chest assures me she's at least still breathing, though I'm beginning to get tired of spending time in this damned room, watching over the unconscious forms of people I care about.

"Well, it looks like we're sleeping in here tonight. There's still a few pillows and blankets from earlier, but I'll get some more." I'm definitely not ready for this to be the room where our bedding just always seem to be; this better be the last time.

My hand rests on Kieran's head briefly as I rise from my crouch, both of us seeking comfort in the brief reassurance of touch. Aria takes the opportunity to climb up my arm and claim me as her new perch, constant contact from the soft creature somehow managing to further settle me. Especially as she hums a quiet tune in my ear, soothing vibrations from her purrs helping to release some of my anxieties.

By the time I return to the room, my arms loaded with bedding, it seems Kieran and Zeke have managed to clean the floor and pull in every cushion from the couch to form a makeshift mattress against Connor's bed. They're just rolling Monty onto the edge of it as I enter, so I drop the blankets and lend a hand. Colonel Stubbs backs into the room, dragging his dog bed between tiny teeth to join us for the night.

"Let's get them cleaned up, maybe?" I lament at the blood on various parts of all three unconscious people. Zeke's already prepared a bowl of clean water with some rags nearby, assumedly from wiping up the area before I got here.

I fill a second bowl at the work sink, sure to wait for the water to warm pleasantly. Peeling Connor's shredded shirt and vest off of him carefully, I realize they're beyond saving and place them aside. It takes an unsettlingly long amount of time to clean him, the bowl of water needing to be changed three times before the task is finally complete. The volume of blood he lost is staggering, but I have to remind myself that his system was set on overdrive by Monty so it's not as drastic as it appears. Even beneath the golden glow he's cocooned in, I can tell his skin is a much healthier color than when he was first brought in. A small amount of hope trickles in that every step they took was necessary, even if we now have three people down for the count.

Untying Connor's high tops, I pull them off as gently as possible, removing his argyle socks as well. Crossing the hall into the laundry bathroom, I drop the socks into the washer and procure a towel from the rack.

"Dry him off for me?" I toss the towel to Zeke, who's already finished with both Dizzy and Monty. "I'll take care of these," I grab the shoes and ruined clothes, walking back towards the front door. Passing through the kitchen, I deposit the garments in our trash can and continue on towards the front door, putting Connor's shoes back into the rack. Just a few stuttered steps backwards, and I'm sitting on the stairs that lead up to our bedrooms.

Elbows on knees, I slump forward until my forehead is buried between them, fingers raking through the crest of my hair to clutch the back of my neck. Aria adjusts herself so she doesn't fall and pushes her wet nose underneath one of my hands, reminding me she's there and giving the kind of comfort all animals seem to instinctively excel at.

Knowing the danger has passed, all of the emotions I was trying to ignore slam into me full-force. Relief that it looks like they're going to be okay brings forth tears that were smothered by the stress of needing to remain as calm as possible and not fuck it up worse. Coming back to my own awareness in that truck to see Connor practically knocking at death's door, knowing that I'd done nothing to help even though I was physically within range shot terror through my spine; a frigid jolt of lightning thrusting agony deep into the base of my skull. An anguish and horror that assault me brutally, now.

The guilt of being so useless, maybe even being part of why he was so hurt, claws at my chest next and shakes loose a gasping sob. When Miriam was dying, I fought against every single diagnosis, spent hours researching and developing cures, lost weeks and months of sleep and sanity refusing to give up for even a moment. And there I was, blind to another person I love inching closer and closer to their final breath, my consciousness unaware I may have had to say goodbye tonight. How would I live with myself if this had been it? I said I'd bring them home safe but I brought our family home in pieces.

My whole body trembles violently with grief, reliving the pain of watching the light go out behind someone's eyes and imagining the same fate for Connor. My heart is ripped out and torn apart all over again, even though I rationally know we're all home and safe and on our way to being healthy. Inside, it feels like we lost; that there are three corpses waiting for me back in the office and I'll have to carry the weight of my failure to save them for the rest of my life.

I'm sobbing, drowning in the dangerous cocktail of anxiety, guilt, powerlessness, and fear. This could have been the end. I've been running scared for years of ever feeling this way again, careful not to let myself get too close to anyone else. It never occurred to me that I still had people left to lose.

Aria slithers down my shoulder, wedging herself between my head and lap. I wrap my arms around her and bury my face in her soft fur, begging it to absorb the secret of my breakdown to hide safely in its darkness. She lets me stay like that as long as I need, continuing to hum gentle coos and purrs as I slowly find the strength to climb back to myself. A tiny piece of the ball in the pit of my stomach releases, the crushing grip around my heart loosening just enough that I'm on my way to finding peace with this situation.

I have to remember that they're alive. They *almost* weren't, but almost doesn't count, damnit. Sitting up, Aria still in my arms, I focus on that fact; we're all still alive. And if we're still alive, we can still fight back. I'll be damned if I ever let this happen again.

Taking a few deep breaths, I rise up and look Aria in her glittering eyes, identical in every way to Dizzy's, right down to the small green accents. "We're going to find this piece of shit and make him pay for ever thinking he could take anyone away from us."

She nods sharply, letting me know I'm damned right we will, then leaps from my arms and flies ahead towards Monty's office.

We walk in on a scene that is part pathetic, part heart-warming. On the exam bed, Connor is tucked in under a blanket, a pillow fluffed under his head. Kieran is backed into one corner of the room, having the best vantage of the door, the windows, and everyone inside. Colonel Stubbs has moved his bed to the same corner, wanting to be a big boy and protect his pack too but also possibly wanting to take a nap. They both huff at me in acknowledgement as I pass.

On the floor in the makeshift cushion pile, Zeke is propped up with pillows against the side of the exam space, Dizzy's head resting on his stomach as he smooths his hands mindlessly through her hair. On their far side, Monty is curled up against them, deep, slow breaths indicating restful sleep. There's already a pillow set up for me on the other side of Zeke, so I slide under the blanket they're sharing and rest my head on it, one arm reaching out to wrap around Dizzy's waist.

"She's incredible, you know," Zeke says, not opening his eyes. "When we tested her, she didn't have the ability to heal. The blood made her panic. This time, she didn't think she couldn't do it, she knew for sure it was a capability."

My fingers move idly along the fabric of Dizzy's borrowed shirt. It reminds me of the purchases we made earlier; hopefully they didn't get lost in all the chaos. "Do you even know what she did?" I ask.

"No." He opens his eyes, stormy blue irises lasering in on me with an electric excitement, "Did you feel it?"

"When she..." I don't really know how to describe what it was, "pulled me in towards her? When all the air left the room? When it felt like a storm was forming but then got pulled away?"

He nods, then closes his eyes again and leans his head back against the bed. "She absorbed all the magic in the air. Maybe in the room. She might have taken some from us, too."

I'm shocked; it's beyond rare to be able to do anything other than use the magic inside yourself, or manipulate materials that have their own magics. "But... That's not normal."

"Like I said; she's incredible."

My eyes seek out her face, serenity blessing her expression while she sleeps. Freckles across the bridge of her nose continue their playful spattering along the peaks of her honeyed cheeks. Full lips rest with just the hint of a smile at their corners, the abundance of life and joy inside her still apparent even in sleep. In her purple hair, Zeke's yellow cloth is still weaved through a small braid, but the stone from its end is nowhere to be seen. She's so beautiful, it almost doesn't seem real that we were lucky enough for her to find us.

Talking about her magic reminds me there's something I need to know, "Hey, what else happened when you were testing her?"

A sly grin creeps up Zeke's face, "She asked plants to grow. They did. And she summoned a fireball, after not being able to light a candle."

I lift my head from the pillow, popping up onto an elbow, "Hold on, a fireball? As in an entire ball made out of fire?"

"Yes."

"Woah, sorry I missed that one. Think she'll show me later?"

"No," he deadpans. "It seems her magic works on an instinct to protect. She likely doesn't know how to control it yet."

I chuckle and shake my head in confusion, "She summoned a fireball of protection? Pretty sure those things are great at destruction," I suddenly realize the implications and get a bit suspicious. "And what the hell were you doing that she needed to protect herself like that?"

Zeke looks at me again, then side-eyes Aria, curled up in the crook of one of Monty's arms, "I believe our furry friend here orchestrated an accident to reveal Dizzy's abilities. Some charms were knocked over and would have resulted in Monty's injury or death. She protected him. Curiously, the only things affected by her fire were the wax charms themselves." He lets the tips of his fingers trace along the curve of her neck, "And she just healed Connor's injuries, even though she couldn't mend a simple cut before. The only magic she easily displayed without dire need was some naturalism, though it was different than expected. We didn't even finish everything we had planned today. I suspect we could test her for years and never be able to define her rigidly."

Even though she can't feel it, I trail my fingers down to her hand and weave them between her own. "Then how do we help with her curse?" A shudder courses under my skin at the memory of pain from today, a sensation likely to haunt me for years to come if I let it.

"I don't know yet. It's possible learning control over her own magic could help with what's plaguing her."

In a way that almost makes sense. "If you think her magic worked to protect Monty and Connor, do you think she can learn to use it to protect herself?"

"Perhaps."

Whatever it takes to stop her from having to go through that again, I'll find it out. The problem is, where to even start looking for help? If her magic is unpredictable, how do we help her gain control? Can it even be used to defend against attacks on her, or is it only for others? What if it's already working and this is it at its best? What triggers the attacks in the first place? And can we develop something to deflect them? If we have to divert the pain she feels, I'd rather take it all than have her suffer like that again.

And then there's the other thing; looks like I'm just going to have to come out and ask it.

"Before we got home, was she... stimulated? Sexually?"

Zeke's eyes pop open and he cocks a brow at me curiously. He studies my face carefully, searching for some trick or inappropriate comment lurking beneath the surface of my question. "Yes."

I take in a long breath and let it out as a deep sigh, "Yeah, I thought so."

He doesn't ask for an explanation, but out of all of us Zeke is the one who would take the information and use it responsibly, maybe actually find a way for it to help her somehow. Very little of me feels shame for anything anymore, but the part that does wants me not to admit how badly I let Connor down tonight, and why. It's the only thing holding me back from almost bragging, or maybe even giving him a compliment if he's the reason she felt that way. Well, the reason we felt that way, I suppose.

"Earlier today, when she was suffering and I felt it, too?" Zeke nods, obviously following along. "It was like I was trapped in the sensation; I could vaguely perceive what was happening around me, but reality took a back seat to the pain. Maybe with practice or a lot of effort I'd be able to separate them, but that became the only real thing in my universe and it overwhelmed everything else." He's looking at me like I'm reciting his own name and birthday back to him; facts that are so obvious they just make me look like an idiot here. Knowing Zeke, he's already figured it all out anyway but I'm still going to tell him. "The same thing happened tonight, at the site.

But it was pleasure. And I couldn't escape it, either." I say the last part wincing, still flinching against a pang of guilt at the admittance.

He smirks at me, "Well, how was it?"

I push his shoulder, "Shut up, you dick." He waits while smiling devilishly like the handsome bastard he is. If he saw me slipping into a funk and is just messing around to help me out of it, it's working. As before, it's likely he already knows but is clearly waiting for me to tell him. "It was great. Nearly came in my pants and I wasn't even being touched by anyone else. I think."

"Good boy."

I squint at him, not sure what that's about but he looks awfully pleased with himself. I have to admit, just like thinking about the pain from earlier, thinking about the pleasure pulses echoes of it deep in my groin. Not particularly wanting to get caught up in fantasies of getting fucked by Zeke while almost everyone else around us sleeps, I lay my head back down on the pillow and try to get some rest.

"It's the same for me," he says after a while. "Her thoughts. I hear them constantly. But I'm starting to learn to turn the volume down, or ignore them. Like background noise. We might be able to control it."

Considering that both times I've experienced her sensations something bad has happened that I'd rather be able to help with, this gives me a small kernel of hope. Though knowing how she physically feels has given me an intimate insight into both what she deals with, and what she enjoys. If we are able to control these connections, it could be an extremely rewarding experience for both of us.

Laying there, contemplating the pros and cons of experiencing the same things as the woman beside me, my eyelids become heavy. My hand, still entwined with hers, loosens its grip. Just as I'm about to lose consciousness, my stomach growls loudly.

Darn. We never did get those kiddie meals.

30. ZEKE

I wake up first, Dizzy's weight on my chest compounded by Lin and Monty's arms crossing her. It feels nice. We're closer.

Removing myself from the pile of limbs without waking anyone is not a simple task, but I manage. Kieran greets me, bumping his forehead against my leg.

"You're still a wolf."

He bumps me again, then goes over and lays down near our friends, head on Monty's ankles. Colonel Stubbs follows me out towards the underused sitting room on the other side of the stairs. Monty's usually the one to feed him, but I'll take care of it today.

I scoop some food into his bowl and grab the one for water, taking it to the kitchen for a refill. Stubbs isn't the only one Monty normally makes breakfast for. I'll take care of that, too.

The clock on my phone says 8:30AM. By now, we're usually at the shop. I'd go there and post a note about taking a leave of absence, but realize I don't care enough to do so. People won't read the sign anyway and I'd rather not waste the time.

Colonel Stubbs' squat face is buried deep in his kibble when I return with the fresh water, oblivious to its addition. He doesn't notice me slip away upstairs for a shower, either. I don't think he's a very ferocious guard dog. He does try, at least.

The house is eerily quiet as I navigate to the fridge, investigating its contents to plan out our meal. My style of cooking isn't always appreciated; I like to combine things and see how they turn out. Like my magic, I enjoy incorporating unrelated items to create something new and unexpected. Both the pineapple and eggs catch my eye. There's potential there.

There are plenty of sweet potatoes in the root bin, and jalapeños from the garden. As I cube the potatoes and place them on a roasting tray, I ponder what else could be amalgamated. To balance the halved hot peppers, I drizzle honey over all the vegetation, adding a roughly chopped sweet onion. Some salt and olive oil are the last touch before everything goes in the oven to roast.

My mind wanders back to the pineapple and eggs as I open the fridge again, a match most would avoid due to the destructive nature of the fruit's enzymes. Volatility has never dissuaded me. The acidic content of the fruit assists in pairing with fats and salts, a thought that causes me to notice the package of smoked bacon. Omelettes. It could work as an omelette.

Before putting it in a pan, I chop the bacon and let it render down until it's just barely cooked, releasing much of its grease. The pineapple joins afterwards, marrying both together until they become one harmonious jam. By the time it's thickened, the roasting potatoes and jalapeños smell ready to be taken out.

Shuffling of feet and a tired groan make their way to me from the hall just as I lay the tray out to cool. Lin emerges, his normally well-kept appearance ruined by skewed, wrinkled clothing and unruly bedhead. He rubs his eyes before focusing on me behind the kitchen island, preparing to put another pan on the burners.

"Mmm," he sleepily mumbles, "what are you making?"

"Eggs and potatoes."

He blinks a couple of times, features slowly narrowing into suspicion. I know he won't accept such a simple response, but I've found that the reception for my cooking is typically better if its description is as vague as possible. I decide it's time to change the subject.

"Are they awake?"

Lin shakes his head, "Just Kieran. And us, I suppose. The other three are still out like a light, which, by the way, the light around Connor seems to have shrunken a bit." He pokes at one of the cooling sweet potato cubes and pops it into his mouth, thoughtful as he chews. "Think high-powered flashlight down from brilliant star in the sky. They're all still breathing, at least." Lin opens the fridge and grabs some carrots and limes, "How long should we wait, do you think?"

I crack a few eggs into a bowl and scramble them with salt and pepper before pouring into the waiting pan, "A week at most. They'll dehydrate if we don't do anything by then."

Lin grinds the carrots and limes in our juicer, looking off at the wall in a daze. When the machine's noise cuts off, he speaks, "How do we stop this from happening again? I need to find the bastard that did this to Connor, and I won't let them go when I do."

A handful of sharp cheddar cheese and a few dollops of the pineapple bacon jam top the soft-cooked layer of eggs. I use a silicone spatula to flip the omelette in half before sliding it onto a waiting plate, now ready to make the next one. "What do we know so far?"

He plucks a few ice cubes from the tray and places them in each of our glasses, scowling at the cups as he pours carrot and lime juice inside. "Not much." Lin runs a hand through the long tousle of hair atop his head, stopping to yank frustratedly at some of the nearly cropped strands further down. "We know it's some kind of shadow, and we know Connor saw it. Aside from that, I was too indisposed to catch anything." He takes a sip of his drink, avoidant eyes wandering around every available surface before landing on the cutting board and going wide.

The glass in his hand is discarded on the counter as he races back to the room we all slept in. I can hear a bit of a commotion, and what sounds like Monty's rich voice. Moments later, Lin emerges with a towel in his hand, the still-bloodied knife removed from Connor's gut clutched within it. Monty isn't too far behind, looking unusually alert and energetic for someone who just over-exerted themselves magically and passed out.

Lin holds up the blue-handled knife in his hand next to the one still on the board, "Shit. I knew I recognized it," he says, waving Monty over. "Do we use the same knives at the shop?"

Monty peers over Lin's shoulder, "Yeah, we do." He turns his gaze to me, curiously examining the omelette being flipped in half. I prepare a third, now that he's here to join us.

"If this knife is one of ours, I can search through the security footage to see if the shadow shows up on screen!" Lin pulls a phone from his pocket and immediately starts tapping away on it with his thumbs. Hardly any time passes before it's suddenly ringing in his hands, an unfamiliar number listed on the caller ID. Lin hangs up, but the ringing starts again within seconds. By the third time this happens, Lin finally answers, "What?! What do you want?!"

Monty looks at me quizzically, but I just shrug in return, adding the toppings to the final omelette.

Lin's face pales, "I'm sorry ma'am, you're right; that was very rude. I shouldn't have lost my temper." He pauses, listening to the voice on the other side of the phone, "Yes, if you and the girls have any insights to give us I would be eternally grateful for your assistance. Thank you for offering it." Once again, he waits, eyebrows raising drastically in shock, "Yes ma'am, I'll tell them that, and we'll come by tomorrow. Thank you, thank you so much."

Lin hangs up his phone, a stunned look on his face as he stares at the device and shakes his head in disbelief. Then he smiles and chuckles a bit before looking up at me. "That was a woman named Miss Fern; a psychic who said her and 'The Girls' could help us out with the shadow looming over us. She told me to tell you that the rainbow moonstone is under your copy of *Applied Astrophysics* in the workshop." He turns to Monty, a look of amusement breaking across his features, "And she told me to tell you that she was sorry you couldn't make it but is grateful for the treats you will have sent."

Monty's face morphs from cocked curious eyebrow into scowling extreme skepticism, "Yeah, okay, let me just get right on baking up a batch of cookies for the mysterious stranger who called you out of the blue. Would you like me to wrap them up before or after you waltz on over there and get attacked again?" He crosses his arms, "How could you even take this seriously?"

Lin's smile is practically giddy, "She told me to bet you $10 that you'll think the pineapple was a good idea, and that if she's wrong she'll pay for a year's worth of advertising for the shop to apologize."

One of Monty's eyebrows arches up high, "What pineapple?"

Lin shrugs. I decline any invitation to respond, choosing instead to scoop some sweet potatoes and jalapeños on all three plates. "She's the psychic, not me. But I'd love to see how this plays out!" Lin pours a third cup of juice for Monty and grabs some utensils from the drawer, "Besides, she's an old lady. What's the worst that could happen? She beats us with her shoe?"

"Famous last words," I murmur, setting the plates down in front of three of the barstools surrounding the island.

"Exactly!" Monty flings an arm in my direction from where it was crossed at his chest, "With what's happened over the last two days, how could you even think about going off to meet with someone we don't know if we can even trust?" He sits down, picking up his fork and forcefully stabbing it into a cube of potato, "What if it's a trap? Both times someone's been in danger recently, we were separated. I'm not going anywhere until I know Connor's okay, and we need to figure out if this was a random attack or targeted before we take risks with our safety. We're more secure together." I watch as his next movement cuts into the omelette, fork poised to take the bite, "How can you not be suspicious of the timing?"

He begins to chew, frowning. Monty's eyes squint, then snap to me. Digging into his pants pockets, he pulls out his wallet without breaking my gaze. "The pineapple was a good idea," He grumbles out, still looking slightly displeased while snatching a $10 bill from the wallet and handing it to Lin.

31. ZEKE

After breakfast, we go separate ways. Monty and Lin shower and change while I return to the office, examining the wards I put up hastily when they first laid Connor down. They deflect attacks, deny entry to all ill-will, and warn of any approach from unknown entities unescorted onto the premises. The spells around our property are more complex and layered, with additions for privacy, spiritual recharge, and overall safety. Kieran and I worked for weeks together to construct and position the pillars and blocks embedded in the soil fully surrounding our grounds. Most are buried, but the cornerstones are exposed as they were the largest.

It's been a while since I checked them. I should probably walk the perimeter, in case this threat from last night tries to slip through. It's been easy to get comfortable here, and that leads to complacency. Now is not the time to become complacent.

Kieran is laying down, pressed against Dizzy's side on the ground with his head facing towards her feet; still able to see the door and window on either side of them. Out of all of us, Kieran takes security the most seriously, especially after what happened with his pack.

I look at him, "Will you check the wards with me?"

He lifts his head and looks between Connor on the bed and Dizzy on the floor beside him before lowering his tawny muzzle back down to rest on Dizzy's leg.

"We can go after Monty or Lin comes back. They won't be alone."

Kieran huffs loudly.

"This room is secure. They will be protected here. It would be even better if we knew the entire area was safe."

He closes his eyes and lets out a long, soft whine, eventually giving a tight nod. Good.

I sit in one of the chairs still strewn around the room, joining Kieran to watch over the sleeping members of our household. My mind wanders to problems in need of solutions. Problem: Connor and Lin were attacked. Solution: Discover perpetrator, prevent further interference with increased protections and awareness. Remove attacker as threat. Problem: Lin losing control of himself depending on what state Dizzy is in. Solution: Possible combination of astral tether to keep his spirit contained, decision stone to help him choose which reality he wants to experience, and studying spell for concentration and awareness. Ah, this is why the psychic mentioned rainbow moonstone. Problem: Dizzy's attraction of harmful magics. Solution: Personal wards against ill-will? What is the nature of her magic and why is one of its base functions the transference of hexes upon her person? If her magic is largely based around protection, as suspected, what would happen if the intended targets receive the curses she absorbs on their behalf? Perhaps a better strategy would be to study and amplify her ability to break these spells, lowering the personal cost in both energy and time? Further information is required in order to plot the best course of action.

My musings are interrupted by Monty walking into my line of sight unexpectedly, kneeling to place his hands on Dizzy and read her. He does the same to Connor, stepping over both Kieran and Dizzy to get better access.

"They both seem fine, almost better than that, weirdly. Trying to read them actually feels good, not just fine." Monty strokes Connor's mop of wavy blonde hair, brushing it off his face in the process. He looks a lot more healthy and clean than when they came in last night. "I wish it had been me," Monty whispers.

"That would not have been ideal. You would not have survived," I remind him. "It's better that you were uninjured and able to provide healing."

"Do you really think that matters? I'm glad he's alive and that I was able to help keep him that way, but I'd do anything to make sure he stays safe. Anything, Zeke." He flops down into a chair, sighing, "And if what you and Lin said at breakfast is true, it's partly my fault that he was hurt in the first place." There's pain in the tightness of his lips as he nods his head in Dizzy's direction, "I was so caught up in how much I wanted her, I didn't stop to think if there could be consequences. We should have known Lin was connected after he felt her pain, or I should have sent them out with more protection after we'd already been attacked once, or just called the whole thing off. It feels like there's so much more I could have done to prepare, and I let myself get so caught up in the urgency of the job that I pushed it when we should have taken a step back instead." He looks me right in the eye, "I feel responsible. And stupid. And selfish."

"Well, stop that," Lin says from the doorway. He comes in and leans against the bed, one hand trailing down Connor's leg lightly, "You aren't the reason any of this happened. Sure, you got a little frisky and it put me down for the count, but first of all, thank you because it felt amazing," Lin winks at Monty, "and second of all, how were we supposed to see this coming? It's not like we've dealt with this particular problem before, so what, you're supposed to know how to fix problems we don't even know exist? Maybe we should ask you for advice instead of Miss Fern, if you're feeling particularly psychic. This isn't on any of us, Monty, not a single one of us. No matter what we did or didn't do, all we've got is now and what comes after. Accept that it happened, and learn from it." Lin hops up onto the bed and scoots against the wall, crossing his legs and putting Connor's feet in his lap, "Me? I nearly lost it at seeing Connor that close to death. Don't forget, I was right there next to him and did nothing to help, but I'm not going to let that become the only thing I focus on and have it stop me from finding out what really happened, why, and how to keep it from ever coming for the people I care about again." He pulls the phone from his pocket, "This isn't going to break me, and I'm not going to lose any of you because of it. I'll check the security footage and do whatever research I can. Don't let this one shitty thing trap you and prevent you from fighting back."

Monty looks down at the floor, turning his head away from us. He doesn't say anything.

I stand and wave my arm in a beckoning motion at the wolf, "Kieran?"

He gets up, turns around, and rubs his muzzle against Dizzy's shoulder. Then, he lifts himself up on his hindlegs, forelegs supported by the edge of the bed, and nudges the side of Connor's face with the tip of his nose. Kieran looks at Lin and lets out a small chuff.

"I'll stay here," Lin says. "Go. If anything happens, I'll scream so loud you could hear it the next state over, even with earplugs in. You need a break; it's not all on you to protect us."

Kieran extends his neck towards Lin, who reaches out and smoothes the fur behind Kieran's reddish ears. The wolf hops down, butts his shoulder against Monty's leg until the despondent man halfheartedly acknowledges his farewell, then we depart.

Eight years ago, when Connor aged out of the foster care system at 18 and Kieran needed a new home after his own was destroyed, Monty bought this house and the five square acres of land it sits on. At first, Kieran was constantly on patrol to keep the area safe. When I joined them a little over a year later, he and I developed a system of wards that are so complex as to actually be bulletproof and nearly indestructible. We layered the spells so even if time or the elements managed to strip away the top layer of our shields, the numerous structures containing its magic are multi-layered, like an onion; making it extremely difficult to fully break through without concerted effort and a long span of time. The woods around our home are still undeveloped and our wards don't go past the official property line, but the wildlife brings its own sort of security and warning system.

Kieran and I walk the perimeter, starting at the end of our long driveway to inspect one of the primary pillars at the junction where the pavement of the road and our land meet. I run my hands across the surface, testing to make sure there is no magical weakening of the spells within. Kieran brushes up against it briefly, then moves along our path to stand above one of the buried points, testing how structurally sound it remains.

It is unique that Kieran can still control his magic while in the shape of a wolf, as most shifters do not have magic of their own, let alone magic they can harness while in their animals. He is the son of an alchemist and a wolf shifter; no one expected that he would inherit both abilities. What's more, on top of being able to control and transform elements as well as control and transform himself, he's able to shift items in a unique way; if the base components to an object can be transformed into something else, Kieran can use them as individual ingredients. He can also shift or exchange objects for something equal to themselves as long as they are either equal in mass or equal in arbitrary value, even if they're unrelated.

His abilities are remarkable, but they're what labeled him as an abomination amongst his people. Bigotry is such a waste of time.

I follow Kieran, bare feet aiding in my own ability to sense the Magics buried underground. It's simpler than needing to raise and investigate each implanted stone, layered with various coatings of inscribed metal.

It isn't until we make it roughly one quarter of the way around that we notice signs of a disturbance. It starts subtle, with patches of grass and leaves slightly more trampled than expected, as though something had paced back and forth along the perimeter multiple times. Eventually, we come across the first space where soil has been dug up in small areas, hidden well within the tree line. Neither Kieran nor myself are able to detect successful tampering with the wards until we reach one of the waist-high pillars, one stone side newly scratched and hacked away at to reveal a metallic layer beneath. The damage is contained to only the surface facing away from our property, indicating no breach was made.

While it is reassuring that whatever did this was not able to come through, it is troubling that the alarms were not sounded at its presence.

"The wards detected it enough to bar entry, but not enough to alert us of its attempts to do so? That is abnormal, and somewhat troubling," I speak aloud. "Can you scent what did this?"

Kieran circles the tall rectangular pillar, sniffing it and the surrounding area. He walks up and down the path our would-be intruder traversed, eventually doubling back to where I still stand. He lets out a frustrated growl, then shakes his head.

There is no evidence as to what is responsible for the attempted damage to our protections, but I strongly suspect it to be the work of the shadow assailant from last night. If I'm correct, it means that we are being targeted and whatever is hunting us is nearly undetectable. Why? Why us? And why didn't it trigger the alarms? I'm interested to see if Lin was able to find it on the security footage.

"Let's repair these and continue on."

32. LIN

"Monty," I wave him over, "What do you see in this?"

He looks at me dazedly, sluggishly rising to retrieve the phone in my outstretched hand, peering at it like it's a mysterious foreign device. Long moments pass before he replies emptily, "It's Dizzy and Connor in the kitchen at the shop."

"Yes, great work there captain obvious. Did you press play, perhaps?" I cock my eyebrow and purse my lips in a look that says I know he didn't.

Monty inhales and exhales in a noticeably troubled way, his focus obviously not all here. Nonetheless, he watches the video; eyebrows raising and jaw dropping the moment I know he sees it. "The shadows moved! Son of a gun, it was there at the shop with us."

"Keep watching, you'll see when it stole the knife from right under their noses. Even worse, it specifically followed

Connor and me out when we left to get clothes and food." The idea is unsettling, and a bit baffling, "Monty, we're being targeted."

He shakes his head in disbelief, "Why the heck would that happen? Seriously?"

I shrug, "Aside from the fact that we're obviously far too sexy for our own good? No clue." At that moment, Aria drifts up from the ground and lands on Monty's shoulder, eyes on the phone in his hand. She hisses at the screen and bares her teeth. We both look at the creature now vehemently expressing her distaste towards the captured footage.

"Ari, do you know what this is?" Her hisses become growls, and then a few sharp, high-pitched yips.

Realization dawns on me. "Monty," I look at him, then at the woman still unconscious on the ground, "If Aria recognizes it, it's possible it's after Dizzy and we're just the lucky ducks in its way." At that, the furious creature on Monty's shoulder becomes immediately quiet. When she stares unwaveringly at me with her large golden eyes, I know without question that I'm right.

But why would anyone be after her, either?

33. DIZZY

They've been keeping her from me. Me. She is mine. MINE. No one denies me access to my property, and yet I somehow find myself barred from bringing her to my side. Our side. I spent much of my night in the woods, demanding she come to me, frustrated that they somehow managed to block my entry; something meant to be impossible. Nowhere is free from shadows. Why not let the boy die if this had no point?

Following them as they travel is a simple matter; We'll just retrieve her when they leave her unguarded. Twelve years. Others have failed, I will not. We will be together, darling, I will free you from these fools. Continue to wait for me. We were promised.

Seeing the Asian one and the blonde one dare to touch what is mine sends me into a frenzy. They will PAY for their dire indiscretions against me. Patience, darling. I will not be patient or merciful in executing their punishments; they are not worth my kindness. Not like you, darling, I can be patient for you. I will show you kind-

ness, I will show them fury.

When these vile idiots finally separate from the group, I know my chance for vengeance fast approaches. I will enjoy watching them be pulled limb from limb; completely unable to retaliate against my superior capabilities. They will know death today. Wait for me, darling, you will join us again soon. We are meant to be together.

***

Groggily, my mind tries to resolve the world it's waking up to. Are there snakes here? That's an awful lot of hissing, and I swore to myself I'd never fall asleep in a snake pit again after the last time it happened. In my defense, it was cool and dark and totally the best place for a nap, all things considered!

The hissing stops. Oh, cool, pretty sure that's just my sleep brain leaving little presents for me in this half-awake state. Though I don't think I was dreaming of snakes? A familiar roiling in my gut tries to make itself known, bringing a sickening sensation to the back of my mind as well as the back of my throat. There's something I'm forgetting, but it tastes like hate and cruelty; the flavor right on the tip of my tongue. I can almost remember what it is.

There's growling, I think, and it distracts me from my thoughts. Shit. Tigers? That wouldn't exactly be a new one, and it's not like giant kitty cats are on my to-be-feared list even though they're definitely worth giving a good berth to if you don't happen to have a giant cardboard box or loop of rope around. Both incredibly effective ways to trap felines of all sizes indefinitely!

Come on Dizzy, get yourself up. Better to get the drop on whatever's out there first and assert your dominance as the superior scary thing in the room. Just remember, you're totally strong and a thousand feet tall and you have the sharpest fangs in the room, and if it turns out you're wrong you definitely know how to run so it'll probably all work out for the best in the end, regardless.

"RAWR!" I pop up into a sitting position, hands formed into claws, teeth bared, yelling at the top of my lungs.

"Son of a motherless goat sandwich on toast!" There's a large dark-skinned man in front of me, holding a hand over his chest. Oh hey! That's Monty! I know Monty!

Oh. Not a tiger den, then. That's honestly kind of disappointing. It shouldn't be, since waking up to a handsome man you've managed to scare the bajeebers out of should totally trump the threat of getting mauled by something only partly cute and cuddly, but it doesn't. Well, it sort of does, but I would have preferred being greeted by both if possible.

"Oof!" A breath is knocked out of me as I sort of get my wish after all! Sure, Colonel Stubbs isn't quite as ferocious as a tiger, but I'm going to count his tiny tackle as a near-mauling and call this a pretty darn good wakeup! "Aw, good morning you ferocious beast, you!" I smoosh his face between both hands, squishing his little white jowls forward because they're soft and I want to.

Delighted laughter sounds from behind and above me, "Welcome back, Love. That's quite a way to wake up! Tell me, is this part of your usual morning routine, or were we just treated to something special?"

I pull Colonel Stubbs' cheeks out to the sides, stretching them like flapping flesh wings. He lets me, so obviously this is acceptable Frenchie interaction procedure, which I expect to be allowed to repeat every day for the rest of eternity. Looking over my shoulder, I can just barely see Lin from my seat on the floor. "All I know is you never know when you're going to wake up surrounded by tigers so it's best to get the jump on them early if you can. How was I supposed to know it was you guys growling! Seems awfully strange, but I'm not going to judge you, just saying. Is that still judgey? Look, it's weird, but weird is fine and probably for the best overall, that's what I mean." My nod is decisive, showing my conviction to accepting these total freakazoids for who they really are.

I keep poking at the pupper in my lap, "Who's got the smooshiest little face out there? You do! You've got a smooshy face!"

Monty gathers his wits about him, clearly having been so utterly terrified by my display of ferocity that they fell straight to the floor and scattered about, "The growling was Aria." He points to my friend, at that moment leaping from his shoulder to mine, burrowing through my hair to curl herself around my neck loosely. "It's... I'm... I'm glad you're up. We had a big night." He hands a phone over to Lin, then quickly turns towards the door. "Excuse me. I have to go... make some treats." And then he's gone, like someone was chasing him with a bouquet of flaming piranha and he needed to get to the closest swimmy pool of fish-unfriendly water.

"Okay, well bye then?" That was fast and awkward. Ha! That's what she said. Womp womp. "He okay?" I ask Lin.

"Give him some space, Love, he's a little out of sorts after what happened last night. He'll come to his senses." Lin slides down from the bed he's sitting on and smoothly glides into a crouch next to me, "How are you?"

I release the face of my squishable captive and raise both arms high, my back arching slightly as I get a good stretch in. "I'm fine!" Well, that's a little bit of a lie. "Actually, I'm really fucking hungry. And maybe my neck is sore. But other than that, totally good!" I rub said neck, working out the tightness in one side, "Why?"

Lin pushes me forward slightly and slides in to sit behind me, digging his thumbs into the muscles around my shoulders. Oh yes, this is definitely how I should start hoping for wake-ups to happen. No more tigers. "What do you remember from last night?"

I melt like chocolate chips in a warm pocket at his touch, "Well, Monty and Zeke tested my magic for a while," A wistful sign escapes my lips at both Lin's hands on me now and the memory of Zeke and Monty's last night. Lin lets out a small, happy hum right after. Then my spine jolts up rigidly, "Shit! Connor!" I look around wildly, realizing we're still in the office he was brought into, "Where is he? Is he okay?! Oh god, Lin, he was stabbed!"

"It's okay Love, he's fine, just sleeping it off a bit." One of his hands keeps working at the knots in my muscles while the other trails a long line along my arm, continuing down the outside of my thigh, "Do you remember healing him?"

I snap my head to look at the man whose face is already hovering next to mine, "I did what now?" He steals a kiss from my lips before resting his chin on my shoulder.

"You healed him, Love. Monty ran out of juice and you stepped in to finish off the job, glowing like a shiny golden god-dess to keep him alive and well."

"Pft. Sure I did. Except I couldn't even heal a cut on Monty's hand last night, how the hell would I have fixed a knife wound?"

I can feel him shrug behind me, "It was quite a bit more than just a knife wound, Love. Take a look for yourself," He stands up, taking my hand in his and tugging me upwards, twirling me as though we're dancing once I'm on my feet. He stands at my back, our hands linked across my front. Sure enough, Con-nor is lying peacefully on the bed, a slight golden glow encircling him. In a way, he almost looks angelic.

"Wow," I reach out and touch his bare shoulder, peeking out from beneath the edge of a blanket draped across him. "He's beautiful." Lin hums his agreement from behind me, swaying us slightly in place. Looking back at him, I ask incredulously, "I did this?"

Twirling once again, Lin positions me to face him with one hand placed on my hip and the other still clasped in mine. "You did."

Sure, why not? I made a fireball yesterday but couldn't light a candle, of course I can heal a stab wound but not a simple cut! Honestly, I'm about ready to believe that I could grow Aria to 1,000 times her size and hop on her back for a ride, or teleport to the center of the Earth with a thought, or just wish for a silver goblet full of jelly beans and the secrets of the universe to suddenly show up! When will I ever stop thinking 'stranger things have happened,' when finally the strangest thing of all happens? Shoot, maybe it already has.

Nah, that time both of my shoes turned into frogs while I was still wearing them is at least a little bit more strange than this. I do miss Icky and Squishy, though; never did find out if their tadpoles grew up to be shoes or not, too.

I'm not really paying attention, caught up in memories of frogs, but I'm suddenly aware of the fact that my foot slips and the cushion we're swaying on is quickly sliding away while I'm still standing on it. Certain I'm about to show off my notorious grace and beauty by either face-planting or doing a sudden split across the growing gap, Lin effortlessly goes all Prince Charming Tango champion on me and bends my slipping leg up against his thigh with one hand, dipping me down while the other supports my back.

"I've got you," he whispers in my ear. His expression is

peaceful, as though he just happens to catch falling maidens every day. Right in the corners of his eyes, I see a tiny glimmer of cocky satisfaction. To be fair, he totally earned it because that was smoother than a baby's butt greased up in baby butt butter-although I'm not entirely sure if baby butt butter exists and I've never rubbed a baby's butt in the hopes of gaining three wishes, so I'm not entirely sure of their smoothness. I'm just going on rumors here, you know?

Plus, I don't have to pretend to stick the landing this time?! Ooh Lin, you're gettin' so many points right now, you're not even going to know where to spend them all! Might as well put them into a savings account and let them gain interest so you can become a points billionaire, and maybe turn into a sexy points philanthropist that goes to those in need and sets up sustainable point economic systems to help those areas flourish. We'll show people how to dig clean points wells, and grow hearty organic points crops. We'll solve world hunger and there will be peace on earth! Until the aliens come, then we'll share with them our points technology and we'll have peace to infinity and beyond! What an incredible empire, all built from this moment where a gorgeous man stopped me from busting my lip open through the power of dance.

Lin has long since pulled me upright, returning us to our regularly scheduled programming while I'm sure my face has locked into a dopey grin. He started humming at some point, but I was too caught up in the fantasy of our future benevolence to notice at first. It's weird, us dancing in a nearly-quiet room while a formerly stabbed man glows beside us and a little white Frenchie tries to look ferocious from a small dog bed in the corner, but it also kind of feels nice.

Except for the clawed demon attempting to make its way out of me through my stomach? It roars its displeasure at how many layers of flesh stand between it and freedom. Wow, seriously, when was the last time I ate?

Still the complete picture of suaveness, Lin guides our dance out the door, feet moving in time to the tune he's producing. I'm pretty sure I smell cookies baking once we're in the hall, and their sugary warmth only proves to make the monster inside me more eager to reach our destination. Which better be the kitchen or the great nation of Lintopia is suddenly going points bankrupt well before its time.

Lucky for both of us, Lin's impromptu waltz leads us straight to one of the barstools stationed around the kitchen island, which he pulls out just enough to twirl me directly onto. He tucks one hand behind his back in a bow while placing his lips upon the one he's still holding. "M'lady," he releases me and backs away, still slightly bent at the waist.

I prop my elbows up on the counter in front of me, resting my chin on the heels of my palms as I watch him grab cabbage and eggs from the fridge. Monty is just pulling out a tray of heaven-scented treats from the oven with his adorable lobster claw potholders. "Whatcha makin', Monty?"

He turns his back to me to face the counter on the opposite wall, using a spatula to slide the cookies onto a cooling rack. "Just some cookies," He replies.

"Obbbbbviously," I blow a raspberry with my lips, "What *kind* of cookies, ya lug? They smell amazing and I want to live inside them, please."

"Ah, like the gingerbread house witch?" Lin grins as he uses a mandolin to shred the cabbage into a large bowl, "Do you plan on luring children into your lair and baking them up in your oven for dinner?"

"I'm not quite hungry enough yet to resort to that, but we might have to reevaluate soon depending on whether or not the ravenous creature inside of me is sated in time." I watch him head back to the fridge and grab a couple more things, then turn my attention to the man silently switching off the oven and pointedly keeping his gaze downward. "So what kind of cookies are they, and can I have one? Or many, if that's an option, too."

"They're white chocolate, cranberry, and pistachio," Monty replies while washing his hands at the sink, back still turned to both Lin and myself. "You can have some, but save enough for the psychic tomorrow; these are for her." He very blatantly pivots from the sink in a way that prevents him from catching anyone's gaze and walks out of the kitchen, pausing near the edge, "And a canister of pineapple tea." Monty continues on and disappears into a room on the other side of the stairs, definitely in no way giving off strong 'leave me alone' vibes.

Yikes. Lin was right; he must be feelin' some kind of way. I can't really blame him for it, either. I remember getting worked up last night because it seems like it's my fault these honestly far too helpful and kind men suddenly have my trademark brand of disaster raining down upon them. Sure, it's actually been slightly less abundant than normal since we met, but less for me is still way more for them, and it's not really fair to unexpectedly have all... this... go on. If anyone knows how un-fun it is to constantly have trouble chasing you, it's me, and I'm trying not to feel fully guilty because it's not like I attract this crap on purpose, but I wish a little bit that they hadn't gotten stuck with me. Just so they wouldn't have to deal with these problems and could go on living their lives the way they were a couple of days ago, without me.

"I don't wish that at all." Zeke's voice comes from around the corner, the sound of claws clicking on the wooden floor following close behind. "I want you to stay."

Lin looks up from the stack of scallions he's slicing, "Were you thinking about leaving us, Love? Because I truly would hate for that to happen."

Sharp teeth gently nip at my exposed thighs and I see Kieran's gorgeous red wolf giving me actual puppy dog eyes. Well, puppy dog adjacent, anyway. "Not really, just... Well, I'm sure your lives weren't nearly this crazy before I showed up here, and I'm just feeling a little guilty is all. And also a little bit selfish for not wanting to leave, either, even though I'm pretty sure my curse is the reason the last couple of days have been so eventful for you guys." I cringe at the admission. Kieran rests his head on my lap and I instinctively rake my nails through his fur, the warmth of him easing away some of my grimace.

"Then I'm selfish too for not wanting you to leave, even if it means everyone in this house gets stabbed, including myself. I felt you, Love, don't forget that. There's simply no way I'd ever let you go back to that alone, so you're stuck with me. End of story, no regrets, now do you want shrimp or no shrimp in your okonomiyaki?" Lin's eyes are blazing with expectation. My what? That better not be code for vagina. Unless shrimp is code for penis? That would be unfortunate as a descriptor, and also somewhat sudden as far as topic shifts go, but it's not like I'd be necessarily opposed. Maybe later, though? I'd rather eat first.

"She wants your shrimp in her okonomiyaki." Zeke answers for me, and I just know he said it that way to mess with me. Especially given how pleased he looks with himself for that comment, and the fact that I'm still not entirely sure what he's just agreed to for me.

Zeke sidles up next to me and sits on the neighboring barstool before speaking in a seductive drawl, "Oh, it's something you'll definitely like. Lin has a lot of experience; he is undeniably the best."

Lin throws a few more things into the bowl and then wipes

his hands off, assumedly ready for me now. Well, this is a big step and lord knows I almost took it last night, but here? In the kitchen? And are Kieran and Zeke just going to watch it go down? Because that's kind of hot, not gonna lie, but maybe a bit much a bit fast?

"I'm happy to supervise if you want. It's my specialty." Oh, don't I freakin' know it. Zeke lifts one of his eyebrows twice, all of his teeth coming out to play in the devilish smile across his face. I squirm just slightly, feeling my 'okonomiyaki' warming at the memory. Head still in my lap, Kieran growls in a low way that almost feels like a purr, only making those good feels down below so much more difficult to ignore.

"That won't be necessary," Lin replies. My breath hitches as he rolls up the sleeves to his white shirt and takes a step towards me. Then another. And another. My heart races the closer he gets to me, the anticipation of his first move almost more than I can take. Lin crouches down less than a foot away from me, face now eye-level with my hot wetness. I feel the muscles in my core clench as he reaches his arm out to open a cabinet door inside of the island and pulls out two large, metal spatulas. Am I into spanking? Is that what's about to happen? Because I'd be willing to find that out today.

"Good to know," Zeke whispers right next to my ear, teeth grazing my neck. His hand swats at my ass, even though I'm sitting on it.

Lin turns and walks back to the bowl of whatever he mixed together, picking it up and bringing it over to the built-in griddle beside the stove burners. Okay, it's probably best to move that out of the way before bending me over the counter and risking it going flying? Totally makes sense with my track record for messes.

Every movement he makes only builds the tension inside me further, from the way he places the two silver paddles down, to how he strides confidently towards the space behind him, grabbing a bottle of oil. Impromptu lube? How thoughtful!

It's about the time where he spreads some of that oil on the griddle that I start to suspect fuckery is afoot, and I'm relieved that it seems he wants to cook what's in the bowl more than lay me down on the hot surface. Though I'm also a bit disappointed and confused. Could have sworn I was onto something here with this whole 'getting bent over the counter and spanked' thing.

"You're definitely onto something with that," Zeke growls out. I glance over at him, pretty certain at this point that he's been messing with me the whole time. The problem is, now I'm all hot and bothered for not the first time with this man, and if the bulge in his pants is any indication, Zeke's feeling the same way.

I clear my throat, "Hey Lin?"

"Yes, Love?" He's casually leaning against the back counter, watching the batter he spread over the griddle as it cooks.

"Just to be sure, okonomiyaki isn't code for vagina, is it?"

Lin barks out a surprised laugh, the delighted smile only slightly clashing with the minor quirking of his eyebrows, "No, it's decidedly not." He pauses for a moment, "Though it could be if you want it to."

"Nah, just had a weird thought." To my right, Zeke's expression is suspiciously blank, as though he hadn't just spent the last five minutes getting me all worked up over... I don't even know what, actually. "So what is it, then?"

It turns out okonomiyaki is some kind of savory pancake thing with brown and white sauce on top. Absolutely delicious, by the way, but just about as far from expectations

as could be given the conclusions I went right on ahead and
jumped to.

34. LIN

After lunch, we all alternate between watching over Connor, or wandering away to tend to whatever catches our fancy. I spend most of the time trying to research the shadow that attacked us, not coming up with much. The books in our house don't list it as a potential magical discipline, and there aren't any matching creatures in the bestiary. It's possible our literature is outdated slightly, but the internet yields next to no results. The only sites that even remotely match my search parameters are run by raving conspiracy nuts, claiming there's an entire society of shadows attempting to kill or enslave casters and start a new world order with mind control and pure, unadulterated evil.

The problem with conspiracy websites is that three hours into reading theories I'm almost entirely convinced that the dark side of the moon doesn't exist, there is an entire dimension that can only be accessed directly by walking into a shadow, and the tooth fairy only collects teeth under the cover of night so it can't be followed back to its fortress of abandoned bones. All of it's crazy, but they really do make compelling arguments that start to make a disturbing amount of sense when all lined up in a row. Enough so that I find myself sending messages, engaging in forums, demanding answers and proof; seeking to sort the fiction from reality.

Trying to use my truth abilities is almost useless in this case, because as far as they believe this *is* the absolute truth. No matter how crazy each theory is, most of them have some kernel of reality buried deep inside that brought the larger conspiracy on, even if it managed to get lost or twisted along the way.

It's fairly late when Dizzy, Kieran, and myself are all in the office with Connor, perched in various positions around the room. Kieran has resumed his post in the corner with Stubbs, though he's been more relaxed about standing watch than last night; occasionally leaving the room to roam elsewhere. He even appears to be taking this time to nap. Dizzy's sitting on the bed with Connor's head in her lap, aimlessly talking about anything and everything to him, including thanking him for picking out the yellow dress she donned after a shower. It turns out that Connor remembered to grab the few bags worth of clothing we'd purchased, even in the midst of all the chaos of my collapse. She directs comments and questions at me every now and then but I only catch half of them between conspiracies, despite sitting directly next to her. It doesn't seem to bother her, though; she's perfectly content to talk to herself.

I realize that's likely due to the fact that she normally only has herself or Aria to talk to, so this running dialogue with no one must be a habit she picked up to combat loneliness. I reach out and link my arm through hers, relegating myself to tapping on the screen with one hand to make a better effort at being present.

She rests her head on my shoulder, "When the glow fades, do you think he'll wake up? Because that's what I hope. But what do we do if he doesn't? He doesn't look hurt any more, but we don't know if whatever happened is keeping him alive and it's a battery about to run out that we should recharge, or if it just up and fixed him. All of this is new to me, and Monty has barely been around so I can't ask him if Connor's all healed, and I don't actually know how to understand any of the tingles and whatnot to read him. But I hope he's okay. You're okay, right, Connor?" Dizzy continues on a mile a minute, not actually expecting any response from either of us. "You owe me a date tomorrow and it's common courtesy to let a girl know if you're planning on cancelling so she doesn't feel stood up. Even if you are in some kind of magical glowing coma or whatever, so just go on ahead and shoot me a quick brain wave or something so I know if we're still on. Because I'd like to still be on if that's okay with you."

Aria flies casually in and drapes herself across Connor's chest, long ferret-like body more than enough to fully span his narrow width. Her leathery wings tuck in tight against her back and sides, almost like a webbed plate of armor. She looks up at Dizzy, and I notice a shift in the way the woman's one-sided conversation is performed.

"Aria, don't lay on his chest! What if you weigh down his lungs and he suffocates and we don't even know it until he's dead?" Dizzy pauses, "Yeah, you don't weigh that much but that doesn't mean it couldn't happen." Aria tilts her head slightly and I swear she cocks a brow, "Sure, you're careful and not stupid, but we don't really know what's going on and I'd rather be safe than sorry. I know you wouldn't hurt him on purpose, but we don't know if it's the kind of thing that could happen on accident or not." The creature sits up and launches off of Connor's chest with a huff, gliding over to curl up with Colonel Stubbs instead, "Hey! You know I didn't mean anything by it, don't be like that! You could have stayed up here with us, still!" A quick squeak is the only sound that reaches us from the ground below, "Okay, I'd want to cuddle up with a cutie-pie like Colonel Stubbs, too, so I can't really blame you, but I'm sorry if it seemed like I was accusing you of not being gentle. I guess I sort of was, but I didn't mean to. And Stubbs?" She pauses, a yip coming from the dog in question, "Thank you for sharing with Aria. And watching over us this whole time. We can go play tomorrow if you want!" Excited little piggy grunts come out of the Frenchie, an affirmative response. "Awesome! You're buckets of fun, Stubbs."

All of the research I've done today has made me more curious about two facets of the conversation I just witnessed.

"Love, could I ask you some things?"

She looks up at me, head still resting on my shoulder, "Of course you can, what do you want to know?"

"What is Aria?"

"What do you mean?"

"I mean what species is she? She wasn't in any of the books I browsed through earlier today, and I've never seen anything like her before, so I was wondering if you know what she is or where she came from or anything of the sort?"

Dizzy shrugs, "I dunno. My mom said she showed up the day I was born and never left, but it's not like that's really helpful. I've always just thought of her as my best friend, since she's the only one who's stuck around and even if she leaves, she always comes back. Only one who ever has. Didn't actually need to know much more than that, really." She plucks at some pilling on the blanket draped over the man in her lap, a sign that something about those thoughts may have been somewhat upsetting. It comes back, likely, to the idea that she's gotten used to not having anyone else to rely on. There's no telling how long it will take before she finally believes she has us, too.

"Is that why you understand her so well?" I set my phone down on the mattress and use that hand just to touch her; a caress on the arm, tapping on her fingers; anything to give her that additional physical reassurance.

"I guess?" She stops plucking at the blanket and instead runs her fingers along the fabric of my shirtsleeves, "I guess it would be kinda hard not to, since we've been together for 28 years and all. That would be a super long amount of time to spend with anyone and not be able to understand them."

"True, but you were just talking to her like it was a regular back-and-forth conversation. Do you... hear her voice?"

"Like do I hear words or whatever when we talk? Nah, I just kind of know what she means. Honestly, it seems pretty obvious what she means, don't you understand her, too?"

She asks it so earnestly, as though it never occurred to her that anyone couldn't understand Aria, "No, Love, nothing like that. I understand her about as well as I understand Colonel Stubbs."

Dizzy looks at me quizzically, one eye squinting and her mouth raising to one side, "Okay, same." Her lips purse out in thought for a second, "Are you saying you also don't understand Stubbs, or you understand them both?"

Ah, that answers it. "I don't understand either of them, aside from generally understanding their mood a little." Her eyes shoot wide open, realization that this is special hitting her. "Zeke told me that you have some naturalism skills, like making plants grow and knowing their properties. A less common ability involves communication with wildlife, both plant and creature." My fingers dance up her arm to brush across her cheek. "It seems like you are a very rare beauty indeed, Love."

"Wow," she looks to be contemplating this new information, "I never even thought about it before. Me and Aria have always been this way, and it's not like I've gone into the woods to hang out with bears and chat with them... although I did know some frogs for a while and it was totally the same, but this is just normal for me! But it's not normal in general?" Dizzy grabs a tendril of her curly hair and starts to flick it between her fingers, "Does this mean they understand me better than other people? Is that why the plants do what I ask? Because they understand me better?"

"Why don't you just ask your friends if that's the case? They're right here, after all."

"Oh! Right! Great idea!" She cranes her neck around me to try and catch a glimpse of the creatures on the floor near the foot of the bed, but I know there's no way she can from this vantage point. "Aria, do you guys understand me better than other people?" She waits for a moment, "Well that felt like a yes and a no, so it's not really all that helpful. Does that mean you understand me better, or you understand everyone, or is this because I asked about Stubbs, too?" There's a cheerful bark, "Ah, so it's Stubbs. Do you understand me better than everyone else, or am I the only one who understands you?"

Dizzy smiles and claps her hands together happily, "Both of us?! So cool!" Her eyes catch mine, "I saw a picture of both me and Monty bright and everyone else in the background; I think he's saying we both do it! Does Monty know? He has to, right?! You guys know way more about this stuff than I do!"

Now it's my turn to question what I've considered normal over the last few years. Monty's never mentioned having any sort of bond or empathy with animals, though it's possible that he was never tested for it, given the extreme rarity. Only the barest percentage of naturalists have the ability to communicate with wildlife, so it would be a waste of time and resources to run experiments if the person being tested hasn't displayed an affinity for it previously. Given that Dizzy didn't even realize this was something she had skill for as it's been the norm, it's possible the same has happened for Monty.

Really thinking about it, he is the one that most frequently speaks with Colonel Stubbs, though most people with pets tend to carry out conversations with their animals so it may just be that. And he did work on a farm with Kieran, that much I know. Is it possible he tended to the animals better because he has an inherent sense of empathy with them?

"Truthfully, I'm not sure. I suppose we could ask him, if he ever stops avoiding us," I respond after considering the possibility. "There wasn't much information in the books that I was browsing about this ability, but one aspect is having an animal bond, which I suspect Aria of being yours. Then there's also the empathy, where you can understand them or they can understand you. Considering that this was broadly described as being a relationship with wilderness, I'm curious to know if there's the potential of a plant bond." My legs are severely stiff from being folded up tightly for so long, given that we've been sharing such a small space for a few hours. I untuck one leg and stretch it to the side, picking up my phone again in the process, "But that's something we can explore at a later date."

When I flip my phone over and light up the screen, Dizzy's head is once again resting on my shoulder. She catches a glimpse of what I'd been working on before we began discussing this deliciously unexpected aspect of her abilities.

"Whatcha lookin' at?" She asks chipperly, obviously still pleased with our discovery.

On the screen is a zoomed-in still from the security footage at the shop, right as the shadow creature is following Connor and myself out of the front door. We have a camera mounted directly above the door frame, capturing the footage of all who exit, should we need to identify them later.

With how brightly the sun was shining outside, both of our shadows are trailing behind us in one large, long mass against the floor. If I hadn't been looking for the unnatural movement of a deeper darkness joining our own, I'd never have noticed anything unusual in the footage.

Through a combination of adjusting contrasts and brightnesses, as well as my own truth magic including the ability for revelation, I was able to just barely make out the shape of a vaguely humanoid form. Within the silhouette of its loosely defined face, the most distinct details are two hateful crimson eyes.

I can feel Dizzy's body next to me tense up, her breath suddenly held; a statue forming against my side. Her hand clutches my arm tightly, "Lin?" She says my name like a question, her voice almost pained, "What is that?"

Not understanding the sudden onset of her distress, I cup her cheek in my hand and divert her gaze to mine, "What's wrong?"

Her eyes look almost crazed as she blindly gestures towards the phone, "What was that, Lin? Where did you get that?"

"It's footage of the creature that attacked last night, from the security cameras at the shop. We think it may have been following us during the day. Why? What's wrong?"

Dizzy looks at the screen in my hand, panic evident in her expression. She gasps softly, brows furrowing in confusion as her voice barely rises above a whisper, "David?"

35. DIZZY

"Most people say you never forget your first kiss, but in my case that's super duper extra true. Really, how can you forget the boy whose face you split open and knocked straight into a coma? Some people probably could, but that moment is forever burned into my noodle right in the regrets section.

"You see, kissing David is pretty much what started everything. The running, anyway. Probably any of the other random disasters beforehand could be blamed for even meeting him in the first place, and if we're really digging deep here, just being born could be blamed for how my life has turned out. But that's a little extreme, so it's easier to say it all started with kissing David Williams.

"When I was 10 years-old, I got kicked out of school after they decided my latest explosion was the last straw and it was too dangerous to have me around everyone else. It sucked at the time, but given how things have always turned out? They probably weren't wrong.

"My mom wasn't around pretty much ever and didn't come up with another school for me to go to, so I mostly spent my time just hanging out with Aria wherever we ended up for the day. At some point, the neighbor noticed us playing in the yard during the daytime and one thing lead to another, eventually ending in her bringing me over to her house and teaching me some things.

"Mrs. Williams was a teacher at one of the schools in town, but she started to let me come over on the weekends so I could learn stuff like Math, and Reading, and Gardening. She'd send me home with huge stacks of books and a ton of homework that I had to do on my own during the week, but it was mostly just nice to have something to do, even if it was a lot of work. Plus, after a year or two I started to get really good at gardening for her, so she left the greenhouse unlocked and permitted me to come over whenever I wanted.

"Sometimes, she even let me watch her brew up potions inside her kitchen, until I managed to knock too many over and she got a tiny bit mad and stopped letting me inside the house at all. But I was always allowed in the greenhouse, and I was always given free reign to do whatever I wanted with the plants.

"Eventually, her son David started coming out and spending time with me. I used to see him peeking out at me from the windows every now and then, but it was years before he finally even said hi. We'd just grow things together in the greenhouse at first, but then he started coming over to my place after school to talk, or explore, or watch TV. I don't know if he was allowed to do all that because sometimes I'd hear him getting yelled at when he went back home, so I asked one day if he was in trouble for hanging out with me. He just said his mom was super protective of him and she worried when he was late but everything was fine. I never actually believed him, but it's not like I knew anything about healthy parental relationships so I tried to ignore it and just pretended nothing was wrong whenever I saw him.

"By the time I was fifteen, we were spending almost every single day together, and he'd started to talk about what we were going to do when we got older. He said we'd run away together and live in the middle of the woods so I wouldn't have to worry about my curse acting up, and we could be surrounded by plants and nature and not be troubled by anyone else.

"Of course, my stupid teenage brain got a big honkin' crush on him, but I didn't really know what to do about my feelings so I added that to the list of things I pretended didn't happen. Besides, he was basically the only boy I ever saw but I know I wasn't the only girl he saw, and there were probably plenty of better people he could have spent his time with.

"Just before midnight on my sixteenth birthday, David snuck into my house and woke me up to say he had a surprise for me, so I followed him out, because of course you do what the boy you like asks, especially on your birthday. Besides, mom hadn't been home for weeks so it's not like there was anyone to catch us and get me in trouble for leaving. He took me to the greenhouse, and there was a space on the floor that had been cleared out for layers of decorated cloths and pillows, and a bunch of different bowls and baskets and other things. There were dozens of candles lit all around, and the whole thing looked pretty freakin' romantic to me by the time we were smack dab in the middle of it all. He brought me down to the blankets and pulled out a little cake and we ate it.

"I don't remember what else we talked about, but he told me he liked me and then told me to be his girlfriend, so then I was. And well, we started to kiss. It was nice, and I liked him, and he liked me, and it was my birthday and I was having a good time riiiiiight up until things went bad. Because they always do.

"Whenever I'm about to be hit with a curse, there's a tingle that happens, and sometimes I lose control of whatever part of my body the tingle is in. That night, my whole body went berserk and I ended up pushing David away. Hard. So hard, he went flying across the room and crashed into a table full of big plants, burying him under tons and tons of heavy pots and dirt and broken shards of table. He was completely still after that-I'm not even sure if he was breathing. A bunch of the candles got knocked over and the cloths I was sitting on caught fire. Before I could try to get up and help David, his mom came swooping in practically out of nowhere and dragged him out even though he wasn't moving. She was gone, I was alone, and the fire was starting to grow a little too close but my body still wasn't cooperating properly.

"Aria's the one who saved me, really. Back then, I was only so-so at breaking curses, and that whole thing had me worked up in such a state that I didn't even know where to begin to get it started. She literally flew in, shoved something in my mouth, and screeched louder than a whole bushel of howler monkeys in a full-on frenzy. We got out of there just in time, because less than a minute later something crazy happened with all the glass bursting inwards and the whole greenhouse collapsed. Everything inside it burned down; all my poor plants reduced to smoke and ash.

"We were standing in the yard, watching the fire burn when Mrs. Williams grabbed me hard by the arm and started dragging me into her house. After I counter a curse, I'm always a little weak and disoriented so at first I didn't realize that she wasn't saving me, she was screaming at me. She called me a bitch and said I'd ruined everything, that her son was in a coma and she would fucking kill me for taking this away from her. That she'd waited so long and it was finally her turn. That

I was her property, consequences be damned she'd get what was hers. It started to dawn on me that maybe whatever was happening wasn't okay, and when she let go of me for a second to unlock some door, I fucking ran. She looked straight up crazy, and not in the charming old lady way, but in the 'I'm going to murder you right here and bathe in your blood before devouring your bones' sort of way.

"It scared me so much that I didn't look back or stop until my body fully gave out on me and I collapsed. I don't know if she followed me or for how long if she did, but by the time I woke up I was in someone else's house and they were taking care of me. That didn't even last a day, though, because I accidentally managed to send one of the people tumbling down the stairs, so I ran again. And again. And again. Every time I get somewhere that seems safe, it's only a matter of time before something big or bad happens and I'm bolting before roots take hold. Things have been like this for so long, I don't even bat my eyelashes at it any more; I just keep going and don't look back to see how things turned out or who might be chasing me this time.

"I lost count a long time ago on how many places I've been and left burning. But no matter how many times I run, I'll never forget that first one; the one where I put my first kiss into a coma. The one where I burned down an entire greenhouse of plants that I'd loved for years and years. The one where the woman I thought was like a real mother to me tried to kill me. The one where I ruined the life of David Williams, the boy next door with unmistakable crimson red eyes who said he liked me on my birthday."

I look up to see an audience of men silently listening to me as I lay my shame out for them to judge and fear. Lin remains beside me, our hands joined though I don't remember being aware of his touch. Zeke is in the doorway, sharp features making his furrowed brow more severe. Kieran stands at the foot of the bed, naked and no longer a wolf, sorrow etched in every line of his expression. There's a certain hellish irony to the fact that I've said all this while yet another man I've kissed and said I like has his head resting on my legs, comatose. Just a reminder that I'm too dangerous to know, especially if that really is David in the video and he attacked Connor last night. I couldn't even imagine why.

"I'm so sorry, you guys." Tears start to well up in my eyes, realizing that this truly is all my fault. "I don't know why this is happening. I don't know why he's here, or why he would have stabbed Connor, or why my stupid curse stuck you guys to me and hasn't even told me how to fix it." My heart is breaking, knowing that this is another time where I'm supposed to run and I'm ruining more lives in the process. Just a few good days I got to have, at least, with these men who took me in even though it put them in danger from some crazy cursed stranger with purple hair and no shirt to her name. A few good days for me, and maybe a lifetime of consequences for them just because I was selfish enough to want to be here. "I'm so, so sorry. I'm so sorry." The dam bursts and I'm completely sobbing, "I'll go, you don't deserve this. Everything I touch breaks and I don't want to break you any more. I need to go-it's better if I do it now, and maybe if David's following me you'll be safe and it'll be okay and I'll be okay. I don't want to hurt you. It's better if I go away." Do it, Dizzy. Get up and go, don't look back, never look back. If you're always moving forward, nothing can catch up with you so you don't have to think about it, or miss it, or get hurt by it ever again.

"Fuck that," Zeke growls out. "You're ours. Stay."

"Love, we've been over this already. I'll tell you it as many times as you need to be reminded, but it's not your fault. And I want you here. If you leave, you take all the joy, and excitement, and life that you bring with you, and I don't want to live without that any more. If you go, I follow." Lin swipes his thumb across my cheek, disrupting the tears trailing down it. "Know that we couldn't possibly blame you for someone else's actions, regardless of whether or not he made them in your wake. *He* made them, not you."

Kieran stomps and stumbles around the edge of the bed until he's in front of me. In his eyes, I see my own sorrow and guilt and pain reflected. Years of loneliness and forced solitude, panic and regret at the destruction always in my wake, and the deep, deep truth that on the inside I will always be the girl whose own mother always left because blood wasn't enough to make her love me enough to care. That no one's ever cared enough to want me to stay, until now. These strangers, whose lives are decidedly in danger because of me, know the risks and said fuck that anyway. They're demanding I stay, not pushing me or themselves away.

The moment I feel just a tiny little shard of my shattered heart get patched up with shaky hope is the moment Kieran's own tears finally fall. He leans over Connor and drags me into a fierce hug, pressing me tightly against his broad chest. It feels the way I imagine love and home are meant to; warm, and safe, and certain, and forever. I let it out, all the fear and frustration and grief and insecurities spill onto Kieran's skin until I'm crying in relief, strength in the arms around me never wavering for a moment. He holds me through all of it, saying more without words than I knew I needed to hear.

Finally, drained and exhausted, Kieran lifts me from beneath Connor's head and lowers me to the makeshift bed below. I fall asleep cocooned in multiple pairs of arms, a tiny flame of maybe flickering to life in my battered but tentatively hopeful heart.

36. MONTY

Most of the day, I avoided talking to anyone else in the house, only really interacting if they happened to be with Connor when I stopped by to check on him. Logically, I know it's ridiculous to feel responsible for what happened-but feelings aren't really known for their logic. So, I'm going to beat myself up over this until the minute he opens his eyes. Hopefully it's only a little while longer. Connor may not be blood, but he's been my little brother since the first day he turned up at my parents' house, 12 years-old and shook up all to hell. There were shadows in his eyes back then, and it took every ounce of my love to bring him out of them. He's been a part of my soul ever since-how could I not take seeing him broken to heart? It's normal to worry about your family, but I don't want anyone else to see me doubting myself like this; don't want them to know my confidence can slide; that they aren't safe in my hands.

Big brothers look out for their little brothers, and I didn't look out for him enough.

It's the middle of the night when I check in on Connor for the hundredth time. The house is quiet, and I'm not surprised to find everyone sleeping in a pile on the floor again. Kieran's human, which means he's probably feeling safer now than he was hours ago; he's always believed he's more capable as a wolf. It's good to see him back after only a day; last time it took months.

I creep across the room and quietly roll my office chair to the head of the bed, sitting with my face barely inches away from Connor's ear.

"Hey kid," I whisper, "It's been a rough couple of days, huh?" The contact of my hand on his shoulder allows my energy to seek inside him for the millionth time today, buzzing its circuit, reassuring me that he's still alive and in one piece. "We're all here with you, waiting for you to wake up. No rush or anything, but It'd be cool too if you didn't leave us hanging any more." His silence wrenches my heart, a response I hate not hearing.

Normally, I'm the one who makes plans and figures out next steps but I've been too caught up in this emotional turmoil to think straight. I rest my head beside him, futilely trying to take comfort in the evenness of rhythmic breaths filling the room. Attempting to let their signs of life ground me in today, let me look towards tomorrow. It's time to decide how we keep moving forward.

The problem is, I really don't know where to go from here. Do I track down the attacker? How? Do I move us far away to keep everyone safe? What if that just puts us on the run indefinitely? Do I call in reinforcements? Who would even come? Do I alert the community so no one else is caught unaware? Why wouldn't anyone think we're crazy for talking about killer shadows.

It's like I'm slamming up against a brick wall every time I try to consider a possibility. Maybe this? BAM, you shall not pass. Maybe that? BOOM, do not pass go. I'm stuck in place, walls closing in and making the options feel even less and less plausible the more I stumble brokenly towards them. I can't see my way out of this maze, one I'm not even sure I remember entering in the first place.

If this psychic of Lin's is legit, I really hope she has some insight for us because nothing quite feels right to try. But it seems wrong to do nothing at all, too.

"I won't let you down again, okay? I'll make this right." Standing, I look down at his sleeping face. The glow around Connor is faint now, what happens when it's gone remains to be seen.

My exit is nearly silent, but apparently not silent enough as I hear Dizzy's voice, slightly roughened by sleep, "It's not your fault, you know."

I let out a deep breath, knowing she's right but not entirely believing it myself. My back is to her at this point, my trajectory interrupted when I was very nearly to the door. "I know. I do, it's just hard to see him like this and not think about a thousand things that could have been done differently so we don't get to where we are now. It's hard for me to let go of thinking I can control everything and prepare for it all when something like this ends up happening." Like it has been all day, my head hangs in shame. I want to be strong enough to keep my family happy and whole, but for the second time this week I'm swallowed up by doubt.

There's rustling and a bit of grunting behind me until I feel a light touch on the back of my upper arm. "Hey," she waits for me to look at her. When I don't, Dizzy circles around and looks up, "Can I ask you something?" Her eyes are weary, but filled with empathy.

I nod, "Sure."

"Did you stab Connor?"

My head whips back, her question a blow aimed directly at my psyche. "What?"

"Were you, physically, the one who took a goddamned knife and shoved it through him?"

I blink at her, not really sure how to go on with this conversation when the answer is so obvious. "No, I didn't."

"No? So you're going to punish yourself and all the rest of us because someone else did something fucked up to someone we care about?" She's starting to look and sound angry, voice gravelly and teeth bared. "Get over it, Monty." Is she actually mad at me right now?

Tentatively, Dizzy takes a step closer and places her hand on my chest. This time when she speaks, it's much softer, almost an apology. "It's not your fault. It's not my fault. We didn't do this to him." She closes her eyes and a tear she'd been holding back comes cascading down her face as she stands on her toes and kisses my cheek. "It's not our fault. It wasn't my curse; it wasn't your kiss." She punctuates each statement with her lips on my jaw, my cheek, my chest; whispering her words like a prayer she can make come true. A prayer I can't bring myself to return.

I realize then, as this small woman displays how large her heart is with just a few soft words and kisses, that she's been feeling almost the same as I have. I've been an idiot for thinking I'm the only one torn up inside by this and chose to leave them all alone while I dug a deeper hole. If anything, this is one of those times where we need each other most, not least.

"Forgive yourself, Monty." She jerks her head at the sleeping forms piled nearby, "That's what these guys forced me to do. Seems a lot like you need to give that a shot, too."

Her arms wrap around me and she tucks her head under my chin, face burrowing into my chest. I let out a long breath, kissing the top of her head. "Thank you." She's right, of course, and I probably would have figured it out on my own eventually, but this isn't the time for me to process slowly, and separately. "Sorry I avoided everyone all day, it's hard for me to deal with this."

"It's hard for all of us, too." She reaches up and loosely drapes an arm over my shoulder, smiling patiently. "Why don't you stay here? Don't go hiding away any more."

Dizzy lightly pulls me towards the cushions, directing me to wedge between Kieran and Lin; the spot she recently vacated. I don't fight it, grateful for the care and acceptance she forces on me. Lin adjusts backwards in his sleep, making just enough space to let both of us into the middle right as Kieran reaches out and tightly wraps his arm around Dizzy's waist, burying his head into her shoulder and inhaling deeply. Despite the movements, everyone still appears to be asleep.

We're both on our sides, facing each other, and I take the opportunity to just appreciate the view of the caring, empathetic, beautiful woman in front of me. When Connor wakes up, I'll finally be able to shake off the rest of these rough feelings, but in the meantime? Being here, with her, with all of them, it definitely helps. I drape an arm across her hip, skimming my fingertips lightly over the soft fabric of her dress in a comforting, absent way, letting the movements clear my mind and bring peace. The vice grip on my heart melts away, my soul settling as sleep creeps close to claim me.

"Oh hey, did you know we can talk to animals?"

37. LIN

"This is for you," Zeke holds out a long braid of yellow material attached to a shimmering, milky stone with blue and purple veins glistening throughout it. "It will help keep you grounded if you experience Dizzy's sensations. You will be aware of yourself and her but be able to choose which to focus on, and how much."

I finger the stone in the center of the length, running the tip of my nail into the symbols engraved on it, "Why Zeke, you really know how to spoil a lucky man with jewelry. First a magic bracelet that brings us a scrumptiously vivacious woman, and now a magic necklace? Next you'll be slipping a ring on my finger and booking us a vacation to Hawaii!" The clasp is simple enough to fasten around my own neck easily, but I woke up this morning feeling flirty so it's time to play. "Let's make it official, shall we? Darling, would you kindly help me get myself all prettied up for our date out on the town?" I hold both ends of the necklace up to Zeke and turn around for him to fasten them together. Romance being completely dead in this day and age, he simply walks away, leaving me to tough it out alone in the harrowing world of miniature hook and eye clasps.

"We'll be here when you get back, and you'd better get back," Monty says as he hands me a tin of cookies, wrapped with a delicate bow. "These are for Miss Fern, send my apologies for missing this meeting and thanks for any help she can offer." He also includes a canister of custom pineapple white tea blend, likely a nod to the bet that had him warming up to her from the start. "If anything goes wrong, or you change plans, or-"

"Yeah, yeah, dad-man, don't worry; we'll call." Knowing he's still sensitive about the well-being of our group, I decide to throw him a bone, "Seriously. We'll call. If it even looks like we're in trouble, we'll get the hell out of there as fast as possible. And we're not splitting up at all." I squeeze his shoulder and lower my voice, "This is important to everybody, okay? I'm not letting anything happen to one of us ever again. Trust me. Trust us."

Monty waves my hand away carelessly, but I know he's doing his best right now to keep from hog-tying us all and locking us in a room for our own protection. The man can be a bit overprotective sometimes, and this week has shaken up our routine quite a bit.

Zeke is already behind the wheel of our bright red hatchback by the time I make it outside with Kieran close behind. It's still early morning, so the plan is to put up a vacation notice on The Tea Kettle and Cauldron before any customers would normally stop by, then continue on to Miss Fern's place, conveniently a scant few miles from the shop.

To me, it's absurd that we've somehow been so close to the absolutely gorgeous victorian-style home our GPS directs us to without ever noticing it. The tall, angular, and many-windowed beauty is located on the corner of its block. Bright teal base with grey and white accents making its large personality unmistakably dominant compared to the rest of the more muted buildings nearby. Somehow, it seems as though the sun is shining more brightly around this one home; a ridiculous thought considering that it towers over everything else and should be casting enormous shadows.

Then I notice that there genuinely are no shadows on the entire premises. I wonder if this would be an effective protection against our dark attacker? If there are no shadows for it to hide in, can it still follow us like it did at the shop?

Somehow, despite still technically being in the city, there's a genuine white picket fence surrounding the impressive property. Perfect gentleman that I am, I skip from our car directly to the gate, flourishing a bow as I open it for my companions. If romance truly is dead, it appears I am the only one mourning its passing given how absolutely unaffected both Zeke and Kieran are by my clear display of chivalry.

"You're welcome!" I cheerily chirp to their backs, continuing my frolic up the impressively tidy white steps of Miss Fern's porch. Just as we make it to the dark grey door, preparing to knock, it swings open and reveals a short, round woman with the largest smile and twinkling pale teal eyes the color of her home.

"Boys! You made it here safely and perfectly on time today! Wonderful, wonderful, come in!" She brushes a few silver coils of hair away from the dark skin of her face as she ushers us inside, "I already put the kettle on for that wonderful tea you brought along, which I do hope you'll bring more of next time you stop by." The canister is snatched out of my hands before I can even offer it up, the thieving woman happily scurrying towards an adjacent room with us in tow. "Oh, and yes, I'm Miss

Fern."

While the outside of the house makes its statement by being decked out in a light but rich blue-green, this room goes all-in on yellow to express itself. There are bright yellow couches, sunflower-patterned curtains, a golden-brown carpet, extremely pale yellow walls, and various bookshelves and tables painted complementary shades of the same color. It may be a little intense to look at suddenly, but the overall vibe is one of incredible positivity and welcoming. It's exactly the opposite of any dark and mysterious atmosphere one might associate with meeting a psychic for the first time, including the utter lack of a crystal ball or fog machine. Though there are plenty of candles and crystals and other magical paraphernalia around the room, hidden amongst pictures of the jubilant woman in her youth, surrounded by different people and places in almost all of them. If these photographs are anything to go by, Miss Fern has always been a fan of bright colors and chunky jewelry.

"Now you boys make yourselves comfortable, I'll go grab that kettle and we can get to chatting about why I asked you here." She hustles away through a swinging door into a room that I catch a quick glimpse of, appearing to be completely purple-themed. It seems we are in a rainbow of a house, which I find utterly enchanting.

"Where the hell are we right now?" Kieran mumbles as he flops down on one of the sunny couches. He looks around suspiciously at every corner of the room, still on high-alert and ready to pounce any threat.

I place the tin of cookies on a squat coffee table already covered in tea cups, saucers, cream, sugar, and tiny sandwiches. A proper tea party, this early in the morning? Amused by the incredibly warm welcome from this apparent stranger, I sit back in a golden high-backed armchair, crossing my legs one knee over the other.

Zeke's attention seems to be snared by the variety of items posted around the room, including a set of wooden masks hanging from one wall, bizarre and sinister expressions carved into them at odds with the pure delight generated by this room. He picks up a wicked-looking black dagger from a small hutch beneath the masks, examining the engravings in its blade.

As I watch him peruse, it occurs to me that the majority of items here, aside from the photographs and general decor, seem to have a darker theme to them. There are shrunken heads beside a bouquet of fresh daisies, a charred hand tucked behind a sun statue made of actual gold, and petrified serpents coiled around shining yellow crystalline formations.

"This room contains curses," I come to the same conclusion just as Zeke says it.

"Bingo!" Miss Fern pushes her way back through the swinging door, kettle in hand as promised. "I've spent the majority of my life fighting against the darker things in this world and they haven't got me yet! Tried plenty, of course, but haven't gotten the drop on me and The Girls in a long long time. Won't for a little while longer if I have anything to say about it, either." At the table, she places a metallic tea ball into each cup, then pours hot water in four of the five settings. She addresses Zeke, still perusing her collection of cursed objects, "Now, mister clever clocks, if you don't take a seat and join us we're likely to spend all day watching you pick apart every little thing in here and you haven't got that kind of time to spend right now."

"Apologies," Zeke nods and takes a seat next to Kieran on the couch, Miss Fern claiming an armchair opposite my own.

"Oh, but I've gotten ahead of myself again! Happens sometimes when you first meet people you already know." She passes out small plates for the sandwiches, which we happily collect and pile with her offerings. "I'm not the best at remembering to start at the beginning, especially when I already know how everything works out in the end. Makes it hard to find the point in all the introductions when we're thick as thieves down the line."

"I, for one, am loving this mountain of vague intrigue you've dropped in our laps," I say, "Maybe let's start with how you got my phone number, and why you called it?" The sandwich I take a bite of is classic ham and swiss, an interesting pairing with our pineapple tea.

"Ah, yes, I should probably explain that. You see, I've always had your phone number because you will have given it to me today, meaning The Girls have all had access to it across our whole line and I've known when it was time to step in for quite a while. Mostly, it was a matter of waiting for David to show himself to you." She holds up a hand to stop us from saying anything, "And yes, I know it's David. Or I will know, anyway. It's complicated.

"You see, the women in my bloodline across all generations and all possibilities are linked. We can speak to one another and share knowledge so long as we don't physically exist in the same timeline. In that case, we do so indirectly by sharing whatever knowledge we need spread to the others. I'm not psychic in the traditional sense, given that I can only know anything any of my past or future descendants would know, but as long as I know I need to know something, it can be arranged that I eventually do."

Zeke is enthralled by this explanation, leaning forward in his chair with a forgotten cup raised halfway to his lips, "How do you avoid causing a paradox?"

"Oh, we don't worry about those silly little things for ourselves," Miss Fern waves her hand dismissively, "They haven't ever seemed to bother us, but it can mess with you lot if we're not careful. Likely has to do with the fact that we exist across an infinite number of probabilities, making it impossible to cause a paradox if the paradoxical action was already a solidified reality to one of us." She chews on the side of her mouth for a second and then shrugs, "Or it's just because magic."

"Fascinating," Zeke runs a hand over his slightly scruffy facial hair, "How long has this been going on? How long will it continue? Is this unique to your family? Why haven't I heard of this before?" Typically quiet and difficult to read, Zeke is unusually animated and alive, brimming with curiosity.

"Hush, now," She cuts off his enthusiastic line of questioning with a raised hand, "That's not what I asked you here for. Though don't you worry your head over none of that right now, you'll figure it out along the way." Placing her cup and saucer on a small side table, the elderly woman stands and makes her way to the hutch positioned beneath those bizarrely unsettling masks, rummaging through a drawer. "I have something you'll need for the path you're on now. We always have a few extra around for when we find some friends in trouble. Ah, here we are!" She withdraws an unassuming black box, just larger than the palm of her hand and so dark as to practically look like a patch of emptiness. Strangely, its coloration is flat in a way that halts highlights from forming to define the corners of its shape. In a way, it's the exact opposite of everything in this violently bright and cheerful room.

Miss Fern shuffles back around the couch and holds the box out to Zeke, opening its lid to reveal a smooth, impossibly clear, ovular stone within. Around the edge of the entire piece is a golden band, inscribed with different symbols.

"If you run your finger around the band clockwise, you can dispel shadows and shadow-touched for an increasing perimeter, up to about 100 feet across. Counter-clockwise can contain a shadow within a shrinking perimeter, starting at about 10 feet across so you have to be fairly close to activate it. You can even capture them inside if you force the circle small enough." She motions with her hands around the faintly glowing stone while describing its instructions, "And if it needs to be deactivated or hidden, this box will completely cut the stone off as long as it's closed." The lid snaps shut aggressively, but is reopened gently as Miss Fern offers it up like a gift.

Zeke takes the entire box, but picks up the stone itself and examines the writing around it thoroughly. As he asks some sort of question, I feel a tendril of warmth spark its way up my spine. A pleasant warmth. A *very* pleasant warmth. Oh my, I know what this is. It travels throughout my entire body, but especially begins to build deep in my abdomen, the sensation of muscles I know I don't have tightening.

"Right, Lin?" Fern winks at me, pulling me back to our surroundings.

"Hm? Oh, yes?" I place my sandwich plate over my lap casually, masking the growing dilemma. I'm not sure what I've agreed to, but it's worth noting that I was able to do so despite my certainty that the delicious sensations building in my nether region are very similar to those that fully incapacitated me mere nights ago. Credit where it's due, that clever bastard Zeke sure can craft one hell of a charm.

"Ah, such a sensitive young man," Miss Fern grins devilishly at me and I just know I've stuck my foot in it somehow.

Kieran snickers between bits from his place on the couch, but is up in an instant, plate of tiny sandwiches thrown to the ground as he snarls at a loud bang from the entryway.

"Grams!" A woman's voice shouts angrily from the hall, accompanied by impressive stomping.

"In the yellow room, dear!" Fern calls back sweetly, smiling reassuringly at us and waving at Kieran to sit back down. He doesn't, but it was cute of her to try.

In storms a tall, thin woman with dark skin and waist-length silver hair. A woman I recognize.

She pauses for barely a second when she sees us, expression softening only slightly. "Oh, hey guys. Was this today?" Lilly, the bartender from The Wood Liquor continues on her war-path towards Miss Fern, who's calmly sipping from a decorative tea cup. "You can't just change my life for me, Grams! I'm a grown damned woman, I don't care what you and The Girls have been talking about, you need to talk to ME, too!"

"Now, now, Lilly Pad, you know we can't do that."

"Phones, Gram! Phones!" Lilly snarls, throwing her hands up in the air in exasperation, "It's like you forget they exist just because you don't need them most of the time. Some of the people in your life live outside of your head, too, you know!"

Miss Fern slowly lowers her cup to its saucer with a clink, a small, scolding look just barely creasing her brows, "Lillian Elizabeth Thorn, I raised you better than to come storming in here like this when we have guests, now straighten your act up right this second young lady or I won't be helping you develop until you remember how to treat people properly."

Lilly glares at her grandmother for a few ticks, makes a sound somewhere between a growl and a grumble, and snatches up the fifth, empty tea cup on the table. Kieran and I share a curious look between one another as we watch the still enraged woman attempt to smother her emotions while pouring boiling water over her metal strainer. Zeke appears too enamored with the creation in his hands to even notice the disturbance, meticulously running his fingers along every inch of fabric lining the now empty black box.

"Well, that sure was a grand entrance worthy of Duke, the 10 foot-tall parakeet," I say, recalling the conversation from our last visit to the pub. With all this excitement, I'm elated to find that my body mostly feels like my own, though a ghost of pleasure is still trailing through my insides; an afterthought in the background that only makes itself known if I bring notice to it.

Halfheartedly, Lilly lets out a breath that has just the briefest hint of humor behind it. She picks up a sandwich and takes an aggressive bite from it, but most of the anger in her expression has been quelled. With a sigh, she turns to address us from where she stands, "Hello gentlemen, It's nice to see you again." Her eyes flash upwards in a motion that appears to be pleading with the sky, lips moving wordlessly as she returns her gaze to the woman patiently waiting from her golden throne. "Grams, apologies for barging in here unannounced while you clearly have guests." Back turned to me, I can only see her fist clench and unclench by her side but imagine she must be gritting her teeth around every word. "I also had an unannounced visitor this morning who rudely informed me that my grandmother had threatened them if they didn't evict me that minute. I'm sure you can imagine how much of a shock it was for me to have my landlord, with whom I'd never had problems before, wake me with her panicked screeching." Lilly inhales loud and deep, "So, Grams, it looks like I'm homeless suddenly, and if you'd like to help me understand why I'd really appreciate it."

The older woman responds, saccharine sweet smile heavily slathered across her face, "My dear, that sounds like a terrible way to start the day. It's a shame you weren't there tomorrow, during the fire and are here now, instead, while three strapping young men are able to help you get settled back in this house."

She looks pointedly in our direction, "You don't mind, do you boys? I'm sure it won't take you much time at all. I'd help, but I'm getting on in years now and my old bones just aren't what they used to be."

Kieran scrunches up his nose and purses his lips, clearly displeased with this turn of events. Zeke is still in his own investigative oblivion, scrutinizing the symbols etched within the golden band encircling our gift. I can't help but admire the masterful manipulation at work here.

"Why, and let a damsel in distress face her fate alone? Of course us dashing heroes are happy to rescue you in your hour of need," I say. "Just need to ring up the boss and let him know we'll be going on a side quest before returning to the kingdom."

Miss Fern smirks at me, "I had a feeling you'd say that."

38. DIZZY

Wetness and a powerful stench wake me from my cozy blanket burrito, courtesy of a wiggly white ball of pudge who apparently is tired of waiting for me to fulfill my promise. I wipe the growing sheen of slobber from my face and swat away the eager pooch, "I know kisses are apparently the stand-ard wakeup call in this house, but yours could use a little work, my dude."

It's a bit difficult to de-burrito-ify myself, and there's lots of rolling and flailing involved in attempting to best my clever blankety captors, but I eventually reign supreme and assert my dominance over the devious fabric. Standing, I'm a bit disappointed to find that, aside from the man still solidly out cold on the exam table and my tiny Frenchie terror, I've woken alone for the first time all week.

"Hey there handsome, you dreamin' up plans for our date today? Watching you sleep has been fascinating and not made me feel like a skeevy obsessed stalker or anything like that at all, but I wouldn't be opposed to seeing those gorgeous eyes of yours open up again. You know, whenever you're ready and such, but consider 'both of us conscious' as one of my baseline requests for this shindig."

The glow cocooning him is so faint, it may as well be nearly imaginary. Whatever magic juice I hit him with is theoretically just about done whatever it's been doing, which is probably quite a lot considering how good he looks. And smells. Even though he hasn't showered in days, he still smells fresh and warm, like slightly citrusy soap and clothes straight out of the dryer. His curly mop of blonde hair is springy and glossy, fair skin smooth, soft, and not splattered with sweat or blood. He looks just a peaceful as yesterday; my very own sleeping beauty.

Leaning down, I place a quick kiss on his lips, just in case that's how to break this spell. Either I'm not his true love, or fairytales are designed to encourage super creepy people who are suddenly glad they're alone with their embarrassment to smooch unsuspecting cuties while they sleep.

"I'll be back soon, don't go anywhere without me, okay?" Smoothing down his hair with one hand, I press my lips to his forehead for good measure. Can't be too careful when it comes to magic, I figure.

Stubbs, like the perv all animals seem to be, follows me across the hall into the bathroom as I take care of business and splash some water on my face to finish waking up. Note to self, probably a good idea to get a toothbrush soon so I don't start to give The Colonel a run for his money in the category of stankiest breath around town. Wouldn't want to break his heart by dethroning him, of course.

"Hello?" My voice sounds hollow as it echoes back through the empty house, "Olly olly oxen free?" No one jumps out from their hiding spot as we make our way down the hall to the kitchen. A folded piece of paper propped up against a crock pot on the counter is the only clue aliens hadn't abducted everyone while I was sleeping and they may have left of their own volition.

Dizzy,

Thanks for straightening me out last night, my thick head really needed it. The last couple of days have gotten me all caught up in my own mind and it's no excuse, but I'm sorry it affected you and everyone else. I'll do better to make sure we stick together through whatever comes from here on out, promise.

The guys left early to talk to some psychic in town who might be able to help us with our shadow problem. I'm not avoiding you, I promise, I'm just out back tending to the garden. Would love your company if you're up to rolling around in the dirt for a bit.

There's oatmeal in the crock pot, and baked apples in the oven. Please, feel free to do/eat/use whatever you'd like. We're all so happy to have you here, we want you to feel at home. I'm so happy to have you here.

-Monty

I fold the note and stick it in one of the pockets of my jacket; a treasure to to keep close when I need a little reminder of goodness. Surprisingly, the oatmeal is delicious and creamy, dotted with tender fruits and a hint of sweetness. Anyone who thinks porridge is a lame breakfast has clearly never had Monty in their house, so... probably just about everyone, in that case. So far, that man has put every tuna sandwich and pack of instant ramen I've ever made pretty darn well to shame. Maybe I can eat his brains and gain his knowledge? But brains are kind of icky, so maybe I'll just see if he can teach me something, instead. Making cookies with Connor turned out wayyyy better than expected, so maybe I'm not a complete loss in the kitchen, as long as I manage not to cause an actual catastrophe in the process!

After cleaning up, Stubbs and I pad out the sliding glass door and down the couple deck steps in search of a chef to kiss. The soft grass feels cool and pleasant between my toes, a crisp breeze licking my bare legs and lightly announcing the impending Autumn. It's still warm enough for dresses and light jackets, but in a month or two I'm going to seriously need to seek out a coat and scarf. Luckily, Lin gave me a sturdy pair of black lace-up boots with the clothes they got, so at least my feet won't freeze off as long as I'm not silly enough to keep up this barefoot practice after we get snow.

"Alright buddy," I bend down and ruffle the small dog's comparatively giant ears, "let's go get Monty! Maybe he'll want to play, too? Is he the playing type? Le gasp! He barely even got in on that game of tag the other day, didn't he? We are owed!"

Colonel Stubbs hops up and down in excitement, then darts to the right towards a huge space lined with raised wooden beds and smaller, ground-level areas sectioned off with stone paths. Squatting amongst the impressive plethora of vegetation, I see Monty in a big straw hat, digging through the dirt with flowery gardening gloves and Aria lounging lazily across his shoulders. Stubbs bounds right up to the man currently losing an argument with some weeds, trampling through what are probably a bunch of healthy and wanted plants on the way. You'd think with all this nature around, there'd be some sort of fence or something up but it looks like this is a household that's big on sharing.

"Wait up, you terror!" I shout while chasing after the godzilla all plants should fear will come and crush their societies beneath its scurrying bean-toes. At least I manage to keep to the stone paths in my charge towards Monty, though I did nearly manage to face plant into a pile of eggplants, the man himself pretty much being the only reason I didn't cause unnecessary vegetable carnage.

"Woah there," His hand clasping my shoulder is firm. So's the one that managed to stop my fall by grabbing ahold of one of my big ol' lady lumps. Monty clears his throat as I steady myself in a crouch, "It's, uh, good to see you both out here. Although it looks like the Colonel's not going to be much help, unless we're supposed to be going to war with the garden today?"

The aforementioned dog has sat his butt squarely onto the base of a pepper plant, snapping and then mauling the stalk with every happy wiggle of his whole body.

"Oh, come here you silly boy!" I hold out my hand and he hops up, yipping excitedly. "You've got to pay attention to where you step!" I'm just about the last person on the planet qualified to give advice on making sure not to break anything, though come to think of it, yesterday went relatively smoothly! Seriously, less damage done than normal, despite damage still being done.

Once I've scooped up the dangerous demon of happiness, I reach out and pinch the pepper stalk between my fingers, rubbing my thumb up and down along the worst of the damage. It begins to knit back together so I start to wave my hand in a beckoning motion, urging it to stand upright again. Ironically, the only reason I know how to get it to do this is because I've managed to smash, bash, and mash more than my fair share of poor, innocent plant-life and had to figure out some way to make amends. Can't be too upset at the little white Frenchie when I've totally done the same thing. Plus, no harm no foul and whatnot.

"Man, that's cool," Monty says. "You're really something

special, you know that, right?"

I roll my eyes, "Yeah, okay. It's not like the plants don't want to grow already, anyway. It's not a big deal to just remind them and let them do all the work themselves. I'm sure you could do it, too. Haven't you ever tried?"

Monty rubs his chin for a second, smearing his dark skin with a smudge of fresh soil. "Can you tell me how you do it?"

I point to a slightly less obliterated plant nearby, "Just talk to it. Tell it you want it to get better, and remind it what it's supposed to look like if it's having trouble."

"Umm... Okay. Uh, plant? Get better?" He puts his hand on the soil around the bent stalk, but nothing really happens. Maybe it moves a little? Probably just the wind.

I grab his hand and place his fingers on the bent portion, holding it there as I think about how the plant would look in its full glory, asking it if it wants any help, telling it I'll try my best to give it what it needs. It responds with a happy pulse of gratitude, then reinforces its wounds and begins to stand on its own again.

Monty's looking at me with a weirdly prideful expression, "Yeah, that was definitely special. I could... feel it. Feel you, and feel it. I don't know how you figured this out because it's definitely not like anything I've ever seen before, but I want to learn."

At first, it seems kind of strange to me that he'd think this is anything but normal boring everyday stuff, since I've been doing it for... well, a really long time at this point. But then I remember when he tried to teach me how to heal his cut, and I realize we basically speak magic in a different language.

"Remember how the other day you cut yourself and told me to send my energy out and use it to find out what's wrong and then fix the problem? It didn't really make sense to me because that's not how I do things, but right at the end I started to almost kinda sorta feel what you meant and maybe understand how to force your cut to heal with what was inside me." He nods as I continue, "Well, what I do isn't like that. I'm not telling things what to do, I'm asking them to do it. It's not like I'm pushing myself at the plant and forcing it to do anything it wouldn't want to in the first place, I'm just asking it to do it on its own. And if it needs me to, sometimes I can feel a bit of what's inside me going towards it but usually because it asks for it, not because I'm making it take what I have. It's like... we work together. Give, take; all of it's the same as long as we're both happy by the end."

Monty contemplates what I've said for a bit, and I get it now how weird what I'm saying must seem to him, since his method doesn't make a lot of sense to me, either.

"You're literally communing with nature," he says. "All that meditating and naked running through the woods to connect with the spirits inside of everything around us that people do to try and get back to their roots? That's what you're doing, but without any of the extra steps."

I shrug, "Yeah, that sounds right. Like I said, you just kind of ask the plant if it's up to doing whatever and then just let it do as it will. If it helps, it's basically the same as having a conversation with Stubbs, where you know what he's saying even though he doesn't speak human." I stand, brushing off the small bits of dirt that seem to have taken my brief garden visit as an opportunity to stow away on the S.S. Dizzy Jones towards a new destination. Stubbs jumps up and head butts my shin, yipping excitedly, "Anyway, I owe this tyrant some playtime, want to join us?"

His face withers, slightly apologetic, "Would it be okay if I stayed here instead? I've still got weeding and pruning to finish up, not to mention I'd really like to try and see if I can do what you just showed me."

There's a pretty substantial path of squashed and snapped foliage, courtesy of the overly-excited pupper presently licking the back of my calf. Even if he gets the hang of it, there's plenty of mending that needs to be done. I'd offer to help out so he's not here for a couple of hours by himself, but a promise is a promise. Besides, he's got Aria so he's not exactly all the way alone, though given how she's gone all boneless around his neck she may as well be a glorified scarf.

As though the black-furred beastie herself heard me thinking about her, she stretches out all four paws and flashes sharp teeth with a wide yawn before settling back down.

"Totally okay, but come and find me if you want to practice together?" I reach out to snag a few fistfuls of sugar snap peas from a trellised vine, collecting them in the skirt of my dress. "We've got some catch to play, right Stubbs?" He barks an affirmative, "Now don't squash the plants on your way out or Monty will be stuck here for the rest of his life fixing your mess!" I lean down and peck Monty's cheek, "Have fun, farm boy."

His laugh is booming as I chase Stubbs from the garden, "You too, nature girl!"

39. DIZZY

Probably the best part about playing fetch with snap peas is that even if your companion doesn't manage to catch it on the first go, they can just snuffle through the grass like a piggy and eat them anyway. And if one or two gets completely missed? No big deal, either! For such a stubby pup, though, Colonel Stubbs can catch a surprising amount of air when properly motivated by food. Maybe those giant ears work like tiny canine wings?

Properly sweatied up and ready to relax, I take a shower before heading back towards Monty's office to keep Connor company. Sure, he's not exactly talkative or anything but I like being near him, so sue me!

Lin's left a few of the books he was reading yesterday laying on Monty's desk, so I grab one and nestle between Connor and the wall, facedown on the exam bed he still hasn't moved from. Feet kicking in the air, I crack open *The Complete History of Shifters* and start reading aloud. The foreword is suuuuuper boring though, so I decide it's probably best to keep to myself all talk of where the author graduated, and how many methods of grass and bug food preparations they learned.

Eventually, they start to tell the actual history of shifters, which is what was promised by that title, and it's actually super interesting. Aside from Kieran, I've never met a shifter of any type in person, but it's not like they're some kind of secret from us human-types or anything.

"Woah! Did you know that the first shifters were animals that chose to take on human forms? I thought it was the other way around!"

"No, I didn't know that," Connor's soft voice whispers beside me.

Gasping, I practically tackle him, even though that should be nearly impossible given we're both lying down. "Connor! You're awake!"

"Oof," he lets out a hard breath as I slam into his torso.

"Oops! Sorry, too hard?" I start to pull back to let him up, but he wraps his right arm around my back and holds me loosely from where I have him pinned. "Gosh, good thing Aria wasn't here to see me practically attack you; she'd never let me off the hook after I wouldn't let her sleep on your chest last night."

Up to this point, Connor's mostly either been sleepily blinking his eyes or looking only at me, but something in his mind suddenly clicks and he dons a look of absolute panic, realizing our surroundings.

"Is everyone okay?" His arm around me stiffens slightly.

"Yeah, you just took the longest to wake up."

"Did I hurt anyone?" Pained look on his face, I feel the heartache in his hurried question. A question I don't for the life of me understand coming from such a gentle soul.

"What? No! You were the only one that got hurt! Apparently Monty and I double-teamed some kind of super healing magic on you and just conked out for a bit, but you got freakin' stabbed so of course it took you two days to come back to us!"

Relief washes over his features in a wave, but I'm still not sure why this was something he felt the need to know.

"Why'd you think anyone else was hurt?"

He whispers even quieter than usual, "Because the last time I gave in to the nightmares, I killed someone." There's a lot of pain in the haunted expression I catch as he turns his face away.

"Oh, no, Connor, we're fine. We're all fine! Even you're all healed up." Wanting to reassure him, I pull down the blanket and run my hand over his bare stomach, an extremely faint scar the only hint that anything even happened. One scar, I notice, among dozens faintly texturing his torso. "So don't worry about it, everything's good now. I promise, everybody's totally okay. Oh, I bet the guys will be thrilled to see you up again!" My fingers still lightly trace the lines marking his skin, hopping from one to another and memorizing the raised feel of them. The feel of him. I don't know where they came from or why he has them, but they're a part of this sweet man beside me, so there's no way in hell I'd think they're hideous. Scars are proof we've survived something that tried to break us, but failed.

Connor gives a weak smile, "Sorry if I scared you."

I rest my head on his chest and we lay like that for a while, his hand on my back tracing patterns as mine does the same on his chest. Even though we're both quiet, it's comforting being there together, awake and alive and in the same number of pieces we started the day out as.

Eventually, I tilt my head to look up at him, "What did you mean by last time?"

For a long while, he's completely silent, hands stilling their subconscious glide across my skin. Just as I start to worry this was exactly the wrong question to ask and I need to divert to something completely different, like how I shot a fireball from my hands a couple of days ago, he takes in a breath and starts talking.

"Growing up, my parents were... not the best. They were addicts, but they were also dealers who snorted and shot more of the product than what they sold." His voice is monotone as he speaks, almost as though he's completely removing himself from the story. "They always needed more money, so dad started to pimp mom out. For years, random men would come into our trailer and have sex with my mother so both my parents could keep getting high. There wasn't anywhere for me to go, so I'd hide under the sink or behind the sofa until it was safe to come out.

"Even when the strangers were gone, it still wasn't really safe. Dad had a temper even at the best of times, but it was always worse if he was drunk or high. For the most part, I tried to keep myself quiet and tucked away so he wouldn't notice me that often, but there weren't too many places to go in such a small space. He always found me, eventually.

"I've always had bad nightmares, really bad, but they started to turn into something else as my abilities developed. At first, being able to hide myself in plain sight was a blessing, especially if I could build a world around me to help block out reality. Escaping was sometimes the only way to stay safe, even if it was completely a fantasy.

"But then I realized that, sometimes, I could make my illusions real. Just small things here and there, like a toy or pen or cup, but they went from being things that only moved as long as I specifically told them what to do, to being real items that other people could touch and feel and move around as long as I kept letting them exist.

"Eventually, I started spending so much time in my fantasies that I stopped being sure about what was real or not, because anything was real as long as I thought about it hard enough.

"That's about when the nightmares started to become real, too. Every now and then I'd see one slip out and do something, even though I never wanted them around, let alone tried to make them real. They became stronger and stronger, and it got to the point where I had to force them to *not* exist, which took so much thought that I stopped being able to hide myself away quite as well. More and more, the worlds I'd build around myself were transparent and flimsy from the inside, and I was forced to face the reality of living in a single-room trailer with two drug-addicted parents who turned tricks on the side."

His voice starts to quiver, but I don't dare move or say anything to interrupt him, not even as his eyes clearly start to water and threaten to spill.

"I was twelve when they brought home a man who offered them something in exchange for having sex with my mother. Some kind of drug they hadn't tried yet, or hadn't for a while, or didn't usually get. Whatever it was, they took it before... well, they took it before. In the main room, where I was.

"As soon as they came in, I'd already hidden myself in one of the corners and put up a camouflage, but holding back the nightmares kept my illusion too weak to stop me from seeing and hearing everything.

"I watched them get high. I watched the man have sex with my mother on the couch. And I watched my father break open a bottle on the table and stab it into the man's neck while he fucked my mother. My father stabbed him over and over and over again, screaming that my mother was a cheating whore and he knew she was turning against him to leave and take everything he'd worked for. He yelled for me to come out, but I was so scared I couldn't even move, so he accused her of turning me against him, saying he knew I was someone else's bastard and he was going to make her pay for making him look like a fool by taking away both her babies tonight.

"My mother was stuck under the bloody man, but my father grabbed her arm and dragged her out and across the floor, so close to where I was even though they couldn't see me. She tried to hit and fight back, and kept yelling for me to run but I was stuck and completely helpless."

He's still talking, but his face is slick with thick rivers of tears, his breaths between words more erratic.

"Already, she was so covered in blood, right there in front of me. I didn't think there was any way there could be more, until my father stabbed her in the stomach. Her scream visits me, sometimes, like a ghost that will haunt me for all time. Every single time he shoved that broken bottle into her, more blood and more screams painted the room... until they didn't.

"I sat, huddled in a corner, coated in my own mother's blood for seconds? Minutes? Hours? I don't know how long. Time stopped, and all that was left was fear as my father started swinging his broken glass around the room, yelling for me to come out.

"It got so hard to do anything except panic, and I knew the moment whatever illusion I had up dropped the second he finally looked right at me and roared that he was going to kill me, too. I couldn't move, couldn't do anything, couldn't even think any more. The nightmares pushed hard against me, and I didn't have any kind of will left to stop them.

"Everything went dark. I don't know if I closed my eyes, or if I passed out, but I felt the nightmares leave me. Sometimes I think I heard my father screaming, sometimes I think it was me instead.

"When I was finally back to myself, there wasn't anything in that whole trailer that wasn't covered in blood. Especially me.

"I found parts of my father everywhere. They'd completely ripped him to pieces right in front of me and I don't even re-member seeing it. But I know I'm the one who made it hap-pen."

He stops talking and closes his eyes, another wave of tears escaping down his cheeks and disappearing into his hair. I scoot up on the bed a little, laying my face even to his, placing a hand to his jaw and turning his head so I can look him in the eyes as we lay side-by-side.

For a while, I smooth out his hair and wipe his cheeks dry even as the tears continue to fall. When I place my lips on his forehead, the strangled sob he tries to hold back shakes me. Even while crying, he's trying to be as quiet as possible because making noise, taking up space, being out in the open wasn't allowed. He hides himself away because it's the only way he knows how to survive.

"Sometimes, I have flashbacks. Lin helps me break out of them when they're really bad, but I couldn't do anything about it the night I got stabbed. The blood... There was so much blood. I can never forget it. And I know it, I felt myself give in to the nightmares again."

I kiss his tear-soaked cheek, its saltiness flavoring the pain I wish I could take away. "You're okay now. We're together. We're safe. There's no nightmares."

His large, turquoise eyes meet mine, boring into my soul like they always do. "I dreamed about you," he says. "You were glowing and golden and beautiful. You're already beautiful, I mean, but the glowing was new and amazing."

Wiping one last tear from his cheek, I reach across his chest and lace the fingers of my right hand through those of his left. "You were glowing too, you know. You looked like an angel." Pressing my forehead to his, I close my eyes, "I was so worried about you when you got stabbed. We all were." With an ex-hale, I let the moment pass and try to shake us out of this funk. "But hey, it's Friday and you owe me a date, mister. You aren't even the first guy to use almost dying as a way of getting out of it so that's not going to work this time!"

He cocks his eyebrow slightly at me, but doesn't ask about the dying thing. "I was thinking about seeing if you wanted to paint with me, but I really just want to spend time with you. What do you want to do?" Throughout our whole conversa-tion, his right hand never left its place on my back, but the more lighthearted topic seems to have made him remember the contact, resuming its exploratory motions.

Leaning in, I nuzzle the side of his neck and squeeze my arm against his chest. "I really missed you. Pretty much the whole time you were out I've been right here, but it hasn't been the same as actually being with you." Sweetly, our lips meet for a soft kiss as I close my eyes and speak against them, "And I was so worried that when the glow ran out you'd just be dead." My heart stutters at the thought, but I kiss him again to reassure it that no such thing came to pass. "But you're not. It was so scary when we thought you were dead, though." I let go of his hand and raise myself up to slap his chest, "Don't you ever get stabbed again!"

Connor chuckles softly, "Okay, I'll do my best."

"I mean it Connor, never again!" I raise my hand to slap his chest again, but he catches my wrist before it makes contact and raises it to his lips, kissing the heel of my palm.

"I'm sorry I scared you, Dizzy." He tugs gently on my arm, pulling me closer as he kisses up my arm, never breaking eye contact. "I promise I'll do my best." His lips butterfly against my skin as they work their way ever higher, climbing towards the sensitive nook of my shoulder. "Thank you for caring about me." Still, he continues along my clavicle, up my neck, until our mouths meet in a long, slow kiss. Even with the added strength he puts between our lips in this moment of clear wanting, it's still a heart-wrenchingly sweet movement.

A slow warmth spreads through my body, as though I've lowered myself into a hot tub of desire while Connor's hand on my back increases the pressure of its strokes. Up and down, up and down, along my spine; each movement building the heat blooming inside us both. Connor touches me in a reverential way that is both controlled and worshipful and makes me feel as though I'm special to him; as though he's never met anyone like me before. Which, yeah, fair enough, but that hasn't really meant anything even remotely good to anyone in a long, long time.

Another little piece of my heart clicks back into place with each oath our lips make to one another. I promise to care about you, I promise to protect you, I promise to keep you; each kiss says something different, and I melt at every new pledge.

My whole body is flooded with heat, and I realize that our caressing has started to travel and explore the canvas of each other's skin. I've somehow ended up with one hand in his wild blonde mane, one leg hiked up and draped over his hip as Connor's finger's skim the curve of my own. We meld ourselves closer and closer in an attempt to not only learn everything about one another, but to become one being with no end or beginning between us.

Slowly, the hand still stroking my back lifts up the hem of my yellow dress and seeks access to bare skin but is denied. There are too many layers in the way, so I sit up, shifting my weight until I'm fully straddling him across his abdomen as both of Connor's hands effortlessly glide to my waist.

There's nothing but adoration in his eyes and I look down at the man beneath me, watching as I slowly peel off my jacket and drop it to the floor. When I crash back down to devour his mouth with mine, his hands slide their way back up my dress, demanding access to the touch they were denied in an ever more insistent but careful manner.

Despite the fact that I can feel his want growing firm in his jeans, rubbing against me with every barely conscious movement of our hips, this feels different than the times I've fooled around with the others. They're usually hot and heavy, commanding in the way they lead our movements, but this is sweet and slow and sort of... loving. Unhurried. Exploratory. Like he's memorizing the exact taste, texture, and scent of every inch of me beneath his fingertips. It isn't any less filled with passion than the others, just in a quieter and more worshipful way.

I have never felt more special, more appreciated, or more desired than I have in this moment; here on an exam bed with a man who just dodged death and should probably not get up to anything too frisky but with whom I definitely want to get a bit frisky. I don't just want to be glad Connor's alive, I want to celebrate it, and celebrate it with him; show him exactly how special he is in this wild and crazy thing we call life.

So I just go for it, because why not, right? Take the happy where you can get it.

I sit up again and timidly lift the bottom edge of my already bunched-up dress, biting my lip as I peel it the rest of the way off my body. In this moment, I'm not really sure what protocol is, but I figure less clothes is at least a solid start.

"I… Ummm…" Connor's brows are knitted together and his cheeks are bright red as he looks away, causing my heart to stutter at the worry that I've somehow read things terribly wrong.

My stomach flips and I'm horrified as I prepare for the rejection, "Oh god, I'm sorry, did I interpret this wrong? Should I have asked? I'm making you uncomfortable and you were too nervous I'd go full psycho to say anything. You don't want to get involved with me, I totally get it, I'm just going to go bury myself in a hole forever." I'm so embarrassed. Kill me now, please; just strike me down with a frozen astronaut turd falling from the skies at high velocity for making an utter fool of myself on top of this sweet and gorgeous man. Burying my hands in my head, I start to try and shift off of my place above him, but his hands on my hips grip me just slightly, pressing me down against him and keeping us connected.

"No! No, I just…" His voice trails off as he looks anywhere but at me, "I've never done this before. I didn't want to disappoint you is all, if I'm not as good as… anyone." He says this last part with a wince, not entirely sure of how I'll react to his confession or what my expectations are. I realize he's feeling exactly as scared as I was just a second ago, thinking he wanted nothing to do with me and like an utter fool.

A huge weight is lifted from my chest, because I can relate so hard to probably everything going on in his head. "Same, though. I'm… I've… I'm a virgin, too." And honestly, it's a relief knowing that we'll both be each other's first. Immediately, I can see it on his face that he's a bit more at ease hearing that there isn't any pressure. If we make it out of this without too much fumbling or breaking our tailbones when we fall out of the bed it'll be some kind of miracle.

"We don't have to if you don't…"

"I do, I do! Unless you don't?" He says.

And I know for sure there's no one I'd rather have pop my cherry than Connor, right here, right now. Though I really wish we had a condom. Like, really wish we had that protection because we may both be disease-free virgins but I'll be damned if we don't have safe sex and end up with a different kind of "first" nine months down the line. I'm about to ask if he knows where we can find a condom, when one just appears in my hand.

Thank you, crazy random magic and your perfect timing.

"I definitely do, too," I hold the foil packet up in response.

My heart warms as he smiles at me, mouth slightly agape at my super cool trick and how awesome I obviously am. He waves his hand slightly and my bra unhooks itself, floating off to wherever clothes float to as he grins at his own super cool trick. Both his hands slide up the outside of my thighs while he admires my body, causing me to giggle a bit nervously despite feeling completely at ease in his hands.

When he reaches my ribs, one hand curves around my back and the other continues its path upward, lightly tracing the curve of my breast, making sure to graze my nipple along the way. Still delicately teasing my skin with his long fingers, Connor tucks some hair behind my ear and beams at me earnestly.

"Wow. I can't believe how lucky I am to be here with you," he says while pulling me down closer to him, the tips of my nipples brushing against his bare chest as I pause to also appreciate how lucky I am for a moment.

When our lips finally meet again, this time we kiss with more purpose; no longer asking and exploring, but with a clear understanding of what each of us wants, and wants now. Our urgency builds, both picking up the pace and increasing the pressure of every movement our mouths and hands make in the frenzy.

I push his face to the side and trail a line of firm kisses along his long jaw, pausing at his ear to gently bite on the plump lobe. He lets out a soft moan and I feel his hips tilt up beneath me, urging me on to give him another nip before continuing my path downward.

He rakes one hand down my back and grabs my ass as I begin to creep down his body, lips trailing the path of his neck and torso as my dampened panties slide along the length of the hard bulge in his pants. Just that contact alone sends a warm wave of wanting fluttering through me, and my hands feel like they're attached to a useless idiot as I fumble with the button of Connor's jeans beneath me. I'm desperate to uncover the prize inside his denim wrapper, but lust and the rough movements of my pussy against his thighs as I ride him off to nowhere have me at a loss for how simple things like clothing are supposed to function.

Connor takes mercy on us both and flicks a finger in the air, popping open the fastening in an instant. Then, he leans up slightly and reaches out towards me to drag a single digit down the center of my chest, commanding his zipper to lower with the same motion. The moment his finger makes contact with my soaked underwear, his fly is fully opened. I raise myself slightly to better tug off his pants and he uses that opportunity to slide his hand in the gap between us, pressing firmly against the outside of the moist fabric acting as a flimsy barrier between his fingers and my pleasure. This time, I'm the one who moans as he slowly rubs his hand back and forth over my wanting heat. Each pass sends a shiver up my spine and I find myself pressing down on his hand in a desperate plea for more.

I've completely forgotten about trying to pull off his pants and am frozen in the palm of his hand as he strokes it against me. I want him; I want him so badly it's all I can think about right now, if the clenching of my empty heat and the fizzles in my brain can be considered thinking.

He turns a finger under the edge of my panties, finally making direct contact with my skin and slipping his touch along my slickness. Connor's gaze is heated, locked firmly on the slit he's spreading my wetness around as though it is the sexiest thing he's ever seen. From my perspective, the way his cock twitches in time with his movements, jumping every time he glances over my clit and makes my breath stutter, is the sexiest thing I've ever seen.

I lean back on my heels slightly, giving him better access to my aching heat, which he easily slides a long, slender finger into. I want to watch him watch himself pleasure me, but my head tilts back on its own as he slowly begins to pump inside me, adding a second finger within moments. Moaning, I close my eyes at the building pressure his movements gift me with, each stroke pushing deeper and deeper, making my hips grind against him as though he were fucking me with more than his hand.

I gasp as he curls his fingers just slightly, hitting a spot inside of me that sends a jolt of electricity straight up my spine. He notices immediately and does it again, and again, and again, until my entire body is burning with anticipation and need.

The muscles in my core squeeze his fingers with every stroke, begging him to never stop, and I know he's going to make me come without even finishing taking off his pants at this rate.

With the hand not buried inside me, he pushes himself up on the bed and kisses my exposed neck without pausing his rhythm in the slightest. I'm moaning shamelessly as he starts to increase the pace of his thrusts, slamming hard enough to hit my mound with the heel of his palm every time. Each movement steals a gasp from my throat and I reach up my own body to pinch my nipples, fully lost in the electric sensations Connor is sending coursing through me. When I feel his lips bat aside my hand and lock onto my breast, I nearly lose myself completely.

"Oh, yes! Oh, god, Connor, yes," I'm somewhere between moaning and screaming as he bites my nipple at the same time as thrusting his fingers inside of me. The sharp but perfect pain at my breast, the curved digits inside of me putting pressure on my g-spot, and his palm slamming my clit all in sync with each other sends me crashing over the edge into an orgasm that is so much better than any I've ever given to myself. The feeling of my muscles tightening around his fingers inside me as he slows his movements continues to draw out my pleasure in languid waves. I can feel my heart pounding in my chest, which Connor is still sucking and biting in time with the contractions of my pussy around his fingers.

For a few moments I bask in the slow, pulsing euphoria of aftershocks before opening my eyes and looking down to see Connor smiling around the teeth clamped to my nipple.

I pull his face up and claim those smug lips with my own, thanking him and asking for more with each kiss I grind forcefully into him. Our tongues and teeth clash in a way that builds desperate. I plan to fuck the hell out of my man for that orgasm he just gave me, if I can figure out how to get him naked.

"Pants. Off." I gasp out between kisses, and I feel the fabric on his legs practically shoot down them with the force of a rocket. I reach between us and grasp his long, hard cock in my hand, pumping it a few times while our tongues tangle in a preview of what our bodies are about to do.

Somehow, I've managed to not drop the condom this whole time and I hand it to him, watching him rip it open as I work to take off my practically ruined panties. In my haste to undress from my awkward position straddling him, I very nearly topple over and fall to my doom, but Connor catches me like it's nothing, righting me and righting my world. His steadying hold is firm, but not as firm as the exquisite love stick gliding along the entrance to my fuck cave. This is good. This is a good man, and a good idea, and good god does that feel good, but a word better than good that my brain is far too fizzled out right now to find.

The moment when I stop fucking around and start actually fucking is like a revelation. Tiny, chubby baby angels come out to sing praises for Connor's cock sinking deep, deep, deee-eeeeep into my hungry pussy, gobbling it all up like a greedy bitch at a hot dog buffet. He groans beneath me at the same moment I gasp sharply, both of us surprised and delighted to feel him hit the absolute end of my wet channel. No vibrator, dildo, or fingertip could ever prepare me for the electric shock of having Connor's length easily test my limits with each movement along his shaft.

Slowly, at first, I move up and down, enjoying the moment most when I'm fully seated on him and he's fully extended in me. But one accidental roll of my hips as I ride him and I'm suddenly realizing there's a whole range of motions to explore and experience. I swear, every time I slam down on him I start to feel it in some new and unexpected place, like the tips of my toes and the roots of my hair. Greedily, I lean down and snatch his hungry lips with my own, stealing every soft noise he makes and drowning it out with my own.

The new angle is a revelation, his magnificent fucking man sausage rubbing against my swollen clit with every movement we make. It's almost more than I can take, and I feel the muscles inside my core squeezing him harder and harder with each surge. My fingers start clawing at his chest, desperate to find a way to express the pleasure the rest of my body is writhing with but having no words other than the scratching of nails against flesh.

When Connor bucks up beneath me while I ride him, I'm not ashamed to say I learned about myself that I am capable of some of the most unladylike grunting in the world. His thrusting starts tentatively, but just like he noticed curling his fingers inside of me was making me burn with pleasure, he damn well noticed that fucking me even while I was on top was a winning strategy.

Growing bold, Connor shoves my head to the side with his mouth, kissing his way down to my earlobe as well and giving it a bite, just as I had for him. But what really sends shivers up my spine is when he rakes his teeth along the entire length of my neck, pausing to nip at the tender flesh every now and then. Each sharp tease causes my hips to jump involuntarily, which only eggs him on more and more, slamming his magic dick harder and harder into me, wiping out all traces of the shy, quiet man who was here just a few minutes ago. Suddenly, there's a sex wizard in the room and he's cast a spell on my being to make me pulse with need from every nerve ending in my body.

While my hands have been busy marking up every inch of him with angry red lines, he's been tugging, pulling, twisting, spanking everything within reach. Each little pinch sends out a spark from wherever it started, straight to the center of my cave of wonders, filling my treasure hoard of pleasure more and more until I can't remember there ever being a moment that didn't feel so shiny and glittering and gold.

"I'm so close... oh, fuck, how are you so good?" I'm practically screaming as I feel my orgasm approach, just over the edge of a cliff right in front of me.

Connor jolts upright, still inside of me as I straddle him, and pushes my shoulders hard, slamming my back onto the bed. From above me, he has a wicked grin on his face as he takes over, thrusting into me like a jackhammer that other jackhammers aspire to grow up and become some day.

The sudden show of dominance from my previously timid man, his slender fingers traveling down to circle my pulsing clit, the taste of his tongue as he shoves it in my mouth and slams his cock into my pussy with wild abandon is all too much.

"I'm going to come. Oh, god, Connor, fuck fuck fuck, aaa-aaaah!" This time, I am actually screaming as I feel my back arch, my toes curl, and my cunt clamp down on his magnificent member at the same time as I am yet again given an orgasm better than I've ever experienced before, including the first one he gave me just minutes ago.

He's still pumping into me and it's making my fingers feel all tingly and magical and warm until I feel him thrust one final, deep time and hold himself inside me, gorgeous turquoise eyes rolling back into his head, blonde hair wild and mussed and sexy as hell above me. I grin dopily, watching him come inside me from the blissful haze of my own release.

We're both panting, but lost for a moment in the feelings and experience. Finally, we look at each other and I giggle just a bit before he lowers himself against me, sweetly kissing my lips like the gentle man I knew before he went berserk and fucked my brains right out of my ears. If I look around enough, I'm sure I'll find them puddled on the floor somewhere. I'd swear he's an angel, glowing above me again in brighter colors than the world used to use, but I'm pretty sure that's just the sex stupids talking.

Connor slides his cock out, laying down beside me and rolling us both so we're facing one another. I'm glad he did that, because I'm pretty sure I've got noodle arms right now and definitely wouldn't have been strong enough for such a coordinated task.

I am coordinated enough to wrap those noodles around him and kiss him a few times, though. When I rest my head on his chest, I sigh in contentment, feeling especially good when he presses his lips to the top of my head and wraps me up tightly in his arms.

"Well, I definitely liked that. A lot. I liked it a lot. I like you a lot. I like to like things a lot." I'm rambling, my nonsense peppered with random giggles. What am I even saying, here?

He hums, and I feel the vibration of his contentment from deep within his chest. "I agree. I agree a lot." I'm pretty sure I feel him smile against my hair, but that might just be my imagination.

40. KIERAN

It's a complete relief when we pull up to our own driveway, hours after we expected to be home. Finally, it feels like I can breathe again.

"Honey, we're home!" Lin shouts as we walk through the front door. There's laughter coming from the kitchen, and right away I recognize Connor's subdued chuckle beneath the sudden shushing.

"Nobody's here, come back later you scoundrels and thieves!" Dizzy responds playfully.

"Then I suppose we must be speaking with the ghost of the household?" Lin fires back.

As we enter the kitchen, Dizzy thrusts her hands out in our direction quickly. "Boo!" She exclaims, really only causing Connor, who's practically plastered to her side, to flinch.

Seeing them both alive and well has my insides twisting and untwisting in a way I don't fully understand, but I know this is a good thing. My pace doesn't slow as I storm up behind them and wrap both in a fierce hug, sticking my head directly between theirs. Dizzy's happiness and contentment ribbon their way through me and take the edge off of some of this anxiety I can't seem to shake. Having the whole pack together feels more right than anything else could, which helps that twisting in my gut calm down a bit more.

"Now now, hunk and a half, you can't hog all the beauties in the room to yourself." Lin strides up to us and clutches Connor's head to his chest "Welcome back, hot cakes. And you," I hear her heart rate increase as Lin plucks Dizzy's hand from Connor's lap and presses a kiss to the back of it, "parting from you was such sweet sorrow. I do hope you managed to greet this stud muffin magnificently in our absence." When Lin nips at one of Dizzy's fingertips, Connor is the one to blush but I scent arousal from all three.

"How'd it go with the psychic?" Monty pipes up from where he's leaning back against the far counter.

Zeke places the black box in front of him, opening it to reveal the clear stone inside. "She gave us this." He gives a brief rundown of how it works, displaying the necessary movements to either dispel a shadow or trap one.

"Obviously, the most sensible course of action is to use it to ensnare your stalker, Love, and rid ourselves of him so his vile misdeeds can't threaten us any longer," Lin says.

"Woah, woah, who says David's my stalker?" Dizzy snatches her hand from Lin's and holds it up defensively, "I haven't seen him in years, this could just be a coincidence! A really shitty, really convenient, kind of scary coincidence. Maybe he's just passing through and decided to get a little stabby with you guys even though you're strangers and..." Her voice trails off for a second before she sighs, shoulders collapsing in defeat. "Yeah, that doesn't make any sense. But why would he be stalking me after all this time?"

"His ritual failed," Zeke states plainly, as though it's obvious what he means by that.

Monty cocks his eyebrow, "You're going to have to explain that one a bit, buddy."

"The ritual he attempted to perform on your birthday."

Dizzy's back shoots straight up, rattling the teeth in my head as her shoulder blasts into my chin. I bristle at the twisted feeling of her anxiety and confusion suddenly assaulting my own emotions. "No, shut up, what?"

"Midnight on your sixteenth birthday. Candles. Cloths with symbols on them. It was obviously a ritual, and judging from the reaction of his mother they had both been grooming you for it."

Stunned, she stops breathing. "Is that... is that really... But... Why? He wouldn't... Could he? David wasn't... was he? But, why?" Her words and thoughts seem to tumble over one another as she struggles to resolve the memories of a friend she grew up with against Zeke's implication of betrayal.

A fiery rage of my own making burns inside me as her fear and sadness make themselves known through our link, burrowing a nauseating sickness into my stomach and stabbing icy claws into my chest. For the first time all week, my own emotions are stronger than hers and of course it's because I'm fucking pissed for her.

"This motherfucker has another thing coming if he thinks he'll ever get another chance," I growl out, my hold on Dizzy tightening fiercely. "I'll rip his fucking throat out if he even tries landing a finger on you, Fireball. What kind of sick fuck chases someone around for 12 years? That's some serial killer bullshit right there and I'll be damned if his twisted ass gets away with that shit in my backyard, with any of my pack."

"Then we're back where we started," Lin delicately strokes Dizzy's arm from his place beside Connor, "We trap him with the stone and take him out of the picture."

"Lin... Are you seriously suggesting we kill a man we don't even know?" Monty frowns as he asks the question.

"I'm saying we do what it takes to defend ourselves," he replies, right as I growl out a "Yes."

On top of everything else, the horrified look on Dizzy's face grows and she pushes me off of her, yanking her arm out of Lin's reach at the same time. "What the hell?! Murder isn't one of those things you just casually bring up at the lunch table! We don't even really know what he wants, or why!"

"He almost killed Connor!" I yell, and I know it's an over-reaction due to her shock mixed with my rage, but it's what's driving me anyway.

She swivels around on her stool to look at me, and I know she's as pissed as I am but for different reasons, "So you think it's okay to take an almost kill and turn into an actual one?! You don't know him like I do, David isn't like that!"

"You don't know him like you think you do! I was fucking there, and it was the scariest damned shit seeing Connor bleeding out on the goddamned ground like that. Does he just get a pass for that? Connor survived, so everything's just fine and dandy? If anyone else had done it, would it still even be a question?"

"Yes, it would still be a question!" She jumps up and pushes me back hard, "I don't care who it is, I'm not killing anybody for any reason, especially not someone I know, and double especially not without knowing why they're even here or what they're doing in the first place!"

"HOW CAN I KEEP YOU SAFE IF HE'S STILL OUT THERE!?!" I'm screaming at her, furious for reasons she doesn't understand yet, "I can't lose another pack. I can't. I will do anything, ANYTHING, to protect Mine. We know he did it, and I don't care why; he will not get a second chance to take away anyone I care about." My face is hot, and I can practically feel my eyes trying to pop out of my head with rage. I clench my fists by my side and close my eyes, trying to let out a breath and bring myself back under control. Right beneath the surface, my wolf is howling for blood and I want to give it to him; give it to us both.

When I open my eyes, I see her approaching me carefully, the anger she was shooting back at me tempered somewhat with concern. Delicately, almost afraid that I might snap at her, she places her hand on my shoulder and I feel shame that she could ever fear me more than an actual fucking threat. This is one of my worst nightmares come true; being the kind of monster that can't make his pack safe at all times. I should never be the reason any of them feels dread, never.

"Hey there, Beefcake, you okay?"

I go to answer, but realize my jaw has shifted and I'm no longer able to use words. Perfect. Just fucking perfect. A knife twists in my heart, knowing I've stepped way out of line but not being able to do anything about it right now. Burying myself deeper in remorse, I yank off my shirt and kilt and finish the transformation, letting my wolf out fully to stop myself from being any more of an asshole. The only thing I can think to do is hang my head, tuck my tail, and dig a hole to hide in.

Dizzy's golden legs fold up into my view, positioning herself to sit right in front of me. She touches one of my forelegs,

"Hey now, don't you go hiding from me." I avoid her gaze, but she grabs my muzzle and forces me to look at her with a yank. "Sounds a lot like there's something you need to let out. I get it; I'm carrying around some shit, too, and it messes with me sometimes, but I'm not okay with you killing anyone. Especially someone I know, and double especially because I can't live with not knowing why he's here. Or if Zeke's right, or if he was ever my friend at all. At the very least, you can't lay a finger or claw on him until I get some answers, okay?"

I whine a response, hoping it conveys how anxious I am about the idea that someone dangerous is out there, and how much I disagree with this even though a part of me knows she's right. Dizzy runs her hand over my head, flattening out the wild fur near my ears.

"I know it's hard. I can see you really want to protect us, but we're safer together, I think, and that means our decisions have to be made and agreed on as a team, too." She looks around the room, "You've all spent days trying to convince me that we're in this together, that I don't need to run away to solve my problems and keep people safe, so let's keep each other safe without abandoning any kind of morals."

She doesn't say it out loud, but I know that if any of us crosses the line she's laid down in the sand, she'll fucking bolt. It sets my teeth on edge knowing that there's some psycho out there with a hard-on for hurting people, but having my teeth on edge is better than being completely gutted at her running and it being my fucking fault. This goes against all the instincts of an alpha, but the goal is always to keep the pack safe and together. If killing this shitheel weakens the integrity of the pack, then it's off limits. Besides, I'm not an alpha here; it's not my job to keep the pack in line.

"Diz, I'm on board with you," Monty leans forward, "we stick together and agree on the best thing for everyone. But

I'm telling you now, and I think this goes for all of us, if it comes down to him or any one of us, I'm not willing to let it be us."

She looks back at him for a long moment before finally responding, "Deal." From her, I feel a wave of acceptance; not the kind that opens your heart up to the future but closes it off, like someone marching towards a firing squad they've resigned themselves to.

"Well then, what's our plan to capture the threat and not kill him or get killed by him? Any bright ideas in those clever heads of yours?" Lin asks the room.

With more confidence than I ever saw coming, Connor speaks up from his seat, "We split up." Dizzy gives him a look that could strip paint, which pretty much mirrors my own thoughts. After all this, that's his first suggestion? Is he fucking kidding me right now?

"Are you fucking kidding me right now?" That's my girl. I shove my muzzle into her hand in agreement, gladly accepting her aggressive petting.

"Both times he's been bold enough to make a move, we've been split up into smaller groups. It's been just Lin and me, actually, and maybe that's for a reason? He either thinks he can take us specifically, or it's just been coincidence as far as when opportunity strikes but that's all we have to go on so far. Our best bet is to make him think the odds are in his favor and split up."

"He's right," Zeke agrees, "It's a small sample size but that is a commonality."

"If Lin and I break off from the group again, he may come for us. I can hide the rest of you so he doesn't realize we aren't alone, but this could be the best way to draw him out."

Monty slams his fist down on the counter, causing Connor to jump, "I'm not putting you in danger like that!"

"We know to be on guard this time so he can't surprise us, and I trust the rest of you to keep us safe if we can't do it ourselves." Connor's tone is even, despite the room's building aggression.

"And why couldn't it be me and Kier instead? We've at least got fight experience! Or Z, with his damned arsenal of spell tats and jewelry?"

Lin scoffs, "I've got plenty of fight skills, thank you very much."

"Have any of you seen him?" Connor sits up straight with conviction, "Because I've seen or sensed him every single time. I'm just about the only person here he couldn't sneak up on, now. It has to be me."

"Then it's you and me, bro. No exceptions." Monty asserts, "If you're putting yourself in the line of fire, then I'm right there with you, or we're digging a moat around the house and never leaving again. That's the only way it happens, or it doesn't happen at all. It would kill me to stand by and watch you put yourself up to be bait without me by your side."

Connor nods. Dizzy leaps up from where she's been sitting in front of me, fingers unburying themselves from the thick scruff around my neck as she practically tackles him.

There's a solid thwack as she slaps Connor hard on the chest, "You promised me."

"I promised I'd try my best. I'm keeping that promise." He grabs her hand and kisses the inside of her wrist, "Let me do my part to help all of us." With an intense intimacy, Connor locks eyes with Dizzy and holds her captive with his gaze, "Can you let me try?"

She glares at him, but I feel the turbulent sea of her emotions threatening to beat a warpath from her chest and drown the whole damned world. Anger, fear, hurt, sadness, worry, and the smallest kernel of hope fight for dominance inside of her. She looks between Connor and Monty, "Keep each other safe or so help me if one of you ends up dead I'll suddenly learn necromancy, bring you back to life, chew you out for being goddamned idiots, and then kill you myself."

"I promise," Monty says. He eyes me and nods in a beckoning way, so I shift back and rejoin the group. "Now, let's work out the details. All of them. And then work them out again until we have a backup to our backup's backup plan. We're doing this, but we're not doing it dumb."

41. CONNOR

"Wife!" Dizzy bounds up to the bar top at The Wood Liquor and practically jumps over it to tackle Lilly with a hug. The skirt of her yellow dress flounces and catches the wind like the mesmerizing undulations of a summery jellyfish. "I thought I'd never see you again, but here you are, and here I am, and here we all are! Isn't it cool?"

They banter back and forth, catching one another up as much as they can over the thunderous jubilation of a Saturday night crowd. Knowing Lilly is an ally is a comfort as she's taken precautions tonight to aid us in our attempt to subdue this shadow man, David, by warding the bar against him. Sure enough, the moment we left the house I immediately sensed his presence, this time tracking his movements with intention rather than ignoring them as the misguided imaginings of my overactive mind. As promised by our silver-haired bartender, the moment we entered her pub, David's influence disappeared. A part of me worries that he'll suspect something by being barred entry to a previously accessible space, but another part of me is grateful that there are more safe places and safe people we can interact with, even if nothing happens tonight.

Kieran is ripping apart a napkin into tiny pieces at the table we've claimed; a snow drift of his anxieties piling up into a Winter wonderland of worries beneath his fingertips. "How is she even real?"

"I assumed you'd have learned this lesson before you were 29, but if I must be the one to educate you in the ways of the birds and the bees…" Lin smirks at his snarky reply, the up-turn of his silky lips only serving to make him more devilishly handsome.

Kieran crumples a napkin and throws it at Lin's face, "Shut up. I mean how is she happy and bouncy and friendly right now? I can't decide if I want to fuck something up or run like hell but it all adds up to not being happy and bouncy and friendly, that's for fuckin' sure."

"Oh hush, like that isn't just your normal setting anyway." Lin lobs the napkin back at its original wielder, setting it sail-ing in a graceful ark landing directly on top of Kieran's head. "Besides, I'm fairly certain being ready to either fight or run tonight may be an instinct worth nurturing for this particular mission."

"She wants to be happy. She works hard at it; actively seek-ing reasons to enjoy life." Zeke is toying with the black box in his hands. It absorbs all light around it, a box-shaped void where nothingness permeates our universe and saps all real-ity exactly from its location. In a strange way, despite being darker than the depths of an endless abyss, I find the box com-forting and unexpectedly familiar.

"Yeah, that may as well be like telling me it's as simple

as making the sun rise from the West-that shit just shouldn't be possible," Kieran rips his napkins more forcefully; a blizzard to accompany the storm of his frustration. The tattooed bands between his knuckles almost shimmer in the light with each forceful movement, nearly indicating what elements were laced throughout the ink. If we weren't waiting for half an hour to make it seem like we're just having a normal night out, I'm certain Kieran would be going for a run right now. Alone. Better he destroy a sleeve of napkins than get himself killed.

Dizzy and Lilly are still smiling and laughing as they walk over to us carrying trays laden with pints of ice water, slices of chocolate cake, a tea cup, and a bowl of cherries. Quick as lightning, a tiny hand flashes out from Dizzy's hood, snagging a glistening red globe and whisking it back into the darkness.

"Figured y'all could use some cake to help fortify you against this dick hole that's been trying to fuck up your day. And as thanks for helping me with my stuff, even though Grams kind of sprung it all on you last minute." Lilly starts passing plates around to us, each with a monstrous slice of chocolate dessert, multiple layers glistening with the promise of richness and sugar.

"Ah, my dear Duke, it was nothing," Lin drawls, "Especially given both her and your assistance tonight."

"Oh, we're definitely getting the better end of the deal! Have you had Lilly's chocolate cake before?! I have and it's a freakin miracle! Miracles more than pay for moving some stuff," Dizzy nearly topples her tray of waters with how animatedly she speaks, the only thing preventing a sudden flood being Lin's lithe hands quickly whisking the tray from hers and seamlessly distributing its contents to the table.

The ceramic plate clinks lightly against our wooden tabletop as Lilly places the last slice down in front of Monty. She leans in and lowers her voice to a raspy hush, "I'll be here all night if you need a place to hunker down, and I can promise it'll be safe," She taps the pendant hanging on a long, golden chain from her neck; a miniature version of the larger stone Miss Fern gifted us with earlier in the day. "Just… keep it in mind. I'm not as keyed-in as my Grams, so it's not like I'm saying this because I *know* something, I'm just saying it because I want to make it clear that you've got my support. Even if it's only moral support." Lilly straightens up, moving aside to let Dizzy slide into the end of our curved booth, Lin pressing hard against me as he makes space for her on the cramped bench.

She says something else before departing, but it doesn't matter to me. I find myself lost in the details, again, of what's around us. The cool, clean, refreshing scent of a rainstorm that always seems to emanate from Lin, the silken texture of his black vest as it brushes against the back of my right hand, the easy and fluid gestures his fingertips play against a glass's rim. To my left, the glinting of light off of one of Zeke's rings combined with his naturally smoky and electrically charged scent brings forth images of treasure accumulated in a dragon's hoard. I am caught between one man who embodies grace and cleanliness, and one who is a little rough, a little dangerous, and has a hidden fire buried within.

Kieran, to the left of Zeke, still carries a stern and serious look on his bearded face. From him emanates a strong, heated sense of power and anger that screams predator so loudly I expect anyone who doesn't know him would subconsciously give a wide berth. The tension carried in his muscular arms as he obliterates napkin after napkin is so tight, I suspect startling him could result in a practically spring-loaded attack that even he wouldn't see coming.

To the right of Lin, I examine Dizzy; the woman who saved my life and very well may save my soul, too. Freckles stippled across her cheeks and the bridge of her nose rise and fall with each laugh she gives herself to, the gold in her eyes lighting up every time she glances my way with a smile, the soft bouncing of her violet curls at every energetic movement she makes. I know without a doubt that she'd find a way, no matter the cost, to keep us all well. She made that clear when she invented a new method of healing without any warning, just for me.

It's comforting to know that these are the people that I'll be counting on to keep Monty and myself safe, even if the metallic taste of nausea does tempt the tip of my tongue at the thought of facing a foe who's almost killed me once before.

"You ready, dreamboat?" Lin whispers and nudges me with his elbow, ejecting me from my distracted observations.

Ambient noise comes crashing back into place, broader strokes replacing focused details. I look up, this time actually present in the moment, and nod. The atmosphere is still tense, but spending this last half hour reflecting on who's with me and what we're aiming to do has helped to settle my nerves. I try to put on the bravest face I have as we file out of the booth, letting the others know that I trust them, and I trust myself. A lot of what we have planned hinges on my illusions, and that's one thing I have unwavering confidence in.

As soon as I'm upright, Dizzy launches herself at me and fiercely encircles my head in her arms, forcing me to bend down to make up the nearly comical difference in our heights. "You promised," she whispers against my ear as I bury my face in her hair, nodding.

"I promise," and as I wrap my arms around her tightly, I hope she feels how deeply I mean it. I'm not going anywhere, and not taking a single moment for granted, but I'm also not letting anything happen to the people I love. This is necessary, and I'm the one who needs to take this risk.

She pulls back, lines between her brows deepening with an expression of forced determination. One short nod, and she kisses me quickly on the cheek, sealing our contract. When she goes to disentangle herself from me, I pull her back, crashing our lips together with as much strength and power as I can muster, proving to her how serious I am about making good on my word. The chocolate on her mouth is dark and sweet, I devour all traces of it until all that's left on her is me and my growing confidence. Lin wolf-whistles in the background, but that doesn't stop us from burning away all uncertainties with our fire. This time, when she pulls back, the storm behind her eyes is calm and I know she's found her belief. With one more small kiss to her swollen lips, we part.

Not done yet, Dizzy sets her sights on Monty and fists the front of his carrot-patterned shirt, creating a shattered web of wrinkles with a twist of her wrist. "You take care of each other, you hear?" In a way, it's meant to be a threat, but I can see the softness she let creep in.

Monty looks down at her, calm confidence exuding from his violet eyes, nearly the same shade as the hair he tenderly tucks behind her ears. His hand lingers on the side of her face, cupping her cheek as he shifts his gaze to me, "Of course we will," a pledge he makes to, and for, us both.

"Good," she tugs him closer to her, "Because I really don't want to have to figure out how to deal with zombies." As she briefly claims his mouth with her own, something inside of me warms. Monty tends to keep a distance between himself and his own happiness, putting everyone else and their needs first without allowing himself a piece of any pie. If Dizzy can bring a bit of the care back to him that he puts out, then that's a real kind of magic worth encouraging.

Monty and I both stride towards the exit, turning to catch one last glimpse of the family we're counting on to keep us alive, tonight. Lin and Kieran on either side of Dizzy, each with one of her hands in their own, all three watching us depart with various expressions of concern or confidence in their posture. Zeke nods at us, shadow box cupped protectively in both his hands. I'm ready.

Looking once more at Monty, we plaster smiles on our faces and open the pub door to stumble outside, more than just the chilly night air sending a shiver up my spine.

42. CONNOR

The moment the door closes behind us, I cover it with a duplicate of itself. Every tumbling, unsteady step we take away from the pub I copy and cover as we pass, ensuring that in five minutes when the rest of our party leave to follow, they'll remain undetected.

I stumble into Monty, intentionally slinging an arm around his shoulders to steady myself, shoving my other arm in front of him to sloppily indicate a direction. "He's here," I whisper. There is a fury and hate shooting at us like blazing arrows from across the street, leaving no question as to the location of our target.

Monty gives me a noogie and laughs obnoxiously, "I got you!" he shouts loudly. To our observer, it's merely two drunk men fooling around, but I know his declaration was for my benefit just as much as our cover.

A thick layer of malice slithers its way across my skin, blanketing us in the sludge of ill-intent. Any thoughts that we weren't targeted and it's all simply been coincidence are thoroughly banished, though Dizzy's right to be curious as to why this is the case. As far as any of us can tell, she's the only link to this attacker, and it's almost inconceivable to think such spiteful violence could truly be intended for her.

Even at our stuttering pace, we manage to quickly traverse the nearly block and a half between The Wood Liquor and the park, our destination chosen for its likelihood to be abandoned this late at night. As we turn the corner and cross through the arched stone entryway, two sensations of movement press and scrape against me.

From across the street, the shadow's presence assaults me as it scrambles past and settles in the darkness of a nearby tree. As hateful as this being is, its aura reminds me of something that's just at the back of my mind; familiar, but buried away.

Behind us, along the path we've just strayed from, a pressure presses against the illusion I left breadcrumbed in our wake. Like a finger trying to work its way into a full water balloon, Dizzy, Kieran, Lin, and Zeke enter the world left behind for them. I hold it, shielding them from detection up to the very edge of the park Monty and I have just arrived at.

Tension and anticipation scent the air like acrid sweat as we bumble our way towards the fountain directly in the heart of the greenery, only drawn out further by the presence of a woman jogging through the grass with a leashed dog. They both pant as they pass us, bouncing happily, completely unaware of the dangers just out of sight. It hardly takes them any time to exit through the stone archway, and I break my illusion just enough to make their departure visible.

Monty and I amble closer to the partially-lit water feature, making sure to conveniently stumble into one of the brighter patches around it. According to Lilly and her grandmother, they can only remain non-corporeal within the shadows and must take a physical form if they want to interact in the light.

Inhaling a breath to gather my resolve, I nod at Monty. Taking his cue, he playfully bumps me with his shoulder, causing my footing to falter and sending me tumbling to the ground, just outside of the small halo of safety.

Time slows the moment my back hits the ground, my mind working on overdrive to experience everything all at once. From his position beneath a tree, our stalker bursts forth and torpedoes towards me, just as I roll away from the strike we had anticipated. As he grazes by me, I feel sharp claws dig into the flesh of my upper arm, slicing three shallow ribbons of pain into my skin. The physical connection of his being unexpectedly pulls at the darkness inside me, both beckoning to one another. My nightmares recognize one of their own.

I've barely finished my roll and Monty's already there, clasping my hand and yanking me swiftly back into the light. A furious shriek is released from the darkness at my swift retreat, in sync with my illusion no longer shielding the pounding footsteps of our backup; both parties breaking free of their respective hiding spaces at the same time.

In a bit of vicious choreography, the shadow's outstretched claw makes a grab for me at the same moment Kieran throws a thin, metallic needle, piercing the attacker's palm with practiced accuracy. Still clutching my hand and only having just pulled me upright, Monty continues the motion and shoves me behind him, using the momentum to smash his fist into the smoky, undefined face just barely within the boundary of our lighted space. The force of his punch sends the shadow slamming into one of the fountain's decorative statues, one which I notice has a jagged chunk missing, bringing it to a dangerous point. Upon impact, a horrific screech of pain rips through the almost surreally pleasant night sky, drowning out the hoots and chirps of an otherwise contented scene of beauty and nature.

His primal agony snaps me out of my adrenaline-fueled observation overload, condensing time back to its normal pace. Almost faster than I can follow, our assailant hurls himself towards the surrounding darkness, slashing across Monty's chest as he passes and disappears into the depths around us. Blood stains the jagged edge of the statue that clearly wounded him, a trail of crimson left in the wake of his escape.

"Coward!" Monty bellows, clutching his bloody chest. "You're pitiful, lashing out when you think we're defenseless. Come and try to take me on like a real man, you pathetic, whiny little boy!"

Dizzy, Lin, and Kieran are at our side and in the light almost instantly, but Zeke makes his approach more slowly, visible only to me through an obscuring shield. Playing a dangerous game, he keeps to the shadows at a deliberate and brave pace, fingers stroking air just above the golden edge of the sphere resting in the shadow box.

Bouncing all around us, a voice that sounds multiplied and layered over and over shrieks, "*You're* pathetic, thieves! How dare you?" It's impossible to tell where he's speaking from, each of my companions swinging their heads frantically in a fruitless attempt to locate his position through the endless echoes. "I will have what is mine, what I deserve! I've earned her, you can not stand in my way!"

"The fuck you just say?" Dizzy's frantic searching stops as she snaps her head definitively in the exact direction I sense our attacker.

Kieran doesn't wait for a response, throwing a handful of flat, metallic disks that blaze to life like emergency flares as they arc through the air. Dizzy and I both track it as our tormentor flees deeper into the darkness.

Despite the fact that David's fractured voice urges every instinct inside of me to take flight, it is almost tender as he responds. "It's okay, darling, I know they're keeping you from me against your will. I'll take care of them, and then you and that nasty bellirae will come with me. Mother says if I bring her the bellirae, you will belong to me. You are mine, darling," his words an icy finger clawing a chill up my spine, "And I will have what is mine. What I deserve."

With that final declaration, he lunges back in our direction, aiming towards Lin, whose back is turned. Unable to find a way to warn him or pull him to safety or do anything even remotely useful, my heart stops dead as, horrified, I reach out in his direction and let out a pitiful yell. Faster than I could have ever imagined, Lin pivots on one foot and swings his leg high, shin solidly making contact with the suddenly physical chest within reach. Following through with the kick, Lin lands on his extended foot and thrusts the heel of his other forcefully into almost the exact same place he already hit, ejecting his opponent from the safety of our bubble of light. Despite Lin's speed, the would-be assassin manages to dig the claws of both hands on either side of Lin's leg, slashing through his black dress pants and digging deeply into his calf.

Kieran throws more flares in the direction our attacker fled in, attempting to herd him closer to our goal by blocking off points of escape. Dizzy's already pulling Lin against her, dragging him closer to the center and stopping him from putting weight on his grisly leg.

"Fuck you, you piece of shit!" Kieran snarls into the darkness, but he's already looking in the wrong direction.

Despite taking his time and lingering in the shadows, Zeke, cloaked in illusion, has managed to escape the attention of the man-no, the creature, hounding us. Also despite the fact that they are finally within ten feet of each other.

"Now, Zeke!" I yell as loudly as I can through the panic attempting to choke my throat closed at seeing so much blood pouring from Lin's wounds. I will not let this take me away from the people that need me, not tonight.

Without hesitation, Zeke swipes his finger along the golden edge of his carefully protected stone, trapping the shadow beast before it ever had a chance to realize it never had the upper-hand tonight. Instantly, a circle of nearly blinding light appears in front of Zeke, a vaguely humanoid wisp of swirling darkness just barely within its perimeter. The second it realizes what's happened, it starts racing around the edge, shrieking in fury each time its desperate attempts to either escape or maim are denied.

Having passed Lin to Kieran, Dizzy storms up to the circle of light, clearly pissed. "David Anthony Williams, what the actual fuck!? You've been trying to kill us?! Why the hell would you do something like that? To me, and to some damned strangers? What the fuck even happened to you! Oh, I'm so mad right now!" Dizzy yanks at her hair in frustration, then slams her fists down by her sides, "I can't even believe this right now!"

Monty and I are at Lin and Kieran's side, doing our best to quickly manage the horrific injury. While I use the tattered strips of Lin's own shredded pants to form a makeshift tourniquet, Monty dives right in and puts both hands on Lin's mincemeat leg, despite not having tended to his own bleeding chest.

From inside his prison, David stops flinging himself at the walls of the circle and turns to her. A smoky appendage raises in her direction, claws flickering in and out of existence on the tips of it. "No, darling, never you. Just these fools who have captured you and mean to keep you away from me. It's okay, I forgive you for not knowing I've been here to protect you. If you help me eliminate them, we can finally finish our joining and I'll keep you safe in the cabin. Mother wasn't pleased we kept it hidden from her, but she's assured me we can make our own life once we return. You don't have to be kept by these vile men, darling, we can free you from them."

"Are you kidding me, David? Seriously?" Dizzy cocks a hip, "I can't believe this isn't the first time I'm saying this today, but you can't solve your problems by killing people! What the hell?!" She starts pacing outside the ring of light, arms gesturing wide and fast with anger, "And let's get this straight right fucking now, I don't *belong* to you, and the only one who's been captured here is you. No idea why you think we have anything to do with each other at all; I haven't seen you since we were kids!"

"Darling, don't you feel it in your soul? I've never forgotten you; never given up. I forgive you for leaving me, they said you would come back and I could have you. These bastards are just another obstacle between us, don't you see?"

"Oh my gosh. You're delusional. You're freakin' delusional!" Dizzy mutters, but not quietly enough.

"No, darling, I'm patient. Ever since mother gave me to the shadows and healed me, I've never stopped searching for you. They warned me that you might not see, but I never stopped hoping we would be reunited, even after all this time. Even after all the traveling. I was always just one step behind, but finally we're together again and I won't let anything stop us."

"You... you've been following me?" She stops her pacing and stares aghast at the shadow now gliding closer to the edge she's on.

"Always." He pauses for a moment, "Though it wasn't always just me, I'm the only one who would never give up on you."

She shoots him a glare so poisonous it could strip bark from a tree, "Did you do all that shit? The fires and the accidents and the people who got hurt? I've felt like I've been in danger every single day, and like I put other people in danger every day. Did. You. Do that?"

"I would do anything to protect you, darling, anything. I always have, when I could. But I couldn't always. Sometimes the nasty beastie got in my way. These criminals aren't the first to try and keep us apart, but they will be the last, now that you know I'm with you."

Dizzy's balled fists start to glow blue as she screeches in fury, "Do you know what I've gone through?! Do you know how horrible I've felt all this time? Do you know how much guilt and anger I've had to shove down every day just to focus on survival? And now you tell me, what, all of this isn't my fault anyway? That you've been the reason I've been trying not to be miserable for the last twelve years? How could you do any of this? Not just to me, but to other people!" She resumes her pacing, the strength of her anger intimidating despite having only one target.

"Because I love you, darling. I've always loved you. Not like these imposters who don't even know you." He snarls, "They just want to fuck you and leave you. They'll never love you; these scum can't even care about you! Nobody will love you but me, and I've always done whatever it takes to protect you. Even the few times you didn't do it yourself!"

"Who said you get to decide anything about my life? What gives you the fucking right to ruin every single small moment of peace or happiness I've ever been lucky enough to catch a tiny smidge of? How can you possibly think that loving me and holding me back are even close to the same thing?" Some of the anger releases from her, and I see cruel tendrils of sadness try to wrap their way around her tired heart. She looks next to her at Zeke, who has remained stoic and watchful during this exchange, "Close him in, for me? I never want to see him again." Dizzy turns away, clutching her arms across herself.

"My darling, wait! Don't let them fool you! I'm the only one who's keeping you safe! The others don't think they need to keep you alive, and you always reacted more when anyone other than me was on your trail. You must know that I do everything for you, don't you?" I see Dizzy shaking at his words, though from anger or sadness I couldn't possibly tell, maybe even a bit of both. Zeke has already started closing the circle, its luminous ring shrinking with each stroke of his finger. Panicked once again, David's voices start to shout and shriek out of sync, each almost seeming to carry its own message and pleas for mercy. "You can't leave me again! I've never left you, don't go!" His tone flips from affection to one of malice so quickly it nearly gives me whiplash, "You dumb slut, I'll find you and rip you to pieces. I'll enjoy it as you beg me to end your life, but not until you've seen me ruin these fools you've run away with. I'll flay the skin from their flesh and force you to eat every last scrap as they bleed out in front of you. You will suffer, you'll all suffer! There is no escape. We are coming."

Despite his face being nearly featureless, I see David's blazing red eyes widen in fear. Before any of us can process what's happening, Dizzy whips around, arms outstretched and fully encased in a massive, electric blue flame already moving to be released towards its target.

Almost all at once, as though choreographed perfectly by a cruel fate, misfortune springs. Dizzy's pivot, while impressively swift, included her arms flinging out, hands slamming shut the lid of the box within Zeke's grasp just as they catch ablaze. By the time her about-face is complete, the shining prison has disappeared; our captive escaping a single sliver of a second before her azure fireball would have hit home and incinerated him to ash. Instead, it carries on through its missing target and explodes against the window of a nearby building.

Horrified either at what she's done, or at what she's almost done, Dizzy gasps and collapses to her knees with a hand covering her mouth. In the distance her fireball immediately snuffs out, but it's clear the damage it wrought was well and truly done.

Strangely, it seems the shadow's chosen to fully leave us, rather than make good on its threat; all of my warning bells completely silent. For now.

43. DIZZY

I tried to kill him. Oh my gosh, I tried to kill him! What the fuck is wrong with me? Twice today, TWICE, I told everyone that murder isn't the solution and I almost committed it on my own without a single thought. Before I even knew what I was doing, it was like my body was moving on its own and trying to crispify someone who wasn't even in a position to fight back!

Right then, I throw up every single sweet morsel of Lilly's chocolate cake into the fresh grass; murderesses don't deserve dessert.

In a manner much more tender than how he usually fists my hair, Zeke is beside me, holding my curling locks back and keeping them from being tainted with bile.

"You did nothing wrong. No regret. None."

I heave and sob and heave again, so many fucked up conflicts swirling and whirling inside of me like a cyclone of contradictions. Horror at my actions and David's threats, relief that I didn't incinerate him despite them, guilt at my relief, anguish at seeing my first crush so twisted and crazed, hope that maybe I can make a life here after all if so much of the chaos that followed me wasn't my own doing. Deep, deep, deeeeeep down there's also a tiny part of me that is happy, proud, and triumphant for reasons I can't even begin to explain, and those feelings rip my innards to absolute shreds. Ribbons of the wretched toxicity inside me project themselves from my mouth to the ground until my ruined guts are all laid out and I am an empty corpse, organs removed and ready for embalming.

Aria slides her way out of my hood, reaching into one of my pockets as she goes. In her hand are mint leaves she pilfered from The Wood Liquor earlier in the week. I snatch them and shove them into my mouth, desperate to erase even the scent of my regret as I bury my face in the scruff of her neck and cling to her silently for comfort.

"You recognized a threat to us. Your instincts are to protect. Can you blame yourself for keeping us alive?" Zeke's expression as I catch him from the corner of my eye is patient and calm, nearly unaffected. It's the antithesis of the roiling conflict I'm clearly not containing, and I can't figure out why he isn't nearly as aghast as I am in this moment. "Because I'm grateful," he says, responding to my inner monologue. "We are wounded, but alive, and we know more than before. We kept each other safe and we will continue to. This has been a victory, even if it wasn't all as expected."

Before I have time to even contemplate his perspective, Kieran practically barrels into me from the side, large hands frantically pawing over every inch of my face and body to ensure I'm whole. Aria springs from my clutches and to the safety of Zeke's shoulder right before the jarring impact. "Are you okay?" His expression is one of utter distress, something I realize is totally my fault since he's probably being completely bombarded with my whack-ass emotional turmoil.

With purposeful effort, I slap a smile on my face that feels weak and fake even to me but hopefully at least does something to show that I'm totally fine, no problems here, not a single one. Nuh-uh. Zero, zilch, nada, HOLY SHIT IS THAT BLOOD?!

I'm grabbing Kieran's completely red-streaked arms and looking over them with the same feverish explorations that he just assaulted on me. My own internal crazy is gone at the sight of deep crimson tiger stripes crusting against his pale white skin. Already I feel a tingling starting in my fingertips, as though my magic is reaching out to lick away any wounds he might be plagued with.

"Are YOU okay?" I shout back at him. He gives me a confused look, and all at once I realize it's not his blood. But that it's still blood, and that means somebody still needs me. Springing up quickly from my crouched position and breaking free from both the men who have a hold on me, I sprint the dozen or so feet to where the rest of our group are tangled together, each with at least one limb draped over one another in some way. It takes a while for me to actually dissect the scene, but I've already tackled Monty before my brain can fully catch up to the logic behind my actions.

Both of my palms slam into his chest, hard, and I'm kissing the ever-loving shit out of him before his back even hits the ground. My fingertips dig into a deep gash across his pecs, causing him to shout with pain against my mouth. Something in me tells me I have to do this, though, and there's a darkness twisting in my already traumatized gut that reacts violently to the increased pressure of my nails against raw flesh.

"Stop! You're hurting him!" Connor cries from beside us,

grabbing my hand to yank it out of Monty's wound. The instant his skin touches mine, it's like a whoosh of fresh air suddenly blows through me, filling me with strength and power and surety.

Deep, creeping, inky smoke seeps from the gash my fingers are dug into. I instinctively know that if this had stayed in him too long, hate and death would have tainted Monty beyond all repair. I don't know how I knew it was there in the first place, or even what it would have done, but as soon as I know the last tendril is fully extracted, I loosen my grip on the edge of his sliced flesh and watch as his wound knits itself closed. Our lips together, I feel some of the lightness and strength pass from my breath into his as he stops struggling beneath me and takes my tongue to his willingly.

Realizing my intention was never to harm, Connor lets go of my arm and the fullness in my chest deflates slightly. Right in front of his eyes, a small puff of pure black hovers and writhes, swirling like an octopus of smoke.

His gaze is briefly scrutinizing and suspicious but shock springs on his face, bright turquoise eyes suddenly wide. "I know you," he says, reaching out to touch the bundle of shadow. In my mind, I'm desperate for him to leave it alone, but that force inside me that demanded I claw at a man I want only to keep safe urges me to keep still and let Connor touch the shadow we just extracted from Monty.

The entirety of Connor's eyes goes pitch black, and despite being unsettling to see, it doesn't feel malevolent. If anything, it seems a little sad and accepting. Especially as he scuttles over to Lin and presses a hand to either side of the wounded man's face. Well, the previously wounded man's face; I manage to notice that his leg is all but fully healed, despite being painted in an opaque layer of dried blood that would suggest the contrary.

Lin's cheeks look sallow and gaunt, his body drained due to the massive blood loss even with Monty's healing. With unhesitating surety, Connor slants his lips against Lin's, drawing out a shocked gasp from the prone man. In the barely perceptible space that appears between their mouths at Lin's surprise, wisps of the same inky spirit are drawn forth and spread, almost completely obscuring Connor's face within seconds. Sitting up from his crouched position, the darkness follows and is fully absorbed through Connor's own mouth, sucked in like a vacuum. His back is straight and sure, shoulders not hunched up to his ears in an attempt to hide himself in as tight a ball as possible. Confidence looks sexy on him, not gonna lie, even if he was just kissing another man. Maybe even a little bit because of that.

As the darkness filling his vision pulls back inside, returning his eyes to their normal bright clarity, a small smile tilts his lips. He pats Lin's stunned chest twice, then stands and reaches a hand out to me. I also rise, and there's something so completely right about his touch, which I'd already way been on board with pretty much since moment one of knowing him. I don't ask what just happened, and he doesn't tell, but it seems to me like maybe I'm not the only one learning a thing or two about themselves this week.

Kieran and Zeke had apparently already reached us while all this 'mauling our friends to get at shadows' business was going on. Even with Connor's hand in mine on one side, Zeke's solid frame a breath away from my other side, and Kieran's warm chest all but pressed up against my back, having my men so close feels comforting rather than suffocating.

I try not to think about the consequences of David's escape as Lin and Monty, no longer wounded from battle, unsteadily rise to their feet in front of us. Instead, I focus on the fact that we're still all here, and we're still all together. Against any odds I thought were stacked against me, it looks a heck of a lot like I've found myself an honest to goodness family.

"Let's go home," someone says. Maybe it was even me.

44. ZEKE

The drive home is mostly quiet, and somewhat tense. Dizzy's thoughts largely revolve around the escaped being, replaying their conversation in her head and attempting to predict what would have happened if she'd said or done something differently. It is not a productive thought experiment but I don't know how to remedy the problem for her, nor comfort her beyond the attempts I've already made.

Instead, my own reflections center around the curious incidents after the escape. Why did he flee? Who is he working with, and what are their motivations? When should we expect another run-in? If this person was able to inject some of its being into Monty and Lin, what is it? What would have happened had it not been removed? How did Connor and Dizzy know it was there, or to remove it? What did Connor mean when he said "I know you?"

There are many aspects to consider of our interaction, and

while it's easy to get caught up in the details of our communication, the more intriguing parts don't involve dissecting dialogue. If this shadow can pass parts of itself on via subcutaneous contact, what is the purpose of such a capability and what else do we need to know about it in order to remain prepared against its attacks? Or prepared in the wake of said attacks. Too much about this element is unknown, and I can not help but work a puzzle once presented.

What did he mean he needed to get the bellirae? I've never even heard of it before! Why would he be after me for something I don't have? Well, he said he was after me for me, but that somebody else wanted a bellirae from me?

"Good point," I tell her aloud. "We should also research the bellirae and determine what it refers to."

"I'll happily look into it, just give me a chance to rest up," Lin replies through a yawn. "It appears I'm frightfully weary after our activities this evening and may need the tender attention of a sexy nurse throughout the night."

"Why Lin, I didn't know you thought I was sexy!" Monty looks back from the front passenger seat and smiles widely.

Lin only falters for a moment before responding in a lazy drawl, "You know darn well you're sexy as hell, honey bear, I don't need to remind you of that, do I?"

"A man likes to be told, sometimes."

Well damn, a man that sexy should get told often. Somebody's seriously been slacking! Oh poop beans, I guess I'm one of those slacking somebodies if you really think about it.

"Will somebody get me out of here and away from these two before they grab each other's dicks right here in this damned car? At least wait until we're home before you fuck."

Dizzy giggles slightly at Kieran's comment, but her

thoughts have started projecting images of lusty scenes with the two men, often involving herself between them. Since the day we attempted to test her abilities, I am fully aware of how much she enjoyed being between myself and Monty; an experiment I'd like to repeat if given the chance again.

By the time we arrive back home, the atmosphere has somewhat cleared. As both Lin and Monty step out of the vehicle, I note the sluggishness in their movements, accompanied by less enthusiasm and alertness than usual. Whatever was done to them, between the injuries and the healing, appears to have physically drained them.

As is often the case with myself, I feel more awake and alive after nightfall, especially when there's a project or puzzle to focus on. If I'm not careful, days of sleeplessness can consume me, as it did when I was working over how to create a prosthetic capable of self-contained transmutation even by those without alchemical capabilities of their own.

Upon entering the house, I wordlessly follow Monty and Lin upstairs, silently offering my support should either of them need it. Based on the way their ankles occasionally almost go out on them and the few times their steps have nearly faltered, it appears they very well may need it.

Aw damn it, if one of them falls down the stairs and breaks all their bones in the process I'll never be able to deal with how dumb a way that is to get fucked up after all the totally more reasonable ways to get fucked up we've had tonight. Although stairs are always up to something, or at least GOING up to something, and they really shouldn't be trusted just because they're typically inanimate. I've known a lot of inanimate objects that looked completely harmless but were just waiting for their chance to strike and totally ruin your whole day, like suddenly starting your period while trying to remain inconspicuous in a swimming pool full of hungry sharks.

Dizzy helps, too.

At the top of the stairs, Monty's master bedroom is directly to the left while the bathroom the rest of us share is slightly further to the right. Confident they're no longer in danger of falling down the stairs, Dizzy and I begin our descent as the two previously injured men head in opposite directions.

"Good night, guys. I'm still kind of wound up after all that stuff so I'm gonna hang out and do… something? Haven't even figured out what yet, or shoot, where do I sleep when I'm ready?" Dizzy tilts her head, plump lips shifting to the side as she chews on the inside of her cheek. *Or who do I sleep with?* She thinks. "Anyway, I'll be downstairs if you need anything but I don't know what you'd need me for, if you needed something."

Looking over his shoulder, Lin addresses our departure, "What, not sticking around to see me get all hot and wet for you?"

"Umm… what?" Dizzy blinks a few times, "I'm… not sure that's how it works?" *I'm pretty sure, anyway.*

"Oh, Love, I'm just so helpless after this whole ordeal, what if I slip and fall in the shower and split open this dashing noggin of mine?" Lin runs the back of his hand over his own cheek, jutting his bottom lip out in a strong pout.

"Take a bath. No falling," I respond.

He huffs slightly, "And if I pass out and drown? I'm still so weak and in need of someone to watch over my body and make sure I stay this beautiful. Wouldn't want to let my standards drop with such a gorgeous creature gracing our household, especially in the company of all you hot hunks." Lin attempts one of his signature devious grins, but it seems less sturdy than normal; lacking in commitment to his usual bravado.

Monty rolls his eyes, "Fine then, I'll call you a supervisor."

With a whistle, Colonel Stubbs comes bounding up the steps, "If he passes out, bite him," Monty instructs, jutting his chin towards Lin. The little white Frenchie yips happily, bouncing in a circle around his charge while wiggling his butt so hard it seems improbable he hasn't already fallen prey to gravity and the other laws of physics. "I'm going to clean up and crash; good night, guys. If I'm not up in time for Walker street... Well, find a way to do it without me. I feel like I've been hit by a bus and plan to be out for a while." With a weak, half-lidded smile that doesn't quite reach his eyes, Monty turns his attention to Dizzy. "Thank you for... this." He halfheartedly waves a hand in front of his shredded shirt, indicating the blood dried across the entirety of his chest, then leans forward and pecks her gently on the cheek before turning the handle on his door and stepping through.

Colonel Stubbs grips the undamaged hem of Lin's remaining pant leg in his teeth, tugging backwards to guide his patient towards the waiting bathroom. Now that he's openly communicating with the small canine, it's a wonder we never noticed Monty had a deeper connection with wildlife.

Dizzy nudges my arm as we start back downstairs, so I wrap it around her shoulder and pull her closer. Tucked against my side, even at half a foot taller than her she still finds a way to fit perfectly.

By the time we're nearly to the bottom of the steps, conversation between Connor and Kieran starts to reach us.

"Yeah, of course you guys getting hurt is one of my nightmares, but that's not what I mean," Connor says.

"Then what the hell did you mean when you said it was one of your nightmares?"

We round the banister to see the two men reassembling our previously stripped couch, extra blankets and pillows still close by.

"I mean the thing, the darkness? It was just like one of the nightmares inside me." Connor fits a cushion back into place, "The ones that killed my dad, the ones I thought killed you when we were attacked at the site. They're always right under the surface, trying to get out, but I've never seen them anywhere without me, before."

"Are you sure they're nightmares?" I ask.

Connor looks up from his task to catch my eye, "What else could they be?"

"Exactly," I reply.

He frowns, brows furrowing. I can't tell if he's troubled or confused; sometimes it's hard to read the less obvious emotions and this could be either one. Silence starts to sink in.

Beside me, Dizzy claps once and bounces a bit on her feet, breaking up the mood and bringing a bit of life back into the room. "Well, I don't know about you guys, but I'm not really ready for bed yet but I'm definitely not up for going out on another adventure this late. What's there to do in this joint? You got any games we can play?"

"Oh Fireball, you've no idea the wolf you're poking at with that request," Kieran's whole face lights up, likely anticipating the thrill of competition while he retrieves a few game controllers from within the television stand.

We settle into various positions on the couch, quickly becoming apparent that Kieran and Dizzy far outpace Connor and myself no matter what we play. It takes a few hours, but one by one we eventually slip into sleep where we are. The last one awake, I choose to remain with them, rather than seeking solitude to sort through my thoughts and theories. Watching the three of them tangled in one another, Kieran's head in Dizzy's lap, her's on Connor's chest; seeing them all at ease brings me comfort. Their breathing nearly syncs; I close my eyes and drift off to their harmony.

45. DIZZY

Mother is already waiting for me when I dutifully return to my room after helping to tend to the garden. Her arms are crossed, and I recognize her stiff posture as one of displeasure.

"I see you two have gotten nice and cozy, just like I asked. Maybe a little too cozy."

Mumbling, I look down, attempting not to confirm her suspicions in any way, "Yeah. She's nice. I like her."

"What's that, darling?" I see her cup a hand behind her ear out of my peripheral, "Yes mother, I'd do anything for you? Why thank you darling, I know you would. You're such a good boy, and it's important that you stay a good boy for mother."

Stony-faced, I nod, my head still downwards; hoping the response is submissive enough to keep her happy.

She steps forward and lightly brushes a hand down my cheek, convincing me for a moment that there is still tenderness in her heart for me and this will be a calm, normal night. That is, until her fingers grip my jaw tightly, nails digging in deep enough to pierce flesh as she jerks my head up and forces me to look at her.

"Look me in the eyes when I'm talking to you, darling."

"I'm sorry mother, yes." Despite every effort, my eyes slide themselves away from her punishing glare; fear of her and deep shame of myself leading my gaze elsewhere. I know it's the exact wrong move, but even my body won't let me pretend any longer to love her.

With a forceful twist of her wrist, my eyes move of their own accord to connect with hers, my entire body locking up in an instant with the strength of her command. Everything freezes, even my lungs, and I become a prisoner paralyzed inside my own mind; helpless to move or speak or breathe if mother doesn't allow it. Even though I know there's no possibility of breaking free, the panic always spurs me on to fight against it for the first few moments until I'm able to force myself to relax and retreat.

"I SAID LOOK AT ME DARLING. YOU'RE BEING A VERY BAD BOY RIGHT NOW." Mother is screaming, flecks of spit landing like hateful raindrops on my cheeks as she makes her fury at me known.

If I could control anything about my life, I'd pack it all up and run away; get out of here and far from her and them and not have to worry about any of this any more. I don't want to do this, any of this; I don't want to be here any more! My eyes well up on their own, partly from the frustration and absolute helplessness and partly because not breathing can really fuck you up. Mother is still yelling, and despite knowing she hates it when I don't pay attention, I can't seem to catch any of her words. It's hard to stay present when the present is so shitty. I'd rather be out there, somewhere safe and far, far away. Maybe in the middle of nowhere, where nobody would ever find me and I'd be safe to just live and be free and not worry.

We. We could be safe.

A blood-curdling shriek cuts through my thoughts, too late I realize it came from me; my lungs and throat my own again, but not as a kindness or courtesy. Mother's hand is on mine, her expression furious.

"You little shit, you answer me right now or I'll break more than just your fingers tonight."

"Y-y-yes, mother," I stammer out through gasped breaths. I don't know what I'm responding to, but she only ever wants to hear my agreement with her.

"Oh, so then you think it's okay to disrespect me like you have, after all I've done for you? After all I WILL do for you?" She sneers, "You're nothing without me."

"N-no mother, no! You deserve respect mother, respect!" Words sputter from my mouth desperately, the only part of myself I have any control of at the moment; words my only possible defense.

Still tightly gripping the hand she's completely shattered the fingers of, mother twists and twists and twists, until we both know my bones are at their actual breaking point. "Remember, darling, you belong to me. You are mine. You do as I say, and you do it when I say, because I say. And if you do not?" With a hard jerk of her arm, my own is in absolute agony. The pops, cracks, and crunches of my bones being obliterated from her strength are completely drowned out by the sound of my screams. "Then I will break you, again and again, until you do. Do you understand me, darling?"

All at once, my body collapses to the ground, no longer frozen in her control. My throat is too tight with sobs to squeeze out an answer quickly, and she stomps on the tender flesh of my torso for my lack of prompt response.

"Do. You. Understand. Me?" Each word is punctuated with the stabbing of her stiletto into my gut.

I nod furiously, bulging eyes desperately seeking hers as I try to swallow every scream that rips its way through my throat anyway. She doesn't like it when I cause a scene, even if there's no one there to see it.

Tutting, mother bends down and looms over me, "My poor baby boy, you really need to learn to mind your manners. Maybe you'll remember to thank me for being so good to you in a few hours when I send Edward down to tend to you." She pulls out a small vial from inside her pocket, filled with a clear liquid, tipping it back and forth in front of my face tauntingly, "In the meantime, I don't think you've earned this, have you? No, I don't think you have at all." She throws the vial on the ground and smashes it with the toe of her shoe, completely destroying the potion that I know from experience would have helped dull the pain while I waited.

I close my eyes and choke on sobs, trying unsuccessfully to compose myself and prepare for the long, painful wait for mother's healer. The clicking of her heels against the cement floor pauses, "Oh, and darling? No dinner tonight. You'll stay in your room and think about what would happen if you try to love any woman other than your merciful mother."

My breathing quickens frantically as she ascends the stairs, eyes still clamped tightly around burning tears. Creak, slam, click, click, click; she locks the basement door behind her, trapping me down here like she does every single night, alone.

For as long as I can, I hold out and try to stay as quiet as possible before finally gasping loudly and giving in to uncontrollable sobbing. It hurts, it hurts so much I can barely think past the blazing throbbing of every single centimeter of my ruined limb. No matter how many times she punishes me, it never stops hurting. The worst part isn't even the physical agony, but the absolute, utter hopelessness in knowing that no one will ever know, so no one will ever believe me or come to save me if I somehow asked. She'll always get away with it.

I try to settle myself into a bearable position, but every small jerk of my body sends a fresh burst of searing pain from my limp, useless arm. If I'm lucky, it'll hurt enough and I'll be forced to pass out, but I haven't been that kind of lucky for a long, long time, now.

***

I wake with a gasp, clutching my left arm and sobbing wildly. "He's hurt, we have to help him!" My heart is pounding wildly in my chest, but I'm already starting to forget what caused it to try and make a fast escape in the first place.

"We're all fine, everybody's fine," a muffled voice grumbles out from my lap. I blink back some of the bleariness from my eyes, slowly recognizing Kieran's face burrowing itself between my legs. His strong arms are wrapped around my waist already, but they pull me tighter and closer to him as I try to shake off the confusion.

Something isn't right. Someone needed... something? Whatever I'd been thinking about has already floated away, like a dandelion's seeds scattered in the wind. Right at the very back of my heart, I feel a last pathetic whimper try to make its way out, joining the tear I find myself wiping away to forget about. There's an echo of something deeply sad playing out inside me, but I couldn't possibly say what for.

There's a light nip at the outside of my exposed thigh, jerking me back to reality the rest of the way. Kieran's looking up at me with a sleepy grin, "Hey, I said we're all fine. You were just having a nightmare, Fireball. Whatever it was, it wasn't real." He pinches my thigh with his fingers, then kisses it when I yelp. "See, this is real," he says through a big yawn, followed by pretty much just rubbing his whole face right on up in my crotch like a damned beardy weirdo. Who nuzzles a freakin' crotch?

Except then he starts growling at my kooch and even

though it's super duper weird, the vibrations from his noises feel oh so very nice, and I'm suddenly no longer thinking about how strange this is and more focusing on how I apparently enjoy a good bit of strange.

Any lingering thoughts of sleep or confusion are poofed right out of my head as Kieran slides his way up my body and buries his face in the crook of my neck, letting his fingertips trail firmly along the path of my flesh on his journey.

"Mmm, I like waking up to you," he says, nibbling at the sensitive space beneath my ear.

Before I can respond with something along the lines of 'yeah, totally, this has been the best week of wake-ups over the course of my entire life,' his lips have charted a course up the curve of my chin and kissed their way to my own. It starts slow, but is by no means soft; each meeting of our mouths growing more and more forceful by the moment. My breath? Totally taken away. Probably also a bit stank given the fact we both just woke up, but I mind his about as much as it seems he minds mine, right now.

We're definitely too caught up in making out with each other right now to notice something as silly as unbrushed teeth, or super mussed hair, or the shifting of someone else behind us.

Shit, the shifting of someone else behind us? I break free of Kieran's lips and turn my head to glance over my shoulder while he takes the opportunity to kiss his way back down my lips, apparently heading for the other set. One of his large hands pushes its way up the inside of my dress, revealing quite a bit more of my torso than could be considered decent in polite society. Like, really quite a bit more, considering I'm now flashing a couch full of men all my greatest assets. The front ones, anyway.

Connor and I lock eyes, and I'm pretty sure he knows as much about what to do in this situation as I do, which is basically no knowing at all considering we're both sort of awkwardly half-blushing and half-pretending this isn't weird at all. I mean, what the heck do you do when you wake up to two people gettin' frisky on top of you? Do you tell them to fuck off? Do you pretend it's not happening and act like you're still asleep? Do you join them?

"Join them," Zeke says from the other side of Connor, rapt attention on Kieran's intended target as my panties are quickly dragged down the length of my legs and discarded who even knows where.

"Oh!" I cry out as a firm tongue grazes its way up my slit unceremoniously. It appears Kieran has no problem with our audience, or he's too wrapped up in getting to my pussy to notice, I'm not exactly sure which but damn his tongue plunging into my cunt sure does feel nice so what does it matter? Zeke crawls the short distance to us and pulls my dress the rest of the way over my head, fully uncovering the black bra I somehow managed to fall asleep in last night. Wearing the damned thing a minute longer suddenly seems like a crime, but my hands are too busy grabbing at random bits of flesh and fabric around me to do anything about it at the moment.

"Touch her," Zeke commands, grabbing Connor's wrist and thrusting the other man's hand into the cup of my bra. Oh, fuck yes! But Connor looks at me with uncertainty, still not entirely sure if he's even supposed to be here right now. From my point of view, that's pretty understandable, but fuck having his hands on me at the same time as Kieran's is so goddamned hot. He's not even doing anything with the hand he's got politely cupping my breast, like a weird chest handshake, but just the extra sensory input is somehow sexy as hell. I wish he'd give my nipples a squeeze, maybe kiss me, flick me, tease me while the tip of Kieran's tongue circles my throbbing clit.

"Ah-ah, Dizzy. Out loud. You know the rules," Zeke calmly states.

Emboldened by his demands, I plead, "Oh, fuck, please Connor, pinch my nips, bite that shit, do whatever you want. It feels so good when you touch me, please. Please do."

"Good girl," Zeke says as he lowers his lips to my neck, rewarding me by biting and sucking hard enough that I know it must be leaving a mark, but the added attention feels so erotic I don't even a little bit care. So what if someone sees it? The worst that happens is they know I've got a claim on some D.

Finally, blessedly, Connor's clever fingers put themselves to work, cautiously massaging my breast at first, slowly building to more forceful twists and pulls as my gasps and squeals of pleasure egg him on.

Also taking my noises as his cue, Kieran easily slides a finger into my pulsing pussy, joining the tongue he's flicking on my clit to send hotter and hotter bolts of electricity straight through my core, kicking my heart rate and breathing into overdrive with each maddening stroke. Desperate to give as well as receive, I reach up and grip a hand behind Connor's neck, pulling his mouth down to mine in an awkward tangle of weirdly-angled motions. My head is still elevated, having been resting on his chest throughout the night in a mostly-sitting position. Zeke digs his fingers deeply into my scalp and holds me up, making it easier to kiss the man still slightly behind me.

Kieran pushes a second finger into me, the rhythm of his hand and tongue intensifying and driving me into an absolute frenzy. My breasts are freed from their fabric and wire prison, giving better access to the flesh Connor is now enthusiastically pinching and rubbing, sometimes hard enough to make me twitch with pain, sometimes soft enough to make me whimper with wanting. My eyes are closed, but I hear two zips and a rustling before Zeke's hand in my hair begins to pull me so I'm fully laying down, my head in Connor's lap, Kieran's head in mine.

I open my eyes and see Connor's long, hard cock sprung free of his opened fly, bobbing right next to my face. If I turn my head just slightly, I could easily taste it. Taste it like Kieran is tasting me, fucking me hard with that skilled mouth of his. The idea of licking Connor's dick while Kieran licks my clit is such a strong one that my tongue is already exploring his hard shaft before I even have a chance to single-guess it, let alone second-guess it.

"You like the taste of his cock?" Even with my face right in another man's lap, Zeke whispers in my ear as I leave a trail of saliva along Connor's length. "Why don't you wrap your whole mouth around him and give it a good suck?" His hand fists my hair more tightly, suggesting with both words and pressure that I follow his recommendation, though not forcing me to in any way.

Besides, I do like the silky taste of him and already want more for myself. As I take the smooth head of his cock into my eager mouth, Kieran's third finger stretching and curling inside my hungry pussy has me moaning out long and low around the dick I'm starting to suck.

"Oh, fuck, Dizzy, shit," Connor starts gasping out almost immediately, and I'm right there with him because fuck, Kieran, shit, has me practically writhing right on the tip of an orgasm.

Just as the muscles inside my core start to tighten in anticipation of release, the cruel man taking me right to that edge pulls his fingers out and abbreviates the pace of his tongue to two long, slow licks that barely breach my parted pussy lips; almost as though he's simply stealing the moisture rather than actually intending to fuck me in any sort of way.

I'd be furious if, as I saw him rise up with his red beard sloppy and dripping, he hadn't been holding a shining metallic square between his fingertips. Oh dear lord, please let that be exactly what I want it to be.

Kieran rips open the wrapper and pumps his cock a few times before rolling the condom down his length, intensely watching me as I suck Connor's cocksickle like I'm trying to get to the soft, creamy center of my favorite kind of treat.

"Let me see you fuck her," Zeke commands from above, no longer the handsome devil whispering in my ear but the demanding one stating loudly to us all. "Don't stop until she comes. Don't stop even if she comes." Oh, I like that last part very much.

Kieran growls loudly as he thrusts himself hard into me, eliciting a gasp that only sends Connor's cock further down my throat. He isn't gentle or slow or anything but fucking wild and powerful as he pounds my pussy mercilessly. Each time his hips slam against mine, it sends a jolt of power through my cunt and up my spine, ending where Zeke's fingers roughly tighten in my hair, only making each pulse of need that much stronger. I need Kieran to fuck me into oblivion, I need to suck Connor senseless... and I need to remember to give attention to the man doling out orders. He deserves a bit of this perfect symphony of pleasure he's had a hand in orchestrating.

I reach above my head, blindly seeking out his steel only to find fingers already wrapped around a cocklesaurus rex of Jurassic proportions. Part of me thrills at wondering what it would feel like to get fucked by a beef stick that thick, but most of me just desperately needs to do something with my hands so I don't end up flailing around wildly and punching someone out. So, fingers wrapped around his, Zeke and I pump his cock together, squeezing harder every time we approach his head.

It's a miracle this whole couch hasn't gone up in flames with how hot my skin feels right now. I'm burning, inside and out; each stroke or touch or thrust or taste from my magnificent men stoking a fire that refuses to be contained.

With a cry around Connor's cock, the muscles in my cunt slam tight around Kieran with an orgasm that nearly locks my entire leg up my toes curl so hard. My choked screams set the man in my mouth off, throbbing as each spurt of salty cum is shot down my throat. A woman possessed, I lick and swallow and suck every last inch of him clean to the rhythm of Kieran's continued thrusts. When he's finally spotless, I turn my head, releasing him with a wet pop.

My grip on Zeke falters slightly; attempting coordination right now suddenly becoming a pipe dream. Haha, pipe. There's plenty of that in this room right now. I try to grip his thick hose harder but he rips the steel away from me, his hand still tangled in my hair tilts my head back so I can see him fully. In that moment, all I can think about is how much I want him to plumb my system with that wide tube of his.

"Good," he says, as he lines himself up with my open mouth, "I want that as well." Kieran thrusts me forward hard, bridging the gap between Zeke's head and my lips in one strong movement. I'm stretched around him so tight, any gasped air almost seems like a hard-earned victory. Between him and Kieran both stealing my breath away, I'm almost light-headed and delirious with desire, enough so that despite my epic orgasm just moments ago, another one starts to build.

If I could, I'd be crying out desperately for them not to stop, to give me more, that I'm almost there again. Fuck, I honestly can't believe I'm starting my day off in the best possible way:

big ol' pork swords impaling me until we all peak with pleasure.

Kieran lowers himself closer to me, tightening the angle of his thrusts and very nearly sending pounding ripples of force up my entire body into Zeke's dick. With the hard sucking of his mouth, he captures one of my breasts mid-bounce and deliciously tortures the hell out of my nipple. No one can fully hear the noises I make at all the shifts in his attention, but Zeke damned well feels them and knows exactly what I want.

"Connor, no slacking now. Rub her clit, and take care of that other tit."

Snapping out of his haze, Connor obeys, snaking his arm in the gap between Kieran and myself. He doesn't hesitate in the slightest, even though he's surely also making contact with the cock mercilessly pounding in and out of me at the same time. My head is upside down, preventing me from actually seeing it, but the thought of what it must look like to have all of these men pleasuring me at the same time is almost too much.

And then I actually see it; Connor's long, slender fingers slick with my desire, pressing against my throbbing clit and brushing against Kieran's stiff dick. I see a hand and a mouth attending to my lady melons, massaging and sucking and biting the ever-loving hell out of them. The chorus of moans and grunts around us seems amplified, as though it's in double surround-sound. Somehow, Zeke has managed to project his thoughts completely back to me and I am absolutely loving getting to watch and be a part of my very own porno.

My core starts to squeeze Kieran, milking his cock, begging him to come for me. As best I can, I swirl my tongue around Zeke's head, trying to give him more than just enthusiastic suction with each plunge he makes.

"Come for her, Kieran. She wants you to. She needs you to."

The man thrusting between my legs picks up the pace, like a crazed sex demon let on the loose, pounding himself into me more relentlessly than I could have ever imagined. It's all too much. Finally, I crest the hill once more, screaming my orgasm so loudly it can actually be heard around the thick rod shooting its cum in my mouth. My back arches up sharply, and I reach around Kieran's neck to slam his head harder against my chest. His movements become erratic, a deep growl bellowing from his broad chest. With one final thrust, he bolts upright with his cock buried deep inside me, howling as he drags his fingernails down my stomach and grips my hips tightly against him.

Holy shit, the man is a fucking animal. In that he is both part animal, and fucks, and that goddamned every single part of this has been incredible and wild and hard and hot.

Zeke slides out of my mouth and I gasp for my first full breath in minutes, relishing the feeling of my muscles pulsing around the man still buried inside me. Then I relax, panting as my hair is finally freed and I flop down the few inches back into Connor's lap.

"Well that was one hell of a show," a voice from off in the mysterious land of things beyond my closed lids drawls. Peeking one eye open, I see Lin, dribbling cock in hand, watching us from beside the staircase. If I were a normal person, maybe I'd be embarrassed or start lying and saying that nothing happened even though there's a whole sausage buffet I've clearly feasted on, but I'm clearly some kind of freak because the sight of Lin having come as well from watching us only seems hot as hell. To be fair, I also got a pretty spectacular view of our activities and similarly thought it was, as he put it, one hell of a show, so it's not like I can fault him for clearly having great taste in spectacles.

Lin swipes the cum off his cock with a hand and licks his own fingers clean, sauntering his way over to us. He bends down deeply and gives me a long, slow kiss, completely unbothered by the fact that there are other men here and he hadn't been invited to this party when it started. "You felt magnificent, Love. I look forward to experiencing more of that again," he says, breaking away from my thoroughly-swollen mouth and lowering himself to sit on the floor. He nudges my dangling leg with his toes, playing a weird post-sex-without-actually-having-sex-with-him game of footsie.

I let out a long, contented sigh, nuzzling the back of my head against Connor's thighs and twirling my fingers through Lin's black hair. "Well, that's definitely been the best way I've ever started a day, do we have anything else planned or is this just a preview of what's to come?"

Kieran lowers himself completely against my chest, careful to not put too much weight on me as I use my other hand to rake through his wavy, red tresses. He chuckles against me, "Well, we did have something special planned for tonight."

"What, and this wasn't special?" I tease. "You just happen to have sudden orgies every morning?"

"This was definitely special," Connor says, caressing my shoulder lightly with those elegant hands of his.

"Yes, Love, definitely special, but I have a feeling you'll think what we'll be up to tonight is quite good," Lin grabs my hand from his hair and kisses it, twining his fingers through mine. "And I promise, it'll be unlike anything you've ever done before."

Given that this, right here, what happened on this couch is already a brand new thing for me and I flippin' loved it, I can't even imagine what else they must have in store.

46. DIZZY

We spent most of the day doing some weird errands that, if I'm honest, were pretty anticlimactic compared to how the day had started. I didn't understand why we were going around to random shops and buying up bed sheets, pillows, and curtains, or why Kieran spent hours chopping up logs when it isn't cold enough to light a fire, yet. We also hauled some weird cubes and a heckload of rocks into a truck I didn't even know the guys had hiding in their garage. Manual labor can be fun for some, I guess, but every time I asked what the point of all this was, they said I'd just have to wait and see.

Finally, long after moon rise, we divided ourselves between the truck and the SUV and went off on a journey with all the random junk they'd insisted on hoarding like a weird colony of garbage-obsessed ferrets. Would that actually just be a group of raccoons? Is there a word for a group of raccoons, like how crows are a murder and lions are a pride? These are important details to divine!

We ended up back in the city, in front of a building that looked like it was maybe one or two good strong huffs and puffs away from being blown in. Connor threw up some kind of illusion that I could tell was hiding us from anyone outside, since anything beyond the sidewalk was suddenly just... gone. At first, I was worried that we were going to do some crimes, or this was another trap for David that nobody had told me about beforehand, but then the guys started... fixing stuff.

Monty used the stones and wood to build a ramp up the front steps, and Kieran shaped some metal into a railing for it. Lin unlocked the door, which by the way, I'm pretty sure he didn't have a key for so that crimes theory is looking pretty legit right about now. Chicks dig bad boys though, right? And I sure do dig these bad boys.

When we got inside, it looked a little bit better but still pretty banged up; poorly-patched holes scattered around the walls, water stains on half the ceiling, scorch marks on the carpet, and the general appearance of grime that refuses to be tamed no matter how many good scrubs have gone up against it. I'd been too confused to notice before, but the beds inside surrounded by torn and worn curtains finally clicked in my head and I realized we were in some kind of clinic. An empty medical clinic in the middle of the night?

Lin went about unlocking all the doors we could see, and Zeke went straight for a refrigeration unit inside one of the rooms, fastening something to the top of it. Connor started taking down the worst of the curtains and throwing them into a pile.

"Ummm.... what are we doing here? Do you guys work here, too? Also, wait, what's been going on with the shop this week because I'm pretty sure nobody's been there for a few days, and now I'm suddenly realizing that means there are bills that won't get paid!"

Lin stops as he's strolling by, carrying a pile of sheets tucked under his arm. He tosses them on a nearby reception desk and leans against it casually, running a finger along the smooth surface as though he's checking for dust. "You know those readings I give at the shop, Love?" I nod, one eyebrow raised in confusion at the mention of his clear scam, "We use those to find people and places that need a bit of help." He pauses, clearly seeing that I don't understand what he's talking about. Sighing, Lin loops his arm through mine and takes me on a tour of the building while he explains, "About a week ago, a woman came in asking if she'd have any luck finding a new job. Through her reading, I found out she was looking for new employment because her current workplace, this free clinic, was in danger of being shut down and condemned for not being up to code. They couldn't get donors or loans for the repairs, either, so the closure was imminent." As we pass by, he points out certain problems, like exposed wiring through a hole in the wall, uneven flooring, and the complete lack of handicap accessibility pretty much throughout the building. "I assured her that her luck would turn around, and we devised a way to help keep this boon to the community not only operational, but actually improve it."

I wrinkle my nose as we pass a room that reeks of rot and possibly death, "Okay, that's cool and all, but why are we here in the middle of the night instead of just hiring a crew like normal people probably do when they need shit done?"

"Ah, well, you see... There's a larger plan in place. What we do isn't strictly legal, so there is a need for a bit of secrecy in that regard. It seems that breaking into a place for any reason, even if you're going to spruce it up a bit is a crime! Especially if you do it without waiting a few weeks for permits," he declares, rolling his free hand around in a dramatic flourish. Leaning closer, Lin whispers conspiratorially, "Plus, we liberate nearly everything we use by stripping and recycling materials from sites that would have otherwise ended up in a landfill. So, really, we're environmentally-conscious Robin Hooded hero-types most of the time." Ending with a wink, he smiles and looks at me, waiting for my reaction.

Do I get outraged here? Is that what I'm supposed to do? Start wailing like a poofy-dressed diva about how she's been deceived by these scandalous heathens and demands they give up their monstrous ways of helping those in need to become regular, boring old shop-owners with no secret lives? Bah. "Well, that's kind of cool," I agree. "Usually I'm the one who's breaking things to pieces, so if I get to actually help make somewhere better? That'll be a first for me!" Thinking about it, it's been almost a week since I've had a steady stream of huge disasters. I know I've realized before that it's essentially been ever since that night Monty nearly plowed me over and they took me home, but now I really realize just how big of an impact meeting these five has had on my life. Maybe I can be Construction Zone Jones instead of Disaster Zone Jones, with their help. Maybe I should change my mind about Tuesdays being the worst if they lead me to this life.

"Oh, and as to your question about the shop? We're closed on Sundays anyway," Lin replies, "Mondays as well. We can re-open on Tuesday, per usual, if everyone wants to but we don't actually need to otherwise." Zeke happens to pass us as we stroll back up the hall and Lin grabs the sturdy man's shoulder, "This stud right here is a bona-fide genius, and we've been living off the profits from some of his inventions for years, now. The shop is mostly just a way to keep ourselves busy, do some good for the community, and test out some of his newest ideas. Probably also to keep us out of trouble, though I suppose jobs like this one have the potential to drop us right back in it if we ever get caught." Lin waggles his eyebrows and I can't help but giggle at his bit of silliness.

"Well then, I guess I'll prepare my speech now for when the

coppers try to drag me off to the hoosegow. They'll never take me alive, of course, but it pays to be prepared!"

I throw myself into the work, honestly delighted to be doing something productive, rather than destructive for a change. Looking around at my men, watching Connor and Monty patch holes and fix furniture, Kieran mold and repair copper wiring, Zeke tinkering with machines and devices, and Lin organizing as well as decorating every space... I realize just how good it feels to finally actually be doing something provably good. Really, really good.

They were right; they really did have something special planned.

The End. (For now!)

WANT TO STAY
UP TO DATE?

Need more? Join my Facebook group, Kat Quinn's Quinners not Quitters! (http://facebook.com/groups/quinners) Come hang out, chat about the books, debate about utter nonsense, and share pictures of your pets! (Yes, really. By LAW, if you are in possession of a cute animal you MUST share pics of it with the group.) We even do giveaways and contests when the mood strikes! Pop on in and give a holla, I'm so excited to meet you! And hear all your theories, as well as see which characters you call dibs on. :D

PLEASE, IF YOU CAN, CONSIDER LEAVING A REVIEW!

I want to make these books the best they can be, and your feedback will not only help me keep going, but help me improve! (Or help me keep doing the things you love the most.)

As a small-time, first-time author, your encouragement is unbelievably welcomed and I am grateful for every single second you spend sharing it with me. <3

AFTERWORD

Wow. I wrote a book. I really freakin' did it! This whole experience has been so unbelievably surreal. One day, I was talking to my word wife and fellow author, Avery Thorn, and the next day I was suddenly writing a book without even meaning to. Sometimes the ideas just slap you in the face and DEMAND you give them attention, you know? I didn't know, but now I do!

This is NOT the last you'll see of Dizzy and her dudes. Right now, at least two more books are "planned" (I use that word VERY roughly, because Dizzy appears to just do whatever she wants no matter what it is I THINK I want her to do) in the Disaster Zone Jones series. However, there are multiple other stories yet to be told from within the same universe! Some characters have either been fully introduced, or lightly teased, and some have yet to let you know they're just around the corner. Regardless, there's plenty more magic and mayhem left to discover.

I want to give a huge shoutout to, again, Avery Thorn, writer of The Nameless Syren series and just the nicest and most helpful danged word wife a gal could ever hope for. Thank you for all the middle-of-the-night meme convos, the uninhibited affection, and free-flowing knowledge. I literally don't know what I would have done without you, because while the answers to all my questions could probably be gotten from Google, I honestly love you more. You sexy tequila worm, you.

Thank you to the naughty bitches over at the #accountabiliteam challenge group, without us torturing each other every week I really would not have finished this. Y'all pushed me to keep going when I wanted to give up, made me laugh on days when I was feeling droopy, and have been an amazingly supportive (though somewhat evil!) part of this community. I love you all, even if I also love torturing you just a smidgen.

To my beta readers, oh my gosh, I could not have asked for a better group of people. The amount of work and thought that you put into your feedback blows me away, and I am so grateful for it I honestly don't even know what to do with myself. Before this, I'd never written anything and y'all took a chance on my unknown ass to help me make this the best it could be. Already, I know I can grow and become better just from the help you gave in this book. Thank you for the color commentary about butt butter, that made me laugh when I was frustrated about editing this for the billionth time. Thank you for making me feel like I'd hit the author goals lottery by telling me I made you cry. Thank you for getting into fights over who gets to have dibs over which characters. Thank you for being so excited about plot theories and this scene or that scene that we stayed up chatting for hours and hours. But mostly, thank you for taking that chance in the first place, because you didn't have to but you did anyway. I love you all so much, you make my heart swell with joy.

Lastly, and I know everyone says this, but thank you, reader. Seriously. I always rolled my eyes at this portion in other people's thanks and whatnot because it's so cheesy, but now that I've written something, myself? I totally get it. Just like with my betas, thank you for taking the chance. When I started this thing, I kept saying that it's my first pancake so I need to mess it up good and plenty to get all the mistakes out now and work towards getting better, later. But you? You're here eating this first pancake despite it being slightly burnt, misshapen, and somehow under-cooked at the same

time. You're even here, now, reading this nonsense about pan-
cakes! That's amazing! I honestly didn't think anyone would,
but you're something special, aren't you? Of course you are.
Thank you. A thousand times, thank you.

If you feel so inclined, please review this book! Write it up
on Amazon or Goodreads or a blog, or tell a friend, or put a
message in a bottle, or train carrier pigeons to fly notes about
it to strangers. Just by telling even ONE person about this,
you're helping, and I would appreciate it so incredibly much.
<3

ABOUT THE AUTHOR

Kat Quinn is a creature sent from the Spoop Dimension to save your planet through words laced with love, lust, and magic. On her way towards writing, she got distracted and took a detour down Doodle Lane, Crazy Cat Lady Avenue, and Cookin' Up a Storm Circle. It's okay, though, now she's settling down 'round abouts Philadelphia in the US, bringing you the best and most ridiculous smut her twirly-wirly brain can provide. She aspires to some day definitively answer the age-old question of exactly how centaurs would wear pants, should they ever, and why. A lofty goal, to be certain, but a worthy one.

MORE BY KAT QUINN

Well, this is awkward. Given that this is my first book, there is no "more"... Yet! Head on over to the Facebook group, that's where you'll see this lack of more proven wrong!

facebook.com/groups/quinners

CPSIA information can be obtained
at www.ICGtesting.com
Printed in the USA
LVHW111115271020
669941LV00006B/230